P9-CEM-129
Hayner Public Library District
0 00 300633311 0

RECEIVED
JUN 19 2020
By

DAUGHTERS OF SMOKE AND FIRE

DAUGHTERS OF SMOKE AND FIRE

a novel

AVA HOMA

The Overlook Press, New York

The poem by Sherko Bekas on pg. vii was translated by the author.

Pg. xi, map of Kurdistan © Peter Hermes Furian / Alamy Stock Photo

Published in 2020 by The Overlook Press, an imprint of ABRAMS.

Library of Congress Control Number: 2019938692

ISBN: 978-1-4197-4309-2
eISBN: 978-1-68335-894-7

Printed and bound in the U.S.A.
1 3 5 7 9 10 8 6 4 2

ABRAMS The Art of Books
195 Broadway, New York, NY 10007
abramsbooks.com

To Kurdish women,
for flourishing in barren fields;
to Farzad Kamangar,
for imagining otherwise;
and
to Ehsan,
for braving the storms with and for me.

What else can you do when your stage is an ember
and your audience a gun?
That's what you had to do.
You had to write poetry with the tip of the flame
And set fire to your fear and silence.
—Sherko Bekas (1940–2013)

CONTENTS

Prologue	xiii
Part I: Leila	1
Part II: Alan	99
Part III: Leila	107
Part IV: Chia	189
Part V: Leila	201
Epilogue	293
Author's Note	299
Acknowledgments	305

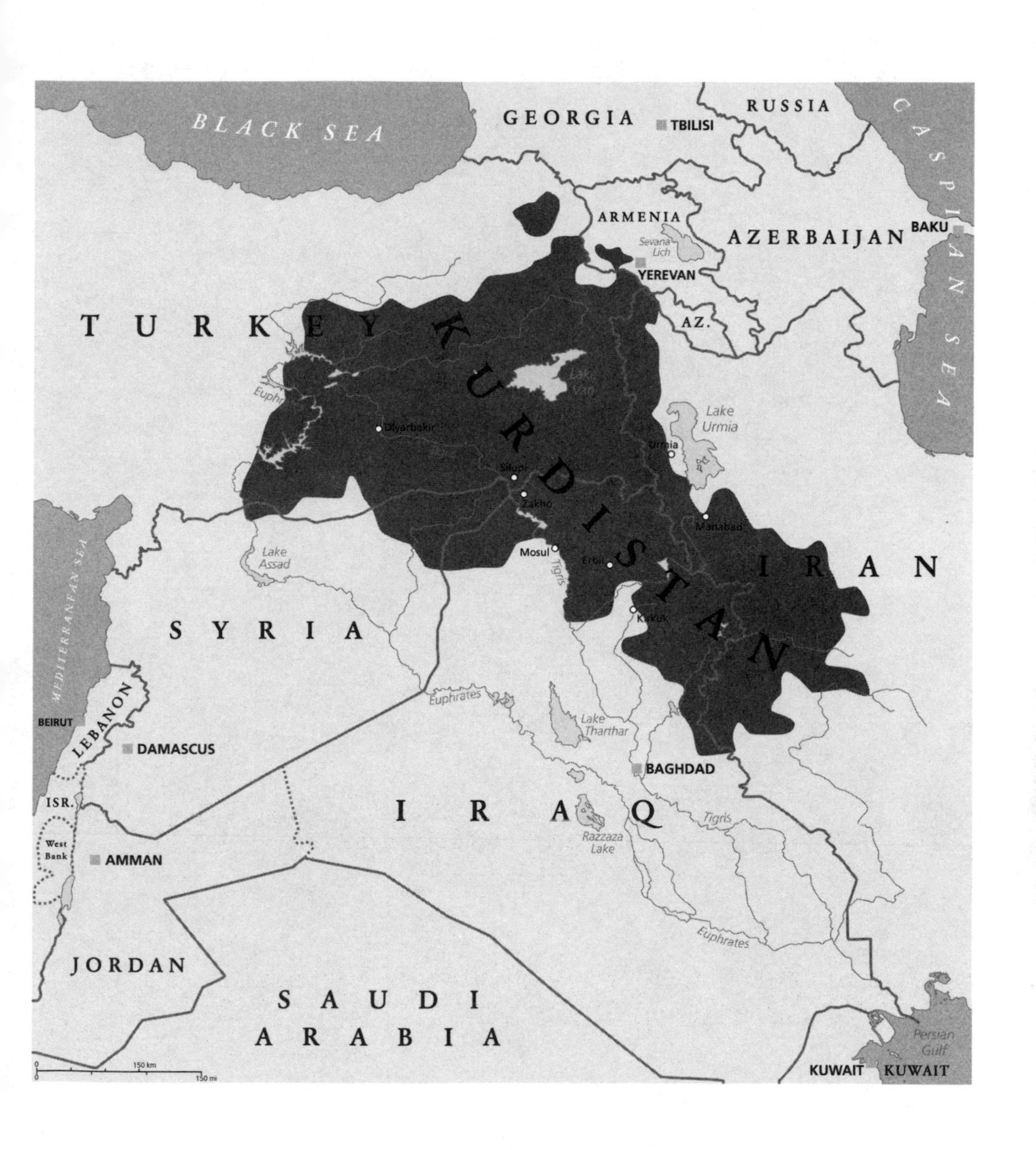
BLACK SEA
GEORGIA
TBILISI
RUSSIA
CASPIAN SEA
ARMENIA
Sevana Lich
YEREVAN
AZERBAIJAN
BAKU
AZ.
TURKEY
KURDISTAN
Lake Van
Euphrates
Diyarbakir
Silopi
Zakho
Lake Urmia
Urmia
Mahabad
Mosul
Erbil
Tigris
Kirkuk
IRAN
MEDITERRANEAN SEA
Lake Assad
SYRIA
LEBANON
BEIRUT
DAMASCUS
Euphrates
Lake Tharthar
BAGHDAD
ISR.
West Bank
AMMAN
IRAQ
Tigris
Razzaza Lake
Euphrates
JORDAN
SAUDI ARABIA
150 km
150 mi
Persian Gulf
KUWAIT
KUWAIT

PROLOGUE

A WOMAN ALONE on the mountain at dusk.

An invisible boot pressed against my throat, making my breath labored and helpless, and yet I couldn't go back and face my parents. Or my stifled future. Hidden behind a boulder, I hugged my knees and imagined my rage and pain whirling into a wildfire, burning down all the injustices.

Could my father have known what was going on? I wanted to tell him, to share this burden with him. My shoulders were already heavy beneath the daily cruelties of living as a woman in *La'nat Awa,* the damned place. This fatigue was incurable.

The sun had sauntered down, disappeared behind Lake Zrebar. A dozen shades of red burst open along the horizon.

Below, the narrow winding asphalt road was the hem around the hill's green skirt, embroidered with clusters of red and yellow wildflowers. The *shiler* flowers stood elegant and tall, flourishing across the rough Kurdistan plateau, defying borders. I yearned to be a shiler, but I was a garden of anguish, of loathing, of torment; my occupied homeland was a birthplace of death.

I stood up, my breath now coming in pants. I wasn't hiding anymore. "*Basa bas,*" I shouted. "It's enough. Enough."

I started down the hill in a tumbling run and found myself unable to stop. Despite the chill of the evening, I started sweating. The wind whipped my headscarf, and I gained speed. I flapped as if I had wings.

As I ran, a wail escaped my chest. I was headed toward the main road, toward the world of men. The streets belonged to them. Judgmental men.

Hypocritical men. Their-honor-depended-on-women men. Cars hurtled around the curve, full of drunk drivers who honked as they spotted me sprinting down the hillside. They were going too fast for this road, too fast for their sluggish reflexes, and too fast for their old vehicles. A white late-model car careened down the winding road, kicking up dust. The wind roared in my ears.

The white car and whoever was driving seemed to seek me out as a fellow traveler. I stumbled on a stone, crushing the shiny red poppies in the grass. And as I lurched, my untold stories tumbled inside me like pages ripped from a book and tossed, crumpled, into the wastepaper bin. An overpowering urge to scream my story, to expel it from beginning to end, seized me. Suddenly I could see the heads of all those Kurds crushed beneath tanks.

Descending the slope at a breakneck pace, my shouts crescendoing, I was unable to stop myself, this crazed woman.

A final lunge and I was airborne.

PART I

LEILA

CHAPTER ONE

MY FIVE-YEAR-OLD MIND could not identify the map drawn on my father's back and neck from the lashed scars of his time in prison. Wrapped in a beige towel at the waist and indifferent to the water droplets sliding down across the hacked frontiers on his bare back, my father packed some of the new baby's clothes and diapers and explained in a hoarse voice that he had to run back to the hospital.

Mama and my new baby brother, Chia, meaning "mountain," had not come home yet, and I was impatient to meet him. The events of that day were etched in some persistent cell in my memory. Baba got dressed, absently shoved my pants and doll inside a plastic bag, and gathered me into his arms. Wrapping my arms around Baba's neck, I saw tears in the corners of his eyes and the fresh drops of sweat on his receding hairline. It was stuffy in the house, the heater still blasting although it was well into March.

"Your head is crying," I giggled and ran my palms over his sharp stubble. "Angry skin. Porcupine." He carried me down the carpeted stairs that twisted in a perfect spiral from our hallway to the basement studio and knocked on Joanna's door.

Joanna opened the door, wearing her face-wide smile. "Congratulations, *brakam*!" She wasn't really my aunt, but she and my father called each other brother and sister. Joanna was dressed in a loose, green, ankle-length dress and a black vest, her hair tied up in a ponytail, her red lips the color of my father's bloodshot eyes. Her golden belt jingled as she walked, its many dangling coins clinking mellifluously together. I loved that she was always nicely dressed, how it set her apart from most women in Mariwan.

"Healthy baby boy. We'll be home tonight." Baba handed me to Joanna. "Could you please take care of Leila?"

Squeezed between them, I inhaled my father's signature smell of lavender soap, which mingled with Joanna's jasmine perfume.

"Of course. Hello, big sister!" she said as she tickled me under my arms. Baba thanked her and set down my bag next to the edge of the wooden door.

"Did you hear the news?"

"Hana . . . ?" Joanna asked.

"No . . . have you turned on the radio today?"

His own radio was always on, its staticky broadcasts a familiar soundtrack. Joanna's radio was usually on too, but hers played only mellow music, often Sayed Ali Asghar Kurdistani's soothing voice. She waved a hand in the air, swatting away the unheard news. "Believe me, I can live a day without tragedy, Alan! You can too. *Newroz* is coming. Your son is born. And we deserve a break, brakam, don't we?"

Baba's face twitched in a futile attempt to dispel the tears that pooled in the corners of his eyes. He turned his face away and crossed the tidy room to the dim main entrance of the walkout basement without another word.

"Let me get you a jacket, Alan," Joanna called out to Baba's hunched shoulders. The chill crept in even after he shut the door behind him, deaf to her words.

"I'm mostly made from water," I announced, repeating the little fact I had learned from Joanna the day before. She was the reason that, at age five, I could read. Her daughter, Shiler, could already spell too, and she was only twenty days older than me.

Joanna sat me in a chair next to Shiler, who was busy practicing the Kurdish alphabet her mother had taught her: *a* as in *azadi* (freedom), *h* as in *hemni* (peace), *n* as in *nishtman* (homeland)—everything the Kurds were deprived of.

Born and raised in her mother's crowded prison ward, Shiler had learned to focus so intently on the task at hand that she completely disregarded the world around her, so she had only just now noticed my arrival.

When Joanna had been released from prison several months earlier, she and her daughter had moved into our basement while she looked for an inexpensive place to rent. My father had said they could stay in our house for free because he'd had a lot of respect for Joanna's deceased husband—his former cellmate, a leftist activist who had been executed. Since she had moved in, Joanna had painted the basement studio a light shade of green, and the grass no longer grew long and unkempt in the yard outside the large, spotless window.

I was thrilled to have a new playmate, but Mama didn't like having Joanna and Shiler downstairs; she was suspicious of how Joanna had secured her release from prison despite being sentenced to death for stabbing a man. Baba had explained to me that in Iranian law, a man's life was worth twice as much as a woman's, so Joanna was to be killed in retaliation for taking her rapist's life. But the decision was eventually reversed.

"And God knows how!" Mama added.

Baba had stuttered when I asked what a rapist was.

"Go play with your dolls," he'd responded. I longed to know why the government punished everyone I liked.

Joanna now held a candy before me. "Mostly from water, ha? But what is the rest of your body made of? Chocolate?"

The orange-flavored candy was inside my cheek before I could answer. "No," I mumbled, mouth full.

"Honey?"

I shook my head.

"Why are you so sweet then?"

I laughed, holding onto the hem of my skirt. She kissed my cheeks. I wished Joanna had always been there, when Baba was too busy feeling bad for himself, Mama was too busy telling the world how wonderful she was, and Grandma was too busy praying for a grandson.

"Leila, have you had anything to eat?" Joanna asked with a hand on her hip.

"I found some yogurt. Ate it with sugar."

On her single burner, Joanna warmed up her leftover *shorabaw*, a traditional soup of beef and beans, though I found no meat in it.

"When will Mama and the baby come home? Do you think they miss me?"

"The baby doesn't even know you," said Shiler, looking up from her finished letters.

"Yes, he does! My brother would recognize me among a hundred girls," I declared. Joanna stirred some bread crumbs into the shorabaw. I slurped the delicious soup and went on: "He'll recognize my voice, because I sang to him when he was in Mama's belly." Joanna confirmed that he certainly would.

"Joanna is sewing new dresses for you and me for Newroz." Shiler was the only child I knew who called her mother by her first name.

"You ruined the surprise, *avina min*," Joanna said.

Shiler took me to the sewing machine in the far corner of the studio, sitting by the cooler that acted as their fridge. On and around the hand-cranked machine, the fabric lay shapelessly, red printed with white flowers.

"Why don't you explain to Shiler how you celebrate Newroz here?" Joanna said as she washed the empty bowls in her tiny sink.

It was Shiler's first New Year's celebration outside of a prison cell, and I excitedly told her all about the gifts we'd receive—usually a crisp note and perhaps a toy—and how thousands would gather in the city center, where there would be lots of pastries, dancing, and bonfires. The celebrations would stop only when the Revolutionary Guards showed up.

"Why was my Baba crying?" I went to Joanna. "He likes Newroz."

She pressed my head against her chest. Her breasts were small, unlike Mama's. "You'll find out someday," Joanna said.

"When?" I asked.

"When you're an adult." She gently stroked the back of my neck and kissed my cheeks.

I pulled away and used the hem of my blouse to rub her saliva off my face. "I am an adult!"

Joanna laughed, a laughter that bubbled up from her core and erupted like a geyser. The wrinkles around her kind black eyes and her narrow mouth made her look older than Mama, though Baba had said she was younger. Mama had smooth skin, high cheekbones, and hazel eyes. No wonder people often assumed Shiler, with her straight black hair and beautiful eyes, was Mama's daughter and I was Joanna's.

"Tell me now," I insisted.

"Something terrible happened when your father was a child . . . I suppose it still makes him sad, especially now that he has children of his own." She straightened up, having said enough for one day. "I know—how about we pick some flowers to make a bouquet to welcome home Hana and baby Chia?"

Shiler and I whooped in eager agreement, and Joanna covered her hair with a white headscarf, grabbed her handbag, and led us outside. We combed the neighborhood for our bouquet, walking to the park to pick the first spring daffodils and poppies. When we picked the flowers, I felt their pain somewhere inside me; the hurt was very real. But I didn't say anything to Joanna and Shiler. When we had an armful of flowers, we stopped at a fruit stand, where a toothless man sold us strawberries so fat I could hardly hold them in my fist.

"Strawberries are my favorite fruit," Shiler said before stuffing her mouth.

"Well, you're very lucky, darling. Kurdistan has the best strawberries."

"Mine is pomegranate," I said.

"It must be in your blood, Leila. Your father is from the pomegranate capital. Halabja."

"I want to go there! I'd eat a hundred pomegranates."

"He is planning on taking you when the war is over. Hopefully soon."

I bit into a strawberry, its juices dripping down my chin, and asked Joanna, "What does your hometown have?"

"Olives. Kobani has delicious olives." Joanna wiped the corner of my mouth with a handkerchief.

The three of us watched as several butterflies, the first of spring, fluttered haphazardly against a sudden gust of wind, their wings glistening like dew.

"Oh, where were you all these years?" Joanna pressed a hand to her chest, shaking her head in amazement, water glittering in her joyful eyes. "What did eight years of bombing do to you? And to the bees and the dragonflies?"

"I'm a butterfly." Shiler sprouted imagined wings, her arms moving up and down in the air. "No, actually . . . I don't want to be a butterfly. I want to be an eagle."

"Though crows live a thousand years, I want to be an eagle." Shiler and I both recited the poem Joanna had taught us, in which a crow reveals to an eagle the secret to longevity: Settle for flying low and feeding on debris, and you'll live a hundred years. *"Chon beji sharta nakou chanda beji,"* the eagle refuses. How long you lived was irrelevant; what mattered was how you lived.

Joanna led us up the trail near the park, where we saw more and more butterflies. "Remember, girls, you can be anything you want to be. Don't allow anyone to make you believe otherwise. See, these beauties were simple worms once."

I thought I'd misheard that. "Worms? Worms can become butterflies?" I asked.

"Only caterpillars," Shiler corrected her mother. "Not every worm."

Among the things I did not understand that day was how right Shiler was. Neither of us knew if we were caterpillars or earthworms. Nor did we know if the tight, dark days of hanging upside down was the onset of death or a necessary part of an incredible transformation.

CHIA AND MY parents did not come home that night, so I stayed in the basement. Joanna tucked me in and crawled under the bedsheets, covering her eyes with a headscarf. Shiler snuggled against her. I lay down too, but my mind whirred with thoughts—of Baba's tears and pomegranates, of whether my baby brother had a song in his heart.

"Can I play with the toys, Auntie?" I asked. Joanna was already softly snoring, so I slid from beneath the covers and played with the horses and elephants Joanna had arranged on a corner shelf. She'd made them in prison out of bread crumbs, beans, and newspaper strips to educate and entertain Shiler. Soon I grew bored and looked around, and my eyes landed on the fat TV set sitting on a chair across from the bed.

When he wasn't watching the news, Baba sometimes let me sit and watch old films with him. Since I couldn't understand the words, I invented dialogue in my mind. I pressed the power button on Joanna's TV.

A nightmarish scene played in an endless loop: people with blistered faces lying on the ground, huddled bodies sheltering against walls. Birds, cows, sheep, cats, dogs—every animal had dropped dead, like they were flowers that had been plucked from the earth.

"—Saddam Hussein gassed Halabja this morning. Within a few minutes, five thousand Kurdish civilians died in an aerial bombardment of mustard gas and nerve agents."

People had fallen on the spot while trying in vain to run away from the chemical attack, trying to protect a loved one, now also dead: a baby, a child, a spouse. They had died with open eyes, open mouths. Flies had nested on their lips and burned cheeks. Their flesh had turned black. There had been no protection from the murky yellow clouds of nerve gas and deadly toxins, not for the civilians.

A tremor of fear sprang up inside my belly, making me shiver uncontrollably, but I was rooted to the spot, staring at the screen. A woman had choked to death while fixing a helicopter toy for a small boy. A girl had died grinning, as if cut off in the middle of a mischievous joke. Some seemed to have perished slowly. A woman was twisted like a rope, vomit and blood on her clothes, her face crumpled with anguish. Thousands and thousands of bodies. Others had collapsed on the outskirts of town, trying to cross the mountains, running to imagined safety.

"Everybody's dead!" I shook Joanna, my tears soaking her blanket. She startled awake, squinted at the television for a few seconds, jumped up to turn it off, and held me tight under the bedsheets. Shiler still slept soundly beside her.

"Are we going to die, Auntie?"

"Hush, my darling. You're safe. You are safe with me." Joanna patted my hair, dried my tears.

"Baba said TVs are liars."

"Yes, they are. Yes, they are." She gently rubbed my back, singing a lullaby: *Ly-ly-ly* . . . Her velvety voice gradually soothed me to sleep.

That night I dreamed that the butterflies I had seen earlier arrived in Halabja, only to be gassed to death. Millions of them lay dead on top of each other, a hill of multicolored wings.

CHAPTER TWO

THE STARS GLITTERED on the long skirt of the sky, indifferent to the knots that snarled inside Chia and me as we waited on the staircase outside the kindergarten, waited to be missed, to be remembered, to be picked up. We remained in the yard, bored and cold, bundled up, peering at the asphalt, leaning against each other's arms. Chia was in the glorious kingdom that four-year-olds saunter in, drumming on a paper cup and muttering a song. I smiled to myself at the silly lyrics, but they couldn't ease the deep pit in my stomach.

Shiler stuck her tongue out at me when her mother arrived to take her home. I held my fists before my face, pretending they were gripping prison bars and that I was crying behind them. Shiler whipped her head away to feign indifference, but I knew that being called a prison child needled her. Kids also mocked her for her chubbiness, but she didn't care about that. Shiler wiggled her bum at me in revenge.

A week after Chia was born and Mama came home from the hospital, she had forced Joanna and Shiler to leave our basement because she said she couldn't trust the "*ghahba*"—whore. They'd left quietly, despite my father's attempt to placate Mama and to get Joanna to ignore "the bitch." I had decided it was better to be a whore like Joanna than a bitch, if I had to be one or the other when I grew up. I'd begged Mama to reverse her decision, but she had banned me from speaking to Shiler or her mother ever again. When we began school, Mama couldn't keep me from sitting with Shiler in class, but I had to steal small moments to remind Joanna that I still loved her, that it wasn't my fault Mama had cast them out.

I played with the spotted green ribbon tied on my short pigtail beneath my headscarf. Now that my corkscrew-curly hair, which grew upward instead of down toward my shoulders, had finally grown long enough to be tied back, I was told that I had to hide it under a headscarf. God would monitor my every move from now on, because I had turned nine, and He would hang me by my hair in hell if I failed to cover it.

"Chia, if God doesn't start punishing girls until grade three, why did I have to wear hijab starting in grade one?" The manteau—the loose, long coat I'd been wearing for two years already—was heavy and uncomfortable, making it hard to run around and play. The compulsory hijab was a shackle on my childhood. "Why can't our headscarves at least be a happy color? Like green?" We girls got into trouble if we wore colorful shoes or socks, if our ponytails made bumps under our scarves, or if our headscarves were not long enough to cover the bosoms we hadn't developed yet.

"Five, six, nine . . ." My brother's almond-shaped hazel eyes—everybody called him *Chawkal,* "Bright Eyes," and loved him because of them—looked up toward the twilit sky as he counted the stars.

"And what's wrong with laughing, Chia? Why shouldn't good girls laugh?"

My brother didn't have to cover his hair or body—not when he turned nine, not ever. During the day, every chance I got, I peeked into Chia's kindergarten, which was attached to my school. I made sure that he was happy, that no one was picking on him, because if someone did, I'd hit them later. All the kids knew this.

It grew colder and darker, and there was still no sign of my parents. The school's hallways had emptied; it was the first time I'd seen them without their usual bustle of students and teachers. The principal beckoned us inside to wait in her office. We sat beside the alphabetized filing cabinet while she balanced on the edge of her plastic chair and shuffled the papers in our file. She made a noise of exasperation. "Strange! No home phone number, and there's no answer at the emergency phone number either." She turned to hide her half-pitying glance.

"I know their father, Dr. Alan Saman." The janitor emerged in the doorway of the principal's office from the half-lit hallway, carrying a large bin of wastepaper. He was a short, skinny man with a large eagle nose; an enormous black mustache obscured nearly the rest of his face. "I can drive them home."

After a moment's consideration, the principal, also eager to leave, agreed.

We followed the janitor out to the parking lot, and he hoisted us into the bed of his small gray truck that was missing its front bumper. "*Barkholakan*, don't forget to knock on the window when you recognize your house or the neighborhood. Sit tight." I liked that he called us little lambs.

But that night every dark narrow street we went down, paved or cobbled, seemed unfamiliar. The windows of nearly every house we passed were illuminated, and silhouettes moved behind curtains as families ate dinner together or watched television. I held Chia's cold hand in mine and made up stories for him, visualizing scenes and directing actors in my head.

"There was a girl whose wishes would come true. Instantly. And she wished her younger brother would be very strong, and all of a sudden he became super-gigantic." Chia looked at me eagerly. "Another time, she saw a wolf creeping up on her brother from behind. 'Die, bastard!' she cried. When she and her brother went to check the wolf's corpse, they saw their father lying on his stomach beneath the wolf."

"Nooo!"

I was now reporting one of my recurrent nightmares. "His back had scratches from the wolf's claws all over it, and—"

Chia peeled his pudgy little hand out of mine and hid his eyes behind it.

"—and he was unconscious, and the wolf's blood was dripping over his face and running down his nose, and his mouth was open wide, and—"

"Leila!" he called, his eyes still covered.

"What?"

"Don't kill Baba, Leila! Please don't kill him." The car lurched suddenly as it hit a pothole, shoving us forward in our makeshift seats.

"I didn't kill Baba, idiot. I saved your little butt." I looked deeper into a silent alleyway that twisted and turned back on itself. It felt as if the houses were huddled closer together here. I heard the call to night prayer from a nearby mosque and wished the truck would drive us toward that voice. I liked the calls, because five times a day they reminded me that God was the greatest—greater than Baba and Mama, or me and Chia, or the principal and janitor. In my head, God was a smiling moon who loved Chia and me.

The truck, to my astonishment, obeyed my wish, and finally I glimpsed the elaborate blue dome that rose above the roofs across from our house. I banged on the window behind the driver's seat, and the truck came to a sudden halt, jolting us forward. The mustachioed man hopped out of the cab and slammed the door in his excitement. "Which one?"

I pointed, and he rang the bell. No answer. He pounded on the rusty metal gate flanked by cement walls too tall for us to climb. Nobody responded to his repeated knocks either. He paced back and forth, muttering to himself. "Man! What type of parents . . . Who could forget their kids like that? I swear they'd be better off in an orphanage." He kicked the gate of our brick house.

He scratched his stubble, deliberating. "I have to run. My wife needs her shot. She has diabetes. I have to run to the pharmacy before they close."

I turned my back on him and wished that he would just leave.

"Forgive me, barkholakan. Sit tight by the gate, all right? Your parents should be home soon. I will check back in a little bit, and if they're not home yet, I will take you to my home." He patted Chia's head and stalked back to his truck, muttering, "And my wife says I'm a bad father."

I sat down, my back against the wall. Chia did the same. We were cold and hungry, hugging our knees, staring at the pebbles on the ground. The truck's exhaust filled my nostrils. My stomach made strange *hee-haw* noises. "I've got a donkey in my tummy."

We chuckled.

Out of the blue, Chia said, "Save Baba."

"You're a fool, Chia."

He was quiet for a while and then asked, "Will you save me next time the wolf attacks?"

"I already killed it."

"Tell me one of your funny stories," he demanded.

"I don't feel funny right now." I laid my index finger across the top of my upper lip and mimicked the janitor. "They'd be better off in an orphanage."

"What's an orphanage?"

"Hey." I pointed to the smiling moon in the sky, and he followed the direction of my finger.

"How about some of Rumi's instead?" I offered. Chia loved those stories. I told him the tale of the parrot that broke the oil jar. Her owner beat her over the head for it, and old Polly lost her feathers as a result. The parrot sulked for seven days. When a bald man came into her sight, she shouted out to him, "So, whose oil jar did you break?"

Chia chuckled and rested his little head on my bony shoulder. Even I was finding it hard to keep my eyes open. I'd told him I had killed the wolf, but what about thieves? What if my wishes didn't come true and I couldn't defeat anyone because I had turned nine, the age when girls must start covering themselves up?

"What are you doing out here?" Mama was panting, coming up the hill from the bus stop.

"We . . . um."

"Inside. Now." She picked up our bags and unlocked the iron gate. It still had traces of the janitor's shoe print on its flaking burgundy paint. We ran through the front yard and the dim garage and mounted the stairs two at a time, but we found we could go no farther, because Baba was passed out across the hallway.

"Alan. Alan." Mama called out. Our satchels looked heavy in her hands.

Baba cracked an eyelid and rolled over a bit, making a narrow pathway for us. "Just like that," he slurred. "Bang."

I kicked over one of the arak bottles on the floor, pretending it was an accident. The strong scent of anise-flavored liquor had become all too familiar in our home since my uncle, Baba's oldest brother, had been killed in the uprising last year.

Mama hugged Chia, carrying him to the bedroom on the right side of the entrance. Our main floor had two adjoining bedrooms: one that I shared with Chia, and one for our parents, though Baba had taken to sleeping alone in the attic.

"What the hell is going on here?" Mama asked me when she returned to the living room. I couldn't answer. "What were you doing outside at this time of night?"

Then she turned to my father, still lying in the hallway. "First my mother is rushed to the hospital, then my kids are out this late, and now you. Why did you let them out? Why are they still in their uniforms?" Then back to me: "Why didn't you two change after school?" She removed her headscarf and fanned herself with it, then turned back to Baba. "What the hell is wrong with you?"

"Tah . . . teror," Baba groaned softly—assassinated. His forehead was pressed to the floor, his arms and knees curled under him like an infant.

Mama sighed and collapsed on her knees. "Mother's dementia is getting worse. She ran into the street today. Three cars crashed because of her, and one struck her."

"In the daylight. They shot him. Baaang," Baba mumbled.

"Who? Who're you talking about? Did you hear what I said? My mother was hit by a car. Who was shot?" Mama heaved herself up and crossed the hall to the kitchen. "You know what? Don't even tell me. I know what it is. Politics again, I bet. Some Kurdish leader got assassinated—another one." She opened the fridge; I was pretty sure she wouldn't find anything in it. "Because that's all you care about. And you care more about that than your kids and your wife." She slammed the fridge shut, gave me a withering look, and retreated to her bedroom.

I felt as though the events of the night had sliced me open and my organs had dropped out of my gut. I deserved all the bad things that were happening to me, because I never completely covered my hair and body. Sometimes my wrists showed. Sometimes hair sprouted out from beneath my headscarf.

Baba tried to get up but crumpled again. Mama's room was dark, but I could hear the low murmur of her voice, whispers that had no audience.

I stole quietly into the kitchen and groped behind the dish cabinet, where I'd hidden a bag of dried apricots I'd purchased with all the cash I'd saved up from my birthday and Newroz. I quietly soaked the apricots and added a teaspoon of salt. There was only the noisy hum of the fridge and the chirping of crickets in the backyard. I covered the bowl with one of the stained tea towels and hid it inside the grimy cabinet.

Noiseless, I then snuck into the bedroom, where Chia was already sound asleep, and climbed into the upper bunk. Baba still babbled away in the hall. My doll was tucked carefully under my blanket. Baba had wanted to name me Nishtman, Kurdish for homeland, except it had turned out to be on the long list of forbidden names the government had compiled. Nobody could prevent me from calling my doll Nishtman though. I brushed her woven hair with my fingers and whispered that Fatima's father had brought a camera to school, and I badly wanted a camera too. She didn't need to worry though; I had a plan to earn some money to buy one.

"Do you know what 'assassinated' means?" I asked her. My doll listened to my whispers, her black-bean eyes attentive. "Listen, you must make sure men don't see your ribboned pigtail." Nishtman fell asleep in the middle of my lecture.

THERE WAS NO school the next day, so Chia and I were allowed to sleep in. Mama boiled potatoes for breakfast and lunch and left for work early, stepping over Baba, who was still snoring in the hallway. After I woke, I checked on my treasure in the cabinet. The grease on the countertop glistened in the daylight, and cobwebs clung to the corners where the ceiling met the wall. My apricot potion, however, tasted just perfect. All I needed to do was to wait for Baba to leave the house. I started doodling in the living room across from the kitchen, where I could keep an eye on my stash. Soon Chia was up too, playing with his toys.

"Ehhhhhh!" he shrieked as one of his toy cars braked to avoid an accident, but then: "Boooom!"

"Your cars sound like horses." I started drawing what looked like a horse, at least to me.

"Your holse looks like a chicken!" he announced, unable to pronounce his *r*'s.

"Roll your tongue," I said. "Say 'rrrrrrr.'"

"Lllll."

"So cute!" I splashed a kiss on his chubby cheek.

Around noon, Baba finally dragged himself up off the floor and showered. The aroma of lavender soap, which masked the strong scent of his body, filled my nostrils as he went to the kitchen to make tea, boil an egg, and gulp down an aspirin. His beige towel covered only his lower body, putting the map on his back on display yet again. I stared at the network of scars from repeated lashings. The sight of them pierced my gut like the point of a sliver blade. I looked into Chia's eyes, and he into mine, but we never talked about the lines cut into Baba's flesh.

He went up to the attic and came down a few minutes later, changed into his loose-fitting gray trousers and a brown sleeveless undershirt. I'd noticed that fewer of Baba's things remained inside the bedroom he used to share with Mama. Positioning a pillow behind his back, he sat down with a steaming cup of tea in his favorite spot in the house: on the handmade rug, one of the few things of his mother's he still had. Firm and finely woven, it was made of symmetrical knots of crimson, white, and blue thread over a wool foundation; its many hues tied together our otherwise mismatched cast-off furniture.

Baba spread a tablecloth over the rug and fed us potato salad. His face was drawn and pale, but otherwise he looked recuperated from the night before.

"Have you had any more nightmares?" he asked me absentmindedly as he chewed. I nodded and started to reply, but he raised the old radio to his ear and turned the dial. It emitted a harsh buzz of static that bored into my eardrums. The government jammed foreign radio signals.

"Baba's radio sounds like a flock of cicadas with sore throats," I whispered.

Chia burst into loud laughter.

"Hush!" Baba warned.

"—Sadegh Sharafkandi, the secretary general of a Kurdish-Iranian opposition party, was assassinated yesterday in the Mykonos restaurant in Berlin, Germany," a cold voice recited. Baba covered his eyes with his hairy hands; his veins stood out. "This comes just three years after his predecessor was killed in Vienna in 1989. The gunmen are believed to be working for the Iranian government . . ."

The radio droned on. I hummed a lullaby, wanting to drown out the broadcast and protect Baba from the news. He didn't hear me, just sat motionless, jaw clenched and face ashen. I motioned to Chia, and we ran out into the backyard. The skinny cherry trees were turning orange and yellow. We wanted to get to the fruit before the birds and worms did, to bite into the cherries without washing them first and snigger at our little act of defiance. But there was no fruit left on the branches.

"Is Baba okay?" Chia asked, kicking the dust.

"I don't know."

"Why do they want to kill us, Leila?"

"I think they want our land."

"But where do we go if we give them our land?" He shook his tiny fists.

"Maybe the underworld?"

"If we lived under the earth, Baba wouldn't be sad?" Chia tilted his head, his brows rising.

"I want to empty Baba's bottles and fill them up with water," I whispered, and we giggled. "Hey, be careful never to mention the bottles at school, okay?"

Children were initiated into an Iranian double life starting as young as kindergarten, when teachers and government agents began questioning students about possible non-Islamic activities that may happen at home. Chia nodded.

"Let's water the trees so they give us cherries again," I offered.

His chubby legs, arms, and cheeks jiggled as he ran to fetch me the water hose. I corroborated what everyone else used to say: "You are bitable."

He frowned. "Biting's bad."

I grabbed the hose and started telling Chia the movie I was directing in my head. "Once upon a time, there was a king who said to his son, 'You should go and kill your sister. She is a bad girl.'"

Chia tilted his head and frowned. "She's a bad girl?"

"She wasn't, but the vizier wanted to cut her head off."

"Why?"

"Maybe he had Alzheimer's."

His hazel eyes darkened in puzzlement. "What's Alzheimer's?"

"Like Grandma. Now she doesn't even like you."

I was too lazy to recite all the details of the story, and I didn't want the girl in my version of this tale to endure so many tests before she could prove her innocence, but I still wanted her to meet the prince.

"So the daughter told her father . . ." I let go of the hose and held onto the trunk of the only cherry tree that the water had not yet reached, turning in slow circles around it. "She told her Baba, 'I will let you kill me, but you should listen to me first.' When she spoke before the court, she showed them all what a hypocrite the vizier was. So her brave words defeated the evil man, her father loved her, and a prince who was present as a reporter fell in love with her courage."

I stopped circling the tree and laughed at the thought of a prince as a journalist and at Chia's confused expression. I ran around the yard, and he chased after me. We laughed.

"Don't soak the trees." Baba's hoarse voice announced his presence before he appeared in the yard, carrying a light jacket over his arm.

Chia explained, "We're watering the trees to make the cherries grow."

Baba turned off the tap. "Chawshin *gian*, you're drowning the trees with the water and me with the utility bill."

I wanted to reply, "At least we didn't forget about them," but my nerve failed me. I was nothing like the girls in my stories.

"Leila, watch your brother, and stay in the yard." Baba shut the gate behind him. Chia pouted and looked to me to gauge my reaction.

I didn't speak, didn't cry, didn't sulk. I jumped on my bicycle. Shrieking like a banshee, I pedaled around the water faucet in the middle of the tiled backyard hundreds of times. Chia cycled after me.

Once I was sure Baba was far enough away, I told Chia about my plans to earn enough money to buy a camera. He could be my model when I became an award-winning photographer, if he helped me. We fetched the bowl of soaked apricots from the kitchen along with an assortment of chipped and cracked mugs, neatly arranged them on top of two boxes, and waited in front of our door for passersby.

Chia, with his big bright eyes and his little speech impediment, turned out to be incredible for business. He boldly accosted people, saying, "Only three *tomans* for a bowl of *malisaw*." Unable to resist him, our customers patted him on the head and dropped their coins into my bag.

Even with Chia's salesmanship, our location was quiet, and business was slow. The town center was full of peddlers, shoeshine boys, young and old men spreading blankets in crowded streets and selling clothing, accessories, fruit, and cigarettes openly—and playing cards, alcohol, and pop song audiocassettes secretly—but the side streets were mostly quiet.

A mother of three who purchased some malisaw and tipped us too advised that we walk down the street to the mosque that was fronted by rosebushes and stocky mulberry trees. We collected our things and headed down the block, leaving the door unlocked behind us.

As we walked, we passed a group of women sitting on the front steps of a rather big house. They were laughing as they cleaned a large bin of parsley, dill, and some other herbs, bantering and gossiping. Some reclined in the shade; others allowed the mellow sun of early fall on their backs. I tried to picture Mama as a member of their group, but couldn't.

We set up shop across from the mosque, and I admired its architecture: the magnificent blue dome, splendid minaret, brick walls, and stained glass windows. The men in folk dress who were leaving the mosque after their evening prayer purchased our product and told Chia just how cute he was. I washed the mugs after each use at the fountain in the mosque's courtyard. The mosque was a man's world, and it was my first time stepping inside one. The high-ceilinged interior was covered with rows and rows of spotless, beautiful rugs, mostly burgundy. A niche inside indicated the direction of the Kaaba in Mecca, before which dozens of men prostrated in humility. Books were arranged neatly on shelves, and there was a box for donations, which I believed had lost its daily share to Chia's magnetism. By the time we had only six apricots left in our big bowl, the change in my pocket was weighing me down.

"Why does the sky turn so red and beautiful at sunset?" Chia asked as we walked home.

"Hmmm . . . I think the sky blushes when the sun kisses her good night."

Chia tossed his head back and showed the little space between his two front bottom teeth.

"Catch me if you can. You are the police, and I am a thief," I said, and ran back toward home.

The out-of-breath policeman whose face was covered in beads of sweat came close to arresting me, but I was an uncatchable criminal.

At home I found some old sour yogurt in the fridge and mixed it with sugar. We ate it with bread to stop our tummies from nagging as we counted our money, coins rolling off the table like marbles. I did the math. If we set aside a portion of our profit to invest in more apricots, and if we were as lucky every day as we'd been today, it would take five years to earn enough money to buy a camera. That felt like an eternity.

"We should work harder." I decided, and we headed back outside to sell the remaining apricots. But the bright vibrant alleyway of the daytime had become a dark tunnel. There was not a customer to be found. Chia and I sank down in silent defeat against the gate, feeling too tired to talk or move. My head rested on his, eyes closed. We must have drifted off to sleep, because we awoke to Mama's furious face, silhouetted by the light of the moon high in the sky.

Mama was hysterical. "Out this time of night again? Are you out of your minds? Where's your useless father? What are these bowls and mugs about? Where did you get apricots from? Oh, God, oh God, oh God!" I sprang up at her shouts. Beads of sweat dripped down her brow. Before I could answer, she swatted me on my bottom.

She went inside, leaving the door open for us to follow. I didn't know how to get out of trouble, and took a deep, ragged breath before entering the house. I rubbed my behind absently; her smack hadn't hurt, not really, but I was worried it was merely a taste of what was to come. Mama had gone straight into the shower. Chia pretended to play quietly with his toy bear, then leaned his forehead near the coal heater when he heard the squeak of the shower tap.

"You have some explaining to do, miss!" Mama was wrapped in a robe, her hair spreading a wide, wet stain over her shoulders, and she sank onto the divan and massaged her swollen legs that always hurt. Chia crawled onto her lap. "Chawkal gian." She kissed his red cheeks. "You have a fever again."

"He's faking it," I declared. "He had his head near the heater to—"

"And you only know how to make a mess for me?" She winced as her eyes traced the trail of yogurt along the kitchen floor. "What kind of daughter are you?"

"He doesn't have a fever."

She touched Chia's forehead again. "Tell me what crazy thing have you been up to?" She sighed.

How could I explain to Mama? She'd never understand my desire for a camera; she'd just call me selfish, tell me there were so many other things we needed.

But before I could answer, the phone rang. She snatched it from the receiver immediately and spoke in a soft voice so unlike her usual tone.

"Just go to bed." She then unplugged the brown rotary phone, clutched it to her bosom, and rushed to her room, shutting the door behind her.

CHAPTER THREE

CHIN IN HAND, I admired the first snow of the year covering the city of Mariwan like a bridal veil, wondering if one could marry herself. I drew a wedding without a groom, a gown made from flowers of all shapes and colors. But I only had a black pen.

"Daydreaming again, for God's sake?" Mama startled me. "We should leave in five minutes."

I had my coverall on. "My school headscarf has vanished."

"Belsima." Stalving. Chia lumbered to the kitchen, rubbing an eye. Now in grade one, he could pronounce his *r*'s, but he also knew how cute everyone found his little speech impediment. His mismatched socks under the open door of the fridge were brightened by the pale winter light.

"Mama! Stalving!" Chia called out on his way to her room.

"Be grateful to God, Chia," she said. "Many people don't have roofs over their heads or heaters in the winter. And no more trouble at school, eh? I have enough on my plate. My mother no longer even recognizes me."

Yesterday Chia had made a scene at school when he stood up for his classmate who had been beaten by the teacher for not being able to speak Persian.

"I only asked a question. What's the point of school if our teachers won't answer our questions?" Chia rubbed his eyes again with the back of his hand and turned to me. He'd asked why students couldn't read and write in their mother language. "What's wrong with learning Kurdish?" The standard response—"One country, one language"—hadn't satisfied him and only led to more questions.

I'd faced this same horror when I began school, and now it was Chia's turn, the inheritance of all the students of Kurdistan and other non-Persian regions in Iran: Beginning in grade one, we were forced to learn to read and write in a new language entirely different from the one we'd grown up speaking, and when we struggled, it was literally beaten into us. Overnight, we were robbed of our language, our heritage. Little by little, we began to understand that our mother tongue wasn't the language of power and prosperity. At a young age, our alienation from Kurdish history and literature—from our roots, identity, and inevitably our parents—began, escalating with each year that passed.

"Ready yet?" Mama called out to me, a hand on her hip. She was dressed in an elegant velvet overcoat, a simple design that gracefully showed off her curves. She must have picked it up from *Tanakora*, the reeking bazaar where second-hand Western clothes were sold for cheap. My mother was indeed beautiful.

Chia turned to me now. "Leila? No bleakfast?"

"You're not so adorable anymore. Speak properly."

I had spent the previous evening arranging my hair into an elaborate braid, tied with a spotted, forest-green ribbon, and hated that I had to cover it.

Baba and his radio came downstairs. His eyes were puffy and tired. "—and four Kurdish villages were demolished by Iran as the government continues to level five more," the radio announced.

"Alan, your children want breakfast," said Mama. "Leila, hurry up."

I frantically searched for my headscarf, worried that we'd miss the infrequent bus downtown. Our neighborhood had a boys' elementary school for Chia, but the girl's school was nearly a two-hour commute away. Chia finally presented the headscarf, all wrinkled. "Did you hide this under your pillow again, *meshkaka*, you little mouse?"

"Don't go to school if you hate it!" he said.

"Listen, Chia." He probably couldn't understand how a girl had to be either pretty or brainy in this world. "The only way I can buy a camera is to get a job, and to do that I need to earn a degree. You should stop hiding my school stuff, and I'll show you my new drawing after I color it at school today, okay?"

Mama and I took the faded blue bus to the city where my school and her counseling office were located. I wondered what advice she would give someone who had a family like ours. I stared toward the front of the bus where the men sat; women were not allowed up front. Sitting by the window in the last row, I looked at the weather-beaten houses, the flats stacked on top of each other without much structure, so different from the stunning architecture of the historic houses I'd seen uptown.

During the long rides, Mama would talk to any woman who sat beside her. It always started with a discussion of how expensive everything was getting, and by the end of the first hour, the woman knew the ins and outs of Mama's life, such as how our landlord lived too far away and was too busy to hound us for the months-delayed rent.

"I'm married to a man who has a doctorate but can't earn a dime and has a separate bedroom, claiming he does not want another child. God's rage will break his back one day," she told a woman sitting next to her today.

Although Mama didn't say that Baba couldn't get a job because he had been a political prisoner, everyone could guess why someone so highly educated was unemployed.

"I am the one who has to feed four mouths, and I cannot work and do all the housework too," she said. By now the bus was so crowded that nobody on it could move, and private conversations were impossible.

I continued to gaze out the window. Most cars already had snow chains on their tires. On several corners, venders sold hot beets. Each time a seller removed the lid of the dome in the middle of his cart to pour out the beets and their wine-red liquid, steam rose and danced in the cold air. My mouth watered.

"Isn't that your daughter?" asked the woman in a folk dress who had been eagerly listening to my mother's endless tirade.

I faced the scrutinizing eyes of the matron. She had a whiskered mole on her upper lip. "If I find crayons at school to color my drawing, it would be the prettiest gown," I blurted out, hoping my talent for drawing would soften her glare.

"Your daughter is big enough to give you a hand. My granddaughter is younger than she is and does all the cooking and cleaning. They'll do everything for their husbands later. Why not for their poor mothers?" She shrugged, and Mama nodded in firm agreement.

After I got off the bus, I sprinted the whole way to school, splashing through the slush puddles, ignoring my wet socks. In the privacy of a bathroom stall, I bit into the stale piece of bread I had hoarded. The walls of the stall were covered with graffitied curses at Khomeini, Khalkhali, and Rafsanjani, calling them murderers and bloodsuckers. The janitor must have given up painting over them. Recognizing Shiler's neat handwriting in the upper corner, I added some profanities of my own, wishing the men would be lashed, tortured, and executed again and again in hell because death was too good for them. Then I noticed an amateur drawing of a worm, or perhaps an arrow, and turned it into a beautiful butterfly, white with black dots.

The school bell rang, and I rushed to join all the girls who stood in queues in the courtyard, respectfully listening as one of the older students recited the Qur'an verses that vowed friends of God never experienced sorrow or fear. Shiler stood behind me in line. Her mother was the only one I knew who often looked happy despite her hard life, or at least peaceful.

Neither Shiler nor I wore gloves, and as the principal lectured us on ethics, we rubbed our hands together, blew on them, and tucked them under our armpits. Shiler wore a loose, short headscarf that would certainly get her in trouble again. "I drew penises in all the bathroom stalls," she whispered and chortled.

I giggled and blushed, realizing just then that what I had seen was neither a worm nor an arrow. I hoped nobody would know it was me who had given the penis wings. Shiler's neck was turning red in the cold, so I reached to tighten her headscarf.

She pulled away. "No. If I wear hijab fully, they'll think I believe in it."

"Aren't you worried that Mrs. Givi will punish you?" The *parwareshi* teacher didn't actually teach any classes; she was an official agent of the government whose job was to browbeat girls into submission and report on teachers and students who didn't comply with religious and political rules. In fact, the only thing that all of the Kurdish regions had in abundance was intelligence agencies; about six of them were active in our small border town, which neighbored Iraqi Kurdistan, alone. There were innumerable spies around town, from cab drivers to peddlers. Even families whose own members had been executed or rendered disabled by torture sometimes turned in other families for cash.

At only twelve years old, the rebellious Shiler was one of Givi's most frequent targets.

"Fuck her!" Shiler said, shocking me with her profanity. "She doesn't scare me and my mother." My friend struck a defiant pose, but the usual audacious glint didn't quite reach her eyes today.

"Plus she has such stinky breath," I whispered to Shiler to prove my solidarity. I secretly believed that the teacher had exchanged her heart for a sewer system in return for the power to intimidate.

Shiler covered her face with her shawl and chuckled, then clutched her belly and winced.

"Are you okay? Did you eat breakfast?" I regretted not sharing my bread.

She swatted away my concern. "I'm fine."

We followed the Persian national anthem with chants of "Death to America, death to Israel." It was the only time we girls were allowed, even encouraged, to be heard. Shiler and I shouted with all our strength as a way to fight the cold and to participate in an unofficial contest to see who had the loudest voice. It was also our shared act of defiance that, instead of saying the slogans, we simply yelled out gibberish, enjoying the sensation of screaming with mouths wide open and cackling about our secret insubordination.

Afterward, we marched in neat rows to the classroom. "I'd show you my new drawing, but I have to find crayons first."

"I love it already." Shiler sat in the back with the other tall girls, where it was easier to giggle and whisper.

The religion teacher, whose endless lectures on sin and the afterlife terrified me, walked around the fifteen rows of seats where three girls in navy coveralls and white headscarves sat on each bench. I pushed my notebook closer to the edge of the desk so she could see that I'd done my homework.

"Tell your mother to wash and iron your headscarf for you every now and then, okay?" she said in a softer tone than her teaching voice. She smelled of rose water, and I thought about all the flowers that had to die to make that perfume for her. "Tell her to sew the hem too." Students swiveled in their seats to look at me. I swallowed, feeling the heat creeping up my neck.

As she moved toward the blackboard, the teacher's massive buttocks jiggled under her dark brown manteau. Everyone continued to steal glances at me through the lesson until Shiler left her seat in the back row and approached the teacher to whisper something.

"Can't you wait?" The teacher was back to her sharp lecturing voice. Shiler looked around nervously and then whispered again. Her forehead was slick, her face drained of blood. The class did not breathe, trying to figure out what was going on. The teacher turned to survey the class and finally said, "All right, go."

Shiler left, and murmurs about blood rose until she reappeared at the door a few minutes later, head bent. An uproar started in the class; not since the end of the eight-year war, when air-raid sirens sounded from the city's loudspeakers and we rushed to the underground shelters, sometimes trampling each other in the chaos, had there been such a commotion. We almost fell out of our seats as we leaned forward to hear the hushed exchange at the front of the room.

"They can help you in the office," the teacher told a flushed Shiler, who then burst into tears and ran out of the classroom. I grabbed her schoolbag and followed.

"I didn't believe Joanna when she tried to tell me," Shiler stuttered, crossing her arms and bending at the waist.

"What did you do?" I asked, and immediately regretted my stupid question.

She looked up at my face with fury. "I didn't do anything. I hate the teachers. I hate this place. I'm never coming back to this dump. I am sick of hearing about the afterlife. Who needs it when this is hell in full flesh?" Shiler snatched her bag from me and threw her textbooks at the hallway wall, one after another. Her religion book hit the large painting of Ayatollah Khomeini. I was flabbergasted.

Shiler spat at the books scattered on the floor, wiped her mouth, and ran down the stairs. I looked out the window of the hallway and saw the shriveled janitor trying to stop her from going out the gate. It was part of his job to prevent girls from leaving and men from entering, unless they were parents or from the government. Shiler argued with him, waving her hands in the air. He grabbed at her wrist, but she pushed him away, sprinted through the gate, and disappeared around the curve of the street. Her black gum boots left traces on the slushy road.

"Saman, get back inside." The teacher was peeking out of the door of the classroom. I made my way back to my seat, trying to recover from the shock of seeing sacred textbooks hit Khomeini's face. Insulting the supreme leader was a crime punishable by imprisonment, at the very least.

A girl sitting next to me elbowed me. "Did you see the bloodstains on Shiler's manteau?"

"Yeah," I lied.

I was trembling the rest of the school day and all the way home, sitting in the last row of the bus and looking outside. All afternoon the school had been full of hushed conversations about bleeding. Trying to solve the mystery of girls and blood, I figured some girls threw up blood sometimes. That couldn't happen to all girls, though, could it?

People in hats and jackets were making snowmen and playing dodgeball. Some mingled under the weak winter sun on their flat rooftops, cracking sunflower seeds and bantering.

"God, I promise to be a good girl." I held my pinkie up toward the sky as I made my pledge, much to the amusement of the bored commuters.

At home, I shared the leftover bread from my backpack with Chia. After eating it all, he confessed that Baba, proud of his son for standing up for what was right in class, had bought him a sandwich before taking him to school.

I pinched his arm. "You spoiled brat. You thief. You ate everything I had. You deserve to vomit blood, not me." He was big enough now to get away from me easily, and he only laughed. It was so unfair that he took advantage of the good looks he'd inherited from Mama. That he fooled me and charmed everyone, even Baba.

But then I remembered my pact with God not to allow the Satan of anger and laziness deceive me in return for keeping me safe from the bleeding that had started in school. "I pardon you for eating my food and forgive Baba for liking you more than he likes me," I announced, and sat down to do homework.

Chia sat by my side with his notebook and started filling the pages. He hadn't had Joanna to teach him his alphabet like I had, but he was still an able speller. We were snoozing on our books when Mama got home. I jumped up, eager to prove I was a helpful, obedient daughter, and gathered the laundry, including my school coverall and headscarf, and figured out how to turn on the washing machine. Proud and victorious, I announced to Chia that we would have clean clothes soon. If only I'd known that I would be beaten later for having poured bleach instead of detergent on the dirty laundry, leaving some with orange streaks that looked like flames.

The stench of rotting fruit made me go to the kitchen to haul out the trash bags. A watery discharge of garbage sludge dripped out of one bag, leaving a filthy trail on the tiled floor that ants would love. Disgusted, I left the bag in the middle of the kitchen, snatched an apple and a cucumber out of the grocery bags on the counter, and hid them under my shirt. But before I could stash the produce in my schoolbag, Mama caught me. "Only one per day," she directed as she came out of her room, now in her ankle-length loose navy dress, and scolded me for having left the garbage in the middle of the kitchen.

The three of us were eating feta cheese on thin slices of *lavash* bread when Baba came downstairs from the attic. "Sign a check for the shelves you ordered," he commanded.

"No money." Mama spoke with food in her mouth, opening wider for the next bite.

I held Chia's hand and thought of taking him upstairs to the attic, where we would be somewhat removed from the fight I sensed was brewing. Chia munched his snack quietly, oblivious to the hurricane that was about to make landfall.

"You owe the guy."

"I have no money," Mama shouted. "Zero money. Nothing."

I led Chia to our bedroom and shut the door. He did not protest that I'd interrupted his meal.

"Why did you order them, then? They'll grab my neck for payment, not a woman's."

"Why don't you pay for once, faggot?" Mama fired back. She'd been throwing that insult around ever since Baba had taken to sleeping alone in the attic.

I felt panic rising in my gut and held my palms over Chia's ears.

"Where the hell do you go every evening, leaving these kids alone? You think I don't know? You think I'm stupid?" Baba raised his voice.

Chia looked up at me. I knew my hands hadn't blocked the sounds, but I didn't know what else to do.

"Where do I go? You really don't know where I go, do you? Eight years. Eight damn years of war." Mama's voice came up through the door. "I had to stand in long lines for hours to get a few kilos of rice or sugar for you and your children. Stood there and fought with fuckers who cut in the line. See these blue veins in my leg? See?" I imagined her pulling up the hem of her housedress. "That's the result. If I don't go to physiotherapy every evening, I can't walk. What the hell do you do out all day, sucking dicks and making no money?"

Baba roared. "Shut that fat mouth of yours, you filthy bitch. I'll set those shelves on fire and burn this entire house to the ground."

The image of our house engulfed in flames shook me with terror. I found some headphones and with trembling hands put them over Chia's ears, plugged them into the old black radio, and turned it on. I turned up the volume, held my hands over my own ears, and pressed tightly. Chia laughed. I wasn't sure what he found so hilarious—my face or something on the radio.

I giggled with Chia to distract myself. Something hit the wall. A glass or some china shattered. Odd cramps panged in my belly. Chia looked cuter than ever in his blue-and-white-striped shirt and pants. My laughs were loud and ugly, but my mouth did not look too big to him, so I grinned freely when we were alone together. I loved him even more because of those giggles, but when I pinched his cheeks, chubby and red, I realized his temperature was too high. I knew he hadn't sat with his head near the heater that evening. Rising alarm made me pinch harder, thinking that maybe I could just squeeze the fever away. But tears formed in his eyes. I bit my lip. I was a terrible sister, leaving red marks on his cheeks.

Oh, God, please don't make me vomit blood in punishment.

I put my index fingers in the corners of my mouth and drew my lips wide, squinting and sticking out my tongue, making a dreadful face. Chia laughed, and the tears rolled down. I kissed his wet cheeks, then got down on all fours and told him to hold the radio in his hands and jump on my back. "I'm too big for you," he said.

"Don't worry. Come on."

Baba roared in fury. Mama screamed words of hatred and contempt. I neighed and barked and crawled around for Chia, who felt heavy. The headphones were still over his ears. He fell off my back and rolled onto the floor, laughing uncontrollably.

Between my legs was unusually wet. I touched my pants and gaped at the rust-colored blood that had seeped through my panties, at my shaking fingers and sweaty palm.

I colored the flowers in my drawing with my red fingertip.

CHAPTER FOUR

FLOWERS WERE BLOOMING; green shoots that had appeared in April and May sprang up, straightening, opening. Walking toward Mama's office on my last day of high school, I daydreamed about attending university, having my own job, buying my first camera, making films. I gulped lungfuls of aromatic black locust and stuffed my mouth with fresh white mulberries picked by boys who freely climbed the trees and shared with passersby. The trees grew indiscriminately in front of most houses, grand and dilapidated alike.

Mama was still busy with her last client, and I had to wait in the counseling office. The walls were painted gray, and the window faced the main downtown intersection where the sidewalks were too narrow for the rush of pedestrians. I perched on the swivel chair by the brown desk where a stack of papers sat beneath a dove-shaped paperweight. Sketching whirling dervishes, I thought about what Shiler had shown me the week before. I rarely saw Shiler since she had dropped out of school—Joanna, now the most sought-after tailor in town, frequently took her on road trips across Kurdistan, visiting ancient sites, listening to folk myths from the various parts of the region, watching all different kinds of rituals, and on nice days, climbing hills to see red-legged partridges—so I'd jumped at the chance to go with her to the *khaneqa*, the Sufi's lodge. I could still feel the rhythm of the *daf*, see the dervishes in a circle, arms locked, until one of them broke the human chain and began to spin in ecstasy.

Mama tucked a bunch of files under her arm after she led her unusually big client out of the office. She wanted to walk despite her arthritis, using my body as a crutch.

"We should get you a cane." I took the files from her as we pushed through streets buzzing with people.

"I'm not that old." She winced and panted.

"Your client looked like a man in hijab," I said.

"She's a hermaphrodite, the most amazing person. Completely unique."

I was about to ask what a hermaphrodite was when a familiar voice rose above the noise of the crowded street. I recognized his husky timbre before turning to see his face. Baba was leaning against a pole, the sole of one foot flat against it, wearing a black cap two sizes too big for him, rows of prayer beads hanging from his arm, calling out, "Only twenty tomans."

Instinctively I called out to him, but when he quickly turned his back to me, I shut up. Mama kept walking as if she were oblivious to his presence.

"These files are heavy. My schoolbag is heavy. You are heavy. I can't walk anymore," I barked. We got on a bus and sat next to each other on torn synthetic leather in uncomfortable silence.

"How's your leg?" I finally asked.

She looked at me sideways. "Since when are you interested in me?"

It was a fair question, but it didn't soften the blow of her accusation.

"Mama, I'd like to know. There's so much I want to understand about you."

"Really?" She turned to me. "What do you want to know?"

I knew she and Baba had met at Tehran University when they were both students and that being among the few Kurds there meant they shared a common historical pain. But it was hard to imagine what had drawn them together. "What did you like about Baba when you first met him?"

Mama said she had found Baba charismatic and intelligent, a knowledgable man of few words, passionate about justice, charming in his down-to-earth manner. She had liked his warm hands, deep dark eyes, his cherubic face that betrayed little emotion.

Baba's mother had come to live with the newlyweds in Tehran, and Mama had thought it was his mother's fault that he soon lost interest in his new bride. Mama had come to understand that his mother was an anchor in his life only after the woman passed away and he became unmoored. It had gotten worse still after Baba was released from prison; Mama had felt neglected, merely another piece of furniture in their home. "He would worship my eyes one moment, and in the next moment, he'd act as if I were invisible."

Perhaps that's why she picked fights, I thought; she needed to be seen.

The bus had grown crowded and noisy, the evening commute at its height, so I stopped asking questions.

When we got home, Mama propped up her swollen legs against the wall, which was stained with footprints from years of this ritual.

"But you two loved each other at one point. What happened? Or do you think it wasn't love from the start?"

"You're too young to understand." Her mouth twisted out of shape.

"Mama, I'm eighteen."

She closed her eyes. Her chest heaved up. "He liked to kiss my eyes. Only my eyes. I couldn't understand why." A tear rolled down. "Turns out the love of his life had hazel eyes like mine. She had died before we met, but he could never get over her. But I was in love. Do you know what that means?"

"I have an idea." I was actually clueless—none of my crushes ever lasted more than a few months—but I didn't want to dissuade her from finishing her story.

"It was the one time in my life I was foolish, and I've paid for it ever since." She shook her head. "Love means being extremely stupid. And I mean extremely. Then one day the hormones subside, and you learn who you've really committed your life to. You're stuck. You can hit your head against the wall all you want. You can't do anything." She stared blankly at the water-stained ceiling. "But no one tells you that. If they did, no one would get married." She turned my way. "Don't look at me like that. Like you said, you're eighteen now; time to get a grip on reality."

She started massaging her temples and then sat up and tied a headscarf tight across the back of her head. She believed the pressure would help with the migraines until the painkillers she swallowed kicked in. I brought her some sunflower seeds and sat across from her. The breeze swept in through the open window.

"Listen . . ." she sighed. "I know I can act crazy sometimes. Don't think I don't know. But it's out of my control."

Now she really had my attention.

Mama cracked a seed. "This isn't the life I imagined. Sometimes I feel like I'm drowning, pulled down by weights." She waved her index finger in a circle. "You know the black hole they talk about in the galaxy? There's one right inside my chest. I never know when it will suck me in again. I kick and scream to be released, and in the process I hurt others—and I hurt myself." She met my eyes, her own verging on glassy. "Your father has no idea how difficult things are for me. He doesn't acknowledge my suffering; he thinks he's the only one who's been locked in a cell. But I'm fighting for my life. I want to live."

I struggled to digest this.

"You don't understand." She cleared her throat and spat out a shell with such force that it bounced off the bowl.

I wanted to ask why, instead of constantly lashing out, she'd never tried being vulnerable with someone, perhaps someone as empathic as Joanna, whom she still wrongly perceived a threat. But I couldn't find the words to articulate how I felt. So I just held her hand in mine and gave it a reassuring squeeze.

"Anyway." Mama steered the conversation back to neutral ground. "I had you when your father was imprisoned, and you were so cute and spunky, sometimes you'd act like you were the mom." Mama smiled. "I raised you on my own in the middle of the war, and do you know what the first word you spoke was? 'Baba.'" She laughed mirthlessly. "My fucking life."

"I'm sorry." I wasn't sure what part I was apologizing for.

"We were lucky your father was released," she went on. "Several thousand prisoners were executed around that time. I had hoped having Chia would help him get over the torture and whatnot, since he had missed your early years. And Chia did help, at least for a while. Your father loves toddlers, but as soon as they grow into people, he loses interest."

"You think he likes dead women and young children because they cannot disappoint him? He can picture them whatever way he wants."

Her face twitched. "Stop romanticizing shit. He's just not right in the head."

Ha. She expected sympathy but refused to offer any in return.

"And quit acting like you're smarter than all of us!" she snapped.

I did have an ugly smirk on my face. "Sorry."

LATE ONE EVENING in August, Baba came home with an unusually thick newspaper tucked under his arm. I was sitting in the living room, immersed in Simin Chaichi's poems, when his glance in my direction interrupted my thoughts.

I detected the disappointment carved into his features, deeper than ever. I gaped at the newspaper. A bolt of realization struck me. The results were in. One national exam—the Konkour. Several million participants. Only a handful got admission to the limited public universities. I wasn't one of them.

I felt as if I'd been pushed from the top of a skyscraper. No, worse. The hand of fate had reached down and crushed the tower of hope I had built, and I was buried beneath the rubble.

"Let me see it," I breathed.

"The government drove a Red Crescent Society ambulance into a Kurdish refugee camp," Baba said to no one in particular as he heaved himself into his chair. "No one tells you how many were killed, how many injured." He still held onto the newspaper.

I wiped a tear but another one spilled onto my butterfly sketch that was serving as my bookmark and ruined it. I snatched the newspaper from Baba's slack grip, gathered it to my chest, and headed to my room to search the list for my name. I ran my finger down the rows of names of the students admitted to public university. Mine wasn't there. I flipped through the pages of a second newspaper tucked inside the first and searched again. There. My finger stilled. I'd been accepted by a private university, the tuition for which I clearly couldn't afford.

I buried my head beneath the pillow. How on earth had I deluded myself into believing my name would appear on the list of the privileged students accepted to competitive universities? I let out a bark of bitter laughter, tossed the paper into a wastebasket, then sobbed.

Mama and Baba started quarreling in the living room. Whose fault was it that cockroaches marched freely across the kitchen? Whose fault was it that there was gum stuck to the sofa?

Baba refused to do "women's work," although he had more spare time than the rest of us combined. "I never get a hot meal in this house," he reproached.

"I have to work full time and take care of a mother with Alzheimer's," Mama yelled back. She said it was my fault that the walls were filthy, as were the curtains, the attic, and the basement.

I opened the door of my bedroom and shouted, "Your house was a shithole long before I was conceived."

It had been obvious from day one, Mama continued, that I wouldn't make the list of the public-university-accepted students—I was too lazy to even keep up the house.

Screwing my eyes shut against the pain of a building headache, I groped my way to Mama's drawer where she kept her pills. The pungent smell of her sweat in the dank, close room made me nauseated. I held my eyes and forehead in my palm.

Mama and Baba agreed on one thing. The only cure for my uselessness, they established, was to marry me off, but since I was not particularly pretty or good at housework, I didn't have a single suitor.

Barely capable of opening my eyes, I found the codeine tablets and swallowed a fistful of them dry.

"She is all your fault." Mama blamed Baba for my failures.

Baba blamed her for my very existence. "I never wanted children. You tricked me."

I crawled back to my room and slammed the door, which flaked little chips of wood on impact.

"You could've learned to control yourself."

"I've learned it pretty well since."

"You're a *kooni*. That's why."

Baba smashed a plate against the wall and retreated to the attic. I willed the codeine to take effect and drifted on the wave of a fever dream.

CHAPTER FIVE

WHEN THE FIRST rays of light slanted through my slatted blinds the next morning, my head no longer pounded, but my limbs protested when I tried to move. Snarling and groaning did not make me feel better. All night I'd dreamed that a man in a black suit was trailing me wherever I went. Mr. Bad Luck, my family's legacy, scoffed at my failed attempts to outpace him.

The house was eerily quiet, which meant my parents were either still asleep or had already left. I went downstairs to the basement studio, now converted into Chia's bedroom, which was bright with curtainless windows. He'd papered his walls with posters of Che Guevara, Gandhi, and Nelson Mandela. No thinker would rebuke Chia for his greasy hair. He was yawning, scratching at his faint shadows of facial hair, and solving physics equations from the open textbook on his desk.

Needing a distraction, I ironed his khaki shirt and pants that I had laundered the night before, as I had done religiously since he was nine. With each year that passed, Chia was praised at home and school for his intelligence, and I was blamed for not being as clever and as neat as he was. I was good at erecting my gallows.

"Don't you want to read some Tolstoy, Leila? Leave that iron. The pants are going to get wrinkled again soon enough," Chia said, head resting on his palm. He was always dismissing chores as a waste of time, convinced that he had so much else to do for this world. Yesterday he'd said, "Why should I make my bed when I have to sleep in it again tonight? I could spend that time each morning reading about the rise of fascism and World War II. So ridiculous that the battles fought by wealthy countries are called 'World War' and poor countries' fights are 'tribal war!'"

I made creases with the iron. I had been trying to serve my family, eradicate filth from our home, but nothing I did was ever enough. Nothing I did could make my parents praise me, make my brother notice my sacrifices, or even make God save me from "sorrow and fear," as advertised in the holy book.

The siren of an ambulance broke my train of thought. Light shone through the mullioned window onto Chia's gray bedding. A copy of *War and Peace* was lying on his unmade bed. "Did you really read all twelve hundred pages?"

"It was a great read." Chia chewed his pen cap. "Did you read the copy of *Nineteen Eighty-Four* I gave you?"

Steam rose from the iron. I did not look at him, but I could picture him pointing a finger at me as he spoke, his usual gesture. I had tried reading it, but Orwell's dystopia was my—our—reality. I needed books that offered escape, not ones that held up a mirror to our suffering.

"I slept in this room on that bed with Shiler and Joanna the night you were born."

"What's eating you, Leila?"

I made myself busy folding his pants. "I miss Shiler. I hardly see her these days."

"What is it really?"

"Your window is filthy," I announced. "There's a pile of clothes I need to iron for you."

I expected Chia to roll his eyes. Instead he got up from his desk and stood before my ironing board. "That's not all, is it?"

With that question, my teenage brother smoothly removed my mask. I broke down. "I didn't make the list. I'm never going to get into a university I can afford, and if I do, it'll be of no use. I'll end up like our father. Or worse, our mother."

"Oh, come on. So what if you didn't get in this year? You don't have to do military. You can study for next year."

"All I want from life," I sniveled, "is to have a college education so I can have a decent job. Make films, tell our stories."

"Stop it with the self-pity already. I'm sure you'll get in next year. You have a year to prepare. Start tomorrow."

I searched his eyes. He believed what he was saying. I put the tips of my fingers into a bowl of water, splashed drops on his shirt, and resumed ironing. I pressed down hard on Chia's shirt, close to scorching it. For a moment I considered holding the hot iron against my face until it melted through my skull and burned away my disillusionment.

"Do you ever think you and I ruined Baba's life?" Chia asked when I'd finished.

"Why?" I unplugged the iron.

"I don't mean deliberately. But look, I was born the day his town was gassed." He scratched his neck.

"Well, I wasn't."

"You know how he wanted to name you Nishtman, but the government banned it?"

"Of course."

"Nishtman was the girl he loved in high school and wanted to marry."

I wondered about this girl who had been called Nishtman, homeland, named after an unrecognized, unofficial, yet beautiful country. I imagined her with inspiring hazel eyes, full of hope, full of courage. "Was it my fault it didn't happen?"

"No, no. She decided to join the Peshmerga fighters, and Baba was accepted into Tehran University, so he decided not to follow her. A decision he must have regretted a thousand times, I suppose."

Peshmerga: those who face death. What a brave girl. An educated dreamer at a time when women weren't supposed to be either. I imagined her holding her head high and walking with a grace that lent her incredible charisma. But Nishtman the girl, just like nishtman the Kurdish homeland, was unattainable. "So she chose the weapon and he picked the pen. And both failed." I sighed. "Mama said she died."

Chia shrugged. "Technically she 'disappeared.' It looks like the powerless in this world are doomed to defeat regardless of what means they pick to fight. And yet resisting and losing is better than dying silently, no?"

"What does that have to do with us ruining his life, anyway? If he wanted to name me after her, he must have loved me or had hopes for me." In Baba's room in the attic was a poster of a man in Kurdish clothing, holding up a picture of a young girl killed in the genocide, showing all that remained of her to the photographer. "I suppose he hoped I'd do something for our people, and I want to—you know how much I want to make films to share our stories—but so far I've amounted to nothing."

"Baba was doing okay before I was born." Chia wasn't listening to me. "The eight-year war had just ended, and he had hoped to take us back to his hometown of pomegranates. But I was born, and his town was gassed. You were conceived, and his house was raided."

"He told you about the night he was arrested? When was this?"

"Oh, a while ago."

I stamped my foot like a child. "Why didn't you tell me? I want the whole story, every detail, verbatim."

"Why?" He arched his eyebrow up at me from the floor, where he was twisted into some yoga pose, his spine ramrod straight, his palms touching.

"Because Baba never shares anything with me."

Chia unwound his legs and stretched. "You better get comfortable."

According to Baba, the very minute Mama informed him she was pregnant, they heard a series of loud knocks on the door. The clock chimed five as the pounding on their door reached a crescendo. Two bearded plainclothes policemen burst through the front door. "Saman?" the taller one demanded. "Alan Saman?"

Baba felt himself starting to shake. "What's this about?

"You'll find out in Evin," said the first man, a giant whose tobacco-stained teeth gave him a cruel appearance.

"Do you have a letter from the court?" Baba asked.

The man punched him in the stomach. "Here's your letter."

Mama pushed in front of her husband, arms crossed modestly over her nightgown. "Please, sir, this must be a mistake."

"Yeah, we hear the same thing in every house," said the other man, who wore glasses above his scraggly beard. "We trust the *Ettela'at* more than we trust you."

The mention of the Ettela'at, the Islamic Republic's intelligence service, would strike terror in the heart of any civilian, law-abiding or not. Baba's mother, whom everyone called Dayah, pleaded, "Please, sir! Take me instead."

"My husband is innocent!" Mama insisted shrilly.

"Cover yourself, woman," the agent with the crooked teeth shouted while the leering one adjusted his glasses.

"Get out of my house." Baba shoved the bespectacled one toward the door, but five more plainclothes agents with Glocks rushed into the apartment, ramming Baba against the wall. At a gesture from the giant secret policeman, the agents began to search the rooms of the house, rifling through drawers, scattering papers, breaking everything in their wake. The two who had first come to the door handcuffed Baba.

Dayah threw herself at the leader's feet. "For the love of God, don't take him. He hasn't done anything. Take me instead," she pleaded in Kurdish. Of course they did not understand her language, nor would they have cared if they had.

"Let go, Dayah gian. Please. Let go. Let go," Baba begged his mother.

One of the men kicked Dayah in the chin. He spat, "*Kafar*"—infidel—and kicked the crumbling old woman again, this time in the chest. Baba growled, shoved the man, and bent before his mother, unable to wrap his handcuffed arms around her. One of the armed men bashed his gun against Baba's temple. He tasted his own blood. Dayah's trembling hands rested on his cheeks.

The secret police discovered two banned political books in the house that night, which became the only evidence of Baba's supposed crime, earning him four years in prison without a clear sentence and repeated torture for information that drew the map of a nonexistent country on his back.

When Mama brought Dayah to the hospital, the old bleeding woman was ignored because she wore a Kurdish dress and couldn't speak Persian. Her heart stopped beating while she waited, waited to be treated, waited for her homeland to be free, waited for her son to return. Incarcerated as he was, Baba couldn't hold a funeral for his mother or bury her beside her husband in Halabja as promised.

CHAPTER SIX

THE POPULATION OF our city doubled as displaced Iraqis fled the war after the American invasion. Most of our neighbors took in refugee families. We did not. We couldn't stand each other, let alone strangers. Shiler had left to volunteer in one of the refugee camps near the border. I was particularly aggressive those days and found excuses to scream at the girls who made fun of my old-fashioned clothes and gray gum boots, at the men who thought I was one of those decadent girls who'd go on dates. If no one was nearby to be the recipient of my contempt, I'd shout at the books that refused to communicate with my brain.

I retreated to my room one evening after Mama scolded me for burning the rice. "But I have to study. That's my job. That's what I must be doing."

"You only care about yourself, you selfish creature," Mama responded.

"Why don't you ask your darling son to make himself useful?"

"He has to study."

"So do I!" I yelled, and my voice reverberated through the house.

"Don't kid yourself. With or without a degree, you'll have to do what all women do. You might as well get good at it."

I pressed cotton balls into my ears, wrote down "9:28 p.m." in the margin of my booklet, and began a sample test in literature, the only subject in which I scored high.

Chia wandered in with his backpack on, his body wafting the pungent, pubescent smell of fifteen-year-old boys, his ugly yellow shirt one size too big for him.

"Get the hell out!" I hissed. He was no longer cute, not to me.

"Sheesh, what's wrong this time?" He held his hands up in mock surrender.

"What's wrong?" I took the cotton out of my ears. "What's right, you should ask, and the answer would be nothing. Nothing is right. Nothing." Having failed the national admissions exam twice now meant my future would be even bleaker than my mother's—at least she had been able to secure some income. With only a high school diploma, I could not find a job respectable enough to win Baba's approval. The city swirled with gossip about what secretaries had to do for their bosses.

Chia was unmoved. "But that's not new, is it?" He flipped through some of my stacked books of photography and film history. He'd grown tired of my complaints over the last year.

"Why do you care? You're not a foster child." At this point they seemed to be only Chia's parents, not mine.

"Are you serious?" He laughed, the laughter of a wise man at an imbecile.

"Ew . . . I can smell the cigarette smoke on you. And you stink. You should shower more often." I theatrically pinched my nose and flapped my hand before my face, as if to disperse his stench.

"I have a few surprises for you. Here, sis." Chia gently placed the old headphones over my ears. I wondered if this meant the headphones had really been soothing when he was little, if this was his way of comforting me, or perhaps it was only a mechanical effort to rewind time. Either way, it made me smile, and I regretted snapping at him.

"Now let's do something about your dull room." He removed some rolled posters from his satchel.

"Might as well," I said bitterly. "Looks like I'll be living with Mama and Baba forever. All of my teachers used to say I was smart. It was only when I started doing all the housework that I went brain-dead." Or when the bleeding started.

"You should shut out all the noise and just focus on studying."

"Do you really believe it matters whether or not a woman is educated?"

He bent forward, palms on my desk. "Are you kidding me? Nothing matters more than education. More so for women."

"Why does it matter?" I crossed my arms. "Mama is educated. Baba is educated. I don't want to be like them. I don't know who I want to be. I don't have options."

Chia was busy stapling posters to the wall.

"I should sign up with Shiler to go to nurse the Iraqi war-injured and refugees." I really didn't care if I died and doubted anyone else would either. If anything, everyone would be relieved.

"Voilà." Chia stepped back from the wall. My two new posters were of poets and their words—Mr. Sherko Bekas and "Ask God to be a Kurd for only a few minutes"; Ms. Kajal Ahmad and "Women and Kurdistan: how similar we are."

"I love them. Thank you, *delala min*."

Baba's heavy footfalls down the attic staircase perforated my brief moment of happiness.

"I want to get him to confess tonight," Chia said with a mischievous smile. His voice dropped conspiratorially.

"You think he's adequately drunk?"

"Saddam has been overthrown."

Baba appeared at my door and asked me to iron his shirt. The same soothing and subtle smell of lavender soap, the same welts on his back and shoulders beneath his undershirt, silently testifying to his infinite suffering. He did not look as irritated as usual though.

Chia winked and left, trailing our father. I followed him as far as the shadow of my doorway to watch, to listen. Chia sat in the living room beside Baba, who was fiddling with his radio knob.

"So, the murderer of so many Kurds is finally toppled," Chia began.

The butcher of your family, your hometown, I added to Baba in my head.

"Was Khomeini or Saddam more bloodthirsty, do you think?" my brother asked.

Baba turned to Chia but didn't answer the question—how could he? Iran had executed his best friend and two of his brothers. Iraq had killed his uncles and grandparents in the 1963 massacre and his remaining brother in the 1991 uprising.

My old man squinted. "Now Iran, Turkey, and Syria are panicking. They're putting much more pressure on their Kurds. Listen!" Baba pointed to the talking box that transmitted nothing but the same static buzzing. He shook his head. "The poor stateless Kurds!"

"Aren't all Kurds stateless, Baba?" Chia asked.

"You don't know about the Syrian Kurds who are denied citizenship?" Baba measured his son's worth based on his knowledge of Kurdish plight. But how were we supposed to learn our history when Kurds were omitted from textbooks and the media didn't teach us either? Mama's snores from the bedroom and the static from the radio made it hard to pick out his words. "The news says there are three hundred thousand of them, but I am sure there are more." He no longer seemed to see Chia or even his mother's handmade rug at his feet. "The children of these stateless people are stateless too. They are the poorest of the poor. You have a legal birth certificate, at least."

Baba abandoned the radio and turned on the television, changing the channel immediately when he saw a clergyman delivering a sermon on the West's "cultural invasion" of the innocent youth by "glorifying promiscuity and drugs." Other channels either showed mullahs or played recitations of the Qur'an. As usual, Baba spat at the screen, cursed the mullahs, and then turned off the TV. And as usual, his simmering rage agitated me, even though I was merely spying on this conversation.

Chia fingered the glossy leaves of the peace lily Baba had been growing. "Why do they torture people who have not committed a crime and who only believe in something other than what they are told to?" My brother straightened his spine and sat cross-legged on the rug in front of my father as if expecting him to be able to explain.

Baba glanced at his son forlornly, then back at the dark screen of the television. It reflected his bald head, his baggy trousers and short-sleeved undershirt. He picked up a newspaper and shuffled the pages. "Rotten propaganda!" He threw it away, scratched his mustache with his index finger.

"How would it happen when you were in prison?" Chia pressed his luck.

"At midnight," he said, "they would call names. We were eighty inmates in one wing—sometimes more, sometimes less. Anyone whose name was called after the sun went down never came back."

I pricked up my ears from my invisible post. Baba's gaze remained on the flowers woven into the rug, his expression neutral, reminiscent. "We would listen for and count the gunshots right before sunrise, and with a fork, we'd engrave the date and the estimated number of people executed on the walls of our cells."

I steadied myself on the doorframe. My brother sat rigidly.

Baba continued stoically. "Every time that loudspeaker crackled, every time a guard turned it on and blew into it, every time someone whose name started with *A* was called . . ." He stopped and glanced at Chia, through Chia, as if Chia weren't there. "The ones who were called had only a moment to give their friends and cellmates any useful belongings they had. A shirt, a pair of shoes, a comb. And they might ask for something to be sent to their parents, wives, or children: their diaries, drawings, handicrafts they had made in prison with inedible dough. Then their friends . . ."

Baba squeezed his eyes shut, bit at the corner of his cracked, bloodless lips. "After the men were taken away, their friends would light a candle if they had one, would pass around some dates if they had any, and would shed tears if they still had some left in them. That kind of stuff. They would gather the few possessions they had to give the executed something like a funeral, an acknowledgement of their existence in a place that wished to annihilate us all."

Chia cleared this throat and asked in a gravelly voice, "Was that the worst part? When a friend was taken?"

My father looked away, rubbed his face, and pressed his fingers to his temples as if he were focusing on something. I wanted to run and grab a glass of water for Baba, whose lips had dried up, but I stayed put. "Once a plainclothed man walked in with a flashlight in his hand." He wheezed. Looked the other way. Memories were crowding in.

I held my breath so I wouldn't miss a single word.

"Three guards followed the man, who was clearly an Ettela'at agent."

"The intelligence service," Chia breathed.

Baba continued. "It was past midnight, and the central lights of the prison had all been turned off. We were about twelve cellmates then, Joanna's husband among us. Their daughter was due to be born the day after. We were ordered to stand in a line and face this figure who walked before us, directing his flashlight at us. He pointed his index finger and ordered an unlucky prisoner to step forward from the line. His blinding light then flashed into my face. I shut my eyes and frowned. On a reflex . . ." Baba's lip stayed low, slurring his speech.

My heart was beating too loudly, and I worried its pounding would drown out Baba's next words.

"And?" Chia prompted softly.

Baba sighed, the deepest sigh. "Somehow the monster decided to move on to the next person and beckoned him out of the lineup. He didn't bother to call names, check the prisoners' files. He was so damn sure he would get away with it all. He could have ordered the light to be turned on in a snap—nothing would have happened to him even then. But he didn't bother. He took eight men."

Baba's features were tight, his breathing so labored I felt he was reliving the terror.

"Did you ever hear what happened to those eight men? Was Shiler's father one of the eight?"

"He was. They are buried in a *La'nat Awa*." Baba didn't wait for Chia to ask what La'nat Awa was. "The cursed place. Mass graves where prisoners are taken after execution, or if they die under torture, or if the subjects are just kidnapped or 'disappeared,' or if their families can't afford to pay the bullet fee . . . Can you imagine? When they executed someone, they made the families pay for the very bullets that killed them just to get the body back. Kurdistan is full of mass graves, all called La'nat Awa."

There was a long pause. "They did all of that. They even raped the young women they sentenced to death because they believed virgins would go to heaven and that those opposing the state should only go to hell. They didn't call it rape. They called it a marriage, to make it somewhat religiously acceptable. They believed all of that. Or maybe they didn't. They knew it was a game of power and lust, didn't they? They must have!"

"Baba," Chia said gravely, "I promise to become a lawyer one day and bring them all to justice."

Baba looked into the distance with a blank expression on his face. Then he suddenly turned back to his son. "But my name was always called during daylight. You think I was one of the lucky ones?"

Chia was unable to answer.

Baba's lips twitched into a bitter sneer. "You do, I see it. All they ever did to me was whip me and then turn me loose so I could live like this, like a dog begging for scraps to feed my children. You can't understand it. I was once young too, had hope, thought that I could change things if only I tried hard enough. My dream was to read stories into a loudspeaker for hundreds of elders relaxing in a large meadow. You won't believe it, but I was a dreamer at one point. You know, son, there is more dignity in death than in a life like this."

He took a pull from the bottle of arak he'd stashed beneath the couch cushion, stood, and made for the attic stairs. As he passed my room, he locked eyes with me, still hunched in the shadow. So he knew I was eavesdropping the entire time. Chia remained seated.

I quietly closed my bedroom door and plugged in the iron. My hands shook as I moved the old heavy thing across another of my father's dark shirts. La'nat Awa.

The whip had indiscriminately left its crisscrosses on our backs. I put aside the iron, hugged Baba's hot shirt, and inhaled the smell of him. My tears left widening dark spots on his clothes.

Our region was one huge mass grave: Some lay silent; some cried out from under the earth.

My father needed nursing just as much as the helpless Kurds in Iran, the homeless ones in Iraq, the hopeless ones in Turkey, and the stateless ones in Syria.

CHAPTER SEVEN

I WOKE BEFORE sunrise and groped for the lamp switch. Today was the day. The university admission results would be printed in an otherwise insignificant newspaper, Chia's and my fates printed in the tiniest of fonts. Each year I'd studied geometry and geography to prepare for the national university admission test, the Konkour, but to no avail. Only private universities had admitted me thus far, and they were expensive. This was my last time taking the Konkour, and Chia's first and last. If I did not get in this year, I would stop making a fool of myself. If he didn't get in, he would be conscripted.

Unable to get back to sleep, I started wrapping a present I had bought for Father's Day. Three years had passed since Baba had shared stories of his time in prison—the reason I'd saved up to get him a gift—and tears still welled in my eyes whenever I remembered them. Since no one knew Baba's real birthdate, I had to wait for a different occasion to show how much I cared for him. His mother, the woman who'd given birth every year for the greater part of her life by then, had said he was born in the spring of the year of the flood. That was all she remembered. A birth certificate issued for a dead sibling had become Baba's hand-me-down identification after he survived infancy. The other boy was also called Alan, the flagbearer.

Without a college degree, I wouldn't be able to bear myself, let alone a flag.

Rebellious tears slipped down my cheeks despite my efforts to contain them, spilling onto the gift wrap, which turned my fingertips green—my favorite color, a tonic in my otherwise dreary existence. Holding my stained fingers under the running water of the bathroom sink, I caught a glimpse of Baba's eyes in the mirror. Neighbors and relatives had commented that I took after my father, but this was the first time I was stunned by the resemblance. If he only understood how his daughter was his prisoner, kept under house arrest.

With my hair cropped short in preparation for the sweltering months of summer beneath my headscarf, I looked androgynous, unlike Shiler—her baby fat, for which she was once teased, had developed into womanly curves. She had a supple bosom and looked prettier than ever with those wild eyes. I sometimes ran into her in the town's bazaar now that she'd returned from volunteering in refugee camps. She had resumed her "degree-seeking mandate" in an adult school.

The green stain on my index finger was persistent. I imagined dipping my entire body into a tub of this color, becoming "the forest-green woman." I could stand in the town square, and people would tip coins into my jar to ogle me, smiles on their faces. I wouldn't need a husband. My hand turned numb under the cold running water, but the stain wouldn't rinse off until I used soap. That sparked an idea.

From under my bed, I fetched some leftover pink wrapping paper, put it in a bowl, and poured water over it. Then, with a small piece of cotton, I colored my cheeks pink. My homemade blush looked natural, my face lively and somewhat pretty despite the boyish haircut and the dark circles under my eyes.

I ran down the stairs and peeked into Chia's room in the basement, excited to show off my improvised "makeup." He was praying. Palms held up to the sky, head tilted backward, eyes on the whitewashed ceiling, lips murmuring words of gratitude or complaint, I couldn't tell. He looked snatched away from this dreadful earth.

I crept into the room, sat in the only available corner of the bright but messy space, and wrote in his open journal: "We are each a thousand people inside, brother, masquerading as one. We are each an intricate plant with petals and thorns, full of hope, full of hurt."

With hands that had received the light, Chia wiped his face in the ritual of ending prayers, a gesture that to my mind was the reason his forehead had a spark that no one but I could see. I hid my cheeks with my palms. A good girl wouldn't rouge her face. Only whores did that. I could not remember the last time my God, the loving moon of my childhood, had smiled upon me.

"Ready?" Chia looked right past my pink cheeks.

"Have been for a while."

We sprinted to the biggest newsstand in the city, where a crowd had already gathered. The rising sun flung a streak of purple into the ebbing indigo of the predawn sky.

"I keep saying the paper won't get here until noon," the vendor said. "If you know people who live in big cities, have them check for you. Stop blocking the traffic now." The frustrated man's logic did not work on the noisy, impatient crowd.

Chia clasped his hands behind his back and leaned against a wall. As the hours ticked by, I stared at the patches of cloud that stubbornly refused to form an apparition of our future, at the sun that shone, indifferent to the mixture of anticipation and dread on the street.

When the papers finally arrived, people snatched for the pages on which their surnames were printed. Some tore apart the pages in their anguish over disappointing results. At least ten people were bent over every page, each drawing a corner toward them as if expecting the paper to stretch. Tears fell. Hysterical laughter followed. There was a jubilant hoot or two.

Chia snatched a copy and pulled away from the crowd. My mouth tasted like coins as the bile rose in my throat.

"I'm dizzy," he said. His finger ran down the list of last names that started with *S*.

He gave me a frightened look and shook his head. A deluge of panic broke my calm façade. A final defeat had been a recurrent theme of my nightmares, a thought I wholeheartedly avoided in the daytime, but which lurked in the shadows of every moment.

Chia wiped a fugitive tear with his sleeve. I grabbed the paper from him, pressed the sheet to the wall, and tried to keep my finger steady as I ran it through the names; there were several hundred Samans. I blinked several times. My vision blurred.

The name next to one of the Samans was Chia's. "I am not imagining," I whispered.

His destiny was spelled out in the code written beside his government ID number. Each student's exam scores alone would decide their academic fate; even those accepted to public universities had little say in the subjects they would pursue. Chia stared down for a moment, shoulders drooping, and reclined against the wall for balance.

"Chia?"

He dropped to the ground and buried his face in his arms.

Despite all his efforts, all the late-night cramming and candle-burning, ranking first in his school, the town, and the province, he could not compete with students from the bigger, wealthy cities, people who had the right books and the right tutors. On a national level, he was merely a mediocre student.

Me? Not even mediocre. In this competition, my rank was nonexistent.

The young men and women who had shared the morning wait with us were now sneaking away in silence to find quiet corners and cope with their defeat after having reached for a dream far beyond the grasp of the working-class families of our deprived region.

Chia wandered away from the broken hearts. I followed him. We took the bus home and sat in our designated areas on the gender-segregated bus.

He'd been selected to study political science, which he didn't care for, instead of law, as he'd hoped. But, like Baba, he had been admitted to Tehran University. This could be his making or his undoing; I would exchange my fate with his in a second. This time I hadn't been accepted anywhere, not even by the expensive private colleges. On the list, "Saman, Leila" was nowhere to be found.

WHEN WE GOT home I offered Chia a distraction. "A family is coming over tomorrow. Will you help me clean up the living room?" My mother had accepted new suitors for me as a contingency plan, the latest in her scheme to marry me off, but I'd held on to the smallest shred of hope that I could cancel the meeting if I were bound for Kurdistan or Lorestan University, if not Tehran. The thought of being touched by a man I didn't like gave me the creeps, but I saw no other way out.

"They come to ask for your hand, not mine," Chia mumbled and lay down in his bed.

I glared at him, already annoyed with his moroseness. Didn't he realize how much I'd give to be in his position? Slowly but discernibly, time had turned us into strangers, even physically. Chia's fair skin had turned brown as he swam in Lake Zrebar and played football with his friends under Kurdistan's abundant sun. My skin had turned jaundiced in my loneliness, my cheeks hollow; I slept poorly, waking with aches in my muscles, stabbing pain behind my eyes. His eyes were still charming, my mouth still big. He was tall and attractive while I was short and frumpy, my head swallowed by a fuzzy Afro of unruly hair.

Perhaps tired of the heaviness of my look, Chia got up, handed me a wrapped book, and said lightly, "Hope you read this one." It was the translated version of Simone de Beauvoir's *The Second Sex*, sold on the black market for three times the price of permitted books.

I had no interest in it, in anything highbrow that he and Baba were immersed in, a club of two.

"Chia," I called. "It's not exactly what you wanted, but you have done magnificently."

"You don't understand. I hate political science. Politics is no science. I wanted to become a human rights lawyer."

"I know. Still, you've done better than almost everyone else in this city—really." I swallowed. "I am proud of you."

"Your nail is bleeding." He sounded like he was reporting the weather forecast.

"Ah." I wiped my cuticles on my black slacks. "Didn't realize I was chewing them." I hugged Chia to reassure him that I meant what I'd said; I savored the touch of his skinny and hairy arms, his familiar and comforting scent.

I shuddered as he jerked back. Our emotional distance was finding a new geographical dimension.

"You're crying."

I wiped my face with my sleeve. "Tears of joy, I guess." I grinned.

"Don't pretend . . ."

"What?"

"I told you to put ironing aside and study, didn't I? Didn't I? But you don't listen. It's not my fault you . . ."

I stared at him in disbelief.

"I would have loved to see you go to college, but you ruin your life and act as if I've betrayed you for wanting an education myself."

"What are you talking about?"

"You make me feel . . . Please just leave me alone." Chia waved his hand in the air as if shooing away a bee.

"You haven't even started college yet and you are already acting like a snob. Just because I can't . . . You have no right to humiliate me."

"You give me this look." He raised his hands and curled his fingers inside as if clawing at something invisible in the air. "That miserable look. You make me feel like I'm a shitty brother, betraying you for leaving you alone here."

"You would be miserable too, Mr. Che Guevara, if you were a woman!" I slammed his door. "I hope you die from loneliness in Tehran," I shouted as I ran up the stairs.

I shrieked at the top of my lungs once I was on the rooftop. It felt good, like when Shiler and I had screamed nonsense during morning assembly, so I did it again.

Then I spat from the roof over and over, timing how long it took for the drops of foamy saliva to hit the street below: only two and a half seconds to reach the gravel. I spat as far as I could and watched the drool evaporate in four seconds. The game went on for several minutes as I expelled these tiny pieces of my being, hoping I was spitting out the bad bits, the parts of me deemed so unworthy.

Dry-mouthed, I went into the attic to drink from Baba's pitcher, the remains of which turned out not to be water. I chugged the bitter liquid, several glasses worth. Within minutes my head was swimming. Reclining on a cushion, I impersonated Baba, happy and proud that my son was following in my footsteps, getting into the same university where I'd studied. I clasped my fingers, stretched my legs, and preened my pretend mustache. My farce would be incomplete without the radio, so I turned it on. Of course it was tuned to the Kurdish station. I wasn't listening at first, but then my ears pricked up.

". . . The fight at a football match in Qamishli broke out between the Kurdish fans of the local team and the visiting Arab team. Security forces arrived at Qamishli and opened fire on the Kurds, killing seven of them. The funeral for these men turned into a violent demonstration."

A Kurdish affairs analyst was speaking about the anniversary of a major conflict in Syria that had happened two years ago, explaining how the Syrian police had killed and injured hundreds and arrested more than two thousand, spreading the Kurdish protest to other cities.

Right away I regretted wanting to be Baba, so I pressed the off button, grabbed the old radio, the source of such horror, and ran back to the roof. With a cry of triumph, I threw the old box over the edge and watched it shatter to smithereens on the ground below. Now we might have some peace.

It didn't hurt when Baba slapped me across the face that night. It did hurt, though, when the devil I thought I'd killed was replaced a few days later by a new one, one with a bigger voice to broadcast our unending tragedies.

CHAPTER EIGHT

"Leila, Grandma needs me. I'm going to stay with her for a while. I can't afford a caretaker any longer. I think her days are numbered." Mama stood by my bed, her new perfume sharply sweet, an orange duffle bag—the color of her lipstick—hanging from her shoulder. The spark in her eyes belied the news she was breaking. Or perhaps she was relieved that this smothering cycle of caring for her demented mother was coming to an end. Mama had seemed uncharacteristically content for some time now, not picking fights with Baba or me and even taking more care with her appearance.

"How long?" I looked up at her from my Jila Hosseini poetry collection, which I'd hid within a chemistry textbook. In truth, I'd given up trying for college, but I had maintained the pretense of anticipation, mainly for myself, my only armor against the despair that was silently and certainly devouring me.

Mama shrugged her shoulders and left the door ajar. But the fat brown suitcase she carried out the front door let me know she'd be gone for weeks at least. She'd been wearing mascara, and Mama's darkened lashes had brightened her hazel eyes, eyes that Chia had inherited. I had last seen him five months and fourteen days ago, when he left for university. My little brother was now in the capital, becoming an educated grown man. As more doors opened for him, just as many slammed in my face.

I checked Mama's bedroom, adjacent to mine, and sure enough, I found her closet nearly empty. Gazing in her bureau's mirror, I frowned at how the genetic lottery had showered my mother's beauty on my brother but left me dry. I'd had only a few suitors over the years, and as much as I'd hated those potential husbands, I longed to be desired, to be given the empowering chance to say no. I sat on my mother's mattress; it was worn on only one side, molded into the shape of a lonely woman. Perhaps beauty wasn't such a blessing after all?

Mama's scratched reading glasses were lying on a book whose dust jacket was covered by a newspaper. It turned out to be a psychology book, and the pages of a chapter titled "Borderline Personality Disorder" were dog-eared. Hostility, intense and highly changeable moods, lack of empathy, strong feelings of isolation, distorted sense of self, impulsive self-destructive behavior. It was my mother to a T.

I made my way back to my room where I had been barricading myself since Chia left, not interacting with anyone, even Shiler. In the meantime, a massive and frightening bleakness inside me kept expanding and rattling. Sometimes I wrote about it in my diary, sensing that if I didn't somehow fill the hollowness, it would swallow my heart and spit out my core. Other times I wished for the emptiness to scrape me off, a permanent erasure.

I was terrified that I was supposed to be living and I wasn't, that I must have some prospect and I didn't.

The posters in my room that Chia had given me over the years had suffered from dust and neglect, and my blinds were always shut even though my window opened onto only our unkempt backyard and the marble-covered wall of the back of the neighbor's tall building.

I catch a glimpse of a stranger trudging inside me, in rare moments when the persistent fog evaporates, I wrote. *In lightning flashes, I notice a tormentor at work when external persecutors are asleep. The wound is said to be the place where the Light enters you, but the Dark can sneak in from the same place.*

The phone rang. It had been nearly two months since Chia had last called. Long-distance calls were expensive. "How are you?" I basked in his fruity voice and sophisticated words as he talked about the extensive market of banned books he could now access through contacts he had made at university; about the students' idealism meeting professsors' wisdom, creating an "educated imagination" ready to reshape society; about the stigmatization of the Kurds in Iran, Turkey, and Syria—our criminalized identity, the "assimilate or annihilate" policy. He didn't ask how I was, but even if he had, what did I have to say? That I found no reason to get out of bed anymore, that I was endlessly tired and sad?

"When are you coming home?" I interrupted his speech about the autonomous and prosperous Kurdish region in Iraq and opened the window. I stretched my palm out to catch a few snowflakes that were racing down, unaware of their fate once they reached the ground. I wondered if there had ever been a rebellious snowflake, one that asked what all the rush was for, sat still on an evergreen and looked on in horror as her friends turned into mud and slush under the heartless shoes of self-immersed humans. Did the witnessing flake die in excruciating pain, more so than the others who faced their destiny without prior knowledge or resistance? Or did she make the best of the remaining part of her freefall? "Sorry, what?"

"Any new drawings lately?" he repeated.

"When did you say you're coming home for winter break?"

"I can't, sis. Sorry. I'm working on a newsletter with some friends after the final exams. We want to wake society up to—"

"Oh, give me a break." I hung up, surprising him but also myself.

In the snow-blanketed alleyway, kids were playing with mitten-covered hands; a beautiful girl was perched on the hood of a parked car, flirting with a man whose tongue dangled out of his open mouth like a thirsty dog. A middle-aged neighbor was shoveling his driveway joyfully, bobbing his head and singing along with the upbeat music blasting from his radio. If I could pack my unhappiness into snowballs, I would throw them at these people.

A man who looked to be in his thirties pushed a wheelchair-bound woman up the curve of the street. All wrinkles, she eagerly watched children sledding, running, and building snowmen. Standing by the window, I folded my cold arms and continued to watch the old woman, who was covered in a green, blue, and white blanket. Her eyes shone as the children shrieked with joy, pelting snowballs. "She loves colors, eh?" I shouted to the man as they passed my window.

He looked up and smiled jubilantly. "Oh, yeah, she loves life." The old woman tilted her head toward me. I waved. She blinked twice, then smiled, showing off her perfect veneers. I saw in her the rapture of being alive. When was the last time I had looked for little excuses to enjoy life? Shuddering, I closed the window and turned on the coal heater. On the roof, the chimney coughed smoke into the sky.

"DANCE WHEN YOU'RE broken open. Dance if you've torn the bandage off." I recited Rumi's rhythmic lines, buoyant enough to temporarily lift me from my depression. "Dance in the middle of the fighting. Dance in your blood." I had the entire house to myself, and I relished my solitude. I twirled like a dervish, challenging the walls to dare enclose me, feeling like I could transcend. I took a deep breath. And then another.

With newfound vitality, I set about cleaning the house. I tended the potted plants, the dying spoon-shaped flowers of the peace lilies, the withering heart-shaped leaves of the silvery-grey peperomia. They wanted to stay alive, it seemed to me, not because of anything, but in spite of everything. I scrubbed the kitchen and tidied the living room, though there was little I could do about things like the spring that broke through the stuffing of our secondhand sofa. Nonetheless, the neat house felt less alienating. In the afternoon, I showered and made *nisk*: pureed red lentils, sundried mint, and mixed herbs.

As the nisk simmered, I read Ms. Choman Hardi's poem about homeland, sitting by the window. Outside Baba appeared around the curve with a wheelbarrow full of potatoes. His breath made little clouds before his face; he wasn't wearing gloves or a shawl. A woman carrying an infant stopped to buy some from him.

An old man came chasing after Baba. "That's mine, you filthy thief." He lunged after his quarry, and his boot landed on my father's hip, knocking him over. I gaped.

The woman's bag split open in her hand, and the potatoes rolled onto the asphalt. "Sorry, ma'am. Are you okay?" Baba got up, ignoring the old ogre.

"Thugs!" the woman cursed as Baba ran after the potatoes and put them in a new bag. She left without her potatoes, without paying.

"What is wrong with you?" Baba cursed.

"That's mine." The old man pointed emphatically to the now-overturned wheelbarrow.

"Get out of my way." Baba continued picking up fallen potatoes, sniffing.

"You think I'm bullshitting you? See, I'll show you."

"Go to hell, you lunatic."

"I'll prove it." The man winced but confidently went to the wheelbarrow, pointed at its right corner, and started to shout. "See, my name. See? Right here."

Under the streetlamp, I saw a sweat break out on Baba's forehead. Shaking my head, I shrank behind the curtains a bit.

"Do you see, or are you blind?" the man cried at the top of his voice, his frail body shaking in fury.

Baba wiped the sweat away with his sleeve and looked down, busted.

"You're still young enough to find proper work. Or this will be your future." The man pointed a finger at himself. Another crushed Kurd. A bitter smile appeared on Baba's face. He did not mention that he'd been about to defend his PhD dissertation when the Cultural Revolution had closed down the universities.

"Fine, fine," Baba relented. "My mistake." Before the man could object, Baba scooped a few more potatoes into his gunnysack, threw it over his shoulder, and hurried through our gate, locking it behind him. I considered helping him lug it inside, but I feared injuring what little pride my father had left. Instead I turned to my journal: "Kurdistan is the land of bravery and betrayal; it asks to be embraced but bites you when in your arms."

Baba looked a little wobbly as he came into the kitchen. Our eyes locked. He wheezed. The lines on Baba's forehead deepened, his voice cracked, and his cheeks and nose were crimson.

I handed him a glass of water and asked if he would like some tea. He nodded and washed his face in the sink.

"Smells like my mother's food." He inspected the pot.

That was the biggest compliment. I served us two big bowls of the soup and sat across from my father. He took a tentative spoonful, then groaned his approval.

"Mama will stay at Grandma's for a while," I told him.

He nodded and took another bite. I hated how he looked so relieved. But I too felt there was now air in the house, as if Mama used to suck up all the oxygen.

"Add more lemon juice next time."

THAT NIGHT BABA did not turn on the television or radio. Instead, perhaps inspired by my soup, he went out and shortly after came back with bags of groceries. He taught me how to make a mouthwatering dish of ground lamb, celery, carrots, eggplant, potato, and tomato sauce. We substituted lentils for the ground lamb. Despite the embarrassing scene earlier, his temporary bachelorhood had put him in a celebratory mood.

"Did you know why they call this food *mala dez*?" He blew on a steamy spoonful.

"Meaning a clergyman would steal it? Why is that?"

"They say if something is good, it will be immediately stolen by either gendarmes or mullahs."

I laughed.

"It's sad." He looked at me with surprise and tasted the food.

"I know, but I love these little acts of rebellion. Naming a food that way."

His taste test burned his tongue. I chortled louder. He threw his head back with glee, showing the empty space where his molars should be.

The food was ready. We relished every spoonful.

"Another teenager was tortured to death today. Only fifteen. Lashed for cursing at the Supreme Fucker." It was a test, but I didn't take the bait. I redirected.

"How did you learn this recipe? From Dayah gian?"

"Everything she made was unmatchable," he lamented. "She was a saint. Every time I had a nightmare she was there, ready to soothe me back to sleep."

"You had a lot of nightmares as a child too?" I had no idea.

Baba told me he had witnessed a massacre when he was seven and how the murderous frenzy of the soldiers still haunted him with rejuvenated potency, in scenes that shifted from a mute, black-and-white motion picture to colorful, three-dimensional, real-life experience.

Chia and I had grown up hearing whispers about that day, the day that had defined my father forever. It was his inheritance, this agony, and I longed to share in his burden, if only to understand what had led him down his path of activism to the imprisonment that was still a chain on our family.

He'd been only seven years old. Baba swallowed, saying he couldn't give details of the day. Instead he shared how he still relived it some nights.

In the nightmares, he was there again, a horrified witness to the parents' shrieks and pleas, the soldiers' mirth, the growl of the deadly tanks, the prisoners' silent tears.

Raising his eyes to the sky, Baba would beg for divine intervention, for an end to the cruelty. Instead he'd find himself in a hole, buried up to his chin, at once a terrified spectator and a panicked captive. He would wait for God to pay attention. He would wait until there was no more waiting to be done and the tread of the tank was upon him. As the tanks rolled in, his inability to scream would awaken him. Grandmother would emerge with a calming hand, in a sky-blue dress, looking like a fairy who had entered through the window.

Outside, a truck's tires crunched the snow. Stunned, I studied Baba's stoic face. I swallowed, wanting to say something, but I didn't know what. That he was a gifted storyteller? That I understood him well because I also suffered, even though my exposure to genocide and incarceration was secondhand? In fact, that was the problem. My imprisonment and motherlessness was figurative, his literal.

"Did you have that nightmare in prison too?" I finally asked.

I summoned patience until he spoke. Ordinarily a morning interrogation would be followed by a flogging in the basement, he told me. But one day his guard was called upstairs, and Baba had to follow.

Baba raised his bruised face as they climbed the stairs. He then saw a row of hanged prisoners framed by the window that opened onto the prison courtyard. "Hearing of executions was one thing, but seeing those limp, hooded bodies . . ." He couldn't finish the sentence.

Baba saw before him his martyred brothers, uncles, and friends, swaying slowly in the breeze together. Their heads tilted to one side. Ropes snug around their broken necks. Hands and feet bound tightly together as if they were hanging from the sky itself.

The guard pulled Baba along, and before he really knew what was happening, he had shoved the soldier against the wall, kneeing him in the groin with all his strength. The guard collapsed, but others swarmed Baba, raining down blows. When they were done, he was thrown into a solitary cell.

That was when Baba, who until then had been the quietest and most introverted of the inmates, started beating his bloody head against the wall. As punishment he was kept longer still in isolation. His tiny cell had no ventilation. For months he sat alone and picked up the scraps of plaster that fell from the ceiling.

I bit the insides of my cheeks to swallow down my tears. Sitting across the dinner table was a man who had paid a massive price for hoping and trying for a just world, who had fathered and then neglected me, who wasn't aware that the rage he harbored had killed all other impulses in him, chewing at the core of his compassion before spitting it back out. And here I was, sliding down a similar inevitable path.

LATER I BUSIED myself with washing the dishes and Baba fetched a videotape from the attic. When I was finished I sat beside him on the sofa and kept peering at him out of the corner of my eye, hoping for more stories, but he was glued to the screen. Soon I became engrossed in the story of *Titanic* too, half of which I had to make up to compensate for the language I didn't understand. He fast-forwarded through all the kissing scenes while I looked down and played with the hem of my skirt.

The next day *Titanic* was nowhere to be found. Baba had removed it to save me from the "perversion and decadence of Hollywood." When I finally summoned up the courage to ask him to bring home some more films, he played Iranian ones in which no couple ever kissed or even held hands and women slept with headscarves on. Nonetheless, I was grateful. Baba's interest in film reignited mine.

One of the recurring images I have of my old man is how he tried to hide a tear while watching Kurdish filmmaker Bahman Ghobadi's *Turtles Can Fly*, which depicted a girl trying to get rid of her infant, conceived when a group of American soldiers raped her. In watching these films, I gained a reason to wake up each morning.

CHAPTER NINE

"STOP WATCHING THAT crap," someone whispered as I was yawning and going through the library's limited movie collection. The voice interrupted the library's reverent silence, which was otherwise punctuated only by the sound of quiet pages turning.

The speaker wore black lipstick and dark brown eye shadow. Her pointed nose and stern eyes were unmistakable.

"Still looking for trouble?" I said. We hugged.

Shiler's unusual makeup would make her an easy target for the police of "Enjoining Good and Forbidding Vice," who strolled around female schools and libraries to "protect" us from perverts. But as usual, Shiler wasn't afraid.

"You're a bookworm now?" She pointed to the pile of film magazines and books I was carrying.

"Look what I found. I bet the staff doesn't know they have this here." I handed her the thin copy of Sadegh Hedayat's *The Blind Owl*, cracked and dry with age, smelling faintly of pipe tobacco and dust.

"Neat. Want some Hitchcock?" Shiler winked.

I beamed. She looked over her shoulder and told me to pick up the DVD in an hour from the far end of the library basement, where spiderwebs wove loosely around books on dirty shelves. "Bring it back next week, same time, same place." With that she disappeared. That girl, looking as if she had emerged from one of the stories I directed in my head, had earned my undying devotion.

Though I was careful not to get caught watching banned movies at home, I replayed *Vertigo* six times before I returned it, and Shiler brought me new movies most weeks at our library rendezvous. Since Baba was barely home, I had enough time to watch anything I wanted as long as I switched to state-run television when I saw him coming through the gate. To return the favor, I wrote Shiler's adult school essays for her. She wanted to read only what she liked.

"Have you ever had *khoresh khalal*?" I wanted to feed her in return for her kindness, especially because she'd let me borrow the DVD of *Scent of a Woman*, our favorite movie, for three whole weeks. I'd kept it hidden between the pages of an English-Persian dictionary that had become my holy book, helping me understand the dialogue I devoured.

Shiler shook her head, blew a bubble with her chewing gum, and sat on the light brown desk instead of the chair.

"I'm talking about the Kurdish food." I poked her gum. "The beef stew with slivered almonds and barberries . . . no?"

The librarian who relentlessly rebuked Shiler for her "unladylike" behavior walked between the tables to check for illicit activities, like writing a love letter. Her wire-rimmed glasses hung on a silver chain midway down her chest, and she raised them to her beaky nose as she prowled the aisles.

"Didn't know you cooked. No more yogurt and sugar for you?" Shiler refused to acknowledge the librarian, who shook her head and let out a loud sigh as she walked past.

"Haha . . . with such fantastic nutrition, it's no wonder I never grew. How is your mom?"

"She's well. This morning she was telling me how your mother smuggled a photo of you inside the prison for your Dad."

"You have to tell me all about it."

"That would be a fifth-hand story. Your father told my father, who told my mother, who told me. Ask your father to tell you."

A girl with thick glasses hushed us and flipped through the pages of her textbook. Shiler made a face at her.

"So do you want to go to my place?"

"Let's do it." Shiler jumped down from the desk and grabbed her coat and her blue knapsack.

In the courtyard, a handful of high school girls were chatting and chuckling. The pond was covered with a thick layer of ice. "You should tell me about the aid work you're doing."

"No." Shiler stopped short, and her stare was intense. "No. It was traumatizing for me; you couldn't handle it. You can't ask me anything about that.

Promise?" The trees on the way to the bus station, victims of last night's violent storm, were upended, their root balls exposed. We walked the next few blocks in ruminating silence until Shiler switched to a lighter topic.

"Have you met any cute boys? Last night I kissed Chris O'Donnell," she joked. "In my dream, of course." Her unrestrained mirth, so in contrast with most girls' self-conscious behavior, earned us looks of obvious disdain from the public transit passengers. The men riding the bus who interpreted Shiler's free spirit as an indication of "availability" got off at my station and followed us, then sneaked by and mouthed their phone numbers. I was agitated, conscious of prying eyes behind windows, of neighbors' headshaking. Oblivious, Shiler kept up her monologue about Chris O'Donnell's wet lips.

We played our favorite film again as soon as we got home. Shiler started tangoing with an imaginary partner, doing an impressive job. I gazed at her shaved head, hair long only in front so you couldn't tell she was bald when she wore a headscarf. She playfully grabbed and twirled me, but I was too clumsy to keep up with her, so I sheltered in the kitchen, busying myself with preparing lunch.

Shiler licked her fingers during the meal, making all kinds of flattering murmurs as she ate. Our old chair rocked when she leaned forward to pour herself a second helping. She gulped down one spoonful after another, hardly pausing for air.

"I have a theory!" I said. "I believe foods change taste and texture based on the energy that flows between the people eating it."

She wiped the grease off her lips. "I sure as hell love my mom's cooking, but I've never tasted anything like this. I'm so full."

We lay down on the sofa. "I miss Joanna," I said.

"You should visit. She misses you too."

We resumed watching our movie. "And I'm here to tell ya . . ." Shiler and I recited as Al Pacino yelled out those words, lines we both knew by heart, sentences that had me imagining the power of being articulate.

Months of this daily parroting had taught me many words and expressions and helped me fake an American accent.

The phone rang, interrupting our joyful recital. On the other end, Chia needed little prompting. "The Constitution ostensibly grants equal rights to all minorities in Iran, article three, section fourteen," he said, sounding all smart and sophisticated but forgetting to ask what I was up to. "But we are denied mid- and high-level government posts and education in our mother tongue.

The intentional underdevelopment in our region creates economic marginalization that severely inhibits us from participating in Iranian public life." I didn't know what some of those words meant.

"Who's that?" Shiler asked.

I palmed the mouthpiece. "My brother."

Shiler snatched the receiver. "Well, hello, hello, Mr. Political Scientist. How's the big city?"

Whatever he said on the other side made Shiler laugh her head off. I forced the receiver back toward me, but all I heard was his guffaw. "What's so funny?" Why couldn't he joke with me?

"Leila isn't letting me talk to you." Shiler crinkled her nose between chortles.

I finally had full control of the phone, but I hung up.

"I thought you wanted to talk." Shiler scratched her bald head.

"Shiler, why did you shave your head?"

She fetched a cucumber from the fridge. "I don't know."

I offered a plate, knife, and saltshaker, but she ignored me and bit into the fruit. "The first time I did it was the day I got my first period. You remember. The day I thought I'd die from embarrassment. Anyway, that day I went straight to the barber, pocketed a shaver, and got rid of my hair."

"You wanted to get rid of your womanhood?" I pulled a pillow onto my lap and leaned forward.

"Maybe." She fingered her lower lip, leaned back in her chair, and looked up at the light bulb in the center of the room, hanging down on its white wire. "I'm in love."

"With Chris O'Donnell?"

"No, silly. With a real man. I mean a man who lives here."

"You have a boyfriend?" I was flabbergasted. "Who's the lucky bastard?"

She glanced at me sideways. "I can't tell you, though I am pretty sure I am the lucky bastard."

"You must." I threw a cushion at her. "Tell me. Do I know him?"

"You'll find out later." She giggled.

I teasingly punched her arms. "Who?"

She wrestled with me and was pinned down. "Tomorrow. Tomorrow I'll tell you. I have to ask his permission first. I promise."

CHAPTER TEN

AT THE ENTRANCE of the central library, a woman wrapped in a black chador checked everyone's ID and outfit. The new two-story building was no place for "idle" people. A large painting on the wall quoted Prophet Muhammad: "Seek knowledge from the cradle to the coffin." The building reeked only of paint, devoid of the dust and musty smells of older libraries I loved. But this one offered the newest collection of books and films.

Shiler showed up at the small booth in the far corner as planned. The bang of her large knapsack on my desk startled me. Sweat glistened on her forehead. "Will you take care of this?" she asked, but she didn't wait for an answer. She was gone as suddenly as she'd arrived. I placed the bag on my knees and kept reading about Yilmaz Güney's *Yol*, recorded when the Kurdish filmmaker was imprisoned in Turkey. The banned movie had won several international prizes.

The loudspeakers announced the library would be closing in fifteen minutes. I looked around for Shiler among the rows of books but didn't find her. The place was almost empty except for "nerds" like me, a word I had picked up from a movie. I checked the bathroom. Still no luck. I thought she might be in the courtyard, gabbing as usual.

As I went down the stairs, the lights of a morality police van flashed through the windows. I stopped. Shiler was handcuffed, but she still had a mischievous smile on her face. I couldn't hear what she was telling the woman covered head to toe in a black chador, one of the female police officers who came in handy because men were not supposed to touch women. She was shoving Shiler forward and shouting at her, calling her a whore, an animal.

At the police station, Shiler could be subject to a virginity test, which she'd hopefully pass, though the sting of humiliation would persist. I wished there were something I could do for her. I retreated to the safety of a bathroom stall and opened her knapsack. So many DVDs and videos. Fifty or so. I couldn't have asked for a better treasure. I had a strong urge to run home and start watching them, stay up all night, not eat, not even breathe. Just watch. Swallow them all. But the banned films were probably the reason Shiler had been arrested.

Dump the bag and run, my wise side said. But its contents were all I wanted from life; it could sustain my happiness for days and weeks to come.

The librarians were locking up, and I had to be quick. I listened for the police, who could come in any second and search the few remaining patrons. Baba would renounce me if I were arrested with even one of these films. I couldn't breathe properly.

"Anyone here?"

This must be it. "Me," I responded, but my throat was too dry to make a clear sound.

"Anyone here?" Louder this time.

I recognized the honeyed voice of the old librarian who had checked out my books and magazines. I cleared my throat. "Just a minute." My shrieking voice could give me away.

"Hurry. We're locking up." Her footsteps started to fade down the corridor.

The bag of riches had to be left somewhere retrievable. Perhaps somewhere between the books in the religion section in a country where everyone had already overdosed on the topic. But the main hall was most certainly locked already. The ceiling was plaster. The trash can was the only option.

With shaking hands, I placed seven films in my handbag and dumped the remaining treasure into the garbage can, hiding the blue knapsack with papers I ripped from my notebook. I might as well have been burying my heart.

Then I stepped out of the stall and soaped my hands. "Wash off that blusher! They're out there," whispered the bespectacled Fatima, who had just come in. I knew her from school. Splashing water on my pink cheeks didn't work. I wasn't wearing any makeup.

There was no choice but to walk right by the police and hope for the best. Trying for nonchalance, I tucked my hair under my headscarf and walked slowly. But then I thought I was going too slow and picked up my pace. What if my bag was searched? The words "Enjoining Good and Forbidding Vice" printed righteously on the police van might as well have said, "Entitled to Harass Anyone We Please." I'd have to go back to the restroom and dump the remaining DVDs. But that could look suspicious. A bonfire was consuming me.

I turned back and impulsively went toward Fatima, who was coming down the stairs, wrapping her black chador around her. "I was going to ask you something."

She rolled her eyes, as she often did.

"I wanted to ask you. How . . .? Um . . . how do you think you will do on the national exam this year?" I had instinctively found a common point. Failure. Fatima was deemed unappealing in a society that valued a woman according to the smallness of her nose and fullness of her lips. But her filthy-rich and religious family entitled her to a sense of superiority. Her underqualified father, the one who'd once brought his camera to school, was the president of the Department of Natural Resources in Kurdistan. His only merits were being a non-Kurd and sucking up to the government.

Fatima said she wasn't too worried about failing the college entry test for the fifth year, explaining that she had several suitors who all wanted her for her "virtues, not for superficial reasons." I listened with faked interest, anxious now that even if the police didn't harass me, Baba would disown me for talking to Fatima. Her family, in Baba's words, were "zombies who stole natural resources from Kurdish land and got fat on our blood."

A bearded man from the police van walked toward us. My breath caught in my chest. Too immersed in narrating her stories—or vocalizing her dreams—Fatima didn't notice how I white-knuckled the shoulder straps of my handbag, barely restraining my legs from running away. "One of my suitors is a handsome member of parliament. I'm not going to tell you which one, but you can probably guess. You know, he wants me for life; a chaste woman is more desirable than one of those women who always turn men's heads," Fatima declared to my pale face.

"Hello, miss." The middle-aged man removed his dark green army hat in respect.

I kept staring at Fatima, still as a statue.

"I have been told to drive you home. Your father's driver called us to say he won't be able to pick you up," he added.

The police were there to give Fatima a ride! Not to arrest Shiler for her films. Oh, somebody's fucking God. Shiler had probably been arrested for her makeup. I had to run to the toilet and get the bag.

"Again?" Fatima stared down at the asphalt as she answered him. A pure woman like her would never look directly into a man's eyes. A "chaste" woman like her would only get people like Shiler in trouble.

"His son is in the hospital."

Fatima turned to me. "Leila, we can drive you too."

I was about to throw up. Luckily I had a good excuse for declining her offer. "Thank you, but no—I live at the opposite end of the city."

"It's okay. I'll tell you about another suitor on the way." Fatima confidently walked to the van, expecting me to follow. If I weren't such an incompetent liar, I would've gone with her for safety, but I worried the police might guess from my body language that I was hiding something. I had never sweated so much before.

"I just remembered," I yelled out. "I must go to my grandma's tonight. She lives right there." I pointed behind me with my thumb. "She's ill, and my mother needs help taking care of her."

"Someone will walk you there," the police said, putting his hat back on.

I couldn't say anything more without giving myself away.

"Bye, Leila." Fatima came back and kissed my cheeks, which were turning hot again. Apparently we had become best friends in the past few minutes.

"You go ahead, miss. One of our men will follow you. You'll be safe," he said, and led Fatima to the car.

I nodded helplessly. "Thank you." The police thought they frightened women less than men did. Cops. That's what they were called in the movies.

I picked up my pace to match my heartbeat and did not look back as I turned from one street to another. I was at Grandma's door when it hit me. The library was open only to men tomorrow; women would not be allowed in.

"Hello to you, young lady." The toothless neighbor appeared, emerging from the front door of the apartment block. I was too out of breath to do more than nod. I glimpsed another green-uniformed cop patrolling at a discreet distance, and I climbed the stairs two at a time to reach the third floor.

Sweat puddled in the hollows of my clavicles and ran down between my breasts. I felt ill. What would happen to poor Shiler? I was so useless, unable to do anything for her.

Mama looked surprised to see me, but she didn't nag, fight, or bang about. She tightened the tie of her headscarf, prayed in the living room, and recited God's hundred different names, pressing the chant-counter's button each time, keeping track of the blessings and graces she was buying herself. Not even my obvious anxiety over Shiler could pull her from her ministrations.

In the bedroom, Grandma, diapered and demented, looked good for someone whose days were supposedly numbered. My frantic pacing back and forth bewildered her though.

"Grandma, my friend was just arrested. Over nothing!" I fretted. "I don't know what to do."

She looked at me suspiciously and asked if I was her sister-in-law. "Wait a minute! I know you," she said a few minutes later. "You're my neighbor."

I sighed. "Don't worry, Grandma. I don't really know who I am either."

It was useless to stay there any longer. I couldn't help Shiler, but maybe I could salvage the rest of her cache of films. After leaving Grandma's I stopped by the library, claiming to the custodian that I'd dropped a gold earring in the bathroom earlier that day and asking to be allowed to retrieve it.

"Go away, kid." The young janitor smirked.

Dejected, I took the bus home.

CHAPTER ELEVEN

"SHILER, CAN YOU hear me?" I placed my fist over my heart and knelt before the open window of my bedroom, praying that my friend would feel my words. "You and I are victims of the insanity of a nation that punishes femininity and the arts and reveres thieves and murderers. But you are not alone. I am with you. I know you will be strong. Please be strong."

Snow swirled onto my hair. My breath turned into steam.

"What's the matter with you?" Baba rushed into my room and shut the window. I was burning up.

"Will you bail Shiler out, Baba?" I jumped up.

"Joanna called. Was Shiler talking to a boy or something?" Baba's clothes gave off a new sickly sweet scent, the bags under his eyes deeper and darker.

"No. Poor thing was just at the library. Baba, what will they do to Shiler?"

"Don't worry. They won't hurt her. Just the usual humiliation, you know. I've found a bail bondsman." He turned to leave. I desperately needed him to sit with me, distract me from my crippling anxieties.

"The drought in Syria's Kurdistan . . . so heartbreaking," I tried, sitting down on my bed.

His icy gaze bore into me. Oppression. Discrimination. Poverty. His old fervor aroused. Those stateless people in Rojava who were starving, whose villages were deserted, who had no money and no documents to seek asylum. The Kurds in Bakur, whose villages were burned and whose women were raped by the Turkish army, who were jailed and tortured for speaking their mother tongue . . .

I watched my father as he sat down and leaned forward on the chair beside my bed, shook his head, and frowned in sympathy with his subjugated nation. The wrinkles creased around his eyes and mouth, the corners of his chapped lips dry and flaky, his receding hairline graying. He was only present enough not to bump into objects, but otherwise he was too consumed by the injustices outside of our home to see his own decline, let alone mine. He went quiet, looking unusually confused, or maybe just tired.

"Baba, you never saw me until I was three, right? Mama says my first word was 'Baba.'" I had a cold sore on the corner of my lip.

"I saw a photo Hana smuggled into prison for me."

"Will you tell me about it?"

"You know, I am starting to think that knowing comes at a price. I think you should curb your curiosity." He got up to leave.

I held his arm. "Ignorance is more expensive. You've always said that."

"You're awfully hot."

"Tell me. It'll make me feel better." I longed for a happy story but figured he wouldn't have many of those. Baba sat back down in the chair and told me about my mother's visit to Evin prison in Tehran, far from home in Mariwan where she'd moved after Baba was arrested.

In the 1980s, prisons around the country were packed with real and perceived dissidents, some merely unlucky passersby captured during protests, some detained for being related to an activist or for having talked to one on the phone. Baba's crimes included being reported by his landlord as "anti-revolutionary," being Kurdish and, even worse, Sunni, and keeping two banned books. One was written by Dr. Abdul Rahman Ghassemlou, a charismatic Kurdish leader who fought for national rights, the other a collection of essays published by a leftist group that prioritized class struggle over national identity. The two Kurdish political parties didn't agree much, but the idealist Baba wanted to read both theories and find their commonalities. When he was arrested, he was accused of belonging to both groups, a bitter irony.

The wings in Evin were so overcrowded, Baba and the other inmates had to take turns sleeping on the floor. But the cells gradually became less populated as more and more "enemies of the state" were executed. Khomeini, the self-appointed representative of God on earth, issued the orders: kill the Kurds, the corruptors on earth; kill the Communists, the prima facie infidels; kill the Mojahedin, fellow Muslims who opposed him.

Baba was well into his second year behind bars before Mama visited. She sat uncomfortably in a chair on the other side of a thick glass pane and picked up the phone. An armed soldier searched through the gifts she had wrapped for Baba. She moved her lips, but Baba couldn't hear her over the mingled voices of other prisoners. She pointed to his phone. He picked it up.

"Sorry, I had to leave Leila with my mother. Bringing her along for the ten-hour bus ride was just too much. All she does is poop and eat anyway."

Baba gazed at Mama's hazel eyes and high cheekbones and realized he had nothing to tell her. He reached deep down in his heart and came up emptyhanded.

The guard removed a tiny picture from the pocket of a blue shirt Mama had brought, shook his head angrily, ready to yell at her for trying to smuggle a photo into the prison, but she was too immersed in her monologue to notice. "Ma'am!" he called out.

Mama put down the receiver and looked at the furious guard. Baba tried to make out what she was saying, but he wasn't much of a lip reader. There was only one thing he wanted to ask her before the time was up.

After a long flirtatious exchange, the guard looked around, put the photo back in the pocket of the shirt, and did up the button.

Mama picked up the receiver again. "What was I saying? Oh, I met your friend's father. What's his name? Dana. He was, you know . . ." She stroked her finger across her throat. "Dana's father was forced to search for his son's body in a pile of corpses. And they were lucky. Most families have not retrieved their children's bodies yet."

"That's how she broke the news of my best friend's execution," Baba said, interrupting his story.

I only nodded in sympathy, knowing that at the smallest sign of judgment he would stop talking. That's why he had kept his stories to himself: his crippling fear of not being understood.

Baba got up, went to the fridge, and came back with a cold beer. He leaned back in his chair and looked past me, into the living room, as he shared the rest of his story.

May 1979. Three years before Baba went to prison eight Iranian tanks shelled Kurdish houses. The Revolutionary Guards, the Pasdaran, killed fathers before the wide eyes of their children. Then they looted shops and sold the products on the black market. The blue skies were smoke stained, the smell of blooming mulberries and poppies mixed with gunpowder, the shoots tinged red by the blood that ran in rivers through Kurdish cities.

I knew better than to interrupt him.

Ayatollah Khomeini was moving to assert control over the restive Kurdish cities and countryside; when resistance was encountered, he did not hesitate to issue a *fatwa*, a religious order, condemning the Kurds as "enemies of Islam" even though the vast majority of Kurds were Sunni Muslims.

Baba sipped at his beer.

Armed with tanks and airplanes, the Revolutionary Guards slaughtered the Kurds. Even hospitals weren't spared. The Kurds were alone, neglected nationally and internationally. Kurdistan was, however, full of youths; similar to those in Tiananmen Square ten years later, they tried to block the troops and the tanks.

It felt as if I were sitting right inside a furnace, sweat dripping down my temples, between my legs, and down my spine. "What did you want to ask Mama when she visited you?" It hurt to swallow.

"I asked Hana where she had buried my mother." He looked down at the discolored carpet with its exposed threads.

She had responded, "In Tehran, of course, where she died. What, you wanted me to carry her corpse on my back all the way to Halabja? Across the border during this war? With what money? I couldn't sell my few pieces of jewelry for that."

"Where in Tehran?" Baba managed to say between gritted teeth.

"I mean, prison is no heaven, but at least you're safe here. Nobody bombs a prison. You have no idea what's it like to run to shelters at all hours with a heavy baby in your arms . . ."

"Which graveyard?"

She looked at him sternly. "I don't know its name. The big one. The one at—"

A loud buzzer signaled the end of the fifteen-minute visiting period.

"Did you at least get her a gravestone? Is her name marked?"

They were talking at the same time, at the tops of their voices, into dead air.

Mama banged on the window. They were not allowed to speak another word.

Later that day, Baba received the package his wife had brought and found a small black-and-white photo of a child with a naked gaze. His daughter. When I was born, he'd named me Nishtmaan in a letter written to my mother from prison. But because that name was banned, Mama had named me Leila instead.

"So you were never offered a furlough?" I asked.

"Once only. Twenty-four hours. Too short to visit you in Kurdistan." Baba had searched for his mother's gravesite at the cold and windy cemetery until he found her photo and the stone where her name was carved in calligraphy. He stared at the cold slice of marble, all that was left of his only source of compassion and stability in life.

I imagined Baba running his fingers over the photo of Grandmother's silver braids and her unsmiling lips set under eyes that seemed to be joyful.

A new question nagged at me now. "Baba." I had a hard time speaking, feeling crippled by fear and fever. "Why did you stay with a woman you—?" I stopped short; "dislike" was an understatement, but it was hard for me to suggest a stronger sentiment.

He squinted at me. "Why what? Are you asking me why I stayed with your mother? Is it not obvious?"

I shook my head, looking into his eyes, where the pain of five decades was engraved.

"Because of you." He said it with such surprise, it was as if I'd asked what his name was.

"Me?" I pointed at my chest, brows rising.

"Of course. You and Chia. Why else did you think? I've wanted to leave this marriage many times. I could've gone too—a couple of times I was close—but I just couldn't. Not with everything that I have witnessed first-hand in my life."

My mouth hung wide open.

"Your mother, she'd remarry in a heartbeat. She wouldn't have much choice—a single mother isn't safe on her own—but with her good looks, she'd have her pick. But what if her new husband hurt you two? This damn country has no laws to protect children, you know. I just couldn't."

I kept staring at him.

"Plus a war could happen any day, with America, with Saudi Arabia. Nothing's certain. And I have seen with my own eyes the things that happen during a war: the lootings, rapes, and kidnappings, the trafficking of women and children." He sipped his imported beer. Wiped his mouth. Sighed. "I have seen parents in refugee camps prostituting their daughters to get some clean water. Get a tent. Feed the rest of their children. War brings out the worst in people, even the people who are honorable in times of peace. Anyway, at least this way I know that you and Chia are safe."

Was my father my prison guard, or was I his?

A key turned in the lock.

"Looks like your grandma finally kicked the bucket." Baba stood up. "Don't be fooled by what your mother claims. That woman was cruel long before dementia broke what little filter she had. She used to beat Hana, just like her husband beat her."

But those footsteps, firm and steady feet walking up the stairs, were not Mama's.

I cut Baba off and ran to the living room.

"What happened to you?" I was startled by Chia's bald head. He loved his hair too much to shave it.

"What are you making a fuss about?" Baba frowned. "He's home to visit his family."

Chia smiled. "Can I get a hug, please?"

I threw myself into his arms.

He touched my forehead. "Leila gian, have you been near the heater?" he teased.

"She left her window open. I think she's coming down with something." Baba grabbed two beers from the fridge, another for himself and one for his son.

"We should see a doctor." Chia grabbed my hand and sat me down on the sofa.

"They arrested Shiler." My eyes welled. "Over nothing."

Chia opened and closed all the dish cabinets. "I can't find one clean towel!"

"Can you come with me to the police station tomorrow?" Baba asked Chia.

"Sure." Chia poured some water in a large plastic bowl and placed my feet in it. He removed his shirt, soaked it, and placed it on my forehead. "Baba, do we have any codeine?"

Baba grumbled and disappeared into the bathroom.

"What's that scar?" I pointed to his shoulder, visible through a hole in his undershirt.

"That's nothing." Chia kissed my forehead, and all the ache disappeared.

"Why didn't you come home for the winter break? And why are you home in the middle of the school term?" His militarized hair was disorienting.

"See, my shirt has already dried. If your fever doesn't come down, I'll have to take you to the emergency room." He fed me some tablets and tipped a glass of water to my lips.

Next thing I remembered, he and Baba were putting me to bed. "Chia . . .

help Shiler," I pleaded weakly, but the words came out unintelligibly.

Every time I opened my eyes that night, Chia was at my bedside, his soaked shirt on my forehead.

AROUND NOON I woke to a delicious smell. "Since when do you cook?" I was less drowsy today, but still weak.

"A boy has to survive on his own." He handed me a steaming bowl of chicken soup with fresh herbs floating on its surface.

"Has Shiler been released?"

He looked at me gravely. "Yes. She's in the hospital." I felt a fresh wave of concern for my friend.

"Let me guess—she got a beating for being defiant?"

"Typical Shiler." He turned his eyes away from me, but I saw something hitch inside him.

Relieved that at least Shiler wasn't in prison, I demanded that Chia tell me the truth.

"What truth?" He put the kettle on.

I confronted him. "You stopped calling. I expected you over winter break. Now the hair. What's going on?"

He waved the match in the air to put it out. Chia explained that he'd dropped out of university, unwilling to complete his political science degree when his heart was set on studying law.

"In this country, we don't even have the right to ask for our rights." His goal, he said, was to eventually bring the perpetrators of genocide and mass executions to justice in an international criminal court. He was certain that was the purpose of his life, and he didn't want to spend four years studying something he saw no use for. But having dropped out, he could no longer use the military exception granted to students, so he had been in a garrison for the past three months, completing his military training. I was furious with him for not having told me earlier, but I felt too woozy from the fever to pick a fight.

"What happens now that the three months of training is over?"

"I'll be sent to teach in an isolated village."

"I hope you'll be sent somewhere nearby." I sipped the honey lemon drink he presented.

"Me too. I'd rather serve my own people."

"Your pretentiousness gives me a rash." I scratched my neck.

He laughed.

Baba came home early that evening, boiling with fury and frustration. Turkey had killed some two hundred Kurds. Our father had noticeably declined; his face twisted with pain.

Chia and I were even, if only temporarily, both equally neglected by our father.

I VISITED SHILER after she was released from the hospital and I recovered from what turned out to be pneumonia. Joanna opened the door and pulled me into an embrace. She looked as though she'd been crying.

"Shiler's asleep. Sit awhile." Their neat one-bedroom basement apartment looked spacious with its cream-colored walls and small white sofa, so in contrast with our yellowish paint and ugly burgundy couches.

"No I'm not," Shiler called out from the bedroom.

Joanna sent me in and went to wash her face. Shiler was propped up on the bed in the corner, pressing her knee up to her belly and squeezing it close. She looked up, and our eyes locked. A large scar extended from her left temple to the center of her forehead, cutting through her eyebrow. A tiny blood spot in her left eye. Face bruised and pained.

I knelt and held her hands. "Delala min, what have they done to you?"

"I'm okay," she winced. "Only lost one kidney."

"A kidney?" I screamed. "You lost a kidney?"

Joanna came in with a tray of tea, eyes now completely dry. "She has another perfectly functioning kidney."

"How? Why?" I tried to release my hands from Shiler's grip, but she did not let go. For the first time I saw fear in her eyes. The firm ground shifted beneath my feet. I'd never seen Shiler so beaten down—not in school, not ever.

"Failed the virginity test. And they found out about my parents' history. Two men and one woman beat the shit out of me. The prison hospital removed the fucked-up kidney. You know what's funny? The woman's finger broke from all the beating." She laughed a bit before squeezing her knee to her chest again.

Joanna pressed her forehead to Shiler's and kissed her hand.

I drew a sharp breath, refused to let my tears fall. "I safeguarded some of your movies. Seven of them. Sorry, that's all I could do."

"I didn't think I would get even one." Shiler's smile was real.

I unzipped my large coat and brought out a bag of discs.

"Oh, girl, I thought you were pregnant," Shiler taunted me lightly. Her smile reached her eyes.

"As if."

We laughed. I got up to place my coat on a chair. *The Second Sex* was on the bookshelf. I never had read it, so Chia must have passed it along. He'd inscribed a note on the first page: *To my militant sweetheart.*

"I didn't know you and Chia were so close." I frowned.

"Please sit with me awhile, Leila. Keep the lights on. Keep the door open," Shiler asked. Five minutes later she was asleep.

I left the bedroom, no longer feeling obliged to hold back my tears. Joanna followed and held my shoulders. "Where the hell is God now?" I said. "Why did this happen to Shiler?"

"Oh, darling. God had no say in this." Her words, already gentle in her soft Kurmanji dialect—much more sonorous than the Sorani dialect Kurds spoke in Iran and Iraq—were especially tender. "It's all human mess, and agency is part of the law. So it's all in our hands. It can be changed, *gulakam*." She called me "my flower."

"I wish I had your faith."

I thought about Joanna's struggles, how, unable to speak Persian, she'd understood only a few words that were spoken in the court during her trial. When she tried to defend herself in Kurdish, the outraged judge changed her sentence from "life" to "execution." He assumed Joanna was a separatist because she spoke in her mother tongue. She wasn't a separatist until that day.

Joanna had wailed and explained that she had been raised in Kobani, Syria, not Iran, and didn't speak Persian. Nobody understood her. Nor did anybody care what a convicted murderer had to say. Joanna swore to God's Kurdish, Persian, and Arabic names that what she had done was self-defense, that the man had tried to rape her while she was going home from work. But the law knew one thing: A man's life was worth twice as much as a woman's. People said he hadn't actually raped her before he was killed. What had she worn that day anyway? Why was she walking alone in the dark? Regardless, she had to either pay the man's blood money or be hanged in retaliation.

The only thing that saved Joanna from the noose was Shiler, growing in her belly. And now the same government that had sentenced her to die had come for Shiler too.

We hugged quietly and cried in each other's arms.

"All it takes is some listening. Remember, crying, even praying, is not listening, *chawakam.*" *You're my eyes.* Her warm look instigated a certainty that I knew I'd lose as soon as I was out of her sight. My friend's body was mutilated and so was my soul.

On the way home, I realized whom Shiler had been dating.

CHAPTER TWELVE

BABA CAME OUT of the bathroom, the same old towel loosely thrown over his shoulders, the same welts, the familiar lavender soap. The pit in my stomach as I looked at the scars was the same too, but that was the extent of it. I was too broken open to dance, feeling trapped once more. Fatima, the rich girl, had killed herself after her fiancé didn't show up on her wedding day, I'd learned. I didn't blame her.

Baba went straight to the pot on the stove, lifted the lid, and inhaled the aroma. I had made Chia's favorite stew of herbs and beef, *sewzi ghawlma.* During the meal I had Baba's attention and Chia's compliments, but as soon as they were full, I was once again as significant as the greasy dishes left in the sink.

Baba lay down on his mother's rug and turned on his radio. "—and Mohammad Sedigh Kaboudvand, editor of the weekly newspaper *Payam-e Mardom-e Kurdistan*, is sentenced to eleven years in prison, convicted of 'inciting the population to rebel against the central state.'"

Baba said the journalist had written about the Kulbar and asked if I knew who they were. I did not. Poverty-stricken villagers, so helpless that they risked their lives and their only valuables, their mules, to smuggle goods, walking long hours and days in the mountains carrying heavy burdens on their backs, sneaking by numerous checkpoints, getting randomly shot by the heartless Iranian guards.

"Baba, I found all the shirts I've gifted you over the years. Did you even try them on? Even once?" They'd been hidden under a large pile of newspaper in the attic, tags still on them.

"Even if the guards don't kill them, the hardship of the job will," he went on, but I detected a hint of embarrassment on his face.

I waited for him to give an explanation, perhaps to say the colors were too happy or the sizes weren't ideal. He stared at me, and I could read his thoughts. How could Leila care about shirts more than the human lives lost weekly to poverty and the savagery of the border guards?

I sighed and headed to Chia's basement studio. His radio was on too, tuned to the same station: "—Kurdish protestors were killed and a hundred and forty-two arrested in Saqez. Government buildings and banks were destroyed."

He paced in the tiny studio, sweating, taking notes, pacing some more. "Iranian troops arrested as many as twelve hundred protesters and killed eleven people . . ." the radio went on.

The birds and worms had already eaten all the cherries in the backyard. Our bikes were rusty and broken. The trees were dying.

Chia started packing for his teaching post.

I went inside his room. "Will you visit every week?"

"Every week?" He looked up from his suitcase.

"You'll be only three hours away."

"The books and heavy stuff should go underneath, right? And then I can squeeze my underwear and socks in the little spaces between books, don't you think?" he asked, as if I knew anything about traveling. Indeed, why would a man immersed in community service waste money on visiting a perpetual straggler, and an aging one at that.

"Don't forget your favorite blue shirt." I handed it over, cleaned, ironed, and neatly folded.

"Ah, thank you!" he said but did not put it in his luggage.

"Explain to me, Professor: What is wrong with having clean shirts?" The anguish of my trivial existence was insignificant to him.

Chia shook his head. "I'm going to a poor village, not to a fashion runway."

"Oh, so you're a saint now, are you?" I said, hands on hips. "You think I don't know you're responsible for Shiler losing her kidney?"

Chia yelped and drew a quick breath, which made me realize my wild guess had indeed been correct. He hunched over his suitcase to avoid my gaze and folded his underwear smaller and smaller, trying to make it take up as little space as possible.

It was all too obvious now. So the progressive souls had been dating and had kept it from me. "You claim you know all about this society, and yet you couldn't protect your own girlfriend? How long has this been going on behind my back, anyway?"

"Shiler had planned to tell you the day she was arrested. We wanted to tell you, honestly, Leila, but the timing needed to be right. You can be such a prude." He echoed the sentiment Shiler had said a hundred times: I was too uptight about sex. "Now will you please go away?"

"Why do you treat me like I'm only a nuisance?" My voice was shrill, a mouse-like squeak.

"We're in love. Do you understand what that means? It's not like I forced her." He wiped his forehead with a trembling sleeve.

"Well, she is the one who was tortured for it, and yet you act as if you are better than everyone else."

He threw a book at the wall and shouted louder than I'd ever heard, "Get a fucking life!"

I had none.

Chia zipped up his half-packed suitcase, left without another word, and slammed the door behind him.

Deflated, I sat at his desk and read his notes. He'd been documenting Kurdish sufferings in our banished mother tongue: Kurdish men made up a disproportionate number of the political prisoners and executions, often more than 40 percent. Women setting their bodies on fire. Smart students expelled from top universities because of their or their families' political activities. On every page he had written the national anthem in large spiky handwriting: *Kas nalle Kurd merduwa; Kurd zinduwa*—Let no one say the Kurds are dead; the Kurds are alive.

I ran my fingers over the words. Alive. Dead. Alive. We were dying but still alive. How was that possible? But it was something I felt acutely. I held a finger under my nose. I was breathing. But I was not alive. Only no one could see that.

Something powerful seized me and would not let go. I was restless, haunted. I wrote: *And here I am, a Kurd who wishes for nonexistence before your eyes, a woman worn down by hurt and isolation, stuck for a thousand tedious years in solitude and invisibility. You see the suffering of everyone but me.*

A red Toyota decelerated at our door and honked. Baba got in the car, dressed up and clean shaven. The driver was the neighborhood dealer everyone called Gravedigger.

I had to get out more too. I filled a small vitamin container with hot water and pink tissue paper. With a piece of cotton, I colored my cheeks and lips. The phony vibrancy gave me the confidence to go out to the town's only park.

The lawns smelled fresh and clean after a light rain. The daisies and poppies were picked over despite the signs forbidding it. I remembered pulling them up by the stems with Shiler and Joanna when Chia was born. I kicked the rotten fruit that had dropped from the trees, half-eaten by worms and birds. The unwanted apples.

Passing men whistled, catcalled, then scoffed at my old-fashioned clothes as they drew closer. They could treat me however they liked. Women came in only two types: whores or dutiful slaves to their families. Good girls would not go to a park alone. Good girls would be content with having men breathe the fresh air on their behalf, take in all the oxygen one required to keep women at bay.

Glancing up at the blue sky as I strolled through the park, I saw two adolescent boys up in a tree, kissing, trying to hide within its branches. They must have trusted that the morality police were not in the habit of looking skyward. The boys could be executed for that.

I bade farewell to the flowers and took to the sidewalk. Cars honked, drivers trying to pick me up. Within a matter of seconds, I made a decision. I was ready to get in one of the honking cars and give destiny a chance. It was common for men with new cars to pick up women, offering rides to see what would come of it—a phone number, a kiss, a date, a fling, maybe something more if there were chemistry.

I stood by the curb. Men braked, looked through their passenger windows, and asked, "Where's this pretty lady going?" I blushed beneath my homemade rogue.

One rubbed thumb and index finger together to suggest he'd pay me.

I sat down on the curb. My heart slowed until there was a long pause between each leaping beat. When the beats did come, my heart heaved desperately, like a fish on a rocky shore, trembling and gasping.

Another car beeped. I raised my eyes to look through the passenger window when a red Chevy braked inches in front of me. My hands were too frozen to open the door.

"What the hell are you doing out here?"

"Oh, hi, Baba." The contempt in his eyes wasn't just terrifying: it transported the magnitude of his hatred to me like an electric current; I was a disgrace to his honor, wearing makeup, sitting on a curb like a beggar, trying to get into a stranger's car. "I was going to see a doctor," I offered.

He rolled up the window without a word, and the car accelerated, dust flying behind. I was being punished for what I hadn't done yet, sentenced in a court from which I'd been excluded.

Utterly drained, I walked aimlessly for a while and then hailed a cab to go to Grandma's.

When I reached the rusty gate of the apartment building, my vision tunneled. I had to support myself with a hand against the wall, and then I lay my head on it and imagined Chia's small head lying on my shoulder. I recalled the days when he enjoyed my stories, the stories that had slowly decomposed in me since he first left for university.

An invisible umbilical cord had connected Chia and me, the kind that formed between siblings neglected by their parents. He was too immersed in the gratification of teaching to remember this now. I should have gone with him to the village, not that he'd offered.

Climbing the stairs to Grandma's third-floor apartment was dizzying. I placed my cheek against her metal door to cool down.

Through the door, I heard Mama speaking in that odd, singsong voice of hers that I had heard late at night while she was on the phone. I couldn't make out the words, but the affection in them was recognizable. I turned my spare key in the lock, pushed the door gently, and saw something I could never unsee.

I would rather have believed I was schizophrenic than register what my eyes saw. Mama was indeed talking lovingly. To a naked woman's tiny penis. She was holding it before her mouth. Mama was dressed in red lingerie the likes of which I'd never before seen—not in her drawers, and certainly not on her. Mama then lifted the woman's penis and licked her vagina. I blinked. Blinked again. Rubbed both eyes.

"Bring me a glass of water, you whore," Grandma yelled. She was in the bedroom, the door shut. Mama was too immersed in carnal joy to notice her daughter or her mother. I shut the door before she saw me, but loudly enough for her to realize somebody had certainly seen her.

CHAPTER THIRTEEN

I TURNED ON my heel. Ran down the stairs. Nauseated and gasping for air, I sprinted down the street. Something chased after me. I retched several times beside a tree, finally coughing up bile. I kicked some dirt over my vomit, then sank to my knees.

After a while, when I felt as though I could stand, I dried my face and hailed the first open cab.

The lecherous look the driver gave me jangled my nerves. In my peripheral vision I could see him leering at me in the mirror. I pushed my headscarf forward, tucked in the few strands of hair that had escaped, and fisted my hands to stop their shaking.

"Where to?"

I told him the farthest place I could think of. I needed to put as much distance as possible between me and what I'd witnessed. My breath grew shallower. I needed air.

"You're hot," the cab driver said when I rolled down the window.

I glared at him. We'd likely crash at some curve soon because he believed women were created to be stared at in his rearview. But the thought of a quick death was tempting.

"I meant 'hot-blooded,'" he went on. "It's chilly today, yet you open the window."

The speed limit was fifty kilometers per hour, but he was driving at least a hundred. I wished he would slow down so I could lose myself in the scenery.

He slowed down, and I had the sudden unsettling conviction that my forehead was glass and he could see through it to read my thoughts, or worse, see the scene of my mother that kept replaying in my head, a trailer of what was likely years-long infidelity.

"You're not from Mariwan, are you?" he asked.

I didn't look like my people. Who did I look like? I could put on an accent and try flirting, but a hand reaching up from deep in my chest had grabbed my voice.

He gave up, either offended or bored. "*Sallahai salla, awin dari tom* . . ." He was singing along to the song by Razazi playing on his car stereo. With his eyes finally off me, I prayed the winding road would never end.

I rubbed my eyes, hoping to wipe away what I'd seen. It couldn't be real. I had lost my mind. That's what it was.

We were approaching the mountains now. I was determined to distract myself. I had to, or I'd completely lose it. Lake Zrebar was too beautiful, too tempting—a three-thousand-acre freshwater escape. In my mind I gave myself to her cool waters like Ophelia, my body floating in the lake while an invisible part of me watched from above.

Checkpoint. I wouldn't know what to tell the patrolmen if they asked why I was going to Zrebar. When stopped, the grinning driver said a warm hello and shook hands with the soldier, whose Kalashnikov dangled on his back and whose nose probed inside the car to ferret out anything illegal: playing cards, alcohol, music, or drugs. The driver put something in the guard's proffered palm. We were permitted to pass.

At the lake, the cab driver asked whether he should wait for me. I gave up all my change and left. "It's not safe, sister," he called after me. "I can come with you or wait for you. I won't charge you."

A wave of sardonic cynicism washed over me. All of a sudden I was his "sister." "You mean it's not safe because of lewd men like you?"

"Ghahba!" He pressed hard on the accelerator, spraying dirt behind his tires.

Inhaling deeply in relief, as if I'd finally surfaced after a deep dive, I watched his cab disappear around the curve of the road. I began to pick my way up the hill, its lush green forest an oasis. I craved something bitter and icy, anything to make me forget the look on Mama's face as she had fondled that woman's tiny penis. Or perhaps that hadn't been a penis but rather a very large clitoris?

I shook the thought from my mind and instead trained my eyes on the lake's glassy surface. When we were children, Joanna had told Shiler and me some of the legends surrounding Lake Zrebar, including the one of its mystical origins: since no one could identify its source—the lake was not connected to any other body of water and rainfall alone could not have formed it—some believed it had appeared by magic. If only the lake could lend me some of its magic now, give me the strength to overcome my shock.

Joanna had said all I needed was to listen. So I did. The snow on the high mountaintops had not yet given up to the spring sun, but the hill was dotted with patches of flowers. Among them, I came across a shiler, the crown imperial lily, a rare beauty. The petals faced downward, and a crown of small leaves sat proudly on top of each stem. Red poppies burned bright under the sun and danced with the breeze. They urged me to hold on a little longer. But a thought nagged in the back of my mind.

Could my father have known what was going on? I wanted to find out—I couldn't stand the thought of bearing this silently, alone—yet I was afraid of his apathy upon hearing the news. I feared his indifference would destroy me more than her betrayal, the unforgivable sin conducted by a pious woman who had taught us such strict boundaries between men and women.

How long could I continue like this, crushed as I was beneath the daily cruelties faced by my people? Denied our language and history, policed and imprisoned, tortured and executed—when combined with my personal failures it was too much to bear. Constantly failing to meet my parents' expectations. Taking the Konkour again and again. Shiler's arrest and beating. And now this. Each injustice barbed me more than the last. I knew that at least this time I hadn't done something wrong, but I couldn't shake the feeling that I myself was an existential mistake. I was an error. Entranced by my own misery, I sank to the ground, seeking release.

I let my headscarf slide down, closed my eyes, and lay down on the grass, palms to the sky, the sun gentle on my face. With my eyes closed, I saw the wind carrying my body above the fields while the poppies sang my requiem.

When I opened my eyes, I watched as butterflies flew overhead, spreading their dotted wings of orange, brown, and black as they moved from red poppies to the yellow bushes of wildflowers, to hawthorns and jasmines, whose fragrance overpowered all the other fresh scents. Almond and wild pear trees were still and serene. The wheateaters, serins, and other birds were singing in a majestic orchestra.

Time passed. I wasn't sure how long I lay there among the flowers, behind a huge stone on the hill, fantasizing about a serene nonexistence. I'd spent hours doing nothing, absolutely nothing: not thinking, not cleaning or cooking, not humming a song, not watching a movie for the millionth time.

The sun started to set, snapping me out of my dreamy state.

Here I was, a woman alone on a mountain at dusk.

An invisible boot pressed against my throat, making my breath labored and helpless, and yet I couldn't go back and face my parents. Or my stifled future. Hidden behind a boulder, I hugged my knees and imagined my rage and pain whirling into a wildfire, burning down all the injustices.

My shoulders were heavy beneath the daily cruelties of living as a woman in La'nat Awa, the damned place. This fatigue was incurable. Despite all the clothes I wore, my skin felt naked in its constant exposure to the thorns of my existence.

The sun had sauntered down, disappeared behind Lake Zrebar. A dozen shades of red burst open along the horizon as the day gallantly made way for night.

Below, the narrow winding asphalt road was the hem around the hill's green skirt, embroidered with clusters of red and yellow wildflowers. Among them, the shiler flowers stood elegant and tall, flourishing across the rough Kurdistan plateau, defying the senseless borders drawn by the Allies after the First World War.

I bent down and cupped the bud of the shiler, slightly trampled by some oblivious hiker yet still intact. As I thumbed the smooth petals, I yearned for the shiler's perseverence. But I was a garden of anguish, of loathing, of torment; my occupied homeland was a birthplace of death.

I stood up, my breath now coming in pants. I wasn't hiding anymore. "Basa bas," I shouted. "It's enough. Enough."

I started down the hill in a tumbling run and found myself unable to stop. Despite the chill of the evening, I started sweating. The wind whipped my headscarf, and I gained speed. I flapped as if I had wings.

As I ran, a wail escaped my chest. I was headed toward the main road, toward the world of men. The streets belonged to them. Judgmental men. Hypocritical men. Their-honor-depended-on-women men. Cars hurtled around the curve, full of drunk drivers who honked as they spotted me sprinting down the hillside. They were going too fast for this road, too fast for their sluggish reflexes, and too fast for their old vehicles. A white late-model car careened down the winding road, kicking up dust. The wind roared in my ears.

The white car and whoever was driving it seemed to seek me out as a fellow traveler. I stumbled on a stone, crushing the shiny red poppies in the grass. And as I lurched, my untold stories tumbled inside me like pages ripped from a book and tossed, crumpled, into the wastepaper bin. An overpowering urge to scream my story, to expel it from beginning to end, seized me. Suddenly I could see the heads of all those Kurds crushed beneath tanks.

Descending the slope at a breakneck pace, my shouts crescendoing, I was unable to stop myself, this crazed woman.

A final lunge and I was airborne.

A squeal of brakes. Tranquil at last.

PART II

ALAN

CHAPTER FOURTEEN

When his grandpa drew a yogurt mustache above Alan's lips, the boy dissolved into giggles. Picturing himself with real whiskers thrilled Alan, who thought that facial hair might make up for being shorter than the other boys in his class.

"Your laughter woke me up, you cheeky monkey!" Uncle Soran, youngest of the six uncles and the only one awake, tousled Alan's hair as he came onto the patio that opened to the yard. They sat around a nylon cloth spread atop a crimson handmade rug to eat breakfast.

Alan laughed again. "*Bapir*, I want handlebars, please."

With a chapped finger, Bapir curled the ends of the yogurt mustache on either side of Alan's puckered-up lips and planted a dab of the stuff on his nose too. Alan collapsed into laughter.

That June morning in 1963, Alan decided that Bapir was the most amusing person on earth. Perhaps he was the reason Alan adored older people and loved to listen to their stories of *maama rewi*, the trickster coyotes. It hurt Alan that most people with gray hair weren't able to read or write, that their backs hurt and their papery hands trembled; his dream was to read stories into a loudspeaker for hundreds of elders while they relaxed in a large meadow filled with purple and red flowers.

Grandma brought out more *nan*, the thin, round bread she had baked in the cylindrical clay oven dug into the basement. Alan made his own "bulletproof" sandwich: fresh honeycomb mixed with ghee. "After I eat this, I can run faster than the bullets," he said.

"Our monkey is growing up, and yet we all treat him as if he is a young child!" Uncle Soran said, making his own bulletproof morsel.

"One's grandchild is always young. That's just how it is." Bapir brushed crumbs from his lap. He winked. "If I were you, Alan, I would make it so I never grew up."

"Growing up is a trap," Grandma agreed, nodding.

"But I like the future," Alan said.

They laughed. Bapir splashed a kiss on Alan's face. "Something a six-year-old would say."

Still wearing his yogurt mustache, Alan frowned. "I am seven."

They cackled.

Father had come to Sulaimani to publish an article he'd written with Uncle Soran illustrating the suffering of the working class in Kurdistan and the rest of Iraq. Kurds had settled in the Zagros Mountains three hundred years before Christ was born, but now Alan's people had no country to call their own. When the Western Allies had drawn the map of the Middle East, they had cut Kurdistan into four pieces, dividing it among Iran, Iraq, Turkey, and Syria.

To visit Bapir with his father, Alan had to ace Kurdish spelling. But Kurdish was not a subject taught at school; Arabic was the only language used there. Father had been trying to teach him and his three brothers to write in their mother tongue, something Alan saw no use for. That morning, Father had skipped breakfast to search the city for a contraband typewriter.

Across the yard, Grandma was watering the pink roses and white lilies. A pounding on the wooden gate in the cement wall that surrounded their plot of land shattered her concentration. She dropped the hose.

"I'll get it." Alan ran across the yard to save her the trouble, but before he reached the gate, six men in Iraqi army uniforms, their faces hidden by striped gray scarves, broke the lock and directed their Kalashnikovs at Grandma's face.

"Where are they?" the shortest one demanded.

Bapir froze, a morsel still in his open mouth. Alan turned to see Uncle Soran leaping over the wall and clambering onto the neighbor's roof. Somebody—Grandma—grabbed Alan and backed him toward the house.

Nestled against her bosom, Alan watched the soldiers invade the house without waiting for an answer. All six uncles were pulled from their beds or hauled from the bathroom, the basement, a closet, and off the roof next door. Alan wiped off his white handlebars with his sleeve and tried to make sense of the chaos, the jerky movements, the incomprehensible noises escaping people's throats. If only his eyes would give him weapons instead of tears!

His uncles were dragged by the neck, screaming and struggling, like animals to slaughter. Bapir's questions and prayers, Grandma's cries and pleas, the neighbors' screams and curses—nothing had the slightest effect on the soldiers, who conducted the raid without a reply.

Alan's uncles, some still in undershirts, were marched out at gunpoint to army trucks carrying hundreds of Kurdish boys and men between the ages of fourteen and twenty-five. Alan peeled himself from Grandma's arms and ran to the street. The men were told to squat in the beds of the trucks, to place their hands on their heads, and to shut their mouths. Alan looked back at Bapir, who remained next to his smashed gate, head bowed.

Along with other children, women, and elderly, Alan chased after the lumbering trucks, their huge rubber tires kicking up clouds of dust as they carted away the men amid the anxious cries of the followers. The older men, unarmed and horrified, searched for weapons and ran up the mountains, asking the Peshmerga to come down to the city to face the armed-to-the-teeth soldiers. Alan trailed after the truck carrying his uncles as it traveled up the hillside at the city center. His heart had never beaten so fast. The truck finally stopped at the top of the hill, and prisoners were shoved out.

On the hard soil, the captives were each given a shovel and ordered to dig. "*Ebn-al-ghahba*," spat the soldiers—Son of a whore. The angry bystanders were ordered to stand back. People obeyed the AK-47s.

Dirt sprayed over the prisoners' bodies, hair, and eyelashes as their shovels cracked the earth open. Sweat dripped down their faces, and tears ran down over hands that muffled sobs. Alan looked at the pee running down the pants of a boy next to him, at a woman behind him clawing her face and calling out, "God, God, God," at an older man shaking uncontrollably, his hand barely holding onto his crutch. Alan did not seem to be in possession of his own frozen body.

Once the trenches were dug, half of the prisoners were ordered to climb down into the ditches, and the rest were forced to shovel dirt up to their friends' and relatives' chins. Bapir had finally made his way to the top of the hill; he had found Alan in the first row of spectators, gnawing his thumbnail as he watched. Alan begged his grandpa to stop the cruelty.

Bapir hugged him. "They will be released in a few days, these young men." He pressed Alan's head to his chest. "They will be sent back home, *bawanem*, maybe with blisters and bruises, but they will be all right. Pray for them." His hands trembled as he squeezed Alan's. "May it rain before these men die of thirst."

Alan searched through the crowd to find Uncle Soran lifting a pile of dirt with his shovel. Soran's grip loosened when he looked into the eyes of his brother Hewa, whose name meant "hope." Hewa stood in the hole, waiting to be buried by his closest relative, a man whom he'd play-wrestled as a boy and confided in throughout his life. "Do it, Soran," he said, his eyes shining up from the hole. A bearded soldier dressed in camouflage saw Soran's hesitation. *"Kalb, ebn-al-kalb!"*—Dog, son of a dog—he barked, and swung his Kalashnikov at Soran, the barrel slicing the skin under his left ear.

Soran growled, almost choking, as he turned. With his shovel, he batted the Kalashnikov away so that the gun hit its owner in the head, cutting his scalp. Alan flinched. Bullets rained from every direction. Soran crumbled. His blood sprayed over Hewa, who was screaming and reaching for the perforated body, pulling him forward, pressing his face to the bleeding cheek of his brother.

Crying out, Bapir tried to run toward his sons, but dozens of guns pointed at his chest, dozens of hands held him back. The shower of gunfire wouldn't cease; it struck the hugging siblings, painting them and the soil around them red.

His uncles, still in each other's arms, were buried in one hole. Half of the prisoners were still covered up to their chins with dirt. The remaining ninety-five men were sent down into the other trenches, and the soldiers buried them up to their heads. Alan stared at the rows upon rows of human heads, a garden of agony.

Intoxicated with power, the soldiers kicked the exposed heads of the prisoners, knocked some with the butts of their guns, and jeered at them.

At the top of the hill, Bapir sobbed with such force that his wails shook the earth, Alan felt. He clutched Bapir's hunched shoulders and felt impossibly small.

A sunburnt man and a neighbor with shrunken features hugged Bapir, then placed the old man's trembling arms around their shoulders and walked him down the hill.

"Where are my other sons?" Bapir gasped for air.

"Let's get you home," the neighbors told him.

Alan wanted to go with his grandpa, but he was afraid to move. If he took a step, the nightmare would become real. He scanned the hill for his other uncles, who were perhaps buried in some distant trench and unable to move. He couldn't see them. Even Bapir was no longer in sight.

The hubbub was dying down. The strangers who'd witnessed the scene were bound by their dread, their exchanged looks the only solace they could offer each other. Their heads seemed to move in slow motion, as if everyone were suspended underwater. Alan breathed in the atmosphere of quiet horror, of paused hysteria.

Suddenly people cried out in terror. From the road below them, several armored tanks were approaching. Gaping in disbelief, Alan staggered back, holding a hand to his mouth. He could neither run away nor slow his hammering heart, which was now threatening to explode. When the panicking crowd pushed forward, guns fired into the air to hold them back.

The tanks advanced.

Alan's mind couldn't process the scene before him. Screams. Curses. Pleas. The devilish laughter of the soldiers. He felt an invisible piece of himself drop away and melt into the ground. He was not Alan anymore.

It took an excruciatingly long time for the tanks to pulverize the heads of the prisoners.

The metallic stench of blood, of crushed human flesh and skulls, the foul odor of death made its way into the spectators' nostrils and throats. The lucky ones threw up. Alan did not.

While the giant metal treads ground his family and the other Kurds into nothingness, Alan sucked in shallow and unhelpful breaths.

BAPIR LAY IN bed at home, tossing in anguish, a hand still on his aching chest. By his bedside his wife shed silent tears. Although they had not witnessed the crushing of their sons, they collapsed that day of broken hearts, one after the other. Someone went to find a doctor.

Father arrived at his parents' home oblivious to the tragedy, having taken an unusual road to safeguard his treasure. His typed article was tucked under his shirt. The joy of achievement and hope for his people glowed in his eyes. Then he found his parents on their deathbed. In bits and pieces, the neighbors told him of the massacre, how Ba'ath soldiers—ordered by President Aref and Prime Minister Al-Baker—had punished the Kurds for daring to demand autonomy.

Father ran to the hill, where bewildered children gathered and clung to each other. Beside them, a group of adults wailed and cried, threw dirt into their hair, and beat their faces in terror.

"The British bastards armed Baghdad to kill us. Their tanks, their planes, their goddamn firebombs and mustard gas that killed Iraqis forty years ago are now killing us," Father said to no one in particular.

Then he just stared with unseeing eyes at the gory mound of his pulverized people, his brothers.

Seeing his father's dazed reaction, Alan finally allowed the sobs he'd held in since he first saw the soldiers to burst forth. Other children followed suit. Tears and snot rolled down the dusty faces of the boys and girls who'd been abandoned by the living and dead alike.

Alan ran to his father and held on to his leg. "Baba gian, Baba!" he cried. It took a couple of moments before his father noticed him and hugged him close.

"We will leave Iraq. We won't live here any longer." A wild urge to be anywhere but here tugged at Alan's gut too.

Some stoic women and a few elderly men tearlessly buried the unidentifiable remains. They laid down uncarved stones in row after row and asked Alan and the other children to pick wildflowers and pink roses from the slope of the hill, placing them in rows too.

Alan sucked on the blood dripping down his index finger, torn by the rose thorns.

"Alan!" cried a woman whom Alan did not recognize. Three other boys turned when she called; one ran to her. Alan was a popular name, meaning "flag bearer." It testified to what was expected of the children of a stateless nation, who had to fight against nonexistence.

PART III

LEILA

CHAPTER FIFTEEN

For a while, all was dark stillness. I floated in nothingness, as if I were weightless in a hollow drum.

But I was alive.

My wild, raw desire to survive—even on the outskirts of life—had scared Death away.

"Twenty-four-year-old female. Motor vehicle accident. Possible concussion. Pelvic fractures. No sign of internal bleeding. Vitals are stable, blood pressure one-thirty-seven over ninety." The words, spoken by a terse, disembodied voice, caused my eyes to pop open, and I was momentarily blinded by the fluorescent light above me.

I was alive. And I was in pain.

I couldn't move my neck, which had been stabilized in a brace, so I cast my eyes around wildly, suddenly alert to the commotion before me.

"On three," someone said, and after the count I was lifted from the stretcher onto a gurney. I didn't recognize the howl that ripped through my throat as I was jostled in the transfer. I caught a faint whiff of bleach coming up from the crisp sheets beneath me, then something raw and primal—vomit? Urine? Blood? My own? I cried, my sobs wracking my shattered body, devastated by my defeat.

I had failed even at dying.

Women in scrubs leaned over me and scissored off my clothes, including my panties, which, they pointed out, had a few drops of blood on them. Someone had drawn a curtain around my bed, but within the fabric walls I was fully exposed to these strangers. I cried and screamed, pulling at the bedsheet beneath me to cover myself. Every atom in my body ached. How was this much pain possible?

The nurses dressed me in a long, loose, cotton hospital gown, fastened in the back, and they covered my hair and tied the headscarf tight. A few unruly strands had caught in the neck brace. I cursed them at each step, profanity I had never before realized I was capable of uttering in an endless stream. Despite my curses, they continued their methodical work, checking my vitals, attaching me to monitors that only added to the chaos with their metronomic beeps. A lanky young man with tired eyes—a resident, perhaps—pulled back the curtain and entered the bay.

"You've been in an accident, Miss"—he checked the clipboard—"Saman. Can you tell me where you are hurting?" His voice was gentle, but even that couldn't calm me.

"Everywhere. Everywhere," I said as I wept. With each gasp, a pain pressed on my chest, like an invisible hand squeezing my lungs in its vice. The doctor placed a soothing hand on my shoulder, a kindness despite its illicitness.

"Let's get her to CT."

The louder my shrieks echoed through the hallway, the faster they wheeled me past massive photographs of the past and present supreme leaders, Khomeini and Khamenei. The edges of my vision went fuzzy.

By the time I was admitted and transferred to a private room for observation, Mama had arrived. She paced the small room in a hysterical circuit like a caged animal, a *tasbih*—prayer beads—dangling from her hand, her entreaties to God loud enough for everyone on the intensive care floor to hear. She'd pulled her white headscarf forward, almost covering her forehead, as if that would make her disappear.

"Leila!" she screamed when the attendant wheeled me in. Her knees gave out as she rushed toward me and grasped the metal railing of my bed. She placed her head on it and sobbed with such a force that my bed shook.

"Stop. I can't take it right now. Please, Mama, stop." My tongue felt thick in my throat.

She reached a hand up to stroke my forehead, but her whisper was anything but comforting. "Leila, they said your underwear had bloodstains on it."

I forced my eyelids open enough to give her a withering look.

"Don't tell your father," she told me.

"Why would I?" I hissed, partly out of rage, partly pain. "If he knows, he'll send me to hell before God does."

Fortunately, the head physician came in soon after to update my mother. "Madam," he said, barely looking up from the chart. "We've assessed your daughter for injuries she may have sustained from being hit by the car. Imaging shows five non-displaced pelvic fractures and two minor fractures on the third left rib."

I placed a hand on my aching chest. "Right above my heart."

"You were very lucky, Miss Saman," he continued. He turned back to my mother. "There don't seem to be any internal injuries to her organs, no splintering. But we need to stabilize the pelvis, and we'd prefer to do it immediately. We're just awaiting her blood work results, and then we'll prep her for surgery."

"What're you going to do to me?" I asked.

"We're going to place your legs in skeletal traction to immobilize the fractures. The surgery is to implant the pins—"

"Pins?" I interrupted. Mama's face had gone white.

"Yes, to keep your bone fragments in the right positions. It'll also provide some pain relief. I imagine you're in quite a bit of discomfort. I'll check on you later."

A bit of discomfort—ha! The physician made to leave, but Mama followed him to the door, whispering something anxiously and grasping the tasbih.

"Thank God." She raised her palms in the air. When the doctor closed the door behind him, she whispered to me that I was intact. "You have not lost your virginity, technically or otherwise. Nothing sharp went in there, did it?"

"Is that really all you're worried about? You of all people?"

"Not anymore. The blood on your underwear could be from the shock or some injured tissue, but . . ." She lowered her voice again. "The doctor says you may not be able to give birth naturally. Caesarean might still be an option, though. We'll have to see how your recovery goes."

"Can someone tell me if I'll be able to walk again?" I screamed, and choked on tears once again.

On the wall hung a poster of a pretty woman in hijab holding her index finger to her mouth, urging silence.

Mama kept pacing the small room, murmuring. Her concern for me waning, she finally asked the question that must have been nagging at the back of her mind all along.

"Did you show up at Grandma's earlier?"

I shook my head, not in denial, but in despair. Protecting her secret mattered more to her than my broken bones.

I held her gaze, noting the conflicting emotions that warred for dominance on her aging face: worry, weariness, guilt, concern, shame, anguish. Mama mashed her mouth into a thin line, saying nothing else to me until the nurses returned to prep me for surgery.

Two orderlies wheeled me to the operating room. With its cavernous ceiling and reverent quiet, the operating room reminded me of a mosque, where I felt small and insignificant. But instead of religious articles, from the walls dangled many devices for cutting. The goal in both places, without so much as asking me, was the removal of that which might corrupt. Men and women in surgical masks and plastic gloves surrounded me.

"Don't worry, miss, I won't look at you," said a bespectacled male nurse, standing at the bottom of the bed and raising my leg while another injected a local anesthetic. I was painfully aware that I wasn't wearing any underwear. Three needles in each knee, and he kept leering. In my head, I clawed his eyes out of their sockets. Finally the woman who held my arms asked the male nurse to switch spots with her, claiming she couldn't stop my squirming. She winked at me. I sighed in relief. My knees grew numb.

I struggled against four strong nurses when the ogling man turned on an electric drill and handed it to the surgeon.

"Sorry. Possible concussion. We can't give you more than a nerve block." A short curtain blocked my view, separated me from my body.

"No! You can't drill holes in me!" I shrieked. "Get away from me. Just let me die."

I was awake, aware, and loud when the sharp metal bore into my bone.

"DON'T YOU KNOW that all the expensive new cars have ABS brakes, Leila?" My brother's gently mocking voice spoke out of darkness the next morning. "And the drivers love those cars too much to drive them carelessly."

Weights were hanging from my footboard. Three kilos each. They were connected like a pulley system to the rods that had been inserted in my knees. Behind Chia, the curtains were drawn, but a little light still slanted beneath in the strip at the bottom of the window. I could see the IV drip dispensing colorless liquid into my vein. Mercifully, Mama was nowhere to be seen. "Why did they do this to me?"

Someone had removed my brace from my unsnappable neck. "Pelvis and rib fractures heal on their own, apparently, so you won't need a cast for them. These weights make sure your legs won't shrink while you heal," Chia said.

"They drilled holes into my knees." I pushed up my gown so he could see.

"I'm sorry. It's necessary, though. To prevent future limping."

With a hand I inspected the bones of my aching face. "Would you get me a mirror?"

"Don't worry. Your face is okay." He sat on a plastic chair by my bed, his hazel eyes bright and affectionate, but worry tugged at the corner of his mouth. "So, sis, were you inspired by that Bollywood railway drama where a handsome man jumps before the train and saves the beautiful woman at the last second?"

"What are you talking about?"

"The driver of the car claims . . ." Chia paused and scratched his ear. "The accident? Was it, umm . . ." He was struggling for a word. He finally finished, ". . . organic?"

I rolled my eyes, but even the smallest gesture made me wince. "No, I used pesticides."

Chia laughed, and suddenly his face changed, colored with relief. "I knew you wouldn't do such a thing on purpose."

"Isn't free will a myth?" I responded.

His expression became mournful and pensive. My brother liked to argue that all humans would make the exact same decisions over again if time could be turned back and the conditions were precisely the same, that their decisions were made in split seconds and that logic did not play as large a role in our actions as we liked to believe.

My gaze drifted over the jasmine and white roses that Chia had placed haphazardly on the windowsill. "You got those for me?"

He nodded. "I should let you rest."

"Painkillers?" I pointed to a box on a small cart in the corner of the tiny room.

Chia read the label and nodded. "Yes, but they've already injected morphine into your IV. I'll get you a glass of water."

I blinked through the fog of morphine and scratched lightly at my arms. "Will they bring me a wheelchair?"

How was I supposed to go to the bathroom? Or shower? I recoiled at the thought of Mama washing my privates. I willed away the vision of her client's blissful expression.

"Why did you do this to us?" I heard my father's voice coming down the hall before he burst into the room.

"What kind of girl would be alone on the mountain so late in the day?" Baba pressed his fist into his palm. "Who were you with?" His expression, a combination of fury and disappointment, was the only familiar part of the nightmarish day.

My brother came back with two glasses of water, which he placed on the cart by my bed. "Baba, not now."

"What trouble could you possibly have gotten yourself into that the only way out was . . . was this?" Baba pointed at the weights accusingly.

Of all the things he had done to me, this question stung the most. He didn't ask, "What happened to you?" or "Who did this to you?"

"How could you say such a thing?" Chia raised his voice.

"The driver and his four passengers say that you leaped in front of their car like a gazelle." Baba raised his elbow in the air like he was ready to jab someone.

"They drilled holes in my knees," I mumbled.

"We should believe Leila," Chia challenged him, their chests inches apart.

"You defend someone who's disgraced you and me?" Baba shoved Chia against the wall, tipping the cart, and the pills fell and rolled along the floor.

I gasped and jolted upright, only to be forced back flat by the pain. "Stop it! Where's Mama?" My words were slightly slurred. Baba released Chia. My father's rage frightened me more than the drill that had penetrated my bones.

A girl of about six peeked inside the room, pointed at me, and screwed up her face in fear and disgust. A man soon came in behind her, and he too winced at the sight of me before quickly averting his eyes and yanking the girl from the room. Drawn by the commotion, a few more people gathered in the corridor, some in hospital gowns.

"How can I live in this town after this?" Baba's voice broke at the end of his sentence.

People gaped. A murmur rose up. "What has she done?" someone whispered. Baba heard that. We all did.

"You're renounced," my father growled, sounding like a wounded bear.

Holding on to the cold bed rails, I pushed myself up. Pain radiated through my knees and hip to my spine.

"Some privacy, for God's sake." Chia chased the other people away.

Baba sighed and turned away from us. He had aged in the span of fifteen minutes.

"Baba, be reasonable. Please, sit down." Chia closed the door and placed his hand on our father's shoulder.

Baba jerked his head up again.

"Reasonable? After all I've been through, what I've endured for you two, this is how you repay me?"

My eyes began to well with tears.

"You. You're as bad as her." Baba stopped short of renouncing his son, took a step back, and pointed at my brother and me in turn. Chia blanched; his placating words died on his lips. Baba had never looked more betrayed. He turned his back to us, rubbed his face with his sleeve, and left.

"I'm not the one who . . . I didn't do anything. I swear!" I called after him, my throat too tight.

Chia paced the room, rubbing his left arm where Baba had grabbed him. "You did not actually try to kill yourself, did you, Leila?" He gazed at me searchingly, his face serious.

I couldn't look him in the eye. I wanted to say no, but that was a lie. So I opened my mouth to say yes, but that was also a lie. Who was the girl who ran down the hill? It was and wasn't me. The IV needle pricked my arm again as I squirmed away from the question.

"I never imagined it would come to this . . . I'm so sorry to have left you behind, gian. I'll find an apartment for us to rent by the time you're discharged. We won't stay in this town anymore. But I do want one thing from you. It's very important that you think about my question. Whatever the truth is, I want to know. Does that sound fair? If you can't answer me now, then write it all down."

I stared blankly at him.

"Here. Make sure nobody sees this." Chia kissed my forehead and slid a notebook under my pillow. "And stop sniffling. It's gross."

I smiled weakly and stuck my tongue out.

Chia held his thumbs to his ears, made antlers of his hands, and crossed his eyes like I used to. We both broke down into giggles, which made my chin ache again.

"What's happened to my face?"

"Nothing."

"How can you expect me to tell the truth when you won't extend me the same courtesy?"

He sighed. "It's pretty bruised, but that'll fade. I asked the nurses. They'll bring you an icepack. And your eyes . . ."

"What about my eyes?"

"The capillaries are broken from the impact. They're bloodshot; there's almost no white around your pupils at all." He must have seen my face, because he rushed to add: "Again, nothing to be worried about. Your vision is fine. The redness will go away with time—and eye drops. But that's the reason the people in the hall reacted like that."

"Are you sure?"

"I'll bring you a mirror tomorrow. Don't forget to put ice on your face and rest. Please write. I expect a filled diary as a housewarming gift for our new apartment."

He left, and I drifted into a medicated sleep.

LATER, WHEN I was all alone in the little room, I shuffled through the pages of my brother's diary, one-third of it full of the stories about his village students.

Students held hands, moving in a circle, singing. The news of Shirin's death passed around like common gossip. She used to be a student in this school. Three months pregnant, she had set herself and her unborn child on fire. I walked to her empty seat and ran my fingers over the phrase carved into the desk that used to be hers: "I wish I were not born a woman."

"Leila's story," Chia had written on the blank page following his last entry. I inhaled the pulpy scent of the cheap paper and ran my fingers over his slanted handwriting.

Over the next week, in the lucid hours between the doses of pain medicine, I grabbed the pen slotted through the spiral of the notebook and wrote:

I don't like to think about that moment. But when I have to, when the images crowd in, I tell myself it was an accident. At times I believe it. Other times a ghostly silhouette frowns, shaking its head in reproach.

During the second week, in the long hours between nurses checking in, I again picked up the pen, pushed aside the hair that fell across my sweaty face, and wrote.

I write so my brother and I can understand how much our destiny was shaped before eggs and sperm united to make us. Because if I don't tell our story, how can I understand why Chia is following in Baba's footsteps with his increasing activism? How the prison guards who tortured Baba torment me too? What it means to belong to a stateless people so crushed under tyranny that self-sabotage has become routine? How can I ever be free if I don't fight my faceless prison guards?

As I wrote, I felt the words mending what was broken within me while the physicians mended what was broken without. When I'd filled the pages of the notebook, I set down the pen. I looked ahead.

CHAPTER SIXTEEN

"LIFE IS PERHAPS that enclosed moment when my gaze destroys itself in the pupils of your eyes." Forough Farrokhzad's poem was twirling in my head as I climbed up a ladder to replace her collection in the poetesses section. In the eighteen months since that day at Zrebar, happiness had become attainable, like the tail of a kite drifting ever closer to the ground.

Chia was now a law student at Tehran University, and his companionship and sense of purpose held my recurrent panic attacks at bay. A small independent bookstore in downtown Tehran had become my source of income—and joy. With this ocean of information and entertainment at my fingertips, I frequently dived into classic and modern books and movies and put my past where it belonged, behind me.

"Oh good, you're still here." Ever-handsome Karo rushed in despite the sign that read "closed."

For a moment I thought I would fall off the ladder. This late customer had a strange effect on my body, making me pulsate at my pressure points. Karo lived in the penthouse of the building where Chia and I rented an apartment. He was a PhD student of computer engineering at the same university as Chia and climbed Touchal Mountain with us every Friday morning. He was fun to be around, but what had happened yesterday was too awkward to be easily dismissed.

For the first time, Karo and I had been alone. Chia had jumped in the gondola lift up the mountain before us, but we were too slow, and the doors shut before we could board. Chia gestured behind the glass, and we hurried to the next one. The group behind us in line did not join our compartment, waiting for their own. Karo's face became first pale, then pink, and finally crimson as he stole a look at my vanilla-coated tongue licking an ice cream cone.

Not knowing how else to relieve the tense silence and the weight of his look, I scooped up a dab of ice cream with my finger and stuck it on his nose. Karo smiled, and his eyes traveled to my neck. I became aware of my headscarf, which had slid down. Something trembled within me. Before Karo, men's eyes on me had always felt predatory, but yesterday it had felt as if his eyes were caressing me like hands, tender and pleasing. In my amplified uneasiness, however, I thrust the entire ice cream cone into his face.

"What the hell!" Karo sputtered. He glared at me when he had wiped the ice cream from his eyes.

I laughed, free from the slightest shame or remorse. "You deserved it."

"I did not!"

Luckily the ride ended shortly after. Seeing Karo's bedaubed face, Chia joined in the banter, and we led Karo to a water fountain. Karo and I stole awkward glances at each other the rest of the day.

I did not expect to see him so soon, let alone at my workplace, which he'd never before visited. "What are you doing here?" I coughed to clear my voice and looked at the empty place where the clock had been—I had recently convinced my boss to remove it, hoping that customers would lose track of time in this fast-paced city and linger to browse the shelves.

Karo held on to the bottom of the ladder as I climbed down, stirring the dust motes into a frenzied dance in the air. The face of his watch was large enough to show that it was 5:23 p.m. The store closed at 5:00 p.m., but Chia wanted to go to the gym after his evening class, and I hated being alone in our rental, where the air was always stale.

"I was hoping to catch you before you left." Karo looked even taller in his black overcoat. He wiped his forehead. Only someone who had been running could sweat in this cold winter weather.

I double-checked that I had locked the cash register. We had made only about seven thousand and fifty tomans that day. At that rate, the owner wouldn't be able to afford the rent, let alone an employee. Thankfully the landlord was a culture-loving rich man who had escaped Iran for Los Angeles after the Islamic Revolution and didn't worry much about collecting the rent since Iranian currency lost its value in the world market regularly. "What's it like out there?"

"Militarized again. I suppose tonight's protests have been called off." Karo sneezed into his sleeve.

The violent clampdown on demonstrators against President Ahmadinejad's reelection—or selection, as some called it—had caused much unrest in the streets during the summer, but it had been slowing down. Protestors who peacefully held signs that read "Where is my vote?" were later told, "Here is your vote" while being raped in prison.

"Did you want a book or something?" I slipped the collection of Kurdish poems by Sherko Bekas, the contemporary poet whose poster Chia had stapled to my wall years ago, into my backpack to read on the subway. Earlier today I had reread his elegy "A Complaint to God," in which the poet writes a letter to God after the Halabja massacre, only to receive a reply from God's fourth secretary, who annotates the complaint: "Idiot. Translate to Arabic. No one speaks Kurdish in God's place, and I won't take it to Him." I tried to read Karo's expression, wondering if he would enjoy the poem.

"Oh, um . . . perhaps. Let me look." He browsed the new arrivals. The woodsy fragrance of his cologne filled up my nostrils. Most of the heavy perfumes worn by the urbanites in the capital irked my sensitive nose, but Karo's reminded me of the forest.

Chia had recently told me Karo was half-Kurdish, and I wondered now if his roots would help him understand a poem about Kurdish plights. Most Persians used our tragedies to say Iranian Kurds had it better than those in Iraq or Turkey in an attempt at whitewashing the crimes of their country and pretending that tragedy could be weighed and measured like so many kilos of potatoes.

Some of the customers would ask me, "Why are Kurds so hated in Turkey and Iraq?" As if I were responsible for dissecting idiocy and ignorance, as if cruelty and racism had a philosophical theory I was supposed to recite because I belonged to its victimized group. No one ever asked, "How does it feel to be a Kurd in a hateful world?"

Karo selected three hardback science fiction novels and payed in full. I decided I'd translate the Kurdish poem into Persian for him later, since an impromptu translation may not do it justice. I gestured Karo out of the store before locking the door, appearing busy to disguise my palpitating heart.

"How come you didn't go to the gym with Chia tonight?" I wrapped my shawl around my neck twice and put on my gloves as we headed to the subway station.

"A friend gave me an extra ticket for a play; I thought maybe you'd like to go."

I met his gaze for a brief second as we turned onto the busy Valiasr, Tehran's longest boulevard. The street was lined with ancient plane trees, irrigated by water channels on each side of the road. When Chia and I had first moved to Tehran, I felt we'd crossed over unofficial borders and instantly understood what my brother meant when he said Kurdistan was intentionally kept underdeveloped. Tehran had wide avenues, skyscrapers, intertwined highways, and innumerable new and chic shopping malls and apartment buildings.

"'Where am I from, and where is love from?'" he added.

He could undress me with just his words. I chuckled.

"That's the title of the play," he explained.

"That's Rumi's poem. Oh, and it's Valentine's Day today." The honking of car horns mingled with the call to prayer in an absurd cacophony.

"The play is about Farrokhzad's life and poetry. I saw you reading her the other night," he added.

"You have *a* ticket?" I raised an index finger to indicate one, looking at him from the corner of my eye, my face partially covered.

"Yes, just one. Chia had plans, and I thought you'd enjoy it more than me. It starts at eight tonight." Theatre tickets were expensive, but Karo's parents lived abroad and sent him what seemed like a lot of money. Or so Chia and I inferred from the Xantia he drove and the lavish lifestyle he led, at least by our standards.

"I wish we had more tickets," I said, "so the three of us could go together."

We continued walking. The street had a pulse of its own; women walked by us in tight, colorful manteaux and loose headscarves, others covered in black chadors; some men wore suits, and some wore tight jeans, all headed toward some purpose. The smell of car exhaust, kebab, and freshly baked pastry, the calling of peddlers, the laughter of flirtatious young men and women—the thrum of the city bolstered me high.

Karo fiddled with the ticket in his palm and said nothing. The air between us felt loaded. As we crossed the square in the direction of the city theatre, Karo's tall frame and chiseled features turned women's heads. Many of these fashionable women were also bandaged across the nose; Tehran was the world's capital of nose jobs.

"Leila . . . there is something I want to tell you," Karo said in a low voice, looking down.

I swallowed.

"Please, sir!" A girl of about five, dressed in a shabby manteau and white headscarf, dirt caked on her face, made a loud noise that was supposed to mean she was crying. But she had no tears. Karo stopped, knelt, and spoke to her.

I looked around nervously. Whoever had ordered her to beg on the street would be watching.

"Wait a second," Karo told me as he stood, then ducked into a nearby convenience store. The girl waited impatiently, hopping from foot to foot for warmth, all the while eyeing me as if contemplating whether I, too, was worthy of her charms.

A few minutes later Karo returned with a sandwich and spoke to the child in a low voice, his words lost in the din of the honking traffic clogging the hazy intersection, which more closely resembled a parking lot during rush hour. I leaned against a tree and looked at passersby, mostly in their twenties or thirties, well dressed and made up. Only a few streets south of this beautiful square, the streets were narrow and unclean, the houses dilapidated, the cars old and unreliable. Tehran was divided by an invisible border, but snobbery was wide ranging, either a custom of big cities or part of the ubiquitous, contagious, and unquestioned contempt for whoever was deemed *shahrestooni*—those who were not from Tehran—who ironically made up the greater part of the city's population.

"Let's go." Karo came back to me, the sandwich still in his hand.

"Sir, sir." The little girl followed, intelligence beaming from her tired eyes.

"You changed your mind?" Karo asked. She nodded. He handed her the sandwich and knelt once again. "I'll wait here until you finish it."

She looked over her shoulder.

"It's okay. They'll know I forced you to eat it in front of me," Karo said. She ravenously bit into the sandwich, looking side to side as she chewed the big bite, and smiled at Karo when she finally swallowed. The baby tooth she'd lost made her grin goofy.

"Well, aren't you Mother Teresa." I winked.

When the girl had finished eating, he trudged on with a smile of self-satisfaction.

After a few more blocks, we came across armed men in riot gear—full-coverage helmets, black bulletproof vests, and knee pads. The protestors had been gathering here for weeks. We walked in silence and with enough distance between us not to trigger the morality police, who seemed downright friendly in comparison to the riot police. Scattered snowflakes danced down, indifferent to the disquiet lurking in the city.

We reached a park across from the theatre. A large group of young men and women holding placards, wearing masks and green shawls, walked the opposite direction. Karo led me past a large central fountain to a quiet corner of the park.

"What did you want to tell me earlier?" I asked.

"Ahh, well, it's not easy . . ."

I got a tingly feeling in my belly. "Say it."

He looked surprised by my impatience. "You know I am half-Kurdish, right?"

"Oh, that." I deflated momentarily but recovered. "Chia mentioned it. But you can't speak a word of our language, right?" I wondered what made one a Kurd and what made one half of that. Having only one Kurdish parent, or was it more about resisting ethnocide, going the extra mile to learn the language, to understand the history?

"Shall we sit there?" He moved to where he was pointing without waiting for my answer. I stood in front of him. The smell of roasted peanuts and diesel wafted in the air. The radio of an armed riot policeman crackled across the street, but the relative peace of the park was otherwise undisturbed. "Not sure if it's wise to be out tonight." He ran his hands nervously across the bench.

I folded my arms. "You're not used to armed men marching in your city? Kurdistan has been militarized for decades."

Karo stared at the sky, the fountain, the ground, at anything and anyone but me as he quickly recited his father's story, as if he wanted to unburden himself of a history he did not know how to handle.

Like my Baba, his father was one of the genius Kurds who, against all the odds, had gotten into a top university in the capital in the early seventies, but from there their paths couldn't have been more opposite.

His father underwent a complete transformation during his undergraduate studies, changed his name and his place of birth on his ID, shaved his mustache and altered his haircut, wore an expensive suit and cologne, and declared his accent was because he had been born in America and never learned Persian properly. Claiming he'd returned to Iran to make investments in real estate, he managed to secure massive private loans and shortly after realized his illusions. Once he'd accumulated enough wealth, he married the sheltered daughter of one of his investors, confessing his origins only after the marriage had been consummated.

"My mom was devastated when she found out the truth."

My face flamed from a rage that bubbled within me as I listened to Karo speak. He looked startled by the wildfire in my gaze. Karo hadn't known me in those angst-filled days in Mariwan. "I think the play is starting soon," he said.

"I don't want to watch it on my own." I headed away from the theatre, toward the subway instead. Rickety motorcycles whizzed by me. Karo followed, but instead of offering to see the play with me, he kept on with his story. His mother had decided to keep the secret from everyone, including their children, but loathed her husband from day one. Karo had only recently learned he was half-Kurdish. His sister from New York had informed him in a letter after getting their mother to confess. "It's clicking for me now why my father was always so tentative at home," Karo said, and I was once again struck by a thunderstorm of emotions. He wasn't sure what to do with this unexpected knowledge and wanted my sympathy.

"Ah, poor you. How can you live with this traumatic information? So you grew up thinking those hillbillies over there were beneath you, but then suddenly—surprise, you're one of them! My heart breaks for you."

"That's all you got from my story?"

"Your mother is a racist."

"She was deceived!" Karo stopped by the stairway leading down to the subway tunnel.

"And that's why you hang out with Chia and me and ask all these questions about history and politics, isn't it?" He needed a walking Kurdish encyclopedia like Chia to decide who he wanted to be, if he wanted to embrace his origins or hang them on the wall like a decorative piece.

"Is that wrong? I expected some empathy."

"I'm truly sorry your father lied to your mother. It's awful. I acknowledge that. I'm even embarrassed. I hope you know that deceptions like that are not part of Kurdish culture. In fact, it's usually the opposite: We're straightforward to a fault. What bothers me is that you barely acknowledge the prejudice at the heart of your story and in the dilemma you now face. Would you have hesitated to declare it to the world if you had discovered you were half German or English, despite their histories with Nazism and colonialism? You know that embracing your Kurdishness comes at a price, a huge price."

Karo shifted uneasily. A murmur went up in the throng of people milling about the subway, and I was suddenly self-conscious, aware of how loud my voice had become.

"Did you ever wonder why your father found it necessary to hide his origins to get ahead?" To me, Karo belonged to people for whom poverty, malnutrition, and lack of decent healthcare and education were problems they did not understand for lack of experience. But as I took in his handsome, downtrodden face, I wondered if I had been too harsh. Before I could try to redirect the conversation, however, I was shoved by a frantic crowd running down the stairs. A wave of people charged toward us. I was rooted to the spot in fear.

Karo looked around, yanked my hand, and we ran as fast as we could. The panicked crowd jostled us in their hurry to flee. Gunshots cracked through the air. People screamed. To the riot police, everyone was a criminal whose innocence was impossible to prove. I ran as fast as I could, but my lungs gave out.

"To the wall. To the wall." Karo pointed. I did as he said. He removed my little knapsack and had me wear it in front, which let the hordes of people pass us without pushing and jostling. But the police were getting closer and pepper-spraying their victims. Karo carefully scanned the area. "Come." He grasped my hand, and we turned onto a side street.

"Small streets are a trap," I panted.

People were frantically knocking on random doors. Every now and then a door would open and someone would pull the first few people inside before shutting the gates again.

"I know what I'm doing." Karo pulled at my arm, and we ran down an even narrower alley.

I was hysterical. "If we get arrested, I'm the one who will be killed, not your half-Persian ass."

Karo drew me inside a medical center to our right, which I hadn't noticed until that very moment. Another couple followed close behind us. "Act ill if they come in."

"What? I can't act." I freed my arm from his grasp.

"They won't feel bad for a man. Just cry and wail like you're in pain. Don't argue, for God's sake! Can you do that?" If only he knew.

A few more people rushed inside the clinic after us, and an older man closed the door. "Better to save a few than none," he said as he turned to survey the terrified crowd. We exchanged guilty glances, but no one objected. Our shame was overpowered by the will to survive.

Karo and I ran down a staircase and crept inside a busy laboratory. "Act pregnant."

"What on earth is that supposed to mean?" I winced against the antiseptic chemical smell.

"We have to act like we're married, or we'll draw attention." Karo then pointed to another couple whom we had seen among the protestors. The woman was resting a hand on her hip and pressing her belly with the other. Sweat dripped down my spine and neck. A lab technician winked at us and gave us some of her medical folders. They were prepared to camouflage us. I burst into nervous laughter.

"I didn't say act high," Karo whispered and grasped my shoulder.

"Congratulations!" The other supposedly pregnant woman wiggled her eyebrows at me. I bent at waist with a hand on my stomach.

"Thank you! It's our first," Karo responded. I looked at his serious face as he rubbed my shoulder affectionately. He looked down at me reassuringly, and my anger and fear evaporated. *Life is perhaps that enclosed moment when my gaze destroys itself in the pupils of your eyes.* Indeed.

CHAPTER SEVENTEEN

A TINY CAMCORDER in hand, I filmed a homeless man across the street, zooming in on his every gesture. His salt-and-pepper hair, unwashed and uncombed, lay limply against his shoulders. His jeans were torn at the knees and stopped an inch above his ankles. Though it was early still, dark clouds were building in the distance, threatening an afternoon storm.

He walked between two old trees, touching their trunks with each pass, talking loudly and animatedly, throwing up his hands and sometimes slapping his chest. Pedestrians rushed past, with or without a glance. Nobody stopped to listen; the man's restless rant was lost in a crowd absorbed in their cell phones.

Chia entered the kitchen in his gray pajamas and undershirt, the side of his face bearing pillow creases, strands of his brown hair pointing in five different directions. A long yawn claimed his face before he could say hello. He then inspected the fridge, reminding me of his days as a boy in mismatched socks.

"Stalving?" I carefully placed the camera on the table without turning it off and poured myself a cup of tea.

"Still haven't put that camera down, eh?" He rubbed his eye and gulped some milk straight from the bottle.

The black camcorder with MicroDVD storage, though preowned and a few models old, was my most valuable possession. I didn't exactly own it yet; I'd only made a down payment and was paying in monthly installments. Still I was thrilled to experiment with pan and tilt.

I had a strong urge to document my little joys, partly because I had an irksome fear that they would be short-lived and partly because I wanted to be able to replay beautiful moments over and over again. I was particularly excited to record Shiler when she visited next week so I could replay her antics on tape when I missed her.

"What were you working on so late last night?" I sat on one of the wooden kitchen chairs we'd picked up at a secondhand shop, desperately in need of a fresh coat of paint.

"I was studying first, and then I read the Bekas collection you brought me, Miss Book Connoisseur. Hold on." Chia left the tight kitchen, passed through the adjoining living room, and entered his tiny bedroom. Gone were the days of his spacious basement; in our Tehran apartment, I had the larger bedroom. I realized the stark walls of the rental building no longer bothered me. It was my home.

Chia came back with the book, sat across from me, opened it to a page he'd dog-eared, and read:

In 1988
all the gods watched
the villagers' bodies burning and spitting.
But they inclined their heads
toward those fires
only to light the cigarettes on their lips.

I inhaled the scent of my freshly brewed cup of black tea with cinnamon and let the steam bathe my cheeks, nodding in agreement with the poem, remembering the day Chia was born, when I had watched a violence on television that my brain couldn't comprehend but every cell in my body did.

Chia put the book on the counter and spread butter and sour cherry jam on a piece of bread. He swallowed a mouthful.

"I heard Mama's client committed suicide a few days ago. The intersex one. Actually, not her client anymore after . . . you know."

"She must have suffered so. Poor thing!"

"You don't sound as outraged anymore."

"Not as much." I sipped my tea calmly. Baba had renounced me, and I had renounced Mama in my heart, so I had no contact with them. Any updates about my life were relayed through Chia. Despite the massive hurt this caused, I also felt relieved, and then felt guilty for feeling relieved. When we had moved to Tehran, I had begun sessions with a therapist, who had explained that Mama's narcissism and Baba's chronic depression meant they hadn't deliberately—or perhaps even consciously—damaged me. Perhaps trauma was a Kurdish heritage, passed down through generations.

"How come you're so cool with everything?" I asked. We still trod lightly around the topic of Mama's affair, the final unjust hypocrisy that had pushed my frazzled self over the edge.

"I'm not. I just think infidelity isn't the only way to betray your spouse. They both betrayed each other. And their children. I feel bad for them now though, aging and lonely."

My hands trembled slightly, sloshing my tea. There was a pain deep in my chest that pierced my lungs with each breath. Revisiting these events I was so desperate to put behind me gave me flashbacks that felt more like experiencing the terrors anew. Chia took my hand in his own.

"Leila, I could use your help to complete this research project I've started. I've called it 'From Self-Reign to Self-Immolation: The Paradoxes in Kurdish Women's Lives,' and it's to be published in a human rights magazine in Canada. I can see how you turn pale and start chewing your nails every time I try to talk about the accident, and I think working on this together will help you, me, and other women who are in danger."

"What exactly are you looking into?"

"Why it is that Kurds had female rulers and governors in the eighteenth century, at a time when that was unheard of among Persians and Turks, but now we have such high rates of suicide by fire. What happened to Kurdish women?"

"What happened to Kurdish men?" I asked. The sound of sirens outside startled me. "I don't think I'm ready yet. Sorry." I wanted to curl up and hide somewhere.

"Okay." Chia grabbed the camera and turned the lens on the man I had filmed earlier.

"How did this magazine find you?" I asked.

"Through my blog."

"Chia, don't you think you risk too much?"

He stared at one of my photos of the snow-covered Zagros Mountains that I'd pinned onto the creamy flowered wallpaper. "Somebody has to do something. And we'll be careful. We'll publish under an alias."

"Last night I dreamed I had a bunch of fish and I couldn't feed them. They were swimming around in a small vase that was placed inside a big pond. I knew they were hungry, but I couldn't find their food. The tiny dears were starving, and no one knew but me, and they kept looking at me, begging for food. It was my job to feed them, but I kept searching and found no food. I still feel bad for them."

"Still having nightmares?

He knew one of my recurring nightmares featured a man in scrubs, holding an electric drill before my exposed genitalia, jeering at me. I shuddered.

He looked up. "Any chance the guy outside may appear in one of your films?"

I opened the cabinet and retrieved the cutting board. "As soon as God sends down a bundle of cash for my filmmaking purposes."

"You should look into ways of getting your work in front of a director." Chia swiveled to look at my direction.

With a large knife, I chopped quickly through a handful of lettuce leaves. "And show them what? Random footage of streets and people, of trees and birds, recorded by a camcorder that's a joke to a professional? Give me a break, Chia." I dropped the knife on the cutting board and turned to him. "You have to know people who know people."

He stared down at the white kitchen tiles with the same kind of blank stare he had when he compared dreams with reality. "You know what you should do?" He combed through his hair with his fingers. "Start talking to the customers at the bookstore. The ones who show up for movies, film magazines, and such. Hmmm . . ." He zoned out again, pinching his lower lip. "If we could find a way to contact one of the Kurdish directors, Hiner Saleem or one of the others, and to show them what you've got, I'm pretty sure they'd be supportive."

I shook my head and resumed chopping. "Show them what? That I have no education, no background, no experience . . ."

"Dreams matter, Leila gian." He nodded, stood behind me, and whispered, "Desires matter. Take them seriously."

I lifted the lid of the pot I had put on the stove early in the morning. "Only if I were Martin Luther King."

"Mmm . . . sewzi ghawlma?" Chia sniffed theatrically when I stirred his favorite dish, the stew of beef, herbs, dried lemon, and beans. I made it every time I wanted him to stay at home longer, stay and tell me that every change in life started with a desire, that the courage to believe in the wildest dreams was what had allowed a black man to run for president of the United States, that women got to be leaders only after they believed in their capabilities. I wanted Chia to speak to me about all these things and let me pretend that I didn't believe him, that he was only being silly.

"Karo would die for this food! Do we have enough for three people?" Chia picked up his cell phone from the table and texted his friend when I shrugged.

"Let me make the salad." Chia fetched tomatoes and carrots from the fridge and started washing them.

I watched his clumsy ways and laughed when he nicked his finger chopping a cucumber.

"What's so funny?" He wrapped his bleeding finger in a napkin. Now I had to do the salad.

"Do you realize why you know so much about history and politics and the world?" I said as I pushed him away and started dicing.

"Because I read."

"Also because you always had me to cook and clean up after you so you could spare the time."

He left the kitchen and flopped down on the squat blue couch with Kevin McKiernan's *The Kurds: A People in Search of Their Homeland* in his hands. I retreated to my room and thought about what to wear for our handsome guest. My striped shirt was a nicer fit than the one I had on and a better match with my tight green skirt. I was so short and petite that I could pick up great clothes in kids' sizes at clearance sales. I tied a forest-green ribbon in my curly hair, applied black mascara and peachy lipstick, and returned to the living room.

Placing headphones over my ears, I sat across from Chia and watched *Crash* on Chia's laptop again to better understand Paul Haggis's complicated intertwined screenplay, stealing glances every now and then at my brother, who was absorbed in his book. But I couldn't focus. Karo stubbornly claimed a space in my head, refusing to leave. The shape of his strong arms and broad shoulders flickered behind my eyelids each time I blinked, and I imagined myself sitting on his lap or my head hiding in his chest, his arms protecting me. Was I confusing my desire for safety with love? Or was that simply what love was, believing you'd found the one person who held the answers to all your needs?

"Every time he is around, I smell trouble," I muttered, pen in the corner of my lip.

"Who? Karo? You blow so hot and cold about him."

I got the tingle one gets when someone guesses their secret. "I'm not sure why you spend so much time with him."

"It's his story . . . it fascinates me."

"That he is a con man's son?" I stuck my chin out. "Funny how his father was humiliated at home. Assimilation didn't work, it seems."

"I don't think it would make anyone happy for too long. Apparently his father disappears for months on 'business trips' to Gulf countries. He sends a lot of money to his wife in Toronto though. So I guess he is financially successful." Chia tapped the side of his nose.

"I bet his identity is not the only thing Karo's father lied about," I said.

Chia yawned. "He married someone who would most likely have rejected him had she known earlier who he really was. Or divorced him, if it weren't such a taboo."

"I would love it if he had a secret Kurdish wife." I giggled.

He looked up at me. "That would make a good story."

"In a far-flung village where nobody speaks a word of any other language, and he probably has nine very Kurdish children who will grow up to become Peshmerga."

"Don't forget to save that in your idea folder." Chia insisted that I take notes for future screenplays, but I never did.

"I'll come to the terminal with you to pick up Shiler."

He nodded. Chia and I continued sitting across from each other, occupying different worlds. By the time *Crash* ended, the sun's rays bathed our kitchen floor and the aroma of a delicious meal wafted across the living room.

"I'm famished," Chia said.

Belsima. I mimicked his childhood speech impediment, but only in my head, because he didn't enjoy the memory as much as I did. By the time we set the table, Karo was at the door: ponytailed, biceps flexing under his T-shirt.

"Mmm . . . so good . . ." he moaned as he ate. His enthusiasm for the meal made the well-mannered Karo speak with food in his mouth, and a grain of crispy saffron rice dropped onto his black jeans. I tucked my hair behind my ear and felt the blood rising to my face. My lonely heart interpreted every friendly gesture as evidence of his attraction to me, but I told myself it was pathetic, wishful thinking. Never before had I so desperately wanted to be ignored by someone, if only so my heart wouldn't go skittering with each smile he cast in my direction.

When we couldn't possibly eat more, we lunged for the sofa.

"I don't know how to thank you two for the feast."

"The usual way is fine." Chia winked.

Karo pulled a USB stick out of his pocket.

On Chia's laptop, Karo showed us some footage he had secretly downloaded from Tehran University's high-speed wireless connection. The clips, mostly filmed surreptitiously on cell phones, documented the government's violent crackdown on peaceful protestors who gathered to object to the disputed presidential election.

The third video made my temples throb. It was hard to believe that what we were seeing was real, not the creation of some fifth-rate movie director. We played it again, pausing several times, our heads pressed together before the screen.

From the window of a city bus, someone had filmed a man dressed in black, wearing a mask and a cloak, who brandished two batons at cowering protestors. Vaulting between two cars, he leaped up and viciously beat anyone within reach. He twirled the batons like some sort of Persian ninja, chased his victims, and didn't stop until he'd rained blows onto their skulls. The video ended when he approached a group of soldiers, who warmly welcomed him, clapping him on the back. I would've thought it was a prank if it hadn't been for his bloodied victims, their howls of pain audible even through the bus window.

"Isn't chaos the best opportunity for the psychopath?" Chia asked.

Karo and I looked at each other; we didn't have an answer, and Chia wasn't looking for one either.

I wandered into the kitchen to make tea and looked outside again as I waited for the water to boil. The homeless man between the tree trunks was hooting with laughter, slapping his knees in excitement, bent forward in a deep amusement. How easy it was to lose sanity, I thought, when you were exposed to such madness, so frequently.

When I returned, Chia was staring at the ceiling, Karo at the floor. We were all tired of discussing the situation in Iran, all discouraged by the political, economic, and cultural deterioration. I placed the tea tray on the table before us.

"There's no getting used to life here because it keeps getting worse and worse!" Karo shook his head.

"So, how does it feel to be beaten up? To be killed because you demanded your basic human rights?" Chia was flushed.

"What do you mean?" Karo asked.

"Don't you think that the mainstream's silence these past three decades is at least partly responsible for this onslaught?" Chia looked back at the screen. I'd never seen him confront Karo like this. "When ethnic and religious minorities were crushed, did you not think one day they'd come for you too?" Chia turned to his friend again and looked him right in the eyes.

I was flabbergasted.

"We . . . people had hope." Karo cracked his knuckles. "They believed in political reform."

"Reform? Don't you think people on the margins have every right to be wary of this new 'quest for justice,' Green Movement or whatever?" Chia's tone was calm, in contrast with his accusatory words. "Our three decades of resistance against the Islamic Republic was dismissed as separatism or violence because it was a poor man's fight."

Karo rubbed his sock-covered toes against the light brown carpet. Where did he stand? He then looked up and noticed my expectant eyes but only glanced at his watch. "We've got to get going, Chia, if you want to make it to your class on time."

I ground my back molars. Every time Karo showed up at our house, he was going somewhere and taking my brother with him. "I'd really like to know what you think about Chia's comment."

"Well . . ." Karo sipped his tea. "What can I say?" I stared at him unblinkingly. Chia went to his room to get dressed. He had vented and was now content; unlike me, he did not expect an answer from Karo. At least not right now.

"It's true, what Chia says. It makes sense." Karo scratched his day-old stubble. "I hadn't really thought about it before."

"Well, it's something you'll have to think about if you decide to reclaim your Kurdish roots. People who are protesting in the streets today sat back and did nothing when minorities were killed in droves. So what does this mean to someone like you, who claims a half-Kurdish identity but has had all the privileges of a Shia Persian man?"

"I'm ready," Chia said from the apartment door.

"I haven't figured that out yet. Sorry." Karo joined him, bending down to tie his shoelaces.

"See you soon." Chia shut the door.

The silence that overtook the space was broken by the rumble of an approaching thunderstorm. I ran to the door and called out, "Do you have to go?" Chia was descending the stairs two at a time.

He stopped and turned to me. "You don't work today?"

I shook my head.

"I'll return in three, four hours, as soon as my class is over," he said.

"Chia!" I called after he had climbed down more stairs. He didn't hear me. I called louder and ran down a few more stairs. "Chia, Chia!" The space was airless and had a moldy, sour smell.

"Gian?" He looked lovely in his new T-shirt, black jeans, and red-and-white sneakers.

"Please stay home. I'll make *dokhawa*! Any food you want." A pause. "I'm sorry I said I wasn't ready to help with your project. I'll do it." I grunted, gripping the cold railings. I hated that I couldn't suppress my fears, that I frustrated Chia with my attachment to him. I hated how pathetic I sounded, and yet he was all I had in this world. "You know it's not safe out there. Please, Chia."

Chia glanced down at Karo waiting on the lower level and looked up at me again. "I can't keep skipping classes." It was true; going back to school had saved him from conscription, but it wouldn't if he failed his courses.

Karo opened his mouth to say something, but he only tongued his upper lip, swallowing his unspoken words. Chia climbed the stairs, cupped my cheeks, then took our old headphones out of his backpack and put them over my ears. They were attached to an MP3 player. He placed a kiss on my forehead. "Don't worry, gian, I'll be home soon." When he hit play, Shahram Nazeri's lullaby washed over me.

Chia left, and I went back inside to the kitchen window to witness a perfect expression of exasperation. The shabby-looking man in the tree-lined street was pulling at his hair, looking left and right, shaking his head. Then he kneeled, tipped his head back, and started talking to the sky, to the drizzle. Curious to hear his words, I cocked an ear, but the sound of the many roaring car engines drowned out his voice.

"It's okay," I leaned forward and called out from the window of our fourth-floor apartment. "You'll be fine." I put down the camera, cupped my hands, and shouted, "We'll be fine."

He resumed pacing and rambling despite the downpour.

I closed the window. *Fine*, I wrote on the window in the cloud my breath had formed.

CHAPTER EIGHTEEN

A SILHOUETTE WAS running toward me. When he drew close enough for me to take in his bullet-ridden body, I recognized him as Baba. I stepped back in terror. "Carry me, my daughter," he pleaded. I was too timid to face a perforated body, too slight to support his weight. "Chia, Chia gian," I called. My brother was carrying a blood-drenched cadaver on his shoulder and reciting a plaintive postmortem letter out loud, too loud. My heart was blasting with long pauses between each beat. I pressed my hands against my ears, pressed them so hard that I smashed my head.

Children in Kurdish clothing danced and played in the dirt, whirled around my bleeding head, their eyes brimming with joy, their laughter inaudible. The children didn't see it, but I did: their crumbled future.

Soaked in sweat, I awoke with a terrible burning in my throat and groped my way to the bathroom, splashing water on my face. Chia wasn't in the kitchen or in his room. My calls went straight to his voicemail. Gripping my hair by the roots, I stood motionless until the thumping in my head slowed down. The hands of the clock lay on top of each other, pointing upward. He should have been home hours ago.

The longer I paced the floor, checked the sluggish clock, and looked out the window, the more real the nightmare became. I turned on the TV, played a DVD, opened a book. Nothing helped. I looked through Chia's room. There it was: the diary he'd given me at the hospital. I rubbed my face and sat on the bed. I flipped to a random page and reread a passage he'd also posted on his blog, Imagine Otherwise.

Girls were secretly reading the history of the Kurds. Sitting in a circle on the hill, among the wildflowers, the students were whispering, giggling, and reading the pamphlet I had prepared for them. The frowning principal was looking through the window of his office, thinking that these shy-looking, pretty village girls were reading science.

I was playing football with the boys.

"Ro-nal-do! Ro-nal-do!" the students cheered for Ali, who had scored a goal, but then he suddenly ran up the hill, away from us.

"Wait, Ali. Wait!" I chased after him. "What's wrong?"

The clock kept ticking. It was one in the morning.

"If I were really Ronaldo, Farhad would be playing as my team's forward now." Ali held his sleeve in front of his mouth and looked down at the poppy fields.

"What do you mean?" I asked the little boy.

I would have liked to think it was the sun, wind, or exhaustion that caused the tears that rolled onto his sleeve. When I reached him and kneeled in front of him, his cheeks were burning and his eyes were volcanic.

Footsteps. I ran and looked through the peephole. Chia wasn't there.

"You will be a great footballer one day, Ali gian," I said softly. "And you can do lots of things for your village when you're rich and famous. How about buying new shoes or clothes for every child in the Newroz? Cool?"

"I could." Ali stared into my eyes. "I'd give Farhad's father money."

I swear I saw a spot on Ali's forehead that gleamed, right between his brows. I still hadn't put my thoughts together to form an answer when Ali ran up the hill again, holding onto his hand-me-down pants. I had almost lost sight of his tiny, fragile body in the distance and among the grasses of Awyar Mountain when I understood what he meant.

I called, emailed, and texted Chia and Karo for the fifteenth time. The streets were deserted. My only shield against my mounting panic was the diary.

You know what he was thinking? That if he could have financially supported his classmate Farhad's disabled father, the boy would not have had to quit school to work as a construction worker, and he would not have fallen to his death from twenty stories up in the city sky. These village kids never cease to amaze me.

I felt the usual sharp pain in my stomach. I wonder if Leila, like me, sometimes feels pains that medicine can't cure.

"Yes. I do. I do, brother," I said. One was allowed to talk out loud to oneself when alone, right? One was insane if they did so in public, but I was all alone in the dark, reading by flashlight instead of turning on the lamp.

I did not know what to say to a ten-year-old boy who had lost his friend to poverty. Quoting the phrases I had written in a countercultural human rights publication could not bring consolation to this young man—"the necessity for instituting a disability pension"; "the desirability of a smaller gap between the rich and the poor."

Was it helplessness that was breaking his little heart? His inability to save his friend and one day himself and other poor families? Was it powerlessness he was tasting for the first time?

"It's not . . ." I stood up and shouted after Ali as loudly as I could. "It's not your fault."

His shaved head was a moving, shining spot under the sun, between the bright red poppies.

I resumed pacing, rubbing my left arm, muttering to myself, looking awfully similar to the man I had watched with pity that very morning.

It took three attempts before Shiler picked up. "What's wrong?" Her voice, traveling all the way from Kurdistan, was garbled with sleep, tinged with slight annoyance.

I could see nothing but darkness inside or outside of my apartment, as if the stars had lost their way home.

"What's going on?" she asked when I didn't reply, not sounding as sleepy this time.

"Chia hasn't called or returned." If my brother were stuck somewhere, he would have called. I shook my head to erase the image of the ninja I had seen on the screen that afternoon.

"You think . . . ?" Shiler did not finish her sentence.

Even if Chia had been injured and taken to a hospital, he would've made an effort to contact me. He had promised never to leave me again.

But if he had been detained . . .

"I don't know what I think," I sniffled. It was the *but*s that made life overly complicated. Buts within buts, creating layers of anguish.

The long-distance call was expensive. Talking was dangerous. Shiler and I listened to the sound of each other's breath. We both knew the injured or gunshot protestors who arrived at the hospitals were taken away by security forces before receiving treatment. We both knew that even the lawyers representing those arrested during demonstrations were sometimes jailed.

"Maybe his cell phone has died," Shiler offered, but the shiver in her voice betrayed her.

My fingernails were bleeding. "His friend from upstairs is not home either. I knocked on his door."

"That could be a good thing. Chia's not alone. They could be hiding, waiting for the curfew to end."

The threat of tears terrified me. It would confirm the terror I was trying hard to contain. "You're right. Chia will be back with a good reason for his delay. I'm just being paranoid. I am."

"It's okay to be afraid, Leila. I'll get on the first bus to Tehran. Call when you hear from him, please."

"I will."

I told myself I was only taking a shower. Tears rolled down my body along with the shampoo, the sweat, and the terror. But they were lost in the stream of water from the showerhead, so they didn't count.

By the time I had towel-dried my body and lain down on my bed, it was half past three in the morning. I placed the old headphones over my ears and pressed the play button. "Ly-ly-ly-ly," I sang along. My hair soaked the pillow.

With closed eyes, I saw Chia and me playing cops and robbers in the yard, saw the days he'd chase after me but never catch me. Or other times when, picking up on some story I'd made up, he would beg me to save him from the wolves. The little head he'd hold near the heater to fake a fever and solicit affection. The story of the parrot and the oil jar that he had me repeat a hundred times. Or the story of the king and his daughter. She was *not* a bad girl. I had been trying to make myself trust that despite what Mama and Baba had made me believe, I was not a bad person. Not at all. But tonight they were both yelling at me for not being able to take care of my younger brother.

Chia was my child. I had raised him. But he wasn't just a child. He was also a protective brother and my best friend, a father, even. And he was a souvenir from my childhood, from the days when we did not know what headaches were, or terror, the days we had no schedules, no debts, no grudges. "Ly . . . ly . . . ly" played from my headphones. The clock chimed four times. "Chia will be home. After the sun rises, he will be home," I said loud enough for every item in the house to hear.

CHAPTER NINETEEN

THE TICKING OF the clocks would not stop. I checked off the days on the calendar, from the first to the thirty-first, and then tore off the pages of each passing month.

Shiler ran along with me from person to person, building to building: hospitals, safe houses, schools, police stations, prisons, anywhere and anyone who might tell us where Chia and Karo were. The graffiti that marked the walls of the city was as frantic and disorganized as our search, an odd mixture of leftism and Islamism, spray-painted portraits of Hollywood stars mixed with anti-imperialist slogans and sketches of political prisoners.

My new routine started each day at dawn. I was sent from one rancid government office to another, and I drew innumerable sketches as I waited in the stale air to meet with authorities who each promised me the next person he referred me to would help locate Chia. I shredded my doodles and tossed them into the wastepaper basket on my way out the door.

When Chia had first disappeared, I'd written to my parents that he'd left for a study-abroad program in Malaysia so they wouldn't try to come to Tehran and hinder my search. I was afraid of being pushed, now that I was trembling at the edge of a cliff. Keeping up the artifice was easy, since we were still not on speaking terms.

One weekend, after navigating the confusing city for months, still no closer to finding answers about Chia's whereabouts, Shiler convinced me that, to preserve our fragile sanity, we must take a day off to hike Alborz Mountain. We climbed up the trails, through bushes and by the prehistoric rocks, and rested on top of one of the hills. I took in the sublime view of the steep green valley, inhaled the fresh mountain air, the subtle fragrance of trees and wildflowers, and allowed the breeze to take away some of my exhaustion as it caressed my face. The hills hummed with frivolity as men clapped and sang upbeat songs, children danced to the beat, and women watched with envious joy. The morality police didn't come up the mountain, their vehicles ill-equipped for the terrain and they themselves averse to the climb.

"We should do this all the time," Shiler said, her face pink from the fresh air and exercise, her headscarf tied behind her neck, showing her large earrings. "I feel alive!"

I did too. We walked down at a leisurely pace. A little river was rushing somewhere out of our sightline, finding meaning in moving more than arriving. At the bottom of the hills, a quaint village called Darband welcomed hikers with its numerous lovely cafés and fountains. At a traditional-style lounge decorated with Iranian handicrafts, I sat cross-legged across from my friend on a large bench covered with a Persian rug. Shiler appeared stoic, but I'd hear her cry herself to sleep most nights as she slept alone in her boyfriend's bed.

We ordered kebab, barbequed tomato, rice, and *sangak* bread. It was a day I'd have liked to have documented, but, no longer able to afford the monthly payments, I'd returned the camcorder and lost my deposit too. These days my paychecks went to bribing secretaries so they'd arrange for me to meet with authorities. But my bribes must have been too little, since most officials weren't available to meet with me very often. I'd borrowed rent money from Joanna, whose soothing hand on my forehead I craved like a plant deprived of water. My energy, however, was unmatched in those weeks; I was up at dawn, running around town all day and working at the bookstore all evening, always getting home after midnight. It was easy. I would've done anything to save my brother.

Shiler winked. "Don't look now, but the cute guys that have been checking us out from across the restaurant are coming this way."

I shrugged, and Shiler agreed that she was in no mood for flirting either, but the gentlemen, educated men with gelled hair and expensive clothes, proved too charming as they offered to share a hookah with us. They joined us on our bench, and the four of us smoked the watermelon-flavored *shisha* we passed from hand to hand, discussing music, literature, how Iranians were migrating in droves only to be deeply nostalgic about this very village we were sitting in.

When the men learned we were Kurdish, they eagerly asked us questions about Kurdistan's nature and said how much Iranian music owed its power to Kurdish artists and melodies. Then we spoke about the Kurdish doctors Arash and Kamiar Alaei, who were arrested for developing educational AIDS programs for healthcare professionals and were accused of being spies for the CIA. The younger of the two charming men, in his early twenties, voiced the need for greater sex education, which was vital in a society where parents acted as if sex outside of marriage was only for the neighbors and schools offered no response to pubescent desire other than to ban it. The other man, in his early thirties, believed that Iranian youth was "lost in lust and hungry for love." I no longer knew if abstaining was a sign of virtue or backwardness in a religious society in a speedy modernization frenzy.

The café owner, who turned out to be a close friend of the men, brought us red wine in gold-rimmed teacups with sugar cubes on the saucers. It was the first time I drank alcohol in public in a country that would lash you for it. When the Police of Enjoining Good and Forbidding Vice came around as the orange sun spread color through the sky, they received their "gifts" and left without harassing anyone.

We drank more "tea," listened to live music, and sang along with the band. The conversations became increasingly flirtatious. Shiler and I laughed a lot that night. The men paid for the food, as was the custom, were offended when we offered them money, drove us home in their Peugeot 206, and invited us to an underground party the following weekend. When asked, Shiler and I both gave them made-up phone numbers and had them drop us off a couple of blocks north of our apartment. It went without saying that neither of us girls would risk attending a mixed-gender party that could be raided.

"Chia would be cool with us having one night of innocent banter after weeks of misery, don't you think?" Shiler asked, holding on to my arm as we walked down the street lined by residential high-rises in the middle-class neighborhood.

"I'm sure he would. Let me tell you though—Karo's far more handsome and a lot more interesting." I didn't confess to the guilt gnawing at me over flirting and drinking.

"You won't shut up about this Karo guy. Are you attracted to him or something?" She teased. "Ooh, or have you fallen in love?"

"Neither! Are you crazy? He's way out of my league. You know the first thing we should do when we find Chia and Karo? Make a ton of homemade wine. Gosh, the wine was lovely."

She agreed. That night I slept soundly, free of nightmares.

CLOCKS TICKED ON. Whatever name the dates bore—July, August, September—they were identical purgatories for me.

The more desperate I grew to knock on every possible door, the more distant Shiler became, asking to be left alone with her "quiet quest," refusing to explain what that meant, taking to hiking to cope.

I was borne on a pendulum between faith and terror, between agitation and paralysis. I'd never felt more alone. Despite Shiler still sleeping in Chia's bedroom, I saw her infrequently, and a chasm grew between us. Although I was sometimes tempted to tell my parents the truth, it was always easier to just keep lying, partly to spare them the panic I'd been living in and partly because there was nothing they could do. I was afraid they'd blame me, each other, themselves, terrified they'd drain what little strength I was able to summon each morning to get through yet another pointless day.

Joanna's presence would have lifted me up, but I couldn't bring myself to leave the city, not when my brother was here somewhere, waiting to be found. My boss was no longer interested in hearing about my hopeless search, couldn't even bear to look at my sallow face. Dust and cobwebs had overtaken the apartment, the spiders even too sick of me to occupy their webs.

Day eighty-six. I sank down to the ground by the calendar, stretching my legs. In the silence of the apartment, I rubbed an eye with the back of my hand and stared at the silver alarm clock on Chia's desk, unsure how to feel about the relentless ticking. Time was both a friend and an enemy. I wanted to fast-forward to a future when I would once again see my brother pressing the snooze button and pulling the pillow over his sleepy head. Yet the passage of each day that ended with no reliable news depleted me.

The door opened. The familiar shape of Shiler's curvy figure appeared. The hallway lamp shone behind her back, illuminating the room through the open door, turning her into a silhouette. "I thought you were asleep."

"I can't really say I am awake," I said.

She sat by my side and threw her headscarf at the wall. "Suffocating piece of shit."

I reached for her hand.

"If he is in a prison, which he most likely is . . ." I began. "How terrible is it? I am sorry to ask, Shiler, but I need to know. Do you remember what it was like? I know you were a baby, but has your mother ever spoken about it? Do you think they . . ." I faltered, my thoughts too terrible to say aloud: Chia being tortured like Baba, being hollowed out, his own map of lashes across his back. Nothing frightened me more than seeing Chia—the man who wanted to bring the perpetrators of massacres to justice—sleepwalk through life like yet another crumbled victim.

She kissed the top of my hair and placed a calming palm on my cheek. I let my head rest on her shoulder. "I was spoiled rotten, living among women who competed to hold me, to play games with me, sew clothes for me. My every fart thrilled them to pieces. Anyway, Joanna often talks about the aspects of prison that weren't too horrible, especially for someone like Chia. He'll meet some kick-ass intellectuals and activists there. There's a camaraderie among political prisoners of similar ideologies that you can't find outside. He'll have a lot of time to read and write. Also, it's not like the outside world is heaven. Chia knows this country is one big prison."

"Thank you, Shiler." I wiped my tears, slightly comforted. "And he'll eventually come out, right? They won't keep him there forever. Even if they found out about his contraband articles and blog and stuff. And when he comes back to us, he doesn't have to hate life like my father. He can become like Joanna."

"I brought him bad luck," she muttered. Born on the day her father was executed, she could not shake off the superstition.

"Shiler, he got to experience love because of you. I'm the one who tired him with my excessive attachment. Maybe he would have stayed home had I not been such a bore, such a burden."

"You know the last thing Chia told me?" She got up and patted his bed as she told me they were lying down on the prickly dried grass on a hill, making up stories about the clouds sliding by in the sky. "A shepherd passed by with a bunch of animals. Chia said he envied the sheep."

"That's not like him. He is quite the lion."

"He said the sheep were lucky they didn't have to suffer because of the way Britain, France, and Russia had drawn the map of their country. Nor did anyone force them to speak in the pigs' language because pigs were in charge."

"Ah, the famous Chia wit." Shiler and I sustained ourselves through sharing memories of him. A desperate attempt to make the abstract concrete, to add to our inadequate reservoir of hope. It was our futile denial of being prey to terror.

Hands clasped under her head, Shiler's eyes were trained on the ceiling, the light in them fading. She'd wake before dawn and climb the hills across from the apartment. By the time the sun was up, she would already be at the summit. I had once spied her on the hills from the window, a tiny shadow against the watercolor dawn.

"What's it like to be on top of the mountain every sunrise?" I asked.

"It's not about getting to the top. The trekking gives me the illusion of surmounting the pain."

"You being a Kurd and all that." I smiled. An archaic saying claimed Kurds had no friends but chia—the mountains.

Shiler swallowed hard, fought to be strong. "I can't go on like this, Leila. We're not getting anywhere."

"What else can we possibly do? I've done everything imaginable." Shiler didn't seem to hear me. I bit the insides of my cheeks, got up to open Chia's closet, to smell him, to find a way to water my spirit in severe drought.

"Leila, look at these." Shiler stood behind me and pointed to a series of four photos on the wall, the ones taken in August 1979 in Sanandaj. The shots depicted the row of blindfolded Kurds who had fallen on a dusty field from the blasts of the Revolutionary Guards' weapons.

"Look carefully. This is still our reality." She knocked on the pictures like there was something I couldn't see. Several AK-47 machine gun rounds were cutting through human flesh. "Here, read what Chia has written."

I had already read that blog post a million times. "With every person who fell from a bullet, a part of our pride and dignity died. With every line of published and broadcast propaganda that named us *mofsid filarz*—corruptors on earth—a part of our heritage shattered in us. We are denied our identity, and when we protest, we are denied life."

I chewed at my chapped lip and held my hand to my throat. "What are you getting at?"

"What do you see in these four photos?" Shiler asked.

The Kurds crumpling at the knees, stuck somewhere between heaven and earth. "He is standing when others are falling. The first man in the row. Left hand wrapped in a bandage. An icon for dying with a straight spine."

"No, Leila. Look at the executioners. These are the people you are asking to help you."

My brain went blank.

"Where do you think the assassins are today?" she went on. "They are the ones running this country. Do you really expect them to have mercy on you and me?"

Shiler was right. We were deliberately kept in limbo. The goal was to deny families a sense of closure—a proper funeral, a grave to visit, a chance to move on—and to threaten their sanity by making them hope against hope, die in a slow decaying despair. When a mass grave was unearthed, a common occurrence in Kurdistan, some families actually found peace after discovering the remains of their loved ones. But others, who had anticipated reunions, had their reason to hope, to keep going, stripped away.

"What do you want me to do?"

"They give empty promises and send you from office to office. They're getting off on your pain. It probably gives them fucking orgasms to look at the desperate face of an activist's sister."

"What other option do I have?" I cried. "Wear makeup? Flirt with them for information? Fine, I'll do whatever it takes. Whatever! This nightmare will end, Shiler. We just have to remain strong."

"Some nightmares only end with the grave," she mumbled, but I heard her. "I have to leave."

"Where to?"

"Out there. On the mountains."

"What? Isn't that where you go every day anyway?"

"I mean I want to become a Peshmerga, join the fight."

"Why?"

"Why? Look around you. You're on a suicide mission. They'll eventually catch you too. It's all useless."

My lips moved inaudibly.

"Don't look at me like that, Leila. I can't fucking stand the degradation anymore. If you are a leftist, they kill you; if you're an activist, they kill you; even if you don't believe in anything and just say 'Yes, sir,' they kill you. Maybe not physically, but they kill you inside. I am sick of it all—the laws from the dark ages, the denigration . . . everything, Leila. In this country we are subhuman. We're women, and we're also Kurdish. I need some dignity, something to hope for. I want to have a real impact. Real fight. Or the rage will turn against me and destroy me. Look at me. I am rotting. Faster than you." Shiler waved her hands in the air and kept talking. "I'm going to die anyway, so why not do it with some pride and honor? Why not kill some of the occupiers first?"

"I don't . . . I don't understand you."

"What's there not to understand, Leila? I cannot tilt my head every single day of my life, say 'Please, sir' to a government that killed my father for striving for equality, put my mother on death row for defending herself from a pervert, beat me up and smashed my kidney over nothing, and then kidnapped my boyfriend. Why would I stay in this dump? What are you hoping to achieve here? How long are you going to keep looking, borrowing to pay rent?"

I held a hand to my chest. "Until I find Chia."

"Chia and I argued about this all the time. He is the idealist, the man of writing and analysis. But this is a dirty war, Leila. We are dealing with Iran and Turkey, not Switzerland and Canada. Do you understand that? We must be realistic. I would much rather get killed on a battlefield than slowly decompose in this morass."

"What about your mother?"

"She'll eventually join me. And maybe you will too. When you get as sick of it all as I am now. Where else would you go? To live with your parents and their curfews?"

"You can't bail on me now, Shiler. You have to stay with me." I rubbed my temples, then steadied myself against the wall. "I need your help to find Chia first. Then maybe all of us will get out together."

She forked her fingers through her hair for the fifth time as she paced across the room. There was only the chirping of a cricket outside and the sound of our breaths. "You should join me, Leila. This is the only way we can avenge Chia's life."

"Avenge what?" I snapped. "You're talking as if . . . My brother is alive. We just need to find him. And I will."

Shiler placed both hands on my shoulders. "Calm down."

"Chia is alive!" I screamed. "I feel it. I know it. I am sure of it."

"You can't be sure. You think the people buried in mass graves and La'nat Awa didn't have family who loved them as fiercely as we love Chia? Do you think—"

"Fuck off!" I shoved her. "Shut the fuck up. If you want to find another lover, go do it."

"You should save that aggressive tone for the bastards you beg every day." She winced and brought her hand to her side as if calming a cramp. "I can't even take a shit anymore. That's how sick I am of everything, and not just this damn constipation and bleeding."

"Then we should see a doctor. I need to get a couple hours of sleep. I'm meeting a parliamentarian tomorrow who is going to help me find Chia." I undressed, got into the shower, and vigorously massaged my scalp. Foam mingled with desperate tears that slipped down my face and body.

"You're a fool for cleaning yourself before going to wallow in filth again," Shiler yelled.

In whose hands was Chia's life? Most families never got the corpses of their children returned. The lucky ones had to pay for the fifteen to twenty bullets that had cut through their loved one's flesh.

My knees gave way on the bathroom tiles. I felt I was being gagged by invisible hands.

In a frenzy, I ran out of the shower, shampoo still dripping from my hair.

"Shiler, please don't leave, not now." She was nowhere to be found. Her backpack was gone too. "Shiler!" I screamed, and my echoes screamed back at me.

CHAPTER TWENTY

MY BROTHER AND Karo would be home soon, and we'd once again go hiking. That much was obvious to me, at least in the daytime before the sunset madness crept into my heart. I sipped my black cinnamon tea, marked day ninety-three of their absence on a calendar, lit a wood-scented candle, and started dusting the phone that had not rung in weeks. Shiler had never looked back. But the curtains, the dresser, the books, everything that Chia had ever touched was faithfully waiting for him to come back and animate the space.

When I moved his mattress to wash his sheets, something fell under the bed. It was the diary he had shared with me, the one with the wrinkly edges and wavy pages, dampened by our tears, shed at different times. I'd read and reread his words when Chia first disappeared, but I later let Shiler immerse herself in them. I had assumed she'd taken the journal with her. I sat on the edge of the bed and opened the small volume to a random page.

Boys were secretly learning the history of the Kurdistan Republic, of Peshawa, who lost his life after having made a dream come true, if only for eleven months in 1945. Ali was reading aloud for everyone. The students were silently listening and nodding, their eyes half-closed against the bright sunlight. Ali knew he must immediately switch to Persian and recite from his legal textbook when the principal came around.

Students held hands, moving in a circle, singing. The news of Shirin's death passed around like common gossip. She used to be a student in this school. Three months pregnant, she had set herself and her unborn child on fire. I walked to her empty seat and ran my fingers over the phrase carved into the desk that used to be hers: "I wish I were not born a woman." I know she would have been collecting signatures for the Women's Campaign had she not been born into poverty.

"Mamosta." *Ali appeared behind me, right by Shirin's desk, staring at the bitter sentence she had engraved with a knife. "Why did she burn herself?"*

I rolled around on the bed, at once pierced with pain and pride. I wanted to be more like my younger brother, detached from my personal problems and immersed in those of others. The sun shone brightly, warming the bedroom.

I confess I feel ecstatic when my students call me Mamosta, making me believe I am a real teacher, not some student doing compulsory military service. But it breaks my heart that this young man did not ask why suicide. He asked why self-immolation. Did he think it was okay, or at least understandable, that she took her own life?

"Are you finished reading?" I asked.

"Someone else is reading. Why fire? Why?"

The last time I saw Shirin's face, she was wearing a white wedding gown—her shroud. Her eyes were full of pain and protest. Her father gave her to a rich man twenty-six years her senior in return for money he had no other way of paying back.

"The groom is well off," the people of the village said. He locked the door, not allowing anyone to see his beautiful property.

Shirin sobbed, "I'm not a criminal to be held prisoner."

"Be grateful he loves you so much," her parents responded.

"It's not you I don't trust, it's the men," the husband justified as he drew the dark curtains tight. He could do that. The law had given him that right, and every other right.

"You talk sense into her wayward head, Mr. Teacher," her parents begged me. But her husband wouldn't allow her a conversation with me.

Gray strands of my hair had fallen on the rug like dead leaves from a tree. I'd dye my roots when I found Chia. For now, the headscarves didn't let anyone know that at age twenty-six, I was two hundred years old.

Ali kept moving his little palm up and down, demanding logic and justice—everything I wished I could offer him and the other children.

Why fire? Why?

Did you know that our region has the world's highest rate of female self-immolation? There. We hold one international record. Despite our long tradition of having female rulers and governors, we've become a nation of burned women.

I ask again, why fire?

I could answer that question. Women who lost all reason to live wanted their internalized burning rage to manifest on the outside too. A dramatic death testified to an agonizing life.

I squeezed my aching left arm and opened the window. Smog had created an impenetrable layer between the sky and the city now that the pleasant warmth of spring had given way to cruel heat. The sun was rising regardless. With grave difficulty, I swallowed some tea, unaware of its taste, wondering where else I could possibly go to look for Chia. Where was Shiler?

"She was sending a message, bawanem." I finally said it and looked away.

Ali wouldn't give up. "Message? What message?"

My stomach turned.

"What message?" Ali asked again. Typical of him to repeat his question until he got an answer, and I was at a loss for words. But I saw a gleam on his forehead and wanted to reach for it, to seek a cure.

I kneeled before his small body and high mind and sang a lullaby for him instead. "Are wa fedai ballat bem aazizem rohze chowar jara . . ."

"Ly-ly-ly . . ." He sang along.

"Ly-ly-ly . . ." I hummed, buried my face in the diary, inhaled its pulpy scent. Despite the pain he'd documented, Chia's words were healing, exuding love and humanity.

I sat on the sofa where Chia used to sit. There was no new place or person to visit. No lead. I hugged one of the cushions, clawed at it.

Chia's book was still on the coffee table. I played and replayed my last video of him that I'd saved on my laptop. "Oh, dreams matter, Leila gian. Desire matters. Take them seriously."

Through the slow dial-up internet I got online and, using proxy servers to break through the filtration of the websites that the government had censored, I logged on to my Yahoo account and noticed a new email from an unknown sender.

Leila,

Tried finding you at the bookstore, but you weren't there. C. and I were captured together; we were filming a gov. truck running over protestors. We were held in custody at Ettela'at but were separated after three weeks. I was released yesterday. He should be released soon too. I might be able to trace him. It seems he was transported to Evin, then to Sanandaj prison, and later to Evin again. Will find out and report back. Stay strong.

I reread the three-day-old email, wishing the crescendo of my heart would let me concentrate. I read the email yet another time before I scrolled down far enough to notice a postscript.

P.S. No words can express how much I regret having taken him out of your home that day. It's all my fault.

K.

This was a scam. This was not Karo's usual email address. He would have certainly phoned to inform me, to save me from the three extra days in purgatory. If he was concerned the phones were tapped, he would have shown up at the door. He might have, though. I'd barely been home.

After pressing the elevator button again and again, I ran up the stairs two at a time to the twelfth floor and pounded on Karo's door. There was no answer. Only then did I notice that in my rush, I had neglected to wear a headscarf. I ran back down the stairs, covered my hair, and wrote a note to slide under Karo's door. "Home all day. Must MUST talk ASAP. Dying here."

Chia was alive. Torn between a mild sense of relief and an unleashed animal savagery, I clawed at my hair and rhythmically beat my head against the wall.

Oh, how I needed to hug someone, but the only person I had in Tehran was a grandmother buried in a graveyard miles away from my place.

"Joanna. Joanna. Joanna. Chia is alive," I cried into the phone. "His friend is released. He emailed me. Once Chia's assigned to a prison, he can contact me; I can visit him. He will be released sooner or later. Tell Shiler." What was the punishment for filming a government murder scene? How many years in prison? How many lashes?

"Avina min! What a relief," she said. "His friend told you all that?"

I paused. "No."

"But you know somehow?"

My heart skipped a beat or two. Then I burst into sobs. I couldn't be certain. Was I deluding myself once again?

"Leila gian, trust your heart. You knew all this time that he was alive when no one else did. And you were right."

I opened the window and shouted to the street: "He is alive. My brother is alive."

CHAPTER TWENTY-ONE

THE TALL STONE walls of Evin Prison, topped with their spiky barbed-wire barrier, became a common sight for me. The golden and scarlet leaves, whether hanging or falling, gradually retinted the city from green to orange and yellow. I marched back and forth on the street in front of the prison, searching for a solution and hoping for a miracle.

Shiler was training in the Qandil Mountains and thriving in her new community. She wrote to me about the camaraderie, the "Kurdistan won't be free until women are" belief of the guerrilla fighters she had joined, the ball games, the bonfires, the hunting, the unique taste of tea brewed over fire, the primitive operas they conducted.

I told her Chia had been found, and she sent me ideas and contacts. I offered bail, found a pro bono lawyer, begged and pleaded, protested before the prison, even threatened to set myself on fire. Nothing worked. But at least, in contrast with the extremely slow pace of the limbo I had been in for so long, the days went fast.

Other than the two emails, the second confirming that Chia was in Evin, the now-free Karo completely ignored my attempts to contact him. He'd shared in our happy days but vanished when I needed him the most. Despite all that, I was not ready to hate him. He could be feeling guilty for being released instead of Chia, or he could have post-traumatic stress from prison. Maybe he was dodging further trouble by staying away from me. Whatever his reasons, little by little I forgot him too.

I met other prisoners' families and bonded with two women and two boys who spoke my mother language. We were introduced to each other as Chia's sister, Shirin's mother, and Farhad's wife and sons. Our names were irrelevant. We lived only to see the prisoners free once again.

These women, and others I regularly came across in hallways and queues, lacked the wealth and influence needed to solve problems in this country. All we could do was summon courage and show up before the armed soldiers. We held hands like schoolchildren, shared stories and memories of our imprisoned beloveds. Unexpectedly, we became shoulders for each other—strangers with a deep connection, who sobbed and prayed and cursed together. Farhad's sons, Hewram and Hewraz, would cling to opposite sides of their mother and observe us in silence as we shuffled through words to find something positive to tell each other. The children's presence, their bright eyes and lovely faces, gave us much courage.

On Tuesdays we could request visitation. Drained faces beamed with expectations.

The bearded prison guard with crooked teeth stamped my application, its bang like a slap.

"Again?"

"Your brother has been here for only a short time." He opened a stained white handkerchief and blew his nose only inches from my face.

I flinched. "But my brother was captured one hundred and two days ago, and for most of those days I didn't know where he was."

"Why do you sound so arrogant?" He sucked back mucus loudly. "Are you a professor or some shit?"

"What?" I looked left and right, heat rising to the tips of my ears.

"No visitation for you until you learn to talk like a proper woman."

I kicked the low cement wall between us.

"Next," he yelled out.

I pulled my black headscarf forward, hid my face in my palms, and ran out of the building. I was immersed in my thoughts when I bumped into a giant.

"Leila!"

I was overcome with frustration, and he'd changed so much that I didn't immediately recognize him—the ponytail was gone, and gone too were his brightly colored sleeveless T-shirts. He wore a formal black shirt, and the skin under his indigo eyes had turned dark.

"Are you here to see Chia? How is he?" The expression on Karo's face was hard to read, and he avoided eye contact.

"Chia is alive, and he will be freed soon," I declared loudly and firmly, as if telling the universe what to do next. Heads turned toward me. My heart threatened to burst.

Karo finally met my gaze in silence. Farhad's wife and sons surrounded me. The boys stood, arms akimbo, ready to defend me. Their mother put her hands on my shoulders. All three of them glared at Karo, who stared at the ground for what felt like a long time. When he finally looked back up at me, his eyes were damp. He hurried away without a word. My eyes darted after him.

My friend placed her palm on my cheek. "Be strong, my dear."

"I'm trying! Believe me. I am trying hard."

She opened her arms, and I felt, for a second, safe in her embrace. Her tenderness reminded me of Joanna. When their bus arrived, mother and sons ran to catch it. I stopped, staring after the trio as they departed for the day. They waved at me from the window of the bus.

Two hours later I was home, toying with the barley soup I'd made days ago, unable to swallow. I couldn't remember the last solid food I had eaten. Mama called to see when her son would come back from his school trip abroad, asking the question so breezily it was if she'd forgotten we hadn't spoken for nearly two years. That she and Baba didn't call my bluff irritated me.

The cell phone beep startled me again.

I couldn't tell you this to your face. The truth. You deserve it. We recorded on my cell phone, not his.

I didn't recognize the number, but it wasn't hard to guess the sender.

I know that makes me guiltier in your eyes. But it gives me hope that he will be released soon.

I felt a sudden unbearable pain in my chest, as if a stingray had stung me. "You killed my brother!" I typed with shaky hands, open mouth, and loud breath.

But I couldn't press send.

Instead I sent: "And yet you're free. He is held. No visitation."

I screamed into a pillow.

CHAPTER TWENTY-TWO

THE PHONE RANG early in the morning and this time brought good news. The bookstore owner wanted to see if I could work full-time that week. It had been more than three weeks since he said he'd call me for a shift. Not that the old man was to blame; I'd kept asking for days off to visit this and that place. When I went into the store, I met the woman they'd hired to replace me. She sported long, painted fingernails and had brought in lots of customers, but sales had only diminished—her admirers weren't there for the books.

New releases excited me, and contact with regular customers happy to see me again was flattering. I was thrilled to have my job back, and because the owner now wanted more than anything else to spend time with his newborn grandson, I began working full time. Once again I had an income and free access to films and books. I had good news to share with Chia when I saw him.

When I got my paycheck, I repaid part of my debt to Joanna and went shopping, thinking about what items a political prisoner could receive. What Chia probably craved the most—thought-provoking books, papers, and pens—were all banned. That much I knew.

This time the first Tuesday of the month arrived faster than ever. It was still dark when I left home, carrying a light jacket for Chia to wear when he was allowed in the yard. I had also bought a couple of shirts and some underwear for him, aspirin, a toothbrush, and a comb. Crammed in among all the passengers on the bus, I kissed my gifts and pressed them to my cheeks. "Carry my love with you."

By 7:30, prisoners' families had already formed a long queue, even though the staff wouldn't arrive until nine. I reclined against a pillar in the lobby and tried to muster patience, to be more like my brother. My cell phone had been confiscated at the door, so I had nothing to kill the time. All the women were required to wear chadors inside the prison, awkward black shrouds that covered us from head to foot except for our faces and hands. I kept tripping on the hem of mine as I shifted nervously in the queue.

A woman with a heart-shaped face and dark black eyes stood behind me. A girl of about six clung to her chador. Their skin was sunburnt. The woman said something in Arabic, but I didn't understand. She didn't speak Persian, so we couldn't exchange more than sympathetic looks and smiles.

"What is 'my daughter' in Persian?" Shirin's mother had once asked me. Never having attended school, she had not learned the country's only official language. Then she told me how as soon as she had asked Shirin, *"Bashy kchakam?"*—Are you all right, my daughter?—in Kurdish, the curtain had dropped over the divider and the line had been cut off.

At her next visit, granted after months of pleading, she mostly pressed her face to the smudged glass and kissed it. Shirin had learned a few words in Persian from her fellow inmates, but the mother didn't know anything more than *"Khoobi?"*—Are you okay?—which she repeated over and over again, pressing her lips and cheeks against the glass, asking Shirin to place hers on the same spot. "Khoobi?" she asked yet again, forgetting the few other words I had taught her. "I have to swallow my tongue every time I am about to say 'my daughter' or ask what she needs." Her daughter Shirin had been sentenced in a court whose language she couldn't fully understand.

At a quarter past eleven, my turn finally arrived to submit my application and present my birth certificate. As I walked to the stall, my leg caught in the folds of the chador and I fell facedown. Those waiting in line held their breath, concerned that my clumsiness would somehow jeopardize their chances to visit their loved ones. The Arab woman behind me helped me get up and brush myself off.

To my great relief, this time I received a blue card that would allow me to see Chia's face behind the thick glass and hear his voice over the phone. Placing a hand on my heart to stop it from jumping out, I joined the second lineup: families permitted—but not guaranteed—visits.

The woman behind me started wailing in Arabic, sounding as if she were praying.

"Next," called out the officer.

But the woman stayed where she was, crying louder, holding her hands over her ears, rocking left and right. Her daughter looked up at her.

"Shut up or I'll call security," the bearded officer shouted.

"She has traveled a long distance," I stepped forward and explained.

The angry man looked at me with disgust. For a second I thought he understood Arabic and knew that I had made that up.

"Mind your own business!"

The young girl directed her pleading look at me.

The woman babbled away, looking first at me then back at the clerk. "See . . . this woman is ill," I stuttered. "She is having open-heart surgery next week and wants to see her husband at least once before then. Please give her five minutes. Let her and the child see him. May God bless you and your children."

The man cleaned his glasses and put them back on, looked closely at the large tears running down the faces of the woman and her daughter.

"She hasn't slept in three days," I continued, gaining courage. "She and her child stayed up all night outside the prison last night. Before that they were on a bus for two days traveling from the south. Please let her see her husband. For only one minute. May God reward you in this world and the afterworld! This might be this poor woman's last chance to see the father of her children."

To my surprise, the officer gave her a blue card. The woman hugged me and showered my face with kisses. I let her place her head on my shoulder and speak to me in her language. I responded in mine. The girl smiled at me, revealing broken, blackened teeth. I winked at her. She was the only one who had enjoyed my improvisation. Together we joined the next queue.

Scowling men in khaki uniforms escorted families up or down the stairs to speak with the prisoners. People whispered, informing each other that there was enough room for more than ten families to visit at a time, but because the conversations were taped, the officials preferred to keep it quiet. We all knew the rules, spoken and unspoken, but the guards who escorted us would stand by and listen to each conversation.

The clock hand kept its pace, impossibly fast and indifferent to our panic that grew with each passing minute. There was no air conditioning in the antechamber, and the water coolers had long been depleted. The heat was unbearable. People whispered to their neighbors, warning that the filthy wards became infested with beetles and cockroaches as the temperature rose.

Each family had twenty minutes to speak through a phone with a prisoner on the other side of the glass partition, but if they ever spoke a word that they should not, future visits would be denied and the prisoner would be punished. Visitation was highly emotional and stressful, even more so for people who didn't speak Persian well: the elderly, the uneducated, the poor.

Those fortunate enough to see their loved ones came down the stairs wailing desperately, shocked by how weak, shabby, and ill the prisoners had become; some bore obvious signs of torture. I braced myself. It's not that the families didn't know what to expect—Evin Prison was notorious not only in Iran and the Middle East but the world over. Yet to witness the boot print of brutality on your loved one's face and body and not be allowed to care for them, nurse their wounds, even hug them, was the family's share of the torture. My stomach churned as I braced myself to see my brother's face, to choke down the sobs that were already clawing up my throat.

Then I thought about Baba in this very prison, where massive signs read "God, God, Preserve Khomeini to Mahdi's Revolution," and how he only had one visitor and was kept behind bars when his mother died and his daughter was born. I thought about a traumatized Joanna, who had once endured a mock execution as a cruel and unusual torture method, about Shiler growing up between the dull walls of the low-slung lockup with overcrowded cells. The malnourished prisoners who died from infectious diseases before they arrived at the gallows. The prisoners whose families were never granted the chance to see their broken features. If the walls of Iranian prisons testified to what they had witnessed firsthand, God's heart would shatter into a million pieces.

I steeled myself. Men and women had formed separate queues, and every half hour, five men and five women were called, but because most visitors were female, I still had a large crowd before me. If I were not allowed to see Chia by five, I would miss my chance for the month. The young Ahwazi girl kept stealing glances at me. She sat on the floor, half closing her eyes in exhaustion.

I sat down next to her. "Would you like me to braid your beautiful hair?" She had spoken to her mom only in Arabic, and I wasn't sure how much Persian she knew, but she nodded. The girl sat on my lap. I looked at her mother to seek her approval, but she was too preoccupied with her thoughts to notice. I grabbed a tiny comb from my purse and started brushing the child's soft hair. The repetitive brushstrokes and gentle tugs must have soothed her as much as it did me, because before long her head was on my chest and she was snoozing. She reminded me of Chia at her age.

Hours passed. The elderly in the long lines complained about chest pains and leg cramps. The more able-bodied started fighting over places in the line.

The large dusty clock on the wall showed half past four. The officers cut down on the visitation time to allow more people to talk to their families. The first people in the lines protested. The little girl woke up. Surprised to find herself in my arms, she clung to her mother. In the men's section, someone in his seventies had fallen on the floor, and even though his name was called right then, he was not able to get up and visit his son. "I can piggyback him up the stairs," a burly man offered, but he was ignored by the soldiers.

"I'm a doctor. I may be able to help him," a woman near the end of the line announced, but she was not allowed to enter the men's area. My heart ticked much faster than the clock.

After all the commotion inside and outside me, I ended up having to leave without getting so much as a glimpse of Chia.

My migraine made it difficult to keep my eyes open as I walked out of Evin and onto the streets. A car I'd not seen honked at me when I passed the intersection. The world had turned blurry. I took some of the aspirin I had bought for my brother.

CHAPTER TWENTY-THREE

My cell phone chimed with a text message when I'd almost finished my shift at the bookstore.

Strike at Evin. It was Farhad's wife. *Demanding to reduce the restrictions on visiting political prisoners.*

I made placards out of old cardboard boxes, as Chia would have done. When I arrived in front of the gates of Evin in the late afternoon, a couple hundred people had already gathered there. Sunlight filtered through leafy jacaranda trees. We chanted for more than an hour, but the authorities ignored us. A few foreign media correspondents showed up, secretly showing us their press badges, and interviewed a few brave people. The reporters were broadcasting live when men on motorcycles appeared, looking threatening enough for the journalists to scatter.

The Basiji bikers, the unofficial militia recognizable by their long beards and striped black-and-white scarves, cut through us. "Go home, filthy animals," they called out. Some carried large buckets of water, which they poured onto the pavement where some elderly protesters had spread towels to sit.

The Basij pushed and shoved us, spat at us, called the men infidels and the women whores. The armed soldiers were entertained by the harassment and mocked our request for protection.

I looked straight ahead in silence. Some of the gang members were as young as thirteen and others as old as sixty. Many were opportunists, others sadists. Some looked brainwashed; some were veterans of the eight-year Iran-Iraq war, had lost limbs fighting for their country, and still believed the government was holy—and that we were threats to be eliminated. If I'd joined a gang when I was in school like them, I'd have been a college graduate today—spying for the government was among the most notorious tactics that got people admitted to universities, while others who scored high on the national exam were denied education because of their or their families' activism.

I snuck out of the crowd and watched from a distance, trying to film the scenes, holding the cell phone under my large and loose headscarf. A man in his forties—hoping to gain release for his teenage daughter who'd been arrested during a rally—lost self-control, pulling a Basiji off his bike and punching him in the face. People cheered, and the thugs rained down blows on the man. Bystanders tried to protect him, and soon it was an all-out brawl.

A woman leaped at and beat one of the attackers with her purse. He shoved her. She fell to the ground. A few women and I, who had been standing nervously on the sidelines, ran to help the woman who'd fallen. But the prison guards were immediately on the scene, ordering us to disperse if we wished to stay alive.

I was pushed forward by the press of the throng, closer to the armed men. Close enough to chant in their faces, "We do not accept humiliation." The rage I'd kept bottled up inside me boiled over, made me brave. I screamed at the guard who told me to fuck off. "International interventions will soon put a stop to your brutality!"

"Yeah," the soldier scoffed, and then laughed humorlessly. "Wait for the world to come and save you. Loser!" Our eyes met. We both paused. His lips curled into a mocking smile before his face turned grave. What I thought was a smirk turned out to be a tic. We sized each other up.

A layer of skin covered the hole where his left ear had been cut off.

He sniffed, then directed the tip of his rifle barrel at my forehead, right where Chia had kissed me for the last time.

"Get out of here before I waste a bullet on you."

The photos of the firing squad formed before my eyes, of the victims holding out despite bullets going through their flesh, others crouched in pain. The deadly weapon on my forehead. The soldier's expressionless face. The cold metal pressing against my skin. His fingers twitched, touching the trigger.

The crowd around me stilled. I held my breath.

"You think we're afraid of death?" My voice was low and even, though my hands shook with adrenaline.

"I swear to my martyred child, we'll kill you if you shoot," a nearby woman threatened the soldier. The crowd chanted in approval, slowly pushed in. A walkie-talkie crackled at the soldier's belt. He lowered his G3 and picked up his wireless device. I backed slowly into the crowd, crablike, still staring at him. He turned away. I squeezed my way out.

Deaf to the car horns and hum of the street, blind to those who passed me, I jogged home, the aftershocks of the confrontation shivering my innards.

Until coming face-to-face with death, I had taken cruelty personally, overlooking how that kind of ruthlessness had roots deep in the history of humankind. It didn't matter if my name was Leila or Njorge, if I spoke Hebrew or Navajo—it was most certainly not about me.

When I got home, I sat out on the balcony as if being between walls would take this little epiphany away from me. I felt light, relieved of my crippling self-pity. I hugged my knees and massaged my aching feet, then stared up at the gray-and-black clouds marching across the sky. Wicked people lived in this world, and it wasn't my fault. It was all part of the game. "Arguing with the rules, complaining about your bad hand . . . none of that works. Shift your focus on playing your hand the best you can and notice the difference," Joanna had said once, and only now did I understand.

The rain splattered down after a loud thunderclap. I lifted my face and palms to the sky. I wasn't alone, I saw then. People in Rwanda, Bosnia, plantations, and indigenous residential schools in North America were standing shoulder to shoulder with the Kurds. I remained in the rain long enough to witness the rainbow that appeared afterward.

In the morning the fog had evaporated. I reread a few pages of Chia's diary and felt nourished by his thoughts.

I knew what to do.

CHAPTER TWENTY-FOUR

SHILER SET UP a video chat for me with her new commander so I could learn some important cybersecurity tips. The all-female militia of her political party elected a new commander every six months to prevent the corruption of power. Berivan—a computer engineer raised in Van whose entire village had been torched by Turkey when she was a child—patiently taught me how to create two-step verifications, avoid easily monitored applications, download encryption software, deactivate automatic backup on my phone, and permanently delete chats.

"You'll be the first culprit in their eyes if his writings go viral," she warned me. "You shouldn't give the monsters any evidence to jail you too. You are playing with fire by drawing attention to his case." Her rifle lay quietly on her lap like a sleeping pet as she had me repeat everything she had taught me.

After she was done, Shiler appeared on the screen.

"You look sunburnt." I was surprised.

"You could use a little vitamin D yourself."

I admitted to Shiler that I was not afraid of the attention that posting Chia's writings would garner, but rather the possibility that no one would care. "Look at the selfie-mania on social media, the ugliness put on full display in the comment sections."

"Do you think the team here is making this much of an effort for him just because I asked? No, *haval*. Listen to me: Chia is going to draw a lot of attention, and not just because you and I love him. You may not see it from where you stand." Shiler picked up the laptop and moved to another room inside her humble base. The wall behind her was peeling, revealing clay mixed with straw, an ancient method of ventilation. "Chia is a unifying voice for a divided opposition, because he is proof that all is not lost in this morass—and he has one hell of a moving pen."

The connection sputtered, and her face, thoughtful for a moment, pixelated on the screen.

"Okay, here's what you do. Type up all of Chia's diary entries, poems, essays, everything. And I've kept all the letters he wrote me over the years, I can share some of those too. When a cellmate is released, he might be able to smuggle some new writing out. If . . . not if, actually, *when* they come for you, tell them you shared his letters only with your parents, who must have shared them with someone else who posted them. Act like you don't understand how the internet works. They'll monitor your phone and wireless connection. Once you post everything, we'll help spread his words."

"Thanks, Shiler. I truly couldn't do this without you. I wouldn't even know where to start."

"I am so sorry I left, Leila. I swear on my mother's life, had I stayed there another day, I'd have completely lost it. I finally understood why so many women do themselves in. Everywhere I looked was a dead end."

"Are you truly happy there? Honestly?"

"I won't lie to you. It was hard on my body at first. But I feel so free. You'd love it here too. Full of butterflies and wildflowers for you. We hunt partridges, and we catch fish and barbeque them fresh. We plant our own garden too and . . ."

"And when Turkish and Iranian air strikes rain bombs on you?"

"We usually outsmart them, and they can't locate our position, but it is heartbreaking when they target innocent villagers. You know what, Leila? The truth is that they don't really want to kill us all. How else are they going to get people to vote for them if there isn't some 'enemy' out there? I see it so clearly now. The end of racism and other fears will be the end of dictators. Our weapons may look like toys before their artillery, but what we stand for scares the hell out of them. So they're more focused on distorting our image than actually killing us, and they can do that. They control the masses through media."

"So what exactly are you doing?"

"A lot of things. Small but good things. We go into the villages and teach women how to make pickles and sell them so they have some financial independence. We give them contraceptives. We teach children how to identify land mines and stay safe. You know, the fields haven't been demined in the three decades since the war, and children still lose limbs because of them. Some die. No one reports on it, but it's happening. Some of the comrades sit with the Imams of the villages and convince them to tell people female genital mutilation is not right. We teach men how to avoid overhunting and be mindful of the ecosystem."

"And what happens when Revolutionary Guards walk in on you?"

"When someone's discovered, if they're not arrested, they run back here or go abroad to continue the work, but they always recruit new members. Leila, people are a lot more amazing than you and I knew. Or maybe the most amazing people are drawn to us because there is very little one can do alone."

"Chia knew all of that, didn't he?"

"He did, but he was more interested in working alone. And not obeying orders. Listen, I'll create a shared email we can both check, and I will send all the updates through it. Never check this from your home internet."

Shiler put her lips on the monitor.

I blew a kiss. We both hugged our computers and laughed.

I TYPED UP some of Chia's journal entries, created a Facebook page, linked to his blog, and shared his words.

I sat at the computer all day and posted as many photos, articles, and stories as I could find. I researched websites and blogs dedicated to political prisoners and submitted Chia's information, emailed every activist whose name I could look up, and asked them to prepare petitions for my brother, whose alleged crime was accompanying someone who had recorded a government's murder scene.

Shiler, who, unlike me, had access to unfiltered internet, joined the effort and recruited her *havalan*—comrades—to translate Chia's words into Turkish, Arabic, English, German, French, Dutch, and more. She moved her massive network, since her party had attracted leftist members and sympathizers all over the globe, especially in Europe.

Chia's words spread.

WHEN MAMA CALLED the week after, furious that I had lied to her about Chia, I realized Shiler was indeed right about his letters going viral.

"I was trying to spare you the heartache. It's nearly killed me, not knowing where he was, if he was safe—or alive, even. And as for lying, did you ever tell

Baba about your affair with your intersex client?" I finally confronted her. She drew in a sharp breath.

"It was a mistake. A momentary mistake. Do you want to tell him now? In the middle of this crisis? Are you planning on giving your father a heart attack? He's devastated. When he heard about Chia, he curled up like an infant and sobbed for hours."

I placed the "Be back in five minutes" sticky note on the door of the bookstore and hid behind the counter. I could hear the fear in her voice. "No, Mama. I'm not going to tell him anything now. I'm just making a point about how some things are better left unsaid."

"When will Chia be released? I've been getting phone calls from TV and radio stations digging for information."

I gaped. "Mama, you should immediately hang up when strangers call. Okay? Remember, it's not safe. Unplug the phone. Or change your number. Do you want to go to prison too? At this age? Do not talk to anyone. Not even one person. If you do, they will torture Chia. Even one word can mean a lot of trouble."

"What can I do? People come to our door. Acquaintances. Everybody has heard about Chia."

My legs began to ache from hunkering behind the cluttered counter, but there was a big grin on my face. I had to hide the smile from my voice. "Just don't answer. They could easily be spies. Even if they look like friends. Remember how your neighbor told on Baba and they raided your house?"

"We want to come visit him."

"I haven't been able to see him, but when I can try for visitation again, I'll tell you. Just be patient until I sort this out."

"I tell everyone my son is innocent."

"Of course he is. Everybody knows this. So please, just don't get him into more trouble. All it takes is one word to the wrong person."

"Your father says you should come home. Living on your own is not safe."

"Is he dis-disowning me now?"

"Please, Leila. Your father wants us to return to Halabja."

"Brilliant! That's an excellent idea. Go. Leave this country. Find a farm there. Chia and I will join you. We will plant pomegranate trees together."

"Not yet! We couldn't leave Chia here. After he's released. When will he be released?" she sobbed.

"Mama, I have to go." I hung up the phone. My knees were tingling. I reopened the store and continued working until eight o'clock.

After closing the shop, I took the bus to an underground internet café I'd learned about from the prison visitors I'd befriended. The café, located in the basement of a fancy shopping mall, was expensive, but they offered unfiltered high-speed internet and privacy, things regulated internet cafés lacked. Inside it was dark and hazy with cigarette smoke, lit only by the blue-green glow of the screens. Each customer wore a headset and was immersed in his computer. I noticed the heavy eyes of the men and avoided looking at their private screens as I made my way to the last available stall to check the email account Shiler had set up.

There they were: the heartening, sympathetic comments and letters from strangers contacting the website where Shiler and I had posted Chia's writing. He had indeed touched a lot of people. Since printouts of the messages would have meant trouble if I were caught, I sat there and reread the letters, trying to memorize the heartwarming lines. One said that Chia's words, his imagination, his ability to communicate the anguish of others made him an icon representing all political prisoners.

That night I left the café in tears. "Aw, did your boyfriend cheat on you?" asked one of the guys.

The protests outside of Evin gained international attention, and the global condemnations regarding the way Iran treated the families of political prisoners finally made the authorities grant more visitations. Meanwhile, not a single piece of evidence was brought forward against Chia; the public and officials alike knew he was innocent.

WHEN I FINALLY set eyes on Chia behind the thick window, 183 days after his disappearance, I couldn't control my sobs. How could I? His hazel eyes were bruised, his skin sallow, his right arm shaking from electrocution. His cheeks were hollow, his formerly full hair receding and graying. His scraggly beard had grown long and disheveled.

He couldn't control his tears either and placed both palms on the window. Chia's endearing terms followed mine, were mixed in mine. I mouthed "*dllakam*"—darling—meaning it more than ever, and I watched him say "dllakam" in return. I wasn't sure if I was at the receiving or the sending end of love as relief fizzled in every molecule of my being.

"Choni khoshkakam?" How are you, sister? Chia mimed the question, pretending to wipe my tears despite the glass. We laughed and we cried together. He placed a hand on his heart, miming "So happy to see you."

"Me too," I mimed back. We didn't need words. We just needed to see each other, and that was the most heartwarming thing in the world.

I picked up the receiver, ready to speak. "You have gained muscles, haven't you?" He had lost a good twenty pounds, if not more.

"I do something like a thousand push-ups and three hundred sit-ups every day."

"Good for you, my dearest. Chia. Chia gian. It's so good to see you." I placed my cheek on the window, and he extended his palm. I'd been hungry for his presence, and now I gorged myself on the sight of him, drinking in each detail, each freckle, each eggplant bruise fading to yellow.

"And guess what—one of my cellmates knows a lot of poems. I've been memorizing most of what he has recited for us. His poetry reminds me of the songs you used to hum. It's such a joy, Leila. I never knew. Poetry is such a cure for loneliness. You see, if you're stuck on an island all alone, somewhere deserted, you can recite poetry and lo and behold, poof! Loneliness fades away. When I am out, we will see which of us knows more *ghazals* by heart."

On a desert island or in a solitary cell?

"Oh, I'll beat you. You know that."

When the authorities didn't allow me to visit him the next week, I threatened to inform foreign media about the signs of torture I'd seen on my brother. They made me promise not to talk to the "hostile media" in exchange for weekly visits and phone calls. I agreed.

Soon Chia and I developed codes and a sign language we improvised, the words mimed or written on the glass with fingertips. We agreed to leave the country when he was released and promised to improve our English language skills. That made me watch more movies, which in turn alleviated my stress. At night I slept well without pills.

Chia wrote new essays in prison with pen and paper he purchased from the crooked guards at ten times the price and read them to me over the phone. I recorded the calls and transcribed his words, reading them over and over until I'd memorized them.

One day Chia painted a vivid picture of the city of Sanandaj, the autumn foliage, things he could not see from the window of his cell but in his imagination. In general he only hinted at agony in his essays; instead he mostly spoke about his moments of falling in love, of listening to Abbas Kamandy's love songs, and of hiking Awyar Mountain. He was distracted from these memories only when the bitterness of the blood he accidentally swallowed threatened to suffocate him.

"My prison guard anxiously checked to see if I'd survived the latest severe beating. I know he would prefer that I die at the hands of the interrogators instead of his. I heard the sound of a wedding's music coming through the prison walls. My guard didn't know, couldn't know, that the music had me imagining dancing at my own wedding, waving my *chopi*—handkerchief—in the air and shouting, 'Cheers! Cheers to all the prisoners' families who are awaiting reunions with their children. Cheers to all the men and women who risked their lives to make a difference.'"

We fed his words to the hungry internet community. UNICEF, PEN, and a few other international organizations released statements about him.

I was called in to Intelligence for questioning and responded that the web followed its own laws. I had no say in how Chia's words were spreading, I said. I was no longer scared of them. If they did anything to me, the pressure to release Chia would only grow.

The authorities had me go on state-run television and make a statement that in the past few months, my brother had been fed properly and allowed to see a doctor and had been given access to soap and other toiletries. It was only when he did receive these basic comforts—which political prisoners were denied, contrary to Iran's own laws—that I agreed to appear on the program. On the air, I parroted their lines and did not say one word more, no matter how cleverly their senior anchor tried to wheedle me into saying that the international news outlets had exaggerated regarding the conditions in Iran's prisons. I kept repeating that I didn't know. When the anchor implied during the live broadcast that I was an imbecile, I asked, "How come you're not asking me how many days it took me to see my brother? Do you want to know how he looked when I first saw him?"

Right then the program "ran out of time."

Shiler wasn't thrilled about my media appearance. She believed Chia must be under tremendous pressure for a fake televised "confession." Some of her friends were former political prisoners and knew Iran's methods.

Chia's lawyer called.

CHAPTER TWENTY-FIVE

I HELD MY knuckles to prevent the dripping blood from falling on the concrete floor, jostled the noisy people blocking me, and pushed my way forward. Outside of the courthouse, I wrapped the end of my headscarf around my fingers and pressed it hard to stop the red stream. The shocking news had numbed the pain in my hand.

"Shahid namre?" Hawrez, the younger of Farhad's sons, asked in Kurdish, pulling on my manteau. His mother had waited outside the courthouse in a show of solidarity.

"What?"

"Shahid regai aazadi namre." This time he pronounced the words as a statement rather than a question. "Martyrs never die. Freedom fighters never die," the little boy repeated.

"Shut up!" I yelled. "Shut up!" Right after the lawyer had summoned me into his office to tell me Chia had been sentenced to death, the last thing I wanted to hear was a little boy repeating "Martyrs never die."

"Freedom or no freedom, listen to me, little man." I waved my bleeding hand in the air. "When somebody dies, they die. They'll never come back. Think."

Hawrez tilted his head, the look in his eyes similar to my brother's at that age.

"Chia will not die." I bent to reach his face. "Nor will your father. Okay? We will save them. They will be free and alive. Do you hear me?" My fingers were pressing the boy's shoulder blade, perhaps too firmly, but he only stared at me in confusion.

Hewram, his older brother, stepped forward and glared at me. I released the boy. Their mother appeared and placed her hands on her sons' shoulders.

"You shouldn't teach the kids these things," I said to her and heard the quiver in my voice. "You must not."

"What would you say, ha? To a seven-year-old?"

I walked away, waved for a cab. I had no answer.

Only after several empty cabs passed by and refused to stop for me did I become aware of the tears mixing with mascara running down my face. Big drops of blood oozed through the scarf wrapped around my hand. I felt faint. I wiped my face with my sleeve and shoved my hand inside my purse. An orange taxi finally braked, the bespectacled owner too old to detect potential trouble. I jumped in and gave him the address, asked him to rush. I had to get home, change, and head to Evin right away. The noise of the car's engine gradually overrode my heartbeat, and I leaned back to place my temple on the headrest.

I hadn't planned to punch the decorative glass scale on the lawyer's table, even though that bogus symbol of justice appalled me. But when the lawyer broke the news, when I heard that Chia was accused of the make-believe crime of *Moharebeh*, "enmity against God"—the indictment punishable by death—I had lost control and smashed my hand down on the scales. Like a scared cat who wished to be mistaken for a lion, my thoughts roared and reverberated.

Back at the apartment, I moved on autopilot. "Exchange the purple shoelaces for black ones. Bring the black headscarf forward so no strand of the hair that has turned completely gray is revealed. Tie your ponytail low so it's not obvious you have one; now tuck it inside the black coverall." I spoke aloud so I could remember and focus. I needed to be invisible enough for this "virtuous" society. "Cover every sign of femininity under your dark chador. Disappear." Rummaging in the drawer, I found a pair of thin black gloves and, despite the pain, forced my swollen fingers inside.

Then I marched hurriedly through the crowded streets, past the cherry blossoms, and concentrated only on the fact that the day had come—finally, after having applied nineteen times—when I could see Chia in person. Not behind a window. The in-person visitation was granted without enough notice for Mama and Baba to make the trek. They had fought over it bitterly; Mama was itching to see Chia and me, but Baba was too proud to visit the home of a daughter he had disowned, too broke to stay at a hotel. The situation suited me just fine though; I was disinclined to share with anyone the few moments I could spend with my brother.

Car horns, road rage, accidents, gridlock—nothing distracted me from my mission. I couldn't change history, I couldn't control the future, but I could save Chia. I would save Chia. I would save Chia. God had abandoned us. Everyone had. I wouldn't give up till my last breath.

After endless hours of waiting in different lines, I was led to a bench where I waited more, avoiding the gaze of the leering guards, checking repeatedly that my hair hadn't sprouted out of my hijab. My chador covered me from head to toe.

To the self-righteous guards, political prisoners' families were bugs that society needed to exterminate. They had a mustached Almighty on their side.

"Chia will be saved; Chia will be free," I chanted silently and cast aside every other thought until my brother's shrunken figure appeared at the end of the hallway and limped toward me, escorted by a guard four times his size. The man was doused in a very sharp cologne. We were led to a small space surrounded by four walls; the only piece of furniture inside was a pale bench.

"Leila gian! *Gola* gian." Chia spoke in a voice so velvety and reassuring that its sound alone was healing. I hugged him, smelled him, and hoped that he would simply let his warm voice roll on.

"How've you been?" he asked, his weak arms barely holding my body, as if embracing me took all his remaining strength. I let go and only held on to his rough hands, pretending that I had not noticed the broken jaw that slurred his speech.

I kissed his cheeks, his eyes, his forehead. "*Ay ba ghorbani chawakanet bem,* Chia gian." I'd sacrifice myself, I repeated. I threw words of endearment at him, words I'd never used before but meant now, just so the glimmer in his eyes would return, so the spasms in his arms would stop.

"Persian!" The guard pounded the off-white walls. The floor and ceiling shook with his rage. We stopped talking.

I used the guard's language, though it tasted bitter on my lips. "I'm good, Chia, dear. I've been working, reading, watching movies. My boss has given me a raise. He's a follower of your letters. How are you? Tell me, how have you been?"

It was easier to hide my agony when I didn't speak in my mother tongue, yet I felt exposed, as if Chia could see through me. He looked at my gloves without asking.

"I've been well too—tons of time to read and think. Prison isn't as bad when you have a creative or inquisitive mind, you know, if you like to reflect on life, on being . . ." He shrugged. "I'm learning English."

A broken gasp escaped my throat; it could've been a loud breath I'd been holding inside so I could listen to him carefully and take in his every word, every facial expression. Or maybe it was an audible smile at the pleasure of hearing him find something positive about incarceration to tell me. Speaking in a language that was not ours made it easier to fake strength. "What have you been reading, Chia gian?"

"There are lots of legal books here. I'll be ready to practice law when I'm out. And I could defend myself in the court, if I ever get there. It should happen soon. I mean, I don't know, but it should. After all, there's no evidence against me. None."

He knew I'd been meeting with his lawyer regularly and had heard the news of his sentence as well. Perhaps, like me, he was ready to fight it. There was no way they would kill an innocent man who had gained global popularity through his letters and poems.

As soon as the armed guard looked away to stuff something in his mouth, Chia slid a letter into my pocket that he had written with a fading marker on a piece of nylon tablecloth.

"So the cherry tree is in full bloom." I wiped a wayward tear and held his hands again. "The little one you planted in the garden. We will have fresh cherries this year."

Chia choked but recovered. "Save some for me, okay?"

"I'll talk to the birds and worms. Here." I gave him the old headphones.

"Does this thing even work?" He laughed.

"It still has its magic."

"I am very pleased to see this," he said in English.

"Look at you!" I stared at him, trying not to blink, to take as many mental snapshots as I could. I memorized the lines of his face as it brightened with a small smile.

"Electronics are not allowed!" the guard barked. "How did you smuggle this in?" He jerked the headphones from Chia's hands in one swift motion.

I closed my eyes so I wouldn't see them break when he tossed them away.

"What the hell piece of junk is that anyway?" His cologne was nauseating.

I flinched and looked around for a window, forgetting there were none. I was short of breath but high from the exhilaration of seeing him.

"Euphoric," he said. "That's the word." Chia kept the conversation rolling, unaffected by the aggressive behavior of the guard, the illogical restrictions, or the broken souvenir of our childhood, the one keepsake of the days I was able to protect him.

"What word, bawanem?" I choked back tears.

"The word for how I feel now. Now that I am holding your hand." He embraced me again.

I whispered, "Delirious is actually how I feel now."

He let go of me. "What is 'headphones' in English?"

"What? Oh, I don't know! 'Headphones' is an English word, isn't it?"

He laughed. "Listen to this." He sang for me, "Twinkle, twinkle, little star . . ."

"Persian!" the guard yelled again.

I laughed hard, an exaggerated laugh. "You're like a five-year-old."

Chia giggled. "I have been aging backward. One of the glories of prison."

I stuck my thumbs in my ears, made antlers of my hands, and crossed my eyes. He let out a yelp of pure pleasure and made a hideous, lopsided grimace. We melted into giggles. The guard touched his gun in the holster. Our laughter echoed off the walls enclosing the tiny space.

When the visitation came to an end, the guard led Chia and me to the hallway where other visitors were also saying goodbye to prisoners. "Look over there. Farhad's sons are here to perform their latest gymnastic routine for their father," he said.

"They are my friends. Those two little boys. Hewarm and Hawrez."

The children showed off their acrobatic moves and ran around the chairs, screaming in excitement, their voices a resonant tremolo of verve and faith. "Out," the guard yelled. I enfolded my brother in my arms and slipped homemade chocolate pigeons into his pockets, ones that Shirin's mother had baked.

"You really shouldn't worry about me, Leila. I am in a place full of intellectuals and artists. We all have rich inner lives no one can take away." Chia squeezed my hand. "I have never been around this many fascinating people at the same time."

The door was shut.

"Don't you ever give up. Don't you ever give in. Together we can get through this." I cupped my hands and screamed for all the political prisoners to hear.

"Fuck off, bitch, before we put you behind one of those steel doors too." A female guard grabbed me and pulled me away. I was very aware of my breathing.

She pushed me down the hallway. Farhad's sons and other visiting young children squealed with delight in their parents' embrace. Their laughter lit up the faces of the prisoners and their families but irritated the guards. Out the door she shoved me.

"Happy May Day!" someone yelled across the street. All the way home, I hummed Kurdish songs of resistance. "We are laborers. We are fighters . . ."

Rich inner life, Chia had said. Rich inner life. One's only reliable investment and the most loyal companion. I was slowly building one too.

PART IV

CHIA

CHAPTER TWENTY-SIX

MY STUDENTS ARE still learning the history of the Kurds in secret, I tell myself. Leila is well, stronger now, and can handle my absence. The call to prayer that reverberates through Evin Prison turns me cold with fear.

Footsteps.

I know the sound of those heavy boots. I know them well. I hear the iron doors open and shut, hear the jingle of the guard's huge keychain, then another metal door opens and shuts, and yet another. The footsteps grow louder. I drop my pen and curl into a ball, shrinking with fear. Three more doors, and then they will reach mine. The pain in my head and face, legs and back, stomach and ribs sharpens. Clutching at the pillow does not stop my arms from shaking.

The footsteps stop before they reach my cell.

Hands up, I think, and almost say it out loud.

"Hands up," the old guard says.

I know what they are doing in the other cell. A blindfold, a click of the handcuffs, and the guards take Ali out, pushing and kicking him.

I follow them in my head as Ali is taken downstairs, dragged nineteen steps to the right, down fifteen more stairs, and delivered to the interrogators. Under his blindfold, Ali will count the shoes in the room: four, six, eight black formal shoes splattered with blood, polished by blood.

The whipping will start soon after the curses. If the man they call Mongrel is there, the interrogation will be longer. Every prisoner knows that man's strange voice, an unusual soft timbre that can detonate in an instant. He'd call the Kurds "treasonous, murdering savages," then show us who the true savage was. It is rumored that Mongrel's brother was killed in Kurdistan thirty years ago when he went there to quash an uprising.

Five, six lashes in and Ali will start thinking about concentration camps, pyramids, the Great Wall of China. He will not feel the whip anymore, I hope.

The number of cracks on the wall numbers 305 today. I sneak a pen out from under my army blanket and take paper, folded six times, from my underwear. *Leila*, I write, but my pen is paralyzed. Guilt gnaws at me for having abandoned her. *My dear students*, my pen gallops. *All I was able to do was teach you our alphabet, our literature, and our history. Please, children, pass it on. Dear little ones, never allow this knowledge to steal from you the joy of childhood. May you keep the memories of youth in your minds forever. It may be the one and only investment you can use later when the agony of earning your bread and butter dominates you, my sons, and the sin of being "the second sex" overpowers you, my daughters.*

Men in prison-blue smocks drag their white flip-flops on the ground. The stairs creak.

> *Remember not to turn your backs on your dreams, loves, music, poetry, and Kurdistan's magical nature. Join together and recite folk songs as we used to do.*

A LAMP IN a metal grating spreads dull light. The steel toilet in my solitary cell stinks. "In me there was a rough prisoner not used to the clanking of his chains," I recite aloud, clinging to the door of my cell, a space that is only five paces wide, wall to wall.

Through the bars, Ali looks so dried up, so weak, but his voice is firm. "Shamlou's poems again?"

I have not seen myself in months—mirrors do not exist in the prison—but I'm sure I don't look much better than Ali.

"What could be more healing?" I ask.

"Not your own poetry then? I wondered."

"I'm not a poet—only a teacher who loves poetry." I try to turn my head toward him, the head that is stuck between iron rods. "Did I tell you I had a student with the name Ali?"

Ali mirrors me and winces. I know that under the prison gown, his body is a web of scars from all the wounds he's sustained. Mine is too.

"What would you do to them, Chia?" Ali's voice is shaking. His cheeks and eyes are bruised and his muscles still. "What would you do, if you could do anything you wanted to these sadists?"

I think about his question for a long time. "I'd send them to rehab."

Ali forces a laugh. "Does your foot still hurt?"

"My entire body does, Ali gian. But this is the pain of a nation . . . and the cure too. So it's not all that bad."

"Make sure you don't forget us, Mamosta, when you are freed."

Ali calls me "teacher," his voice growing fainter. Even though his body is stronger than mine, I know he is too frail to stand or speak much longer. I spent eighteen days in an emergency room after my open sores from the interrogation sessions became infected. I was barely allowed to sleep, not allowed to use the washroom more than twice in twenty-four hours, and was kept in cold lockdown. All I had to wrap around me was a once-white mat.

They must have played "football" with Ali too. The interrogators, the "players," stand in the corners of the room, tell "the enemies of God" to strip, kick our bodies around, curse us and our ethnicity, kick our heads, kick us harder where we are already injured, threaten our families, threaten to rape us. We cannot stifle the screams that satisfy them so much.

Do not worry, Ali gian. Your cries are not a sign of weakness. I write down in the margin of a state-run newspaper what I cannot say to his face. *I have seen a child's birth. Cries and struggles are the first signs of life, not of weakness. "A mountain begins with its first rocks and a human with the first pain."*

"*Are wa fedai do didai aazizem show bi khawt bem, ly-ly-ly-ly . . .*" I sing the lullaby Ali used to sing for his daughters when they were babies. I wonder if he will see them this week or if he will have to wait until the bruises on his face, at least, heal a bit.

Ali weeps, and I sing louder. "*Ly-ly-ly-ly . . .*"

My lullaby passes through the concrete walls. Other prisoners, political and nonpolitical, are quiet. My lullaby soothes them even though not everyone speaks my language. Some sob like infants.

"*Ly-ly-ly-ly . . . Kazhollei chaw kazhallem . . . ly-ly-ly . . .*"

EIGHTEEN, NINETEEN, TWENTY . . . I count the cracks in the ceiling. My lawyer is presenting documents to the judge. Here it is hard to breathe. The room reeks as if the walls were made of corpses. The judge leaves his seat and walks to the door that convicts cannot use. It is only for him. The attached light brown desks divide His Honor's space from that of the non-honored ones.

"Chia Saman is absolutely innocent, Your Honor," my lawyer says for the third time. "He is not a part of any political group, Your Honor, separatist or not. Nothing in Saman's judicial files and records demonstrates any link to the charges of terrorism brought against him."

There are only three of us in the room. Five minutes have passed, but the judge seems not to be listening. I wait for him to speak.

He tucks some papers under his arm and walks to the door only he is allowed to use. "I am going for my afternoon prayer."

"Your afternoon prayer!" I shout. I cannot help myself.

He stops.

"I have been in prison for five hundred and forty-five days." The words jump out of me. "For a hundred and twelve of those days I was not allowed to contact my family, seek legal counsel, or even know what my crime was supposed to be."

The judge touches his gray beard. I imagine he houses dead mice there. Every step he takes toward the door makes me speak louder. My arms and legs tremble with pain as I lurch toward him, courtesy of the jolts of electricity.

"I was proven innocent of all the charges of terrorism. Why don't they let me go? They haven't bothered to make up a single document against me."

The judge does not heed me. Worms wriggling in his ears must halt my words from getting through.

"Absolutely zero evidence has been presented against Saman, Your Honor. Zero," the lawyer says.

The judge holds the door handle. He looks back, glances around the empty room, ends his search at the camera installed over his high chair. "Ettela'at ordered your death," he whispers. "There is nothing I can do."

And he turns his back, leaving the room abruptly through his private door. My lawyer gapes. I scream, "Ahhh!" and the scream bounces off the walls and back to me.

A security guard runs and presses my wrists against my back.

"I wasn't speaking with my hands," I say softly, feeling almost numb.

"Hush, brother, hush," the young, sunburnt guard whispers with a heavy Azeri accent. He is short but sturdily built, and his tough look shows that he is a hardworking village boy, probably on obligatory military service.

The lawyer shakes his head and waves his hands in the air. "Only five minutes behind closed doors and not even a word of explanation?"

Hush, Chia, hush, I think, *not because there isn't much to say, but because speaking here is a threat to national security and enmity against God.*

The door shuts behind us.

I FINALLY SEE my sister in person, without cruel glass sitting between us. Leila, aged heavily now, stares at me. Fighting seemed right to me, but Leila's accusing eyes tell a different story. Farhad's sons are here again to perform their latest gymnastics moves for their father. Despite everyone else in the room and all the chairs, despite the bruises on their father's face. "See, Leila, I realize now that these children are not just innocently entertaining their father. They are aware, you see?"

Leila is too quiet, and this kills me. I gambled with both of our lives, not only mine. I make silly jokes, sing an English children's song for her, but nothing can diminish the elephant in the room. What will happen to her when I'm gone?

When the fifteen-minute visitation is over—fifteen minutes we have been counting down the days toward—I have to warn her. "If they do anything to you, Leila gian . . . Please stop protesting in front of the prison. Please."

I want to repeat it a thousand times, but the lump in my throat stops me.

Leila bites her lips and chokes back tears. "Sitting by the other people makes me feel stronger, bawanem. I get to console families whose loved ones have been hanged."

I repeat "hanged" aloud to hear it in my voice.

"Hey, don't you worry," she says. "Your letters are widely circulated, and national, even international, campaigns have been started to save you."

The guard is unlocking the door for her to leave.

"You are different from other prisoners, Chia; you have a voice, an impact. Soon you'll be free. Your lawyer has written letters to hundreds of members of parliament and other authorities saying he will resign if anyone finds any evidence to prove you're a criminal."

The door is waiting, open for only her.

She speaks louder. "I receive calls and letters from people that I don't even know. Kurds in Turkey, Syria, and Iraq are supporting you."

She runs to me, hugs me, and slides something into my pocket. She is taken out, but I hear her voice. "Don't you ever give up. Don't you ever give in. Together we can get through this."

"Yes, we can. Yes, we can," I shout back, hoping she hears me.

"Yes, we can. Yes, we can." Other prisoners chant along. I am shoved back into my cell, but this grin that I have cannot be wiped away.

THE NUMBER OF cracks before my eyes is infinite today. The homemade chocolates Leila gave me are by my bed. She also smuggled in a mini pencil and paper. *"Are wak bakhchei bi aw aazizem teshnei waranm . . ."* I murmur the lullaby late at night.

I take a few deep breaths and write:

No, I will not let them kill me. Not inside. After all, the high walls here can't stop me from seeing the moon and stars. Being enclosed behind bars cannot stop me from knowing that out there the Zagros Mountain dances slowly to the sound of the tambour. The cricket is my witness. She knows that, despite the injustice inside the prison, the day and night do not steal each other's turn in their freedom.

When I am freed, I will dance. With Shiler, with Leila, with my students, without sharing the story of the walls, without counting cracks in every room I find myself in. Chocolate melts in my mouth. Delicious. Heavenly.

I continue scribbling despite my swollen fingers.

Sleep, Chia, sleep.

Not because it's time to sleep, but because being awake is a sin here, and the punishment is beyond what human bones can stand. I should remember that words are sinful in this forgotten part of the world. Thinking is a "crime," writing is "enmity against God," and talking is "terrorism." The newspapers are blank, the walls are spies, television is the greatest liar, and speaking out is off limits. I feel strongly that there is a mysterious, underground power that has recently given the poet the right words, the writers their subjects, the elderly bravery, and the youth hope. I need to remember what I am told when I am beaten: that in the Islamic Republic of Iran, there is no such thing as poverty, protest, oppression, discrimination, lies, or immorality. These are the enemies' terms, part of their "plot."

I will eventually escape this place. "The butterfly that flew away in the night told me my fortune."

Heavy iron doors open and shut. Keys jingle. Footsteps. Heavy boots.

I am not shaking, and I smile at this victory, at the courage that writing gives into me. It's too late for their usual visit. It must be dark outside. The pen and paper are quickly placed under the army blanket. The footsteps reach my wing. *Hands up*, I think, and almost say it out loud.

"Hands up," the old guard says.

"After-hours interrogations?" I ask the old guard I have known since the early days of my imprisonment, exactly 454 days. I speak informally to him. He knows I have a pen here and pretends that he doesn't. We have one thing in common: counting the days, the guard toward his retirement from a job he despises and me toward a future yet to be determined. We both try to keep our sanity by doing mathematics.

I look at the two huge men standing behind the familiar face.

"Number A-1332," the old man says, "stand. Collect your things."

I nod in recognition, turn my back, and shove my letters inside the pocket of the shirt Leila bought me. I place all of it in a plastic bag, vaguely hoping they will be given to my sister.

The usual shoves follow, the usual handcuffs and blindfold, but not the same path, not the same number of steps. I'm counting blind now.

When they remove the cloth covering my eyes, I see Shirin, Ali, Mahdi, and Farhad. We are in the prison yard, and dawn is breaking. Twenty-five armed guards stand together, surrounding five handcuffed prisoners. I peer at the sky.

"The sun is checking to make sure it's not counterrevolutionary to rise today," I say, and the four other handcuffed people laugh.

The guards push us toward the western corner of the yard, thrusting and kicking to urge us along. Farhad is also limping. We both lag behind.

I give him a half smile. "Were you a football too?"

When he was first arrested, Farhad did not have gray hairs in his mustache and eyebrows. Now he looks at me, not offering a word.

"Did you meet the Mongrel? Did he play football with you too?"

"That was your special treat. They were boxers with me."

I laugh, and the guard hits me between the shoulder blades with the butt of his rifle.

"You know what?" I sense death, my guard's rifle pointed at my chest. I become daring. I know what will happen to us soon. There is nothing left to be scared of. "The sun will rise regardless of what you do here today."

The guards ignore me, waiting for an order, and we stand still. Chocolates. I reach into my pocket with difficulty, with cuffed hands, and take them out. "Have some," I say to the tallest guard, the one on my right.

The bearded guard tries to hit me again, this time with his fist, but the tall one holds him back. Unable to move forward, he swears at me, at the other four prisoners, at all Kurds.

"Rise, sun. Rise and be our witness," Shirin shouts and receives more blows and curses.

I'd like to tell her I had a student whose name was Shirin.

The sun is in no rush.

"What's wrong with sharing chocolate?"

Nobody responds. The guards are too busy quarrelling among themselves.

I limp toward Shirin, whose guards watch us warily.

"Can I take two?" she asks.

"Please do, sister. No more dieting for you and me." I wink, surprised at myself for being so calm.

Shirin holds a chocolate in her mouth and closes her eyes to better savor the taste. I smile.

"This is our graduation ceremony, you know," she says.

"With honors."

I hobble toward the other prisoners, passing the chocolates around, indefinably relieved that today ends the daily humiliation of being trapped in a place that tells you every single day that the world is better off without you. The other prisoners take chocolates from me, but the guards refuse. I still haven't finished giving away all the pieces when we are pulled back so the soldiers can tie the four male prisoners' handcuffs together from behind with short lengths of rope. They tell us to walk in a line. Around the corner in the main square, five chairs wait on a high stand.

Farhad is struggling. "You can't murder us like this. Where are our lawyers? We haven't even said goodbye to our families. Who ordered our dea—"

One of the guards kicks Farhad in the groin.

Everything seems familiar to me in a curious way. Even Farhad's face, crimson with anger and pain.

When we are up on the platform and the guards are tying our feet, I see that Ali is silently crying and biting his lower lip. The fatigue I had not allowed myself to feel envelops my body, dulls my senses.

"Ey reqib . . ." I start singing the ancient anthem. *"Kas nalle Kurd mirduwe; Kurd zinduwa/Zinduwa qet nanewe allakeman."*

The others join me. "Oh, foes, the Kurdish nation is alive and its flag will never fall. It cannot be defeated by makers of weapons of any time. Let no one say the Kurds are dead; the Kurds are alive."

The angry executioners do not speak our language. *Kas nalle Kurd mirduwe; Kurd zinduwa.*

More ropes. These are placed around our necks. I know the media here will announce, "Five terrorists have been hanged."

I also know that the sun will rise, that the cracks will one day bring the prison walls down, and that students will one day be allowed to learn the history of the Kurds openly. Leila will be strong.

THE CHAIRS ARE kicked away. Above the ropes, the chocolates melt in our mouths.

PART V

LEILA

CHAPTER TWENTY-SEVEN

THE WIND GUSTED through Chia's bedroom, slamming the door. I pulled the vacuum out from under his bed, pried a pair of navy boxers from the hose, and turned off the machine. The radio I had turned on to relieve the silence was tuned to a London-based Kurdish station and was playing a Kurmanji song: *"Men biria to kerie, bavar ka . . ."* I miss you, believe me that I miss you. Ask the birds. Ask the flower. Ask the prison walls. I miss you.

The last piece of Scotch tape gave up, and a calendar page fell to the floor. I fetched the orchid spray from the living room.

"Iran hanged five prisoners today, four of whom were Kurdish, for the fictional crime of Moharebeh," the radio announced when the song ended, then listed their names. My ears perked up upon hearing Shirin and Farhad identified. "Chia Saman." I froze. My brother couldn't be the only one with that name. In a daze I returned to Chia's room—now spotless—and sprayed the fragrance. In the living room I heard the radio repeat Chia's name, the most famous among the list of the executed.

Suddenly my ribs tightened. I found balance by pressing them and sitting at the edge of the bed.

A stinging terror crept in under my skin, deep inside my bones. But Chia lifted my chin, smiled, and kissed my forehead. When I raised my eyes to look into his, he disappeared.

I got up, twirled and sprayed the orchid scent, twirled and sprayed until I coughed so hard I had to stop. With a nimble flick, I shut the radio off.

Joanna called. I told her the Kurdish media must have gotten the news from the government, which was obviously lying. "When have they ever told people the truth?" I asked.

She said she believed me but asked if she should visit anyway, or if I wanted to visit her.

"We will. As soon as Chia gets out."

"Remember, my arms are always open to you. I love you like I love Shiler."

Shiler, I remembered. "Please tell her to ignore the lie."

Upon hearing the bogus report, which had now spread like wildfire across Kurdish and state-run media alike, Mama and Baba were a team for once in their lives, united by tragedy. They forgot about how disgraceful I was and invited themselves into my apartment before dawn. They left their luggage inside and headed for the Evin morgue. I turned off my phone, which was now flooded with sympathetic emails and interview requests by the local and foreign media that had believed the farce. My parents came back empty-handed. I sheltered in Chia's room and locked the door. Mama pounded on the door and screamed, but I could not let her or anyone else touch Chia's things.

"You godless woman!" she yowled. "You didn't tell us. We had to hear it from strangers." She was just another sound to block out while I floated in an unidentifiable time and space.

Mama's tenacity and unmatched skills at getting on people's nerves made the authorities promise to return the body under the condition that the deceased's family signed documents under oath, guaranteeing that they would neither hold a funeral nor bury him during daylight. Even after all this, it took them days to deliver the body they claimed was Chia's.

My brother and I winked at each other, secretly mocking others for believing the deceit. He was four again. His chubby arms and legs jiggled as he ran to me, bit into unwashed cherries and giggled.

A truck carried us and the imposter's body to Mariwan. "I need to pray," Mama said when we entered the city. "Drop me at home first." She thanked God as she climbed down from the truck, straightened her shoulders, and walked away without looking back.

In the wee hours, Baba, the truck driver, and I arrived at the graveyard. The gates were locked, but Baba talked to the night guard, placed hands on his shoulders, slid some cash into his palm, and, using a flashlight, walked into the darkness, silent, head bent, shoulders hunched.

With shivering knees, I followed the men. The driver, quite strong and well built, helped Baba retrieve the body from the truck. They placed the stretcher on their shoulders, shepherded me past the older section of the cemetery—the little gardens where used needles were scattered—to a section with holes dug for graves that hadn't yet been assigned. Baba stopped, and I watched in silence.

Baba laid the body down inside the hole, meticulously tucking the shroud around the limbs, and climbed out of it. The weak beam of his flashlight scanned the wrapped corpse. Only its size resembled Chia's. The government paid attention to these details. Baba froze. The truck driver shoveled dirt into the hole. Baba was only a silhouette.

There were only the sounds of our breathing, the sinister whooshing of the wind, and the lethal silence of the graveyard.

"Cannibals!" Baba's sudden outburst rattled the cemetery. "Cannibaaaals!"

His shoulders shook, wracked by feral sobs. Huge tears ran down his cheeks and lost their way in his week-old graying beard.

I blinked at him in disbelief. Where was my proud father? Or was this his clone? Had this all been staged, right down to the foreign mourner before me?

"It's a lie," I whispered.

Our eyes locked. The pain in Baba's eyes was real. Shocking in its vulnerability. The saddest person I knew, who subsisted on sorrow like air or water, was now testifying to a catastrophe bigger than anything he had experienced. In that one look, I knew the truth.

"Chia, tell him it's a lie!" I clambered down into the grave and pushed the dirt away. Placed my hand under the dead man's head. Removed the shroud from his face.

"No, Chia gian. Brother, wake up!" I shook his shoulders. His pale lips did not move, and his head dangled limply. "Say you won't leave me!" I wailed.

Baba turned off the flashlight. "Hush, Leila." Baba's soothing voice was not his. It was a voice he had borrowed from another.

I pressed my brother's lifeless face to mine.

What escaped my throat wasn't a sob, a lump, or a breath. Rapid, noisy air burst from my heaving chest. I was sinking and straining for air.

I WOKE UP in my childhood room. The sameness shocked me, the old shabbiness and the layers of dust. In this room I had studied to get into a university, had kicked out Chia when he'd peeked in to spy on me, had spoken to the suitors I'd resented. The clock had stopped ticking. I sat up, drew my aching body upright, took in the silence and the darkness. The full moon glowed with a smile in spite of Chia's absence.

I swiftly separated from the girl who was sitting cross-legged on the bed, her shoulders heaving up and down in noiseless sobs. Defying gravity, I flew up, feeling numb and free.

When the sunrays finally beamed through the dusty air of the room, I became one again with the anguished body. "God! Hello? Mr. God!" I jerked up and opened the window. "Wake up!" The sun's face grinned, suspended in the dawn sky.

"Are you even alive, Mr. God?" I roared in a voice that was louder than I thought possible. My scream echoed down the narrow street where we'd once sold apricots. "Are you? Or did they place a noose around your neck and strangle the life out of you too?" My plaintive cries merged into a long keening noise. I bayed like a wounded animal, a coyote whose pup had been slaughtered before her. An early-morning shopper stopped before our home and looked up at me incredulously.

Loud thumps on my door didn't stop my tirade. "You're the one who should be buried in the earth, not Chia."

Baba broke the lock and rushed in. *"Astaghforella,"* Mama said. "Alan, get her to stop this blasphemy, will you?"

"Enough, Hana," he hushed my mother. She slammed the door to her bedroom.

Baba pressed my wrists, shook me like a rag doll. I looked at him. There it was, in his face: an age-old pain that was still young in mine.

HUNDREDS OF PEOPLE showed up at our door uninvited, at the same ramshackle house in which Chia and I had grown up. I hugged my knees in a corner and watched the comings and goings, the whispering mourners who could be caring strangers or daring spies. Old and new neighbors, the baker, the butcher, convenience store owners' wives, classmates, Chia's students and their families, anyone who thought they knew my brother in some capacity showed up.

Chia had the best-attended secret funeral.

The old cassette player repeated the rhythmically recited verses of the holy book all day, promising that friends of God had no fear or sorrow. No sorrow.

People stole dreadful looks. They exchanged knowing, condescending glances when talking about "the martyr's family." Mama was thankful to her God for making her feel special again and providing her with all the attention she craved but didn't know how to handle. She left the guests to pray ten times a day, then walked back and forth through the crowd, repeating that she was the blessed mother of a martyr.

Baba was a ticking bomb, a silhouette in the flickering candlelight. Like Shiler, he'd hike to grieve. I pictured him climbing up the Zagros Mountain, hands clasped behind his back, head bent, counting the number of steps, searching to find the best rock with which to entrust his weight, assuring himself that nobody had ever been condemned to experience such a horrific sequence of misfortunes as he. He rarely showed up at the mosque, where a man's job was to appear sad but reserved, unshaven and messy. A heart attack was more acceptable than shedding tears.

Then she showed up. Joanna.

"How could this have happened? How?" I asked, collapsing toward her. My vision blurred with tears, but I noticed that time had left its mark on Joanna's face. Or was it worry?

We cried in each other's arms. "Leila gian, dalala men, *kechakam. Nazarakam,*" she said soothingly.

Dressed in white from head to toe and showering me with terms of endearment, Joanna didn't offer answers, only listened and calmed me. She managed to feed the guests during the three days of the funeral and nurse me too. The custom was for the female next-of-kin to utter the most heartbreaking sentences loudly, pull at her hair, and claw at her face so everyone would weep along. I failed. Some guests helped Joanna provide dates and halva, others made and served tea, and the woman next door, a self-appointed expert mourner looking to turn funerals into howling contests, took matters into her own hands. When the crescendo of her wailing peaked, she orated, "Chia, son, how's your new home, darling? Is it too dark there? We were looking forward to celebrating your wedding, young man. It wasn't your turn to leave; why did you have to get ahead of everyone else, darling?" Her questions were soon lost in loud sobs.

I got up to leave this theatre of mourning. My limbs were numb and heavy, as if the amount of noise I had been exposed to had stemmed the blood flow to my extremities. At the door two women in their early twenties hugged me and sobbed, telling me they had been following Chia's letters from prison and were shocked by his execution.

There was much they could have done prior to May 9. And yet, all these people who claimed Chia had changed them had done nothing. "Thank you. But there are still many more political prisoners you can save." I walked down the alley.

"Excuse me," a short man with salt-and-pepper hair asked. "Do you know which mosque men should go to for the young man's funeral?"

It took me a few seconds to recognize him, but the now-gray, still-large mustache was distinct. "Two blocks south of the main street," I responded. "By the way, I think you were right. We would've been better off in an orphanage." He gazed at me for a second and left.

There was one thing I needed to do: preserve what little sanity I had left. After some pacing up and down the street, I snuck back inside my room, packed a bag of Chia's childhood toys and notebooks, and threw it into the yard from the window of the bedroom. When the mourners were busy sipping tea, I slowly walked downstairs, and after hugging Joanna goodbye, crept across the weedy garden and grabbed my belongings.

The dried-up sticks standing erect by the cement walls used to be apple and cherry trees. The rusty bicycles—their front wheels stolen—had given up on life.

My body no longer felt like my own, only a rental, as if I could be subject to eviction any day. Perhaps that day I'd reunite with Chia, who had dropped his body.

CHAPTER TWENTY-EIGHT

THE ORANGE GLOBE of the sun was visible in the sky when I got off the bus at Tehran's West Terminal and transferred to the local bus. The smell of hot beets and baked potatoes wafting from the sidewalk carts had me drooling, but an anxiousness tugged at my heart, urging me to head home immediately.

Stuck in the morning gridlock, I remembered that I had failed to pay the rent yet again. With the news of Chia's execution spreading, the landlord must be outraged and afraid for his safety. Chia's notes and diaries could be soaked and muddy on the street, the lock changed. Since the city transit was at a standstill, I got off and ran the rest of the way home.

Blankets and kitchenware had been thrown in front of my building, but they weren't ours.

"Miss Saman, Miss Saman," Kajal the building cleaner called as I took the stairs two at a time. She only spoke Persian in public, even to her daughter, although she had told me she craved Kurdish.

"Sorry I missed Mariam's twelfth birthday. I've picked out a new book for her, but I haven't been by the store," I responded in kind.

"Mariam was sure you wouldn't forget." Kajal grinned from ear to ear and leaned on her broom as if it were a crutch. "I told her you were traveling."

"You were right," I lied. "See you soon."

"Miss Saman, I must show you something."

"I have to go now. I'll talk to you later."

"It's urgent." Her voice was lost in the sirens of an ambulance and my footsteps. But I was already taking the stairs two at a time.

Mercifully, the key to my apartment worked and everything seemed to be in its place.

Ignoring the notice scrawled on a slip of paper and squeezed under the door, I dashed into Chia's room and dove into his closet. His scent still lingered faintly among his folded and hanging shirts.

My throat seized, and a searing pain radiated from my shoulders down my arm. My fingers ran over the calligraphic characters of Shamlou's poem posted inside the door: "In me/there was a rough prisoner/not used to the clanking of his chains."

In the drawer of his bedside table, I found Chia's notes and an eighteen-page draft of an article titled, "From Self-Reign to Self-Immolation: The Paradoxes in Kurdish Women's Lives." What had happened to the Kurds in the casino of life? Snake eyes? Double zero? Or chips taken away one by one?

It was easy, indeed joyful, to look at his published articles. But the half-finished one that I had promised to help complete . . . I hugged my knees, sitting in his closet. I should have stopped him from leaving home that day.

Chia, in his blue-and-white-striped shirt and pants, munching on a hard crust of bread, materialized before my eyes. Mama and Baba screamed at each other, and the floor shook. Small and slim, deeply anxious, with messy hair and a muddled head, I carried Chia on my back, crawled on all fours for him, tried to protect him from the panic that had descended on me. "*Ly-ly-ly . . .*" Chia's lullaby soothed me into a nap.

Next Chia was hanging from a rope. Unable to breathe. No matter how badly he wanted to inhale, he couldn't. He felt life leaving his emaciated body. He knew he was dying, but there was nothing he could do.

I was unbearably powerless as I watched him gasp for air. I gasped with him. Someone knocked. I called Chia's name. More knocks.

My eyelids snapped open. I was suffocating in a tearless nightmare. I got up to open the door but felt dizzy and lost my balance.

"Leila. Miss Leila."

"What's going on?"

Kajal was at the door, head tilted. She looked around. "I found this," she said, a navy headscarf with tiny printed flowers hanging from her hands. "I thought it might be yours."

It was the same scarf she had been wearing for the past two years. "I don't have time for this right now." I resisted the urge to shut the door and went to the kitchen to splash cool water on my face.

She briskly stepped inside and closed the door behind her. "I have to tell you something," she whispered.

I palmed my face to stop the light-headedness. She had invited herself in for tea before and had shared how she'd fled her village to save her daughter from a drug-addicted father. She worked three shifts to make ends meet and pay for her daughter's schooling so the girl wouldn't suffer the same fate as hers. Today I was in no state of mind to listen.

Kajal drew the curtains closed, turned off the light. "Miss, a couple of men have been asking for you," she whispered in Kurdish. "They claimed they were your relatives. I didn't give them any information." Her voice had dropped so low I wasn't sure I had heard her correctly.

"Men! What men?"

"They asked if you usually have a lot of guests or if the same people come here often, what time you leave, what time you come back, if you carry big suitcases. Miss, I pretended to cooperate. They thought that because I am a simple cleaner with an accent, I am stupid. They told me to call the next-door notary office when you came home. They said if I didn't, they'd have me fired. Please, miss, you have to move out immediately."

I had to sit down.

"They might come back any day." She kneeled before me, her voice barely audible. "They got here this morning right after you went upstairs. Miss, I am so glad you didn't hear me when I asked you to stay. I could have . . . you know . . ." Tears welled up in her eyes. "They gave me this number and some cash and asked me to call them when I saw you. I accepted so they wouldn't be suspicious, but I swear upon my daughter's life, I would never . . ." She threw herself into my arms.

"I'm grateful, Kajal gian." I was too weak to hold her.

"You shouldn't stay here. Leave right now. I'll help you pack."

I looked around. Chia had passionately discussed his ideas sitting on this chair, had voraciously read on that sofa, had eagerly eaten at this very kitchen table.

"I can't." Come what may. If they ever showed up at my door, I would jump from one of the windows before I let them take me.

"If you have nowhere else to go, at least make sure you don't turn on the lights at all or go near the windows, even with the curtains drawn." Kajal got up and unplugged the phone too. "No internet. Do not open the door for anyone, even your own father. I will bring food for you. We should agree on a way to knock, or you can give me a key. Oh, wait, I have a better idea." She rummaged through a large set of keys. "Remember Karo? The handsome man on the twelfth floor?"

I nodded.

"His apartment is empty, and he gave me the key."

I shook my head.

"Yes. Yes. You must."

It was either that, or my place would be my solitary confinement before they detained me.

"Hide in his apartment until you can make arrangements to travel. Go to some far-flung village, or wait—go to Iraqi Kurdistan. You'd be safe there. I might be able to find you help from my village to smuggle you across the border if your name is on the list."

"What list?"

"Of those who cannot leave the country."

"Oh, yeah." Iran didn't send dissidents into exile but instead made them rot in living hell.

"I know these things, miss. My cousins are Peshmerga."

Maybe I could join Shiler. "I really need to connect to the internet."

"That's another reason you should stay at Karo's. At least at night. I will get you an internet card and some bread and milk."

"What if he comes back? Or another tenant moves in?"

"He owns the apartment, miss, and he is not renting it for another year. He told me so. I think he went abroad. He gave me his key so my daughter and I wouldn't need to commute every single day. We have stayed at his place a few times. Most of his personal stuff is packed, but there's a bed, utensils, a sofa, and a television. Don't let any of the neighbors see you. Be extra careful." Proud of her plan, Kajal left to copy me a key and buy groceries.

The note that had been placed under my door wasn't an eviction notice, rather the beginning of a barrage of threats to remind me that I might yet suffer the same fate as my brother. Chia's writing had spread on social media ever more quickly after he was hanged.

In the silence and darkness of Karo's apartment, loss settled in, diminished the fighting and denial.

It wasn't just that I had lost Chia, but also the part of me that found meaning in being his sister. Who was I now? Without the part of me that was attached to my younger brother, without the role of big sister that I'd taken on so early in life, who was I now?

When I finally got online, I found my inbox filled with requests for underground public speaking. The worst had already happened, and there was nothing more to be afraid of. I had to carry the torch that Chia had involuntarily passed on to me.

Some seventy strangers were sitting in a damp and dark basement, waiting for me to begin. Having so many eyes on me would have made me nervous at any other time, but my senses had abandoned me.

It was no secret that plainclothes Ettela'ati could be here, one of those who had placed a noose around Chia's neck, looking for their next prey. Yet I was determined to respond to my calling in life.

"Chia, my brother, carried the pain of something larger than himself on his shoulders. From a young age, he was intelligent, sensitive, and profoundly observant." I bit my lips to force down the howl rising in my chest. "His selfless dedication to justice made him an unwitting hero. And that's what terrorized them. Dictators are nourished by fear, hostility among the citizenry, and above all, apathy." My voice was hoarse. I had to pause.

I caught a glimpse of a familiar face looking down, hiding behind a pillar. His stealthy glances started up a fire in me.

The attentive audience in the basement, old and young, looked defeated. The gathering was being held in a wealthy part of the city, right by the Touchal Mountain and not very far from Evin Prison. We all felt thwarted in our fight against the state, exhausted from the endless pain of having lost loved ones or borne witness to their physical or mental torture.

I swallowed and took a note from my pocket. "Chia couldn't stop his torturers from breaking his jaw . . . but he was able to maintain the life within him."

Everyone turned toward the door at the back of the basement when it creaked. I kept reading.

"He had a rich inner life that no one could take away from him, its currency insightful books and people and the processing and application of the wisdom he had gained. He kept repeating that he wouldn't let them kill him inside, and he never did."

A middle-aged, bearded man entered, and I wasn't sure—perhaps no one was—whether he was an unofficial militia or just a man with an untrimmed beard.

"Like Nelson Mandela, like Leyla Zana, Chia was *not* broken under torture. That's where his victory lay."

Nervous eyes traveled the room. I had to continue to fill up the frightening silence, to keep going on Chia's path until my last breath, and then someone else would take my place, maybe someone sitting here tonight. "Chia wanted all of us to understand what it meant to suffer poverty, genocide, and ethnocide: the loss of language and culture." I spoke slowly but with emphasis, as if I were reading words written in a foreign language.

Suddenly the breathing of the crowd turned very noisy. The fluorescent lights above my head glared. Karo had moved forward, no longer trying to hide.

"Chia Saman was not a *jodai talab*," a middle-aged man whose voice shook with anger yelled.

Jodai talab—a separatist—was a slur in the Iranian vernacular, equivalent to "traitor."

A woman with bottle-blond hair sticking out from under her headscarf adjusted her eyeglasses and shouted, "Didn't I warn you Kurds are all filthy separatists? I would much rather that fanatic clergies rule my country than see Kurds, Turkmen, and the rest divide my country into pieces."

"Wait a minute." I tried to regain control of the room like my stern religion teacher. "So every time minorities speak about their tragedies, it automatically makes them separatists? And why do you act like that's a crime, anyway?" I looked around in complete disappointment. It was no surprise that Kurds were singled out and oppressed even among the opposition, but I'd assumed the crowd that had invited me would be different. A murmur of speculation and suspicion spread throughout the room and soon dominated it. This was not the government silencing me. This was the opposition.

Karo walked toward me. I didn't need his help. I knew what to do to overcome prejudice: invoke sympathy. "Let me put it this way. Imagine if Persians were living under a brutal government run by the Kurds, and your children couldn't read or write in Persian, couldn't read Hafez and Rumi, couldn't understand the maestro Shajarian. Think. And then, when you've been debased this far, think of what we have actually endured: You are to be hunted down, abused, tortured, exterminated . . ."

"*Nefrat parakani nakon.* Stop spreading hatred. In this country everyone suffers equally." The phony platinum-blonde was not to be placated with reason.

"No. People do not suffer equally in this or any country. Talking about our reality is not spreading hate. It's inviting understanding." I shook my head in despair.

An angry middle-aged man coughed for silence and said: "History has shown . . . Excuse me, brothers and sisters, please listen. History has proven that these tribes, all of these tribes . . ."

I knew him from somewhere. "Tribes? Did you just call a nation a tribe?" I peered at his goatee; his glasses hung from his neck on a thin chain. I remembered.

He looked up. I had dared to challenge "the intellectual." He was the one who always showed up at the bookstore, who would make everyone in line wait while he ogled me. He always found an opportunity to accost me with some nonsense about the Russian and French Revolutions and then, finding me an unwilling listener, would leave the store without making a purchase. From an object of flirtation, I had been downgraded to a tribal interloper in "his" homeland.

"Tribes start by asking to learn their mother tongue, and next thing you know, they want independence. Independence, ladies and gentlemen!" He spat out the word.

Blood rushed to my face. "The moral of the story is a large group of people should be deprived of one basic right so they won't ask for their other rights?" I pointed a finger straight at his face. My glare was riveted on his contorted features. How naïve of me to risk my life to speak to people who valued acres above humans. "Can't you hear how similar you sound to the government you oppose?"

"We like Kurds. My cousin has married a Kurd," a voice called out. I searched the crowd but couldn't identify the speaker in a sea of moving lips. A buzz rose, and the words "democracy" and "the right to self-determination" popped up from different corners of the room.

Oxygen became scarce. The room was dank and musty and thick with tension. I started to feel faint. "I see. Freedom is good, but only for the privileged few." I left the podium.

"We Marxists support the right to self-determination." A tall thin man raised his fist. People turned and started attacking him instead of me. Some young men and women stared at me with pity and nodded. "Kick out the separatists!" someone said.

There was a tightness inside me. Fear of fear. "Stop," I said, either in my head or out loud—I didn't know which.

"Unfortunately Miss Saman does not feel well enough to continue speaking." The familiar voice became clearer with each word. "She has been through a lot, as you all know. Please excuse her."

Karo softly took my arm and pulled me through the press of people. But his actions only alarmed me, suggesting a larger threat. My arm went rigid.

"I knew it," he muttered, feeling my resistance. "I knew it."

The rising din of these disgruntled listeners was a hammer beating on my head. As Karo sent women and men scattering, I felt as if I were in a movie. He guided me outside and into the parking lot, lay me down on the back seat of his Xantia, and drove me home.

"You must leave this country, Leila."

When the cradle of the car stopped rocking, I rose from the back seat. Karo held the front door of the building open for me. He held my arm when I was at the edge of collapse and kept a grip on me until I unlocked my apartment. He laid me down on Chia's worn-out blue sofa and went into the cubbyhole kitchen to put the kettle on.

When I opened my eyes, Karo was holding a glass of hot tea and softly calling my name. Steam danced just above the rim, and sugar whirled in its bottom.

"You should leave. Go somewhere safe."

"Didn't you say that before?" I asked.

Karo sat down. "I'm going to have to find you a safe place."

"I've been staying at your place at night."

"That's not very safe either." His breath felt warm on my face.

Energy was returning to my limbs, coursing up to my brain. "It's dark comedy, the way tiny tyrants demand democracy."

Karo patted my shoulder. "Sometimes the people you fight for become your worst opponents. Anyway, my sister said something interesting about the Kurds. She draws a parallel between Kurds and the indigenous people in North America."

"How?"

"Well, Kurds are more native to the land than the people who rule them. And the genocide. Subjugation. Cultural appropriation, whatnot."

My chest felt heavy. He gently squeezed my hand. When our gazes touched,

I recalled Farrokzhad's poem, that "life was perhaps this enclosed moment." He then looked down and played with his fingers. I stared at the gray linoleum. "I'll find a way to get you out."

"What happened to your ponytail?"

His fingers drummed on his shaved head. "I'm a soldier now."

"Chia would have been graduating now too if . . ." I ran my fingers around the rim of the glass he had brought me.

"You look flushed," he whispered.

"Isn't it too hot in here?" I didn't wait for him to answer. He was still in his sweater. "I think it must be the tea."

"I told everyone I dropped out. The truth is I got kicked out. I couldn't take it anymore."

I started unbuttoning my coverall.

Karo lowered his head, his chin pressed against his collarbone, as if struggling to admit to some deep disgrace. I stared at him intensely. "Chia's popularity and influence . . . they backfired."

"What do you mean?"

"What you tried to say tonight."

"What did I try to say?"

"That if he hadn't become a hero, he'd be alive."

"What? That's not what I said, but do you—" I got up, my hands clenched. "Are you saying it was my fault? That I killed him by sharing his writing online?"

"That's not what I said!" He raised his hands in surrender.

"It was his fault then? For being so endearing, so influential?"

"Leila!" He stood tall before me.

"What, Karo? What? What are you trying to say? That the goodness in him and my desperate attempts to save him killed him, not the fascist system? Not . . . not your hands?"

"Me?" He sat down again, deflated.

"They didn't know you were Kurdish, the interrogators. Did they?" I pressed my lips together firmly, biting the insides of my cheeks. "You hid that fact well, I bet?"

He looked up, down, at the wall. "I wouldn't be alive if they'd known . . ."

"It was your damn phone. And you're the one who took Chia out that day."

"It wouldn't have helped Chia if they knew my origins. And Chia had an accent, a Kurdish place of birth. They later learned about his blogs and articles, about the illegal Kurdish teaching, everything." Karo's voice was low and rough.

"You used your privileges to save yourself, but you didn't do anything for my brother." I tasted the bitter salt of my tears.

"What privileges, Leila? I was tortured and humiliated. They just didn't find me worthy of their bullets or ropes because I was a nobody. Chia was somebody to begin with, and he became a bigger and bigger threat. I am not saying . . . You did the best you could under the circumstances, but the support, it was small. Do you understand what I mean?"

"No."

"If the *Guardian* or the *New York Times* had written about him, Iran would have modified their charges, but only the Kurdish media outlets and a few Persian ones mentioned him. Even PEN and UNICEF have limited reach. And he had too many local admirers. It terrified the state that he was becoming an icon." He placed his hands on my shoulders.

"Oh, go to hell." I shoved him. "You and the rest of these phony people. To hell with your affection when it means doing nothing and worrying about your interests first."

"You think it's easy for me? Do you know how much Chia meant to me?" He turned to me with those vast eyes that reminded me of the evening sky. I hadn't looked up to see the sky in so long. Karo squeezed my hands, and I pulled them away. He said something, but I couldn't make out the words. My eyes brimmed with tears. I sat and rested my head on the sofa arm, wrapped myself in a blanket, and inhaled deeply to catch the last remaining scent of Chia.

Karo stood before me with a box of tissues. I wept. He kneeled before me and spread his arms wide open and enclosed me in his embrace. His chest heaved against mine, his fingertips gentle in my hair.

CHAPTER TWENTY-NINE

When I awoke, my head was on Karo's lap, his head lolled back on the sofa, his palm heavy and warm on my waist. He breathed deeply and slowly. I wiggled to free myself, but he only gripped my hip more firmly.

I was fully dressed, and so was he. "Karo," I called softly. He opened his eyes, taking in his surroundings for a moment, then jumped. "Sorry, sorry." He untucked his shirt to hide the bulge in his pants and practically ran out the front door, almost slamming it behind him.

I stared at the closed door and released the air trapped in my chest. How on earth had we gotten so intertwined? Did I just see Karo with an erection?

Even in the vacuum created by his abrupt departure, I still felt Karo on my body, a sticky, invisible presence. I drew a bath and soaked under the foam.

Bewildered, I ran my fingertips along my hip, right where his hand had been only minutes ago, then across every inch of my body, exploring sensations. When I reached my left breast, I imagined it was Karo's palm cupping it. I bet he could hold it and its twin in one giant hand.

This estranged body of mine, introduced to me as something to be covered and spurned because it was a source of sin—and only men's sin—was in and of itself a meadow of desires; my body was appealing, but it was also fully capable of choosing, of yearning.

If only Karo hadn't led my brother to the gallows.

I lingered in the bath until the water turned cold. A door slammed somewhere in the building, making me jump, and I eyed the window for any sign of

The Men. Reluctantly I stood and wrapped myself in a towel, and my fantasies washed down the drain with the last remaining suds.

Munching on a jam and butter sandwich, I opened my laptop. The red battery light on the computer flashed. I connected through the dialup internet and logged into my email account, hoping I still had a few minutes left on my internet card. A lot of messages from unfamiliar senders and eight from Shiler sent over the past week. She'd said I could go to the UN office in Turkey to apply for asylum, or join her, or go to the autonomous and prosperous Kurdistan Region in northern Iraq.

I began typing a reply to Shiler. "Surprise, surprise—I was given a platform but was pulled down as soon as I mentioned Kurdish plight. Don't think I'm ready to join your feminist revolution though. I still prefer to live for a cause than to die for one . . . I need help. A safe place. ASAP."

As I scrolled through my inbox, I played some music. The burning sadness in the Kurdish singer's voice and the piercing sound of the daf stung and soothed me.

"Write back to me immediately. No money. No trustworthy person or place. Home could be raided any second. I've packed some of Chia's notes and diaries and some of my own. Your blue hair clip is included in the small package. Please hurry."

I wrote to Karo too but deleted the message, retyped it and deleted it again. As I logged out, someone knocked.

My stomach dropped. I tied my robe tight. Could The Men have seen me come inside last night? Noticed the candlelight? Seen the emails just now? I walked backward to the kitchen window. More knocks. I should get dressed. At least wear panties. Knocks.

The voice muffled behind the door got louder. "It's me."

I went to the door. But what if Karo was forced to knock at a gunpoint? Why hadn't we thought of a safe word?

"Come on. Come on! Hurry up!"

I held a big kitchen knife behind me and cautiously opened the door with my left hand.

"It's okay. Nobody saw me." Karo swiftly snuck in.

"It's crime enough that I am 'counterrevolutionary.'" I placed the knife back in the drawer. "I can do without ethical allegations."

"I am sorry I stayed the night. Your eyes," he said. "Obviously you have not slept well. I wanted to sit still so you'd get some rest, but somehow I gave in to exhaustion too."

"I didn't mind that. But you coming back only makes things worse for both of us." I fetched a long coat and headscarf from my bedroom to hang by the front door so I could put them on quickly next time someone knocked.

"It's easier to be in prison for anything other than politics." He winked.

"Not if you are a woman. Lashing. Maybe stoning. Who knows?" I brought a trash can with a lid, placed the large silver knife inside, and covered it with dish towels. "Imagine being a virgin and getting lashed for adultery!" I mumbled.

"You're going to stab armed men?" His raised eyebrow gave him a comic look.

"Myself, if need be. And we need a safe word. How's . . . umm . . . I don't know. Think of something."

"Ice cream on my face?"

I smiled at the memory of our happy hiking days. "Okay."

"Can you sit for a second? I have something I've been meaning to tell you, and I want you to consider it carefully before saying an impulsive no." Karo scratched his ear.

I sat across from him. "I should have been out of here last week."

He clasped his hands. "I've made arrangements for a place for you to stay until things get safer."

"Until Chia is forgotten?" Something clawed at my heart.

"We should pack the absolute essentials and leave. Right now."

Books on the shelves, food in the fridge, clothes in the drawers. "Where's this place, and how do I know it's safe?"

He stared at me in silence for a few seconds. "You still don't trust me, do you?"

"Should I?" My wet hair dripped down my spine.

Karo plugged the phone back in and played the messages. "Ms. Saman, report to your local police station immediately. We know everything." Click.

"I don't know if you have a better option." Karo's shoulders drooped.

"How did you know that message would be there?"

"It wasn't hard to guess, was it?"

I got up and paced the apartment. "They're just trying to intimidate me. Otherwise they'd be here right now." I didn't care if Karo heard the tremor in my voice. "Unless they know they can trust the public to silence me before they do."

Karo held my shoulders. "We have to get out now."

He stared at my mouth. I swallowed, expecting his lips on mine any second, unsure how to react. The knot of my robe was already open. He put a fingertip to my lip, and it came away red.

"Oh!" I tasted the blood on my lips. I had been chewing them.

"I will try to pack some stuff while you get dressed."

The robe slid down before I got to my room. The weight of his look on my hips. In a few minutes I was covered head to toe in black. Karo picked up the suitcase I had packed earlier. "Anything else that is absolutely vital?" he asked.

"Personal stuff."

"We will get you new stuff. I parked three blocks to the east. Leave in exactly ten minutes and walk toward the police station. Go inside the shopping mall across from it and take the first elevator to the parking garage. Level five. I'll wait for you there."

"Be very careful with my luggage. All Chia's photos and journals are in there."

I squeezed a few more things into my purse, donned sunglasses, and pulled my headscarf forward before hitting the street.

I tried hard to walk with confidence but couldn't help looking behind me every few minutes. My shadow had never been more petrifying.

I picked up my pace before the police station. That was a crazy move, but I had no control.

When I got to the fifth level of the mall's underground parking garage, Karo's silver Xantia was nowhere to be found.

This was a set-up. Karo was with them. That's why they had released him. I kept my purse before my chest, my hand touching the silver knife inside.

An empty parking lot was the best place to be murdered, and the state wouldn't have to bother with arrest and execution. No one would find out.

I walked back to the elevator, constantly checking my surroundings, terrified by every sound. Three trucks were parked in the dimly lit garage.

I kept pushing the button, but the elevator was too sluggish. I tried the stairs. The sharp smell of urine emanating from the dark staircase made me want to throw up.

I looked around at the amateur graffiti, the gigantic sketch of an ejaculating penis on the wall.

The roar of an engine. A car skidded.

"Great timing." Karo rolled down the window. I stared at him.

"What are you waiting for?" He reached over and opened the passenger door.

I got in and held my breath until we left the garage. The smog blocked my view of chia, the mountain. The honking cars freely voiced their frustration. I let go of the air trapped in my chest.

"There's another thing I must talk to you about," he said.

I looked at his pensive profile. Karo drove inside another garage. "Where are you going?" I looked left and right.

"What's the problem?"

"I hate underground parking garages!"

"Since when?"

"Since now!"

He made a U-turn and parked on the street before the shopping mall.

"Why are we here?" I asked.

"We need to clear our heads first."

"I hate shopping malls!"

"Stop hating things and think for a moment." He raised his voice. "Don't make this harder than it is, Leila. No one would look for you here."

The storefronts of the posh clothing retailers lining the block glittered in the afternoon sun. In the window displays, the mannequins' nipples were cut off. Scarves were draped over their misshapen heads—also cut off right where the brain should be—so the mannequin's faces were only visible from the nose down. Plastic legs were sloppily concealed by newspapers and Scotch tape.

"I can't stay in this country, Karo. It's not just because anything could happen to me any second. I simply can't stand it any longer. I don't belong." I looked back at his face. "I never belonged, but I used to have reasons to stand it. Now I'm desperate to get out. I need to be anywhere other than here."

Karo mashed his lips together.

"I only need to find somewhere safe to stay until Shiler connects me to people who can smuggle me across the border. A day or two at most. I need to figure something out. Maybe I can stay with Joanna until then. Though if they don't find me in my apartment, they'll surely look for me in Mariwan."

Karo turned on the engine. "Wait, I should get in the back seat, no?" I didn't wait for him to respond and slid over the center console. The last thing I needed was to be pulled over by morality police for driving with a man. This way we could pretend he was driving me for a fee. "Sorry."

For a while Karo drove in silence, and I took my last looks at the bustling streets of the city that had sheltered, then demolished me. The hushed derisive message had been: Live here, but you'll never be one of us; try catching up, but you'll never arrive.

"I don't know how to say this, but . . ." Karo was barely audible in the driver's seat. "I was thinking about this all night. I want to . . . I mean, I can if you want me to . . ."

"Sorry, I can't hear you well."

"I can . . ." He coughed to clear his voice. "I can take you to Canada."

"You can what?"

We came to a stoplight. "You're probably thinking . . ." He raised his hands in surrender. "That I'm a shark like other men."

"What're you saying, Karo?"

He cracked his knuckles and looked left and right. "I'm offering only because I am sure Chia would want me to. I'm sure he would do this for my sister."

"Do what?"

The light turned green, and he sped through the intersection, cutting off a Mercedes before making a sharp right. He pulled over and turned on his hazards. "Okay, listen. I can take you to Canada, and there you will be free to go your own way. I swear upon my honor that I'm not trying to take advantage of you. Chia's sister is like my own sister. I promise."

I met his gaze in the rearview mirror and shook my head in confusion. I remembered that his family was in Toronto and that he'd had a Canadian permanent resident card too, although he'd never stayed there long enough to become a citizen. But how could he take me there?

"I can apply for your Canadian visa and get your papers in a year or so." He looked at me, then back at the road. "Once there, you can get your own permanent resident card, then you'll be free to go your own way. No commitment. No risks. You'll just have to remain discreet in the meantime."

"Why would you do such a thing?"

"How?"

"Well, why and how?"

He checked his side mirror and reentered the flow of traffic, heading north of Tehran, toward the prison. "You lost a brother, and I lost my dearest friend. I can help his sister. I wasn't able to save Chia, but I can protect you. You know better than I do that Chia has become a sensation, and they're afraid of you too . . . I don't want to ramble. News to me is history to you."

"But why would Canada give me residency? Shiler said that I should apply to the UN office in Turkey for asylum. I have more than enough evidence to prove that my life is in danger, but I don't understand how you and Canada come into play. If I ask for asylum, I could ask to be sent to Canada, but they may not allow that. Also the process takes three to five years, not one."

He pulled a bottle of water from the cupholder and took a sip. "Marry me." I gaped at him. "You'd have to marry me. But only on paper."

I started laughing. His indigo eyes looked solemn in the mirror. He stole a quick look at me before focusing on the road.

My stomach was quivering as I fought a new gust of giggles. My life felt like one of Samuel Beckett's absurd plays. Tears rolled down my face.

"Stop it."

The harder I tried to stop cackling, the more hilarious it all became. He splashed some water on my face.

He laid on his horn as a car cut him off, holding it longer than necessary. "What's so funny? I'm giving you the best option you can have. Who knows how many years you'll end up waiting in Turkey? I've heard of people waiting up to eleven years for asylum. I've heard of people with actual torture marks on their bodies being rejected. Meanwhile you won't be authorized to work or study. Best case scenario it'll be four years of your life down the drain."

The scenery changed as we left Tehran behind us. Undulating hills in shades of brown lined the highway, and cedars flashed by us at a nauseating speed. Karo was right. I'd heard many similar stories, including one shared by a woman I had met in front of the prison. She'd had to work illegally in Turkey while waiting for her asylum application to be processed. Her daughter needed warm shoes, and she started cleaning at a motel while thinking about her next revolutionary essay. The day she was supposed to get paid, her boss came into the room she was cleaning and unbuckled his belt. She barely made it out of the motel, grabbed her daughter, and came back to Iran. She spent eleven years behind bars, released just in time for her teenage daughter to be arrested for protesting.

"There are no checkpoints, are there?" I asked, suddenly concerned.

"What?"

"Where are we going?"

"To a safe place."

"A safe place?"

"Yes. I promise."

We drove down a six-lane highway and passed by a dozen flags dancing in the breeze. Flags! How I hated them, glorified symbols of division and bloodshed. To get out of the country that wasn't mine, that had killed my brother in cold blood, I had to trust that Karo wouldn't let me down yet again. How could I?

"So, seriously, Leila, what do you think about my plan?"

Karo gripped the steering wheel, white-knuckled, while he waited for my reply.

I sighed and sat back in my seat. The sky had grown gray and foggy. "My father would never give permission, not in a million years."

"That won't be a problem as long as you're okay with the plan," he responded calmly. He was right. In a country so corrupt, forging Baba's signature wouldn't be difficult at all.

"What if Canada finds out we are lying?"

"About marriage? We won't be lying. We'll actually get married. They won't make you go through a virginity test there."

"I'll go to the Kurdistan Region," I said. "The autonomous part of Iraq. It's booming, and I would love to live in a place run by Kurds for a change. Or maybe I'll even join Shiler." Karo's expression had soured in the rearview. "Where is the safe place you're taking me?"

"My sister's cottage in Lavasan. It's been vacant for a while."

"How come? Is she still in Canada too"

"Awin moved to Toronto years ago on a student visa, but she works in New York now."

"When did she leave?"

"Eighteen years ago. More. Twenty? She hasn't been back since. At that time studying abroad wasn't common. You had to look universities up in catalogs, mail them letters asking for application forms, complete and return them, and then wait for a yay or nay for half a year or so. But she made it."

"My father did the same thing. He was admitted to a PhD program at UCLA, won a scholarship too, but the revolution happened, and then the American hostages. His story and timing could have been scripted by Chekhov feeling spiteful." Silence. Karo didn't want to talk about his father.

I continued, "What inspired your sister to study abroad? She was single when she left, I suppose."

"'A third-world country is comforting only to a third-world mind.'"

"That's what she said?"

"She sure did. Although now she says it's not politically correct."

"So she thought her brain belonged in a developed country?" I asked.

"I suppose so. You've always reminded me of her."

"Well, does she still think that?"

His light laughter put his perfectly arranged set of good teeth on display, another testament to his comfortable upbringing. "I think so. She seems happy. A top manager. She never got married, though, and lives far away from my parents."

"Your parents have lived abroad for over a decade, haven't they?"

"Well, they sure take care to look modern despite their traditional beliefs." Karo winked. "I'm starving."

We pulled off the highway and found a small restaurant, where we ordered kebabs that melted in my mouth; it tasted better than anything I had eaten since the day Chia disappeared, when the three of us—Karo, Chia, and I—sat at our table and devoured a whole pot of stew I had made. I realized I hadn't cooked much in the years since then.

"I don't know as much about Kurdish history as Chia and you do, but I remember him saying the Kurdish dream, when fulfilled, was always short-lived. I am sure the Kurdistan Region is much safer than here, and freer, but can you study film there? Wouldn't you have a better future in Canada?"

"I need to be with my people."

"Let's face it, Leila. You and I are not revolutionaries. Chia was different. Going to the Kurdistan Region or joining the Peshmerga won't be any better."

He was right. If jailed like Chia and Baba, I would collapse on day one. "But education is expensive in Canada. I can get my bachelor's in Kurdistan and then go there for graduate school. I'll save up some money by then."

"That will only delay your life for at least four years, and no amount of money you could save in dinar would be enough to pay tuition in dollars. But once you have a residency status in Canada, you can stand on your own two feet, get student loans, apply for grants or find donors for your projects. Chia will live on in your work, and I'll feel I've paid my debt to him."

"What debt?"

Karo put his spoon down, clasped his fingers, and cradled his head in his hands, thumbs pressed to temples. "Chia was a real inspiration in my life. I loved that man. And I'm sure this is what he would do. He'd do a lot more than I have done if our positions were reversed."

My chin started quavering. "Ever since he's been gone, I miss him more every day. Not less. More."

"Me too. But we will honor his path—and that would be much more doable in Canada than anywhere else."

I needed Chia to appear for at least one second and tell me what to do. I had enough reasons to trust Karo and just as many to distrust him.

"Here's the plan," Karo said when dessert arrived. "Sleep at my sister's tonight, and I will stay with a friend. First thing in the morning, we will register the marriage."

I pushed the saffron ice cream around the bowl with my spoon. "Happy people marry for love. You'd be marrying me out of obligation. And I guess I'd be getting married out of desperation, to stay alive."

He looked at me. His lips opened. But he swallowed his words.

We left the restaurant after he paid.

"So will you do it? Will you marry me? Out of desperation, I mean." He smiled.

"No, but I'd like a ring anyway and wouldn't mind seeing you on your knee."

He cackled heartily, the laugh reaching his eyes, and he seemed to relax.

"We'll be there in about twenty minutes. I'll pick you up early tomorrow morning for the paperwork. Don't forget your birth certificate. I'll ask the cleaner to take what she wants and sell the rest of your belongings, if that's cool. After we leave the notary office, I'll book my flight to Toronto."

WHEN WE ARRIVED at Karo's sister's place, I got out of the car without a word. My joints were stiff from the car ride, and as I stretched I took in this would-be haven. Here in Lavasan, there were gorgeous mountain vistas, crisp air, and winding country roads. The neighborhoods were dotted with luxurious mansions, whose grand architecture made me think they were owned by celebrities or top state authorities. The streets were serene and quiet, a world away from the hubbub and hazards of the city. Karo was right; unless we'd been followed, nobody would think to look for me here. I was safe. But would this change in scenery diminish the pain of loss?

"Wait, there's something we must do before I leave." He unrolled the passenger window. "We'll need to go to a studio and take some wedding photos. That's vital to the case."

"There is one thing I need to know," I said. There were, in fact, so many things I wanted to know, I couldn't choose a single one. I sat back in the passenger seat. "Can we arrange it so your name won't appear on my birth certificate?"

"Do you care to explain why?"

"If Canada rejects my application and you don't come back to divorce me for whatever reason, I'll remain 'married' for the rest of my life."

"And what's wrong with that?" He winked. "I believe we need all the legal documents to make our case valid, but we could 'lose' your ID and apply again. So yes, I can arrange for that too."

"Without the need for my father's documents and neighbor's testimony and what have you?"

"Without a hassle for you. We should oil quite a few mustaches though," he said. "Keep both IDs. So I can get you out of trouble, if need be."

If I got detained while he was away, he could help me only if we were related.

"Is that all?" he asked.

"No."

He turned off the engine.

"What did you want to say," I asked, "on Chia's last day? When you were on the stairs and I was begging him to stay."

"I . . ." He looked sideways at me like a rabbit looking at his hunter.

"The truth," I demanded.

"I swear I was going to ask him to stay. The clips had frightened me too."

Long pause. "Well, why didn't you?"

Karo clasped his hands behind his head and leaned his forehead on the wheel. "I didn't want you to think I was a coward."

"If you'd let me think you were a coward, Chia would be alive," I whimpered.

He reached out and took my hand. "I will make it up to you, I promise." The dam broke and we sobbed in each other's arms.

CHAPTER THIRTY

KARO HUGGED ME, and it lasted longer than it should have. I looked around for the Police of Enjoining Good and Forbidding Vice, scanned the faces of the people who noticed our touch.

"This is the preboarding announcement for flight 759 to Austria . . ." said the loudspeaker.

"I will see you soon, invincible lady." Karo patted my shoulder, his straight black hair falling across his forehead.

I avoided his gaze to hide the hurricane churning within me. "Are you making fun of me?"

"You stare into chaos and see past it. Nothing gets in the way of your composure."

This wasn't his usual vocabulary. "Are you reciting poetry now?"

A mischievous smile. "Please be extra cautious and patient until your visa arrives, Mrs. Wife." He kissed the corner of my jaw, but his lips met only my headscarf.

I stared into his indigo eyes and then took one last look at his full lips. A kiss on my forehead. The roar of a plane landing. The lingering smell of his woodsy cologne seconds after he walked away. I searched for the exit sign.

"Leila!" he called in the sweet way only he could pronounce my name, more like *Lee-la*. I looked back. "Take it easy, please," he said, and turned on his heel.

"Call me from Vienna." I cupped my hands around my mouth as I called after him. Iran Air planes were flying coffins, thanks to the US sanctions. His Air Canada flight to Toronto after the six-hour layover would be less scary.

The only way to find out whether or not I was on the blacklist of those forbidden from leaving the country was to make an attempt, and that required a visa. A tremendous amount of luck would be needed for so many details to fall into place and let me be free. If luck was hereditary, I wouldn't ever be getting on a plane.

I watched Karo pass through frosted glass doors that only admitted passengers. My head spun, making me feel seasick. There walked a man who had held me close yesterday in a portrait studio and—momentarily uniting our breath and body—gently placed his lips on mine at the photographer's command. But he had never pressed them.

THE LARGE WINDOWS of the bungalow in the town of Lavasan, north of Tehran, presented a world of wonder, a mess of weeds and fallen branches in the front yard. The interior was tastefully decorated with wooden statues of birds and framed paintings of landscapes, yet from the noxious smell of decay from dead vermin in all the rooms, I could tell that rats had taken up residence before me.

In my suitcase, Karo had left a framed photo of him and me at our staged wedding, touching cheeks and smiling, staring directly into the camera lens as if daring whoever saw the picture to challenge the validity of the union. But it was the only picture there. I searched frantically for the photos of my brother between the folds of my packed clothes. I wanted to climb to the top of a mountain and scream my lungs out.

"Vienna has one neat airport. It's 2:00 a.m. here," Karo reported on the phone.

"Why did you steal all my photos of Chia? How dare you?"

He hung up. I hurled the wedding photo, which hit the wall, and the glass shattered into dozens of pieces. I was not sure where, but I ached. I was internally bruised, all blue and purple.

The first week, I scrubbed and vacuumed and dusted the old cottage that Karo said had not been rented out for a few years. When the place was finally livable, my weary soul began to revive. I hit the garden, trimmed the dead stalks and watered the live ones. In time Chia's shadow no longer haunted me—it was more like a companion, piecing me together.

Two weeks had passed since I'd last heard from Karo, aside from one curt text informing me he'd arrived in Toronto. He was punishing me for my outburst.

The empty fridge had been disappointing, but the stress of risking arrest to go grocery shopping was more than I could handle. I found stale chips and canned beans, wrapped a blanket around me, and sat on the patio with a cup of fresh tea.

Under the dawn's rose light, a stray cat, gray with white stripes, climbed up the short cement wall surrounding the gate. "Wrong place," I said. "No food for you, kitty. Lots of cash, though, if you can digest that, left by my pretend husband, who thinks he has the power to simply blow grief away like he's Aladdin's genie."

My words did not stop her beautiful saunter. "You're pretty fat. Where I come from, cats are the size of Tehranian mice. Mice there are the size of the cockroaches here." She meowed. I made a meek high-pitched noise to communicate—if not commiserate—with her, the first living being I'd seen after two weeks of solitude. The cat shamed me into sharing my chips and fetching water for her. "So what do you fear in life?" I asked as she lapped her water. She turned her back on me and jumped lightly on top of the wall.

I sighed. I couldn't avoid leaving the gates of my sanctuary forever, not if it would take over a year for my visa to come through. So I put on sunglasses, covered myself head to toe in black, and cautiously peeked out the door. No one was out on the street at midday, not when the heat was this oppressive and the air thick. That gave me courage to stand in the doorway and inhale the sweet fragrance of vining shrubs of jasmine on the brick walls of the next-door neighbor's house, another humble bungalow. The mountains were a sea of green. The rest of the cottages on this street were luxurious. Perhaps my best tactic was to disguise myself as a wealthy vacationer, dressing in the clothes in the owner's closet. But I couldn't bear the attention it would arouse. I was more comfortable looking like a maid.

A cab braked before me at the intersection. The local supermarket was only a five-minute drive away. Quickly I purchased enough food to last me for weeks, wearing my sunglasses inside the building too. The same taxi driver was waiting when I was done, and I jumped in, preferring to see as few people as possible. He asked me on the way if I was raised abroad. My outfit must have stuck out in this ritzy resort town, where the Iranian upper crust came to ski.

In Toronto, I said. "The capital of Canada?" he asked, and I confirmed, though I was not actually sure. I made a mental note to check later. He helped put all my bags inside the yard, and I tipped him handsomely to appear like someone used to spending dollars, not toman. When he left, I sighed in relief and realized I knew nothing about Canada and that my English needed a lot of work too. Before closing the gate, I picked one of the neighbor's jasmine flowers that had grown onto my wall.

I SETTLED INTO an uneasy pattern, trying to preoccupy myself by preparing for my new life in Canada, should my visa actually come through, all the while looking over my shoulder. I'd discovered a small library in town, open to women three days a week. I perused the shelves, looking for encyclopedias, travel guides, English language dictionaries—anything that would help me acclimate to my new life abroad. I tried to force myself to study English for four hours a day, but too often I slipped into old habits, watching film after film borrowed from the library and planning storyboards in my head.

My plants pushed through the fertilized soil, transforming into tiger lilies and impatiens. I spent long hours in the garden, spritzing each leaf carefully, hoping to cultivate something within myself as well. Karo and I had weekly video chats, where he babbled on about his life in Toronto and quizzed me on English vocabulary until I wanted to chuck the computer across the room. And occasionally Shiler called, updating me on her missions with her political party. I never called my parents, save for one call to inform them that I was leaving the country. But aside from these video calls and the few people I encountered at the library and the supermarket, I avoided contact with everyone, worried my neighbors would learn my identity and call Intelligence on me.

One day, long after the sweltering stretch of summer gave way to crisp autumn mornings, I woke to my phone ringing, a call from an unknown caller. I stared at it until the ringing ceased. A formidable pain enveloped my limbs like my bones were being crushed in a giant, invisible fist. It could be Karo, using a calling card. Or it could be Shiler, who also had not called me for weeks, since she was undergoing some intensive combat training. Syria was torn by civil war, and she was going to the Kurdish north of the country to rebuild the neglected area.

I ignored the phone and went out to the patio. The caller didn't leave a voicemail. The sun radiated through purple clouds. Near the rusty gardening gear in the shed, I found unmarked seeds in a plastic bag and planted them, trying to recall Rumi poems. "In this imaginary plain of nonexistence/I am your spring of eternal life."

Someone rang the bell and knocked on the gate using a coin or keys. I froze.

The knocking continued. I held my breath and walked backward, expecting soldiers to scale the cement walls.

I slipped inside as quietly as possible and tried to get one of the messaging applications to work—Skype, Google Talk, or Yahoo Messenger—but none did, thanks to the government's almighty web filters.

I paced the house frantically, grasping my hair, which weighed unusually heavily on my scalp. I couldn't even call the police if someone broke in. A gun was what I needed, and some training in how to shoot it.

Rummaging through cabinets, I collected and sharpened all the big knives in the house and hid them under the pillows and doormats, atop the fridge, and inside a dresser by the main entrance. I'd die with dignity; I would not let a filthy Islamic Republic agent or a burglar touch me.

When I went to shower that evening, I stood before the wide mirror of the bathroom, held the largest knife, and mimed stabbing myself.

My survival instinct might stop me from cutting myself deep enough to save me from a state agent or random rapist. A plan B was required.

I placed razors in every part of the house and inside my coat pockets. Wrist-cutting was more doable and efficient if it came to that. I bathed and scrubbed away dead skin.

I wrapped a towel around my hair, threw my stiff body on the bed, and stared at the ceiling. My thyroid was swollen, and I imagined my entire body gradually inflating, turning me into a gigantic balloon, stretched so that my skin paled until it disappeared into the ether. I flew up and up, so high that I could leave this country, this earth, get where no one could reach me, not even Chia.

I once again stood naked before the mirror and turned on the light, surveying my tiny breasts and protruding hip bones, changes I had not noticed until then. I was practically gaunt, with prominent collarbones; my ribs even protruded when I lifted my arms. If I kept on losing weight like that, I'd disappear entirely before the Canadian embassy made a decision about my case. Somewhere between my bones and my skin, blisters had invaded my flesh. Only I could see them.

I held up a pair of scissors. I'd lost my brother; I'd lost our tie; I'd lost the me I'd understood myself to be; I'd lost my safety. For me, grieving was like crackling in a hot furnace. Yet I was alive, perhaps capable of rising from my ashes one day.

Each lock of hair that fell eased a portion of my burden. With a trimmer, I shaved the rest.

When the hair was swept up and flushed away in the toilet, I was no longer sizzling.

CHAPTER THIRTY-ONE

THE NEXT MORNING I closed the door behind me and walked down the road only to see a woman turn onto my street. I shifted my focus to the houses, pretending that I was looking for an address.

"Leila!" She startled me. "Is that you?"

I gaped. I knew that breathy voice.

"Finally! I was about to go home! Why didn't you open the door?"

Tears pooled in my eyes, but I was also grinning.

She went on, "I knocked on your door a few times yesterday. Is there something wrong with your doorbell? I thought Shiler gave me the wrong address or . . . Are you okay?"

I looked over my shoulders, took Joanna's hand, and led her back down the road and inside the house.

"Would you like some water? That's the only thing I have to offer." I fetched a pitcher from the fridge and two glasses before she answered. Then I double-checked that all the doors were locked.

"Come here, my daughter!" she said, patting the sofa.

I broke down before her, crying uncontrollably. She held my shaved head without a word.

It took a while before I was able to speak. "It's been brutal. I think I'm losing it."

"I understand, avina min," Joanna said. Shiler had been worried about me, holed up and mistrustful of everyone, so she'd sent Joanna to check on me. She'd jumped in her shabby car and driven for some ten hours to stay with me for as long as I wanted. Because I hadn't answered her knocks yesterday, she'd had to sleep in her car.

I told her what had happened yesterday. "I think I've developed paranoia. Every sound freaks me out—the wind, the raccoons. I had sleep paralysis this morning. It's too awful. I'm losing it."

"You're not, my sweet. Remember that you're very strong and this is only a phase. You can rest easy now. I'm here." She led me to the bedroom, and after I lay down, she pulled the sheets up to my chin.

"Will you sing me a lullaby?" She made an eye mask for me out of her headscarf and sang in a soothing voice.

I now understood why she and perhaps other mothers sang lullabies: to prepare children for all the sorrow awaiting us along the way while putting us to sleep.

I WOKE TO the smell of chicken and *ghabooli*, rice made with pomegranate paste and walnuts. Joanna was singing by the stove. "Joanna, thank you! But you should have rested first." I was salivating.

"I had my power nap." Joanna placed plates and utensils on the dining table and served dinner. I was reminded of the afternoons I'd visit Shiler and Joanna after school, before Mama got off work. Often Joanna was seated behind her brown-and-black sewing machine, tailoring dresses for the community. She'd remove her glasses, hug me, and feed me, no matter how many times I lied about not being hungry. The simplest food she made tasted heavenly, especially her dokhawa, the steaming soup of yogurt, rice, and barley with parsley and dill drifting on top of it.

As we ate, I told her about my audiovisuals and books that taught English to foreign speakers. Through the role-playing scenarios, I had practiced explaining symptoms of the flu to a doctor in English, shopping for clothes, complaining to a neighbor whose dog barked at night.

Joanna rose and cleared the dinner plates, then began dicing pistachios for a batch of baklava.

"I cannot thank you enough for the meal. I'll cook for you tomorrow. I haven't cooked a proper meal like this in years! Since before Chia . . ."

"Practice giving your recipes to your Canadian neighbors," she interrupted.

I smiled at the thought of sharing food with neighbors in peace. If I didn't get arrested in the airport. If I survived the challenges of the first few years.

Within a few minutes, the smell of hot honey and toasted pistachios wafted across the kitchen and had me drooling all over again. As Joanna retrieved the piping-hot tray from the oven, I rummaged in the kitchen drawers for a serrated knife, already imagining the crispy phyllo melting on my tongue. I turned to a drawer in the buffet near the dining table, instead coming across a stack of papers I'd not yet discovered. There was a piece of mail with the address of the bungalow, but it was made out to a Reza Azimi, not Awin Shokri. I forgot the dessert in an instant. With a pang of realization and annoyance, I stormed off to demand some answers from Karo.

A collection of pixels on my computer screen formed a blurry image of Karo. While the stars had appeared in my sky, his was still blue and bright.

"Leila!" he answered when the video finished buffering, his crystal-clear smile at full wattage. "How are y—"

"So you said this place was your sister's? Awin's?"

I expected Karo to demur, perhaps blame an invented weak connection, but he admitted he'd been renting the bungalow and made the story up so I wouldn't feel I owed him an even greater debt.

"What else have you made up, Karo? Does Awin even exist?"

"You're going too far, Leila."

"How do you expect me to trust anything you say?"

"You don't need to. Just let the papers come through, and then you can do whatever you want, and with whomever you trust, if you trust anyone at this point. For God's sake, Leila, you pick a fight with me every. Single. Time."

I hung up.

I padded on bare feet back to the kitchen, where Joanna stood at the sink, rinsing the dishes.

"Sad thoughts again?" She tilted her head.

"You're a mind reader?" I looked down in embarrassment.

"It's all over your face."

I didn't want to burden her with another litany of fears, but I could no longer bear the weight pressing on my chest. I told her about distrusting Karo, leaving out the fact that after spending some time with him, it had physically hurt to say goodbye. She did not interrupt me once and listened with interest even though she'd likely already heard most of it from Shiler.

Then I confessed that I had lied to my parents after Chia's funeral and told them that I was leaving to study in Canada. "I asked Mama to let me talk to Baba, and I stood there at a pay phone. People were waiting in line behind me. I thought now that Baba and I had a loss in common, you know, perhaps we could talk about our grief. He wouldn't talk to me. Can you believe that? How can he be so stubborn?"

Joanna gave me a caring look but didn't answer, assuming I was still only venting.

"Seriously, Joanna, I need to understand. Please talk to me." I picked up a dish towel to dry the plates while she washed.

"Your father has been depressed for twenty-five years. You experienced depression at one point yourself. His is ongoing." Joanna talked about how torture broke people in irreparable ways. He had never found the chance or the tools to heal.

When the kitchen was spotless and filled with the smell of baklava and freshly brewed black tea with cinnamon, we sat at the scrubbed table, sipping from our mugs. Joanna told me that after the funeral had slowed down and people started to forget, as people do, Intelligence called my father in every day for a week and questioned him all day, telling him how his failures in life had gotten his son killed. "Who did you gamble your life and you son's life for? Your people? Do you not know that they report on your every move?"

Joanna said I had done the right thing by telling my parents I was in Canada. Because that's what Baba in turn had told the agents; he had said they couldn't touch any of his children any longer.

Joanna gave me a slip of paper with my father's handwriting on it. "They moved." It was their phone number and address in Halabja.

"He wrote this for me or for you?"

"He asked me to give it to Shiler so she could send the information to you."

"Do you think I should contact them?"

"I don't know, bawanem. But you will know. When the time comes. Enough for tonight?"

"Joanna, it's so hard to love parents who don't know how to love. It's even harder to love yourself when your parents didn't love you." She nodded, but I wasn't sure she understood how, after a life of motherlessness and loneliness, I opened my heart easily—and how many malicious forces competed to fill that vacancy.

That night I dreamed that I was slowly lifting my head out of a swamp buzzing with lots of noisy flies and other insects.

The inexorable ticking of clocks continued.

CHAPTER THIRTY-TWO

JOANNA AND I gardened, cooked, and talked all day, every day. Every time grief lunged at me like a shark, she offered me her shoulder. The house shone spotless, and more poems reappeared from my dusty memory: "A heart filled with love is a phoenix that no cage can imprison." But every time a gust of wind howled or a door slammed within earshot, every time someone spoke too loudly outside of the house, I jumped uncontrollably and my hands shook.

Then the day came. A postman left a package in the mailbox. A sudden breeze ruffled the leaves of the trees, sending them into a frenzied dance. I twitched as I tore into the envelope.

The papers felt heavy in my hand. I was invited to go to the Canadian embassy for a visa interview. I felt like I grew inches in height. Tears rolled down my face, but these were different from those I'd shed over the years. They were at once hopeful and fearful. I felt tall as I walked back across the porch and into the living room, where Joanna was reading. She looked up at me from her Sufi book, and she knew. "Sixteen months of waiting is over," she said as she hugged me.

I sensed a panic surging in my chest. "It hasn't happened yet."

"You'd have to mess up the interview really badly to not get that stamp in your passport."

"Tehran-Ottawa relations are sour these days." Individuals' destinies didn't matter.

"Oh, stop with the worrying!" She played music, waving a handkerchief in the air, moving her hips. I held her hand and danced the *halparke*: right foot in front, left one in back, shoulder pushed forward and back, celebrating my first step toward freedom. Miserably clumsy and uncoordinated, I danced along and was soon too enthralled to be touched by fear. The irony wasn't lost on me that a people with one of the most tragic histories had created such a happy music and were always ready to dance and celebrate good fortune.

I booked the first available slot for an interview with the Canadian embassy. On a frosty morning before sunrise, we got into Joanna's car and drove to Tehran. As we navigated the winding mountain roads, I didn't have anything to say, but I couldn't bear the silence either. I gripped the seat. Even if by some miracle I got the visa, I could be on the blacklist. I fiddled with the radio dial for a distraction.

I clenched my jaw as Joanna parked, and we made our way to a small office with its doors closed. A crowd of nervous Iranians in hats and shawls shivered before it, sharing stories of wild visa rejections and of Canada debating whether to close its embassy. Joanna left to find us some food, and I had a sense she couldn't bear the tension. I clutched at my coat and stayed rooted to the spot, hoping that I wouldn't break down, reciting poems to deafen myself to the frightful chitchat.

Just as Joanna finally made it back to the queue with two sandwiches, they called my name and let me inside the embassy.

The frowning middle-aged woman at the counter did not have to cover her hair. She didn't bother with niceties and asked question after question about how I met Karo and where we held the wedding, checking my answers against the document we had provided last year, then told me to wait outside again.

I hugged myself tight, leaning against the wall across from the small window of the embassy, waiting for it to reopen and another name to be called. The staff was on their lunch break. I paced the small street.

"Do you miss him?" Joanna wanted to know if that was why I couldn't eat.

It didn't even occur to me that she was talking about Karo. "I feel there's a limit to how much and how long we can yearn for someone." My heart had shrunk so much that it was not capable of missing Chia anymore.

"Do you feel somewhat numb?" Joanna wrapped her shawl over her nose, which was turning red in the cold.

"I feel grateful." It was true. After all, I felt a faint sense of appreciation for having had Chia in my life even for a short while.

"I'm not too sure how you feel about the move."

"You're not alone!" I wanted to get out of Iran so badly, and yet I was terrified of what could happen in Canada with the mounting anti-immigrant sentiments. The Iranian and Canadian flags, erected over the door, danced in the cold breeze. Neither of the countries was mine. One had crucified my brother and threatened to kill me. One had killed its own natives at one point and I wasn't sure it had a place for the likes of me.

The steel-barred window opened at two. Names were called. I wasn't too sure if the Leila they finally called was me. Joanna shoved me forward. A man slid my passport along the counter. I clasped it and stumbled back. Joanna placed her hand on my shoulder, and we walked through a curious crowd.

My hands were shaking too much to open the document. Joanna found the visa page for me. I ran my fingers over the glossy page. It was real.

We headed back immediately to make it home before dark.

"It won't be easy to have to accommodate someone else's needs and schedule when you get to Canada," she said.

It was true—I had been able to read whatever and whenever I wanted, completely ignore what the clock dictated, and sleep anytime, anywhere in the house, in whatever piece of clothing I wished.

"That's the least of my fears, Joanna."

That night, she taught me how to bake an apple cake and had me blow out candles. We celebrated a rebirth that had not happened yet.

In bed I held my stamped passport to my chest and could not fall asleep.

Dawn broke as I sat up, soaked in sweat, and shook my head to dispel the recurrent nightmares of getting lost in Toronto, forgetting all the English I had practiced, being abducted by human traffickers. I wrapped myself in a robe and went out to the yard.

The chirping birds were invisible, and their nests, high up in the branches of the weeping willow tree, looked vacant. A cool breeze whispered under my robe and raised goosebumps on my moist skin.

Surrendering to the biting weather, I unlocked my folded arms and, stepping onto the dewy grass in my slippers, bent toward the small garden that had grown out of some mysterious and neglected seeds in a plastic bag. I kneeled to feel the support of the earth beneath my palms. I was closer to freedom than I had ever been. All I needed was to make it on to the plane and feel it take off.

Then I held my hands up to the sky and gazed at the rising sun.

CHAPTER THIRTY-THREE

I DRAGGED MY life behind me, condensed into two suitcases. I didn't want to leave Joanna's embrace. It was the safest place I'd ever known. I soaked her shoulders with my tears, wishing she were my mother and that I could crawl into her womb and be cared for and safe. "I have never been this happy and sad at the same time," she said as she wiped my tears.

My destiny was to be decided today, a year and a half after Chia's execution. I crossed the departure area between the embraces and murmurs of the passengers and their companions.

"Traveling alone?" The customs officer did not make eye contact.

"Joining my husband." My breath was noisy.

"His permission?" He extended his hand.

"Whose permission? Oh. Right. My husband is waiting for me. He's sent me an invitation." I provided every document I had, none of which was Karo's official letter allowing his wife to travel abroad on her own. Of all the possible scenarios, I had missed the most plausible one. A nervous sweat broke out on my face.

The man had me follow another officer to the waiting area where suspicious travelers were kept. I still had three hours until boarding, but panic roiled inside me. If they had not looked into my records yet, they would now. Time mercilessly slowed down and stretched. An oversized picture of a pretty woman in hijab gazing down read in Persian and English: "Respected ladies, complying with Islamic dress code is mandatory."

By the time I was called in for further questioning, my cuticles were bleeding.

The dark old room smelled putrid, like escaping sewer gas. The metallic blinds were closed. A large uniformed man with a long untrimmed beard was looking for a folder wedged somewhere among many others. Behind his chair hung a refrigerator-sized photograph of Khomeini and Khamenei, the Supreme Leaders who had slaughtered countless thousands of "God's enemies."

The armpits of the secretary's shirt were wet. On his chest, white traces of salt had formed isolated atolls. He looked annoyed as he thumbed through the file drawer of his battered metal desk. "Leila Saman?" he asked in an angry voice. On his lips my name was another crime. I'd be dragged into a prison cell right now. The rotten-egg smell made me want to throw up.

"You deaf? Are you Leila Saman or not?"

His beady eyes drilled into me as I nodded slightly.

"Is it easier to move that big head rather than a small tongue?" The crude man laughed at his own joke, looked through some papers he'd fished out of a battered folder, and signed in a few places. How would they put it? *We'll send you to the place we sent your brother?* I wondered if this final relief would be a favor. It was better to die once than a hundred times a day. And who knew what would happen to me in Canada if I made it there?

The officer made me stand there. The room had no window, no air conditioner, no plants; a ceiling fan hung still above shelves overflowing with dusty files and yellowing papers. The odor of sweat and mildew was suffocating. His terrible breath filled up the airless room.

I stared above him at where the ceiling met the wall. "My husband is a resident of Canada. I'm going there on a dependence visa. That proves he wants me to join him. You can contact him."

"Why didn't your parents choose a name for you from the Qur'an?"

A bucket of ice cubes poured down my spine.

He had a prayer bump on his forehead from frequent friction with the *mohr*, the Shia clay tablet. My ID revealed that I was born in Kurdistan, among people Khomeini called corruptors on earth.

The guillotine, I'd heard, was a lot less painful than the firing squad. Death was a friend now, had faithfully walked shoulder to shoulder with me these past two years.

"Why don't you and your husband serve your own country?" he went on.

My eyes traveled down from the ceiling and wall to the folder, to the large man's indifferent face as he absently scratched his beard. "We will, once we graduate. That's the goal—to mix Western technology with Islamic ethics."

He nodded in approval, started searching my luggage, meticulously unfolding each pair of underwear I'd packed, including the silk lingerie I'd bought on a whim, and sneered when he found a zipped-up plastic bag at the bottom of the second suitcase.

The officer recoiled when he realized he'd been touching my sanitary pads. Without another word, he showed me the door.

I dissolved into laughter after I closed his door behind me. God bless infidel-saving pads.

My passport was stamped. The boarding pass did not evaporate or melt or shatter into pieces like I had dreamed. I went through the frosted doors that did not admit the silhouette chasing me. The past was another continent.

I was the last person to board the Aeroflot flight.

I walked down the narrow aisle, blind to the other passengers. This was real, this breaking up with life as I knew it, this one-way journey to the unknown. When I settled in my seat, I relaxed my shoulders despite the tug of grief in my chest.

The engines rumbled beneath me as the plane began taxiing to the queue for takeoff. I took a steadying breath to calm my nerves. Raindrops formed into lines of water that slid sideways across the tiny oblong window as the plane took off. The clouds skated under the plane.

The layover in Moscow was eleven hours long, and because of my Iranian passport, I was not allowed to step outside into the city I was so eager to see. I browsed the terminal, taking in details of life outside the 636,400-square-mile prison named Iran.

Tall and slender women flaunting shapely legs in short skirts sold cigarettes and liquor to endlessly waiting passengers. People passed in front of me, talking, chewing, laughing, frowning, and directing their looks away from me. After an hour, I sat on some stairs, my palms touching the cold blunt stone. A smiling, pretty blonde reclined on the stairs in front of me. Five male admirers surrounded her, cutting each other off to make jokes for her. She laughed at what would frighten me.

I continued to stroll around and came across a mysterious door that I hadn't noticed before. This nearly imperceptible door was made of opaque black glass and was emblazoned with Russian words. I walked by but found myself across from it again, and I waited there awhile before pushing the door open. The dark stairs looked menacing. I stepped back. An older man in a black suit and tie bowed to two sharply dressed businessmen and led them down the stairs. I followed.

Downstairs was cool, a significant contrast to the heat upstairs. The old man said something to the receptionist and led the two to a modern, chic room with lots of chairs, desserts, and drinks. Internet—there were three connected computers. Two were busy, one free. I could send an email to Karo, let him know I had dodged incarceration.

"Excuse me," called the receptionist in English while I stared excitedly at the monitors.

"Oh . . . hi! Could I use the computer for five minutes?"

"Did you fly business class?" He looked at me from head to toe.

My throat went dry. *I bet you can figure out the answer.*

"Sorry, if you had flied business class, we could have helped you."

Shouldn't that be 'flown'? My left hand was still pointing toward the free computer.

"Do you have an invitation letter?"

I shook my head and climbed back up the stairs. In the economy area, I slid down a wall and sat on the floor, bracing myself for more exclusions and for what would inevitably be more embarrassing situations in which I'd fail to understand unwritten rules.

After a tormenting ten-hour wait, I made my way to the security screening area and emptied my purse for a gruff border officer's inspection, removed my shoes and belt, passed through the intimidating metal columns, and let them conduct their "random" search.

While we were boarding, a man in uniform sized me up and smiled in approval, as if rating me. He then scrutinized my passport, and his smile suddenly froze. He looked me up and down again, but his expression was so different this time, I couldn't help but chuckle slightly. "The pilot has asked that you let us hold onto your passport for now."

"Randomly again? But he can't do that. You don't have the right."

My glare did not shake him.

"We will return it to you once we land at Pearson."

I looked at myself and wondered what made me look like a terrorist.

"To hell with you and the rest of you," I said under my breath as I walked away and found my seat on the massive Air Canada plane.

I felt numb. The sting of distrust burned, but that was yet another penalty I had to pay for having been born in Iran, in that wicked land where, just like in James Joyce's homeland, "the old sow eats her farrow." My birthplace would follow me everywhere, making me a criminal in the eyes of a stupidly cruel and prejudiced world.

I found my seat and wrote in my diary:

Life has happened to me without much agency on my part. Baba and Mama brought me into this world, into Mariwan; Chia took me to Tehran; and now Karo is taking me to Toronto. If I make it there alive, I vow to take the wheel: find a job, "a room of my own," get into a college, pay back Karo, carry on Chia's legacy. So long, smothering grief.

A pretty woman with a shy smile sat beside me and said hello. She was wearing a blue sari and had large dark eyes, long braided hair, and a bindi. Before the plane took off, she swallowed some pills from her cupped palm and gulped down a full bottle of water. "I am a mail bride," she winked.

"I am an imposter bride." I winked back.

CHAPTER THIRTY-FOUR

I GOT OFF the plane after ten hours. The sun still shone in the middle of the sky, just where it had been when I left Russia. The man who had taken my passport in Moscow ran after me and returned it. Every man who set eyes on me looked like a human trafficker. I braced myself for the arrival process and made my way to customs.

A clean-shaven, blue-eyed officer asked me questions, looked over my documents, then brought me to a spare, well-lit room with several cubicles, sat behind a desk, and asked more questions. I gathered all my mental faculties, but he spoke so brusquely that I could understand only a few words in each sentence. Guessing at his questions, I tried to answer, resulting in many awkward misunderstandings, repetitions, and corrections. I was worried to death he'd interpret my language barrier as dishonesty, which was also part of it, perhaps the real reason for my palpitations. He told me to wait and left.

It all dawned on me: Karo didn't really want me. I had no money. My English was terrible. I'd saved myself from the threat of prison only to die alone in a foreign land.

I looked around at other people conversing with officers. A shabby-looking woman broke down and started shouting. All I understood was her very liberal use of the word "fuck." Two giant uniformed men grabbed her arms and took her out. I held my scarf over my mouth for fear of throwing up.

My officer returned with a neutral expression and handed me my passport and a bunch of documents and application forms. He spoke in a soft voice, too fast for me to understand. I stared at him blankly, got up, and followed the exit sign.

Once at the baggage carousel, I looked back. No one was following me.

My suitcases heaped onto a luggage cart, I made my way to the arrival hall and looked for Karo. The Canadian flag with the red maple leaf hung from the high ceiling. A sea of faces swam around, expressions ranging from ennui to excitement. A woman in her sixties stood out among the crowd, with tanned skin and blond hair, dressed in a tight, knee-length, black-and-pink dress and tottering in high heels of the same colors. She wore too much makeup. Her bulging belly stretched her tight dress. She stared at me too. I could read her lips saying in Persian: "Is that my daughter-in-law?"

The man next to her, bent over a backpack and battling with its zipper, was Karo. He waved at me. I waved back, but my hand froze in the air, suddenly self-conscious about my bedraggled appearance: my ugly sneakers, the turned-up cuffs of my jeans, my ill-matching white, purple, and blue shirt, my boyish hair, which I'd kept pixie short.

Karo's mother shook hands with me, leaving me slightly bewildered by evading my attempt to kiss her cheek. I admired her majestic height.

Karo gave me a warm hug and kissed me on the top of my head—headscarf-free for once. His mother held her hand over her mouth, tittered, and then let the laughter shake her body. "Don't you worry, honey. I know a place that sells gorgeous wigs."

I didn't respond, but she didn't seem to mind. We made our way to the parking lot, where she got into her white BMW. Karo, who had come from work, indicated an old Toyota and moved his work files to the trunk, atop my luggage. He slowly drove toward the parking lot exit.

The awkwardness of our reunion was unexpected. After exchanging pleasantries in tight, clipped sentences, I finally asked, "What did you tell your mother?"

Karo tilted the rearview mirror to check out his face and ran a hand through his hair. "Nothing."

"She doesn't know the marriage is a charade?" My body twisted toward his.

He drove up to the parking exit and inserted a ticket and a credit card into the slot machine, and the gate opened. "Don't you want a bigger audience for the show?"

"Not funny." I moved uneasily, restricted by the seatbelt.

"Did you tell your parents the truth?" We merged onto a highway called the 401 East and navigated our way into Canadian traffic.

"I couldn't."

"Same here."

"But mine are far away, and they don't need to know."

"Correct. No one needs to know."

"But your mother is here. She'll figure it out. Why lie to her?"

"Because she'll be happier this way."

"And what are you going to tell her when I leave?"

Karo eyed me. "Your short hair looks so different in person."

"Why does your mother assume I want a wig?" He didn't answer. I unrolled the window and stuck my head out to let the wind comb through the short curls that could breathe from now on. I felt a slight thrill at being so exposed. The rising heat created shimmering pools that disappeared beneath the many cars' tires on the expressway, leading us to a city unlike anything I'd ever imagined. Knots of intertwining four-lane highways whisked us through a canyon of towers, so lofty and modern that Tehran's Milad Tower would be right at home in Toronto's skyline. Fast cars savagely cut us off, speeding through the dense traffic as though they were jets traveling down an empty runway. We puttered along in our shabby little vehicle. As we pulled off the highway and drove through the megacity, I marveled at the spectrum of skin tones outside my window. Some women wore miniskirts, and some were covered by headscarves—by choice, I reminded myself. Some men wore ties, and some were in shorts. It was like a scene from the dozens of Hollywood films I'd watched back in Mariwan. But this time I was inside the movie, unsure of my lines or my role.

We arrived in North York at a sleek, modern house with expansive windows. Trying for nonchalance, I explored the interior decorated with furniture in quantities and styles I had seen only in the late king's palace, now a museum. Antique burgundy love seats and sofas with mahogany legs, large sculptures of leopards, lions, and warriors, buffets loaded with crystal and decorative dishes, finely woven handmade Persian carpets spread on the hardwood floors, a splendid fireplace in the corner. Not even one decorative bookshelf.

Taken aback by the display of extravagance, I began to feel insignificant. The distance I'd traveled descended upon me. I did not belong there. We put my luggage in his mother's finished basement, which was mostly a storage space crammed with older furniture and many labeled boxes but had a finished bedroom at one end of its hallway and a bathroom at the other.

In his innocently excited manner, Karo explained that his mother was offering us some privacy by letting us stay in the basement instead of the guest room upstairs and said she'd like to take us out for dinner that night. Worn out after more than twenty hours of travel, I asked if we could stay home instead.

"We can order takeout. What would you like?" he asked.

With great effort I mustered a smile. "Something Canadian."

"I can find you any other type of cuisine you may fancy: Ethiopian, Korean, Chinese, Indian, you name it."

"Canadian."

"There's no such thing."

"How is that possible?"

"Okay, they have one dish. But I warn you, you won't like it. It's called poutine and is mainly made of potato and some cheese. Wait, even that's French! So no Canadian food. How about Italian? Greek?"

"Poutine." I chose it because I found it amusing to eat a dish whose name meant "boot" in Kurdish. Let the absurd theatre reach its peak.

I changed into a comfortable T-shirt and pants and must have dozed off, because next thing I knew the food had arrived. We sat on the edge of his bed and indulged.

"We should get a little dinette down here. I've picked out three but was waiting for you to pick one of them. We'll go to IKEA this week."

I had no clue what IKEA was. "This is so simple. But tasty. What was it again . . . poo-tin?"

Karo laughed. "No, we are not eating the Russian dictator. Pou-*teen*."

"Whatever!" I caught him studying me again.

"The new hair." He inspected my face.

"It'll grow back." I looked down.

"I wanted to say it suits you. Long hair hides your face. I like this."

I squirmed. "Someone on the plane asked if I'd finished chemotherapy. I said, 'kind of.'"

Karo flopped onto a twin mattress on the floor. "Sometimes people make an effort to connect with you and end up saying the absolute worst shit. Others, like me, are so afraid of saying the wrong thing that we don't make conversation. Listen. My mother." He fetched an extra pillow and blanket from the wardrobe.

"When she talks about things like, I don't know, taking you to a makeup artist or plastic surgeon, she's only trying to bond with you."

"What? Plastic surgeon? Has she cooked up a complete makeover for me in her head? What's wrong with the way I look? I mean, I know I'm not beautiful like her, but I don't want to be either. I have other priorities, at least for now." And I was too busy surviving, I thought. How much of her own face and body had been retouched?

Karo lay down on his mattress. "I'm not saying you should listen to her. I prefer women's natural looks myself. I am just saying that she isn't being cruel when she says those things. That's her world. She is inviting you into her world. You know what I mean?"

"I should brush my teeth." I headed to the bathroom. My God, if that was her way of being nice, I'd hate to see her truly be mean.

In the bathroom mirror I examined the exhausted, unattractive face of a girl who'd wished for death and failed, tried to save her brother and failed, and now imposed herself on this wealthy beautiful woman who was embarrassed, if not downright horrified, by her ugly daughter-in-law and her son marrying down, just like she had done. I brushed my teeth, painfully conscious of the missing molar that she may not have seen yet. I needed to get into the habit of covering my mouth when (if?) I laughed. And I needed to find a way to leave Karo and his mother as soon as possible.

When I returned to the bedroom, Karo's hands were clasped behind his head, and he was staring at the ceiling. I stood by Karo's mattress. "You should take the bed."

"I said a horrible thing, Leila." He sat up. "I am such an idiot. I wanted to make sure you wouldn't be hurt by her assumptions, and I hurt you myself. Look, she does these things to herself all the time, and she feels flattered by them, not insulted. So when she says . . ."

"Please, Karo. Just get up and sleep on your own bed. Let me sleep on the floor."

"I'm very comfortable here." Karo slid under the sheets and drew them over his face.

"Well, I'm not. You're used to your bed. I'd be more comfortable on the floor. Trust me."

He pretended to be snoring. I stood there and looked at him, reeling from the absurdity of the situation, my whole reality. The pixelated image on my laptop screen had now become this handsome man who slept in the same room as me but not with me, who temporarily hosted me but was my "husband," who—albeit inadvertently—had killed my brother, yet saved me from the threat of death.

I crawled into his bed and stared at the flat ceiling and freshly painted, opal-white walls all night. When I did finally fall asleep, I was back in front of Evin, watching men and women being hanged.

CHAPTER THIRTY-FIVE

SWEAT DRIPPED DOWN Karo's face and neck as if he'd been under a leaking faucet. "A hundred and fifty push-ups. Enough for today. Do you want to go downtown?"

I rubbed my eyes. "I dreamed coming to Canada was a dream."

He laughed. "Pinch yourself."

"Why would I? I don't want to wake up from this dream." I stretched my arms out and yawned, my jetlagged body mildly achy all over, my brain still foggy. His sturdy naked torso glistened with sweat. I averted my eyes, an ice chip slipping into my belly.

"Let's make it the best dream ever, then. I took the week off to show you around." He wiped his face with a light green towel. "Pack your bathing suit. But bring a sweater too. Canadian weather can surprise you."

"I have no bathing suit. Besides, I need a job, not a tan. Does your company hire anyone other than computer engineers?"

"It's a start-up with one CEO who does nothing and six engineers who do everything. But I'll ask around next week. Today we're doing something fun."

"Fine." I rolled my eyes but relented. I sat up and pointed to his bulging pectorals. "I still need a bathing suit, then. And you need a bra."

He laughed and left the room. "We'll buy some beach stuff on the way."

I heard the shower turn on. The room was rather big and neat, but it didn't have a window. I hugged my knees. How could a room not have a window? How could one live without the light and air? A dark bronze chandelier with eight little lampshades hung too low from the ceiling, a poor replacement for sunrays. There were no clocks in the room, and I was unable to tell the time. The black TV screen facing the bed reflected my body back at me like a fun-house mirror; I squeezed to take up less space. I stuck my tongue out at the image, and the reflection did the same. A PlayStation and a pile of comic books were placed under the TV.

I made the bed, then inspected the walk-in closet to my right. It was also meticulously organized, its clothes arranged by season and hung on matching hangers, tops sorted from bottoms, jeans and sheets folded, wires and other electronics arranged neatly in a bin, several bottles of whiskey lined up. I did a double-take seeing the bottles displayed so openly. Oh, yes—one wouldn't get lashed for it here, I reminded myself. My suitcases were placed carefully by the wall, and the shelves atop them were unoccupied. I wondered if Karo's head was also that neatly compartmentalized, offering a temporary corner to the sister of a dead friend. I was envious, tired of the mess that I was inside and out.

"These shelves are all yours, and I can give you more space too if you need it. I laid out some towels, and the soap is in the bathroom cabinet. On the right." Karo stood behind me as I tried to decide which stuff to take out of my luggage. His soap smelled like sandalwood.

"What's that thumping sound?" I pointed to the ceiling.

"My mother is on the elliptical machine. Hercules, her trainer, is barking at her. And he needs a bra more than I do."

I gathered my toiletries to my chest and made my way to the narrow basement hallway. There was a small rectangular window high upon the wall at its end, a laundry room and bathroom to the left. There was the steady noise of a vacuum cleaner, and I couldn't comprehend how his mother could be working out and cleaning too.

When I stepped out of the bathroom, freshly showered, I saw a smiling woman with chubby cheeks lugging the vacuum down the stairs.

We got dressed and drove to the station. During the subway ride, I was relieved to learn I was not the only one for whom English was foreign. Some of the riders spoke different languages, making me feel I was not in one new country but many, all at the same time. The teenagers standing there and speaking perfect English were a mix of Asian, European, and African. "Will you help me find a job?" I asked Karo.

"Leila, you've barely been here twenty-four hours. We should get your residency paperwork sorted out first. You can't work in this country without a social insurance number. Also, your first real job is to prepare for your English exams and put together a list of nearby universities that offer film studies." Karo looked uncomfortable but added that he would be happy to help.

Nearby? I'd attend any college in Canada that offered some sort of financial aid, nearby or not. "So, that's a no? To helping me with the job hunt?"

"Why are you so impatient?"

"I want to repay you."

"You will. What's the rush? You have a lifetime to do that. You could dedicate your first film to me. How about that? That would be a lovely repayment."

As the train came aboveground and an automated woman's voice intoned "Arriving at Rosedale, Rosedale station," the train car was filled with a cacophony of dings and beeps, notification tones from all the cell phones regaining service at the same time. The door slid open, and a man wearing a hoodie boarded, nodding his head rhythmically to a beat, making me feel like I was listening to his music. We got off at the Dundas station, where people jostled and teenagers ran.

"It's not even rush hour," Karo said.

"When is rush hour here?"

"Nowadays in Toronto? Almost all day long."

"Aaa! You come from Tehran, and you complain about the traffic here?"

His face brightened into a charming smile. In the daylight, his indigo eyes looked darker. "I suppose I carry too many expectations of a developed country."

We ascended the stairs to the sidewalk, where a sloppily dressed man with long, scruffy hair carrying a large bag on his left shoulder rummaged through the garbage. "Dear God. Poverty everywhere? Even in Canada?"

"That's what I was talking about. Expectations." Karo grabbed my bare arm, which made my temperature suddenly rise. "This is Dundas Square."

I twirled, taking in the many large buildings and numerous billboards. The moving image on top of the H&M store showed anorexic-looking girls in bikinis running on the beach and posing for pictures. An instant later they were back on the beach and running again. And again. And again.

We continued south on Yonge Street and entered a large big-box store called The Bay to buy bathing suits. I tried on a yellow one-piece swimsuit the color of sunshine; it offered more coverage than all the skimpy bikinis on display. Though still relieved about not having to wear a headscarf, the idea of wearing a bathing suit in public was uncomfortable, especially before Karo, who'd now see how scrawny my body was. Joanna's meals had helped me regain some ten pounds, but I still had a shrunken look about me. Oh well. It wouldn't change anything anyway. And dipping into an actual lake was a long-held desire of mine. I had to be brave. I was brave. I didn't panic before a gun held to my forehead.

I stepped outside of the dressing room and looked around at the preoccupied shoppers, wondering if anyone else had ever had a gun pointed at their forehead. In a country full of refugees and migrants, mine couldn't be the craziest story.

Karo appeared with two beach towels and blue swimming trunks draped over his arm. "Let's find a Canadian Tire," he said, taking my yellow suit and heading toward the register.

I couldn't fathom why we'd want a tire for the beach. It turned out we didn't—it was just the name of another huge store. I walked down an aisle and saw a woman in a loose-fitting and stained black shirt, one trouser cuff up, one down, brushing her gray hair and smiling into a mirror. A green tag reading $5.25 dangled from the brush. Karo patted my shoulder. I looked back and saw the toothless corner of her mouth as she smiled broadly at her jubilant reflection. "I think she's going on a date," I told Karo, who looked around to see who I was talking about. "Perhaps with the shabby man outside the subway station."

"Where do you get these ideas from?" he asked. I remembered Chia and his constant nagging about my idea folder, and my heart flickered.

I gaped as we walked down a different aisle toward the registers. "So many colorful crayons! Lots of them. Look—there are five shades of red! Hundreds of crayons." He stared at me as I almost danced on the spot, moving my arms and wiggling my hips left and right. "I bet you didn't yearn for these when you were a kid." I bought a pack of a hundred crayons for only three dollars.

At the waterfront, we stood in line to board the ferry for some time. I looked at the people passing by, carefree, dressed however they pleased. I wanted to stop them and ask if they were thrilled to be in Canada. But they didn't look as overjoyed as I expected them to be. Looking back at what I had observed in the past hour, I almost understood why.

We boarded the ferry to Centre Island and sailed over Toronto's equivalent of beautiful Zrebar, named Lake Ontario—but unlike Zrebar, it didn't have a mystical source. The water, shining silver under the sunlight with the glint of a thousand mirrors, flooded me with exhilaration. As the ferry pulled away from the city I looked back at the skyline, at the CN Tower rising up, the high-rises growing smaller on the horizon.

Centre Island was our hostess through the rest of the afternoon and into the evening. Children ran around, shrieking with laughter as they played, reminding me of my jubilant childhood days spent at Zrebar, running around with Shiler and later Chia.

"That cloud looks like a fluffy little monkey." I pointed and twirled.

We rented bikes and pedaled along the boardwalk by the lake. The wind brushed through my hair and over my face. "Look at that grin," Karo said, cycling by my side.

He'd have one too if the ruling clergies had deemed biking inappropriate for men. "I haven't ridden a bike in twenty years."

I cycled away. *Chia, where are you right now? Right this moment. I wish you could see me growing younger with each pedal, reclaiming the years stolen from me.*

I pedaled so fast that it felt like the wind was slapping me, but I carried on, faster and faster, tears sliding sideways down my face. *Chia, you used to bike after me. Now you're the uncatchable one, no matter how fast I ride after you . . .*

I didn't stop until I'd completely run out of breath. When I looked behind me, Karo was nowhere to be found. I pedaled slowly back in the direction I'd come from to find him, too afraid to ask anyone simple directions in English, too guilty after forgetting about Karo like that.

I found him sitting on a rock across from the bike rental booth, running a stick over the asphalt, writing a diary entry visible only to him.

"I'm so sorry." I had made a spectacle of myself.

He looked ahead and away. We returned the bikes, changed into our swimsuits in the mildewy changing booths, and hit the beach. I went barefoot to feel the sand, squish it between my toes, but the sensation of being so exposed slowed my steps. The sideways looks from my fellow beachgoers prickled my skin.

We spread a beach towel on a patch of sand and sat down. Silence. I gazed blankly at the life forms around me: shore birds, kids in motion, stationary adults baking in the sun, some bobbing their heads to radios, some reading, some napping facedown.

A middle-aged couple was sitting on a dune nearby. The woman put a small piece of sandwich into her partner's mouth. The man bit her fingers. She laughed. Louder than a woman was supposed to. Was there a permitted female decibel level here? I looked around and imagined the Police of Enjoining Good and Forbidding Vice swarming the beach, their stampede toward women scantily clad in bikinis. Of course, they didn't show up.

Lying down in the sun, taking in the scenery, the sight of happy and relaxed people, I felt I had died and, having received some undreamed-of and unhoped-for special pardon, was now in paradise. Perhaps for the rest of the crowd my heaven was just another nice day.

Several times, I caught Karo staring at my chest. "What are you looking at?" I finally blurted out.

"Ah, I think you should put on sunscreen."

"I'm going to . . ." I stood up and pointed to the lake.

"Swim? Want to swim?" He moved to rise, frozen in a strange position between standing and sitting, his palm on the ground, his hip up.

"Ummm . . ." I needed to be alone.

"Ah, okay, go ahead." He sat down and wiped the sand off his palm.

The waves tugged me forward, and I struggled to keep my balance. They swept away the tiny pebbles of the beach and tickled the soles of my feet. I rocked in the water and felt like I was part of infinity, a relative to the sun and the sky. I waded in the shallow tide and let the water surround me like a loving mother hugging her tired, wounded daughter. At least I belonged to Mother Nature.

When I made my way back to Karo, he wrapped a towel around me.

"Will you put some sunscreen on me?" He lay down on his stomach.

I kneeled beside him and tried to cover his back with the lotion, dismissing the warning tug in my gut. His skin was soft, warm, and moist, his muscles hard, his neck and shoulders already red from sun exposure. "We should have gotten one of the sprays." I handed him the lotion so he could do the rest himself.

"Are you dry yet?" he asked.

"I don't need sunscreen."

"Oh yes you do, unless you want to scratch your back every night while your skin peels off."

My skin tingled under his fingers. Once we were both well slathered, I followed him back to the water, unafraid of the waves. Immersed in our game of Frisbee, I forgot my inner struggles. With his hair pressed to his scalp, water dripping down his face, and with his eyes squinting at the sun, Karo was a dazzling titan.

"Please, Karo," I said when we got home that night. "I feel like a colonizer. I'll be much more comfortable if you let me sleep on the floor."

"Good night." He hid his head under the blanket, and not long after, his rhythmic breathing revealed that he was asleep. I stared at the ceiling again until my eyes gave in to exhaustion.

The next day we went to the top of the CN Tower, daring one another to lie down on the glass floor. We took pictures and put coins in the telescopes to magnify the view of the city.

"Having a good day?" Karo put an arm across my shoulders in the elevator. I felt his breath on my face.

"Oh, I can't remember being this happy since . . . you know." Since the day you urged my brother to come with you. I placed my hand on his hand, but only to remove it from my shoulder. Then I took the camera from him to snap my own photos, to crush the stinging memory under my shoes like a cigarette butt.

On day three I witnessed the grandeur of the Niagara Falls, which put the smallness of my wounds to shame. I felt that a cover had been torn away from my senses. The sinister forces that had beset my life started to recede. That night I dreamed my chest expanded. It cracked open, and a phoenix rose into the air.

By the weekend, my massive sorrows began to shrink as I walked among the roses, impatiens, and lilies in the lakeside Music Garden and the West End's High Park. Occasionally during the week of sightseeing, I felt a deep peace as my overwhelming rage and fear shifted to calm acceptance of my trials. Could I possibly exist above my history? At a café in Allen Gardens, while Karo went in search of a washroom, I wrote on a napkin: *Trees and flowers bloom despite human barbarism. Maybe I can too?*

Karo took too long, and I got bored. I strolled out of the café and breathed in the scent of flowers. I touched the bud of a peony lovingly and, for the first time in a long while, felt the pulse in my wrist and fingertips strengthen. I hadn't noticed how numb I'd been. Karo appeared before me with a smile so broad and beautiful it startled me.

The dark shapes of the birds were etched against the sunlit sky. Before Karo's concerned eyes, I lay down on the damp garden grass. The cool spray of a sprinkler landed on me. I pressed my eyelids and welcomed the intermittent shower on my face and hair. When I opened my eyes, the trees were greener, the red, yellow, and purple in the peonies and roses brighter.

A shout arose from my throat, a long-stifled cry was released.

CHAPTER THIRTY-SIX

KARO AND I dealt with the issue of our abstinence by stubbornly refusing to acknowledge it. Each day I let my eyes linger on him a little longer when he changed shirts or came into the room wrapped in a towel. Each night, as he snoozed on the mattress at my feet, I listened to my body yearning for his.

I was amazed by his incredible willpower, and yet I couldn't help wondering if he had a problem or maybe a safety valve. Could he be so traditional to assume intimacy was "using" a woman? Shiler and Chia used to say that I was too uptight. Could Karo be concerned that I'd be troubled if he made a move? As for me, I could only initiate in my fantasies, afraid of the implications and consequences, afraid that my attraction was one-sided.

But Karo wasn't the only thing that made my head spin in this new, beautiful country. The English vocabulary I used with ease in my mind came out garbled whenever I faced a native speaker. My ears weren't used to such a variety of accents, and my own mispronunciations erected walls between me and almost everyone I wanted to talk to. Too shy to ask people to speak slowly or repeat their words, I often ended up confused, misunderstanding and misunderstood. The city was filled with newcomers, and not many Torontonians had patience for so many individuals handicapped by their limited means of communication. Any gain in confidence was instantly dissolved with one mispronounced word. Even a small mistake like catching the wrong streetcar triggered frustration and defeatism. Even the doors were puzzling; accustomed to doors in Iran, which could only be entered from one side by pulling, I was constantly tugging on doors meant to be pushed.

At night, after Karo fell asleep, I silently recited poems until my eyelids felt heavy. Chia's face was all I could see when my eyes were closed. "Acclimation can be a lifesaver," I declared one night.

"What, dear?" Chia asked, surrounded by poppy fields.

"Conditioning and familiarity. You believed they were 'the end of creativity' and 'the killers of inquisitiveness.' Had it not been for the power of adaptation, I'd have been irrecoverable."

"Habituation is brain-deadening." Chia was now swimming in Lake Zrebar.

I stamped my feet. "And brain-saving! Saves it from exploding."

"What is it that you are trying so hard to get used to?" Chia asked, now behind bars, his eyes full of enthusiasm for life, his broken chin shivering.

"Leave me alone, you. Let me be. I love you. I love you, but let me be. You didn't listen to me when I begged you to stay away from trouble. You ignored me. Let me be." I woke up drenched in sweat and bit into my pillow to stifle my sobs. The tears soaked into the cotton pillowcase. I longed to crawl under Karo's bedcovers and ask him to hold me until my shudders ended, but the possible ramifications stopped me. His friendship was all I had left. His steady snore was the most reassuring sound.

AT THE END of my first month in Toronto, Karo and I went to Earl Bales, a vast park not too far from home. My mother-in-law and her friends showed up uninvited, which was a surprise, since she and I never exchanged many words beyond respectful pleasantries. I was conscious of her complicated feelings toward the Kurds, her hatred of her husband's deception, how she had denied her children the truth of their heritage. I assumed she was cursing fate for having me as a daughter-in-law as well.

She and her friends were overdressed for a picnic and showing off bright red lipsticks and matching nails and toes, perhaps dropping by before heading to a party. The women were making fun of a new girl at their hot yoga class who had a wealthy husband but whose family and background nobody knew anything about. She was a snobbish girl, they said, who arrived early, always carried a book, and ignored the others.

Self-conscious before their gazes, I isolated myself in a way that could only be interpreted as aloofness.

"God knows what she's up to," one of them scoffed. "Loners always turn out to be someone with something to hide."

I took the first bite of my egg salad sandwich but found it hard to swallow.

"These *bi-kas-o-kar* women!" my mother-in-law spat out. Her friends laughed, but their Botox didn't allow their eyes to crinkle, making them freakish in their amusement.

The morsel got stuck in my mouth, refusing to move down my gullet. The epithet bi-kas-o-kar—literally meaning "who has no one," implying "of no account" or "unreliable"—rang in my head. My throat constricted, and I breathed with great difficulty through my nose, suddenly feeling the onset of a panic attack. Glancing up to look my mother-in-law in the eye, I tried to determine whether she and her friends were indirectly attacking me—as if one could tell just by looking.

I squinted at her, hated her. These women had left their roots behind and struggled in Canada to escape dictators. Little did they know that they had become tyrants themselves. If Chia were alive, no one would dare call me this.

Karo laughed, talking on his cell phone, unaware of the army that had beset me. I excused myself and marched away briskly. The past, with all its ghosts, swirled around my head like a colony of mosquitoes. I spat out the salad, sat on a bench with my back to the people and my face to the stagnant water. I missed Chia desperately; I felt I was being stabbed in the throat.

The next morning I left the basement before Karo woke and strolled aimlessly along Bayview Avenue, wondering if people could tell that I was breathing with an invisible dagger still in my throat.

I ordered a small black coffee in a ubiquitous Canadian café called Tim Hortons and sat near the window, watching the few yellow leaves fall on the cars waiting in the drive-through lane. "Didn't I tell you/that they will kidnap you from the path?/They will steal your warmth and take your devotion away./I am your fire, I am your heartbeat, I am the life in your breath . . ." I recited Rumi silently, but it offered no solace.

"Shiler, where are you when I need you?" I typed on my new cell phone. "Karo's married me but doesn't touch me, lest he disrespect me. His mother thinks his son is too good for a bi-kas-o-kar like me. I traveled over the ocean to suffer the same discriminatory mentality I thought I had escaped. Admitting that I am attracted to Karo feels like betraying Chia. Denying it is a lie. I need Joanna, I need a country, I need you. How are you doing on top of the mountains? Getting bombed every day? Are you also done with crying? My tears have gone on strike, because each time they appeared I deported them. How's your home on the hills? Are the mountains actually friends of Kurds? The apparent splendor of Western life is so alienating."

"I've seen you around, haven't I?" The red socks this elderly gentleman wore glowed between his black shoes and bright blue pants. I wondered if he expected me to confirm that he had indeed seen me. I shook my head, hoping he'd go away and leave me to my email.

"I live around here. You live near here?" he asked.

"Sorry. No English." I looked at the clock behind the cashier. I still had two more hours before my English class, and right away I felt bad for having rejected such a cheery person. He was probably lonely too, but I was in no mood to hear "pardon me" and "what's that" a million times. "No English" was the easiest way for an immigrant to refuse people who'd perhaps think, "Why the hell are you here, then?" The old man heard my words, looked at my dark eyes and black hair, and yet pushed a chair back and sat down opposite me. I smiled wordlessly, a puppet without its ventriloquist.

"It's supposed to rain tomorrow," he said.

I nodded and wanted to say that I liked the rainbows. But I was afraid of speaking, of suddenly bursting into tears like a maniac.

"John," an older woman standing at the door called out. "Hey, Caroline." My potential interlocutor got up to join her.

"Shiler, I miss your goofy grins," I typed, and let the email fly away across the planet, from the side that manufactured weapons to the side that used them.

My coffee wasn't steaming anymore. I walked down a side street off Sheppard Avenue until a "Hiring" sign at a café called Soul beckoned me. The place had couches on one side and tables and chairs at the other end.

"You worked before?" The expressionless Asian owner asked, his accent thicker than mine.

"I've worked." I kept crossing and uncrossing my arms. "I am a . . . I am a quick learner. Experienced at customer service."

"You speak Iranian? Lots of Iranian customers here."

"Yes, I do. Yes."

"You look good. Start tomorrow? Tomorrow at two. Afternoon."

I looked down at my striped green shirt and black tight skirt, feeling unworthy of being hired. "Really? Yes, I can. Of course I can." I didn't jump, but my voice did.

"Trial. Two days. Okay?"

I didn't know what "trial" meant. "Okay. See you tomorrow. Thank you!" I left but then came right back. "You will train me, right?"

"Yes. Must learn fast."

I took a photo of the menu with my cell phone and by evening, I'd memorized it. After my English class, I went home and checked the pronunciation of the words on the menu, watched videos on YouTube about how to make each of the special coffees, and searched for tips on how to be a good barista. I was walking around in the bedroom with an empty tray, smiling at my imaginary customers, when I remembered my days of studying for the national exam. Fear of failure crippled me. I sat down at the edge of the bed. Karo's mother called me from upstairs.

"I brewed fresh tea."

"I don't want any. Thanks," I said.

"Come up for a minute," she commanded.

"Okay." I instantly regretted my tone, how quickly I'd acquiesced. There was such a delicate line between politeness and cowardice.

She had poured tea and sliced some blueberry pie, her eyes scrutinizing me. "How's your family?"

I thought she was my family. "Pretty good." I leaned back on the love seat and clutched my fingers around a kneecap.

"We like the Kurds," she said.

Sure, I thought.

"My brother, Amin, had to leave Iran in hiding, and some Kurds safely smuggled him past the border. They saved him and many others. Many exiled Iranians owe their lives to the Kurds."

"And yet when we're mentioned, we are only smugglers? Even when the world itself relies on the Kurdish army to defeat the Islamic State?" I asked in a barely audible voice.

She pretended not to hear. "Will you get those photos from the kitchen counter?" She crossed one bare leg over the other.

The silver picture frame was made up of five flowers, each holding a meticulously placed tiny photograph. The top one was of her wedding, with a black-and-white photo of her parents in the center, one of Karo on the right, and one of her daughter, Awin, on the left. Karo had inherited his high cheekbones and bright eyes from his father. The man in the bottom picture must have been her brother. On the marble counter lay a check made out to her for

$1,500 for "June rent and groceries," signed by Karo. It was unheard of for an Iranian family to charge their child rent, especially for a crappy basement. And groceries too, when we barely ate at home?

"Amin and I were very close."

I sat back on the love seat. The home phone rang.

She waved her hand as if sending the ringtone away. "Karo has mentioned that you were close to your brother too. Chia."

I flinched. It was wrong, his name on her shiny red lips.

She went on. "My brother lives here in Mississauga. I don't see him because his wife doesn't allow it. She's never liked me, you see." She looked down. "So they act as if I don't exist." She examined the backs of her hands, her nails perfectly shaped and painted, three big diamond rings glittering.

She searched my face for sympathy. To my surprise, I recognized the loneliness in her eyes.

I stared at the pictures to stop myself from feeling sorry for the person who had hurt me only the day before. When it came to the Olympics of misery, I was the reigning champion. "Your brother is alive and well." I put the frame on the glass coffee table, the base of which was a statue of a lion.

"I wish I knew if he was well and happy," she said pointedly. "I was ten when Amin was born. I raised him. He's like my own son. And now he's been taken away from me." She bent forward toward me, the exotic perfume she wore nearly causing me to cough. "I'd certainly die if someone took my son away from me too."

I stood. She sat back and stared at me, checking the effect of her prepared speech, tapping the arm of the sofa. She was not threatening me; she was manipulating, trying to provoke pity.

"One can't offer contempt and expect kindness in return." I headed to the basement.

Unconsciously—perhaps something I had learned from Baba and Chia—I opened the laptop and started reading the news: "Several hundred Kurdish prisoners have begun a hunger strike in dozens of prisons across Turkey. Among their demands is the use of their language in Turkish courts. President Erdogan plays down the hunger strikes, calling it a 'show.'"

Was engaging with world issues a defense mechanism to trivialize personal pain, or was I doing it to be aware and responsible?

The sound of a key turning in the lock put an end to my dilemma. I flopped onto Karo's uncomfortable mattress on the floor, assuming this would force him to sleep on his bed and rid me of my guilt.

With his jacket hanging from his index finger, Karo winked and lay down next to me. "Welcome to my bed!"

Embarrassed, I got up and slid between the blue sheets of the queen bed.

Karo pressed the remote. A familiar show appeared on the screen: the story of a New York comedian, his pathetic friend, and an intrusive neighbor. Nothing about it seemed funny to me, and I couldn't believe people in real life slept around so mindlessly, as if having sex were no more intimate than a handshake. Karo, however, found the show hilarious, and I ended up smiling and even laughing along with his thunderous guffaws. As the episode came to an end, I watched Karo clutching his belly and gasping for air. His unrestrained laughter filled me with envy.

"Come." I tapped the sheet. "Come sit on the bed for now. You're not comfortable there."

He surfed the channels, quickly skipping CNN, CBC, and other news stations, the opposite of what my father or brother would do. I wanted to tell him that I could be fully employed if the next two days went well, wanted to explain why I had left in the middle of the picnic yesterday. But Karo poured himself some Johnnie Walker, joined me on the bed, and started laughing at almost every line of a sitcom, sometimes throwing his head back and slapping his knee. The smell of alcohol mingled with the pleasant scent of his hair or his aftershave. His aroma was mild, like the distant whiff of faraway wildflowers when you drive by a field with the windows down. It was alluring.

After some more channel surfing, Karo closed his eyes and leaned his head against mine. The touch of our temples created a shudder of discovery. This was how he coped with his grief: Denial. Comedy. Whiskey.

"Good night." He kissed the crown of my head and crawled into his makeshift bed, pulling the blue duvet up until it nearly covered his head.

I lay on the edge of the bed and watched Karo in peaceful slumber. His serene outward form camouflaged an agonized inner life. I stretched out a hand and lightly ran my finger along his profile, the line of his cheeks, nose, lips. His warm exhalations caressed my palm.

CHAPTER THIRTY-SEVEN

At the coffee shop, I learned to prepare every item on the list, work the cash register, and communicate with customers in Hollywood-derived English. I nodded awkwardly at chatty customers, trailing behind in one-sided conversations full of phrases and slang words that I couldn't decode. It wasn't unusual for me to misuse common expressions, like saying "no headache" when I should have said "no worries." "Thank you, and have a good day," the boss made me yell after each customer, and after a while I did it automatically, desensitized to my ineptness.

Because of the evening and weekend shifts at work, I rarely saw Karo. My mother-in-law and I avoided each other and exchanged nothing more than a few clipped greetings. Torontonians discussed the weather, the traffic jams, or the reduced size of the Tim Hortons cups.

One July morning I read on Facebook that Turkey had shelled the Kurds who fought the Islamic State. Several were killed. On the bus to work I searched Canadian media to learn more about the butchery, but not a single word was mentioned about the attack. I'd noticed that when the culprit was an ally, the news would go unacknowledged—even when a NATO member brutally killed a vital anti-terrorism partner. The beginnings of a headache drilled my skull. I had a premonition but lacked the courage to check my email, afraid that it would bear bad news, more anxious that there would be no news.

My boss surprised me that day by giving me an extra twenty-dollar bill. "You're a good employee. Save it to buy warm shoes later. Winter in Canada is very bad." He left me by myself for the first time. The café was slow then. I sneaked a look at my email.

Shiler's letter was there: "Loss is an inevitable part of a Peshmerga's life. Death confronts you often, smirks and takes away a friend, a relative, some new Peshmerga who hasn't had a chance to practice fighting. The woman or man you've been having tea with every day . . . one day, they are no longer there."

Something collapsed inside me. In her previous emails, Shiler often talked about the fun on the mountain, the ball games, bonfires, camaraderie.

"Leila, my friend Shaima is gone. The cluster bombs killed her. One moment she was there laughing, singing a folk song while I played the ancient keyboard I told you about—the one that's held together by so much glue. I played, and we sang together, and then the next day, they stuffed what was left of her body into a bag to be buried under a tree."

Shiler's stretched arms—imagined wings—appeared before my eyes, her unmatched stamina and piercing black eyes. I was relieved she hadn't been the target and yet was all the more afraid that one day I would no longer hear from her and would be forced to sizzle in a new purgatory of waiting.

"After two years of fighting, of seeing decomposing bodies, of digging graves . . . you'd think so many casualties would make death routine. But I see Death Almighty everywhere, casting his eyes on me, carting off a part of me with each friend taken, aging me every time."

Unable to conceive a response, I mopped the floor, wiped the counter, and cleaned the bathroom. A dozen students entered, and I rushed to brew more coffee, offer larger smiles to mask the heartache. Young customers sat all day in the café over cold cups of coffee, tapping away on laptops.

I sent what I could recall of Abdulla Pashew's poem to Shiler later that day: "I say, sir/Place your wreath under any tree/Near any stone/Beside any collapsed wall/By any riverbank/Bow your head and place your wreath/They are all my unknown soldiers' graves."

A gray-eyed man came in and asked for a latte. "Out of curiosity," he asked when I returned his change, "are you Portuguese?"

"For here or to go?" I made myself busy selecting a cup.

"Spanish?" He kept scrutinizing my face.

I wanted to yell, "I'm one of the people your government's NATO ally kills in daylight and your media ignores." I said, "Your coffee will be ready in a minute."

The heaviness in my head transferred to my limbs. I weighed a thousand kilos. The tears I did not allow to run down made me nauseated, as if threatening to come out of my throat any second.

An older man with a lovely smile came in and asked for green tea without reminding me that I sounded or looked different. When I delivered it to his table, I told him I loved his long white beard. He said he was a writer from Manitoba. I said I was a dreamer from Kurdistan. He didn't ask me to repeat myself, didn't ask where Kurdistan was. Instead he got up from his seat, stared into my eyes, and hugged me. "You're the first Kurd I have met in my life."

I wanted to tell him my friend was a freedom fighter, but he kept talking about everything he knew about the Kurds—the genocide.

"Yes, Saddam Hussein put cemen in the springs so people would die of dehydration."

He asked with wide eyes open, "Semen?"

"Sement?" I tried to correct myself.

"Oh, cement!" He sounded relieved but wouldn't explain. I checked the dictionary and blushed. We laughed.

EARNING A SMALL but steady paycheck and scoring high on the TOEFL enabled me to apply to the film departments at the University of McMaster and the University of Western Ontario, relying on government loans to underwrite this expensive undertaking. I clipped the classified pages of rooms for rent and searched online.

My mother-in-law wouldn't even return my greetings anymore. I couldn't make sense of her. If she was afraid that I would take Karo away from her, as her sister-in-law had done with her brother, surely she didn't think this hostile behavior would prevent that, did she? Or did it somehow appeal to her to be the victim, the deceived woman abandoned by her husband and children? Whatever her reasons, I needed to live without friction, already dizzied by my new life as it was. But she made me feel I was dirt to her as much as I was to the government she disliked. I barely saw Karo, and when I did, I was always tired, always preoccupied with work or studying.

A good-looking woman who had straight hair that curled gently at the ends started coming to the café every day around three, making special requests for the preparation of her macchiato. Her nasal voice and haughty attitude made understanding her orders a challenge. I had no choice but to ask her to repeat herself and then ask for another confirmation to make sure I got her order right. While this was going on, she'd ostentatiously look at her huge designer rose-gold watch, never bothering to enunciate clearly.

She would then settle into the middle of a couch, claiming it all for herself, take her *Cosmo* out of her Gucci bag, put her feet on the table, and smack her gum. Every other day at about two, my heart palpitations began. She made me remake her drink every single time.

You're such a moran, she wrote on a napkin one day and placed it on the counter before she left. I did not let any customers see my tears.

"When your best is no longer enough, when your name is no longer pronounceable, when your identity becomes an obstacle to human connections, you know you are an immigrant," I wrote to Shiler that night. "Nowhere on this planet is there a place willing to embrace you and me, but maybe we can find a peaceful corner? When will you put down your gun as you keep promising, build the safe Jinwar village, and bring Joanna? I am tired, Shiler. I am scared for you. For Joanna's loneliness with you so far away."

The next day before two o'clock I corrected the customer's misspelled word to *moron* and, before taping the napkin to the counter, wrote beneath her sentence, *You're so smart you can't spell in the only language you speak.* "How can I help you?" I asked when she appeared. She exhaled loudly when she noticed the napkin and left, never to return.

On a crisp September day in Toronto, I visited some available apartments, walking for hours from one side street to another, checking out house numbers. I finally found a room in a basement I could afford for 65 percent of my pay. The kitchen and bathroom had to be shared with two guys and another girl, but that was okay. I needed a space of my own.

I was drying my hair when Karo got home. He held up an envelope in one hand, untying his shoelaces with the other. "Happy birthday!"

"Oh, gosh. I'm so old I forgot my birthday!"

He held a tiny gift before my face and then moved his cheek forward, expecting a kiss. I almost turned away. Karo felt my hesitation, and his disappointed eyes shamed me into placing a splashy kiss on his cheek. I accepted the gift and tore open the envelope. Under his anxious gaze, I tried to make sense out of the words written on two pieces of paper: *TIFF, Visa Screening Room (Elgin).* I was about to confess my confusion when a familiar name popped up before my eyes: Mehmet Aksoy, Kurdish filmmaker. With a burst of recognition I remembered what TIFF was: the Toronto International Film Festival.

I screamed with excitement and hugged Karo. "How thoughtful!"

"The director will most likely be there too."

I held the ticket to my chest. "Thank you, thank you! This is such a thoughtful gift."

"You're welcome, Leila gian." He put his hands on my shoulders and looked down toward my mouth.

I leaned in. Our noses almost touched, his breath brushed my cheeks, and suddenly my lips pressed against his: soft, warm, and gentle. It felt as if a butterfly had landed on my face. A glacier melted within me.

When the kiss was over, neither of us knew what to do with it. I busied myself with the computer. He leafed absentmindedly through a comic book.

In the morning I pretended to be asleep until Karo had dressed and left. Slowly and meticulously, I combed through the room in the basement and packed my life back into two suitcases, one of which now had a tear in its covering from being tossed around by baggage handlers.

At work, the regular customers commented on my tired appearance. I waved my hand in the air. "No, never better." I needed to believe I was excited about this new chapter and push away the incommunicable grief and guilt tugging at my heart.

I was allowed to end my shift at four, and on the subway ride, I wrote the letter I'd been drafting in my head:

Karo, I've found a small place of my own. This was our plan, right?

See, I've always been scanning the horizon for a savior. I don't know who I really am or who I am going to be in this wild world, but I can see now that I could have been my own rescuer, that I shouldn't have become so dependent on Chia either.

I used to believe that something was fundamentally wrong with me and that's why I went through what I did in life. But now I see that suffering is not unique to me and my people. Also, I am not going to allow ANYONE, your mom included, to put me down for things that are not my fault.

I can see my weaknesses, Karo. I nurse wounds and won't let go of longings and disappointments. That's why I collapse. I have to find my own way. You will be happier without me. I see you have in abundance what I lack—tranquility and ease.

Thank you for everything you've done for me. I've taken notes on how much I owe you and will gradually pay you back, with much gratitude.

Farewell,

Leila

I resisted the urge to revise the note and tucked it under his pillow. Before closing the door, I looked around at the room, at the bed I had occupied for months, at Karo's stack of books.

Since cabs were expensive in Toronto, I mapped out the easiest route to move using public transit. My phone vibrated when I closed the door.

"Are you done at work?" Karo sounded as if he were at the bottom of a well. "Shall we go out for dinner tonight?"

The handles of the suitcases were heavy in my hand. I let go of them.

"Can you meet me at Union Station?" he asked. "I am leaving the office now. I should get there by five thirty-ish at the latest."

CHAPTER THIRTY-EIGHT

When I reached the station in my green summery dress, Karo was sitting on a bench, hands clasped, his baseball cap pulled low on his forehead.

I applied another coat of lipstick to my already beige lips before approaching him. "Where are we going?"

He raised his eyebrows and grinned like a schoolboy. "Centre Island. There's a nice restaurant there."

I didn't object. We'd spent our first fun day together there, and perhaps we should spend the last one there too. I sat by his side on the ferry, seeing with perfect clarity that he was disoriented. People around us chattered and chuckled.

"The greatest power parents have is in screwing you up, better than what your worst enemy could manage." Karo's abrupt comment astounded me, shattered the web of thoughts and puzzles I had knitted together.

"True. They give you life, then ruin it in a snap."

On the wooden bench of the ferry, he held my hand. I turned to him, surprised. He took the other as well. Now we were facing each other. His gaze was intense. "Is this going to be our last meal together?"

"What are you talking about?" I didn't know why I lied.

"Can we at least stay friends?"

I pressed my lips together. How did he know? "Don't be silly. I'm going to the deck." I watched as the engine bore a white tunnel into the blue lake, the way it disturbed the surface's peace and made water froth and churn against itself. But I couldn't escape his sorrowful, sagging eyes. The image was burned in my mind, and my stomach tightened with hot pinpricks of guilt. But I had been walking down the path onto which he had led me.

The ferry arrived at the dock with a jolt, and we walked off and onto the crowded path. Birds bathed in a small puddle, shaking their heads and wings and dipping again into the muddy water.

At the seafood restaurant, the host showed us to our table on the patio, which wasn't nearly as chic as the tables inside—dark walnut with flickering candles. A young woman in a low-cut top appeared and took Karo's order: two shots of Johnnie Walker Black on the rocks. I got "water on the rocks." The fish and chips we ordered took too long to arrive. Karo ordered another drink. When the waitress returned, she slammed down our glasses and never apologized or cleaned up the spill. After taking such pains to deliver impeccable service myself at the coffee shop, I was taken aback, but I assumed that she was new at her job or having a particularly rough shift.

"I want to try your special drink."

"You should start with something lighter and perhaps fruity."

"You of all people tell me that?" I pointed to his drink.

"I'm more practiced than you."

"What's the point if you can't loosen up a bit?"

He ran his fingers across his brows. "You're right."

The sky was gradually turning purple.

"Look at how politely she's treating the other customers." I pointed to the waitress, who was now speaking pleasantly with a couple seated at a nearby table. Their hair was lighter, their skin fairer than Karo's and mine. "We will never belong here."

"Don't say that. She's the one who doesn't belong, not us—Canada isn't for racists. Watch this." Karo waved at her and in a very strong Middle Eastern accent asked for "a bomb."

She went pale.

"Car bomb," he said. Before she ran to call the police, Karo added, "Irish Car Bomb. You never had one? Very good," pronouncing the *r* in a theatrical manner.

We burst into laughter before she was far enough away. Karo went to get the drinks from the bartender directly so she wouldn't spit in them. He taught me to drop the Baileys shot into the Guinness and drink it immediately. It tasted like a bitter chocolate milk. I let myself soak in the ambient music for a while.

When the awkward silence lasted too long, I asked, "So, does your father . . .

I mean. How is he?" Karo's mother never mentioned him, a trait her son had inherited.

"He says he's away on trading business. Somewhere in Duhok or Dubai. He hasn't called me for . . . I don't even know how long . . . over six months. He hasn't heard about my Kurdish wife yet." Karo looked straight into my eyes. "Perhaps don't ask me any more questions about him? I don't know anything, haven't seen him in three years. More."

I looked at the busy corner of the restaurant. A group of women in their thirties were clinking glasses and laughing. Men in suits gesticulated to their associates as they did business over their meals. A couple sitting at the next table got up, laughing over some shared joke, making me envy their ease and happiness.

I needed words to fill up the raw gap and wanted to know what it was like to grow up with a rich absent father. But then Karo might ask questions about my own father, and that was painful territory. The plates finally arrived along with a bottle of Shiraz. I had little appetite but kept sipping the wine.

Karo seemed to enjoy the silence that terrified me. "Are you sure that all this lying was the right thing to do?" I was getting maudlin.

"Do you think staying in Iran was the right thing? Do you think there is such a thing as 'the right thing'?"

"So you don't want to tell the truth to your parents? Or at least your mother?"

"Nobody wants the truth, Leila. Everybody wants to hear what gives them the most comfort."

We sipped on, mute, immersed in separate thoughts. The weight of our unspoken words was crushing me. Leaning back in my chair, I entwined my fingers behind my head. "Tell me about Chia, everything he said and did the last time you saw him." If this was to be our last meal together, I wanted the full story.

He sighed, sucked his teeth. Sighed again. "I . . . I told him to forget about filming, that it was too dangerous, but he wouldn't give up."

I sat up straight. "Wait. What are you saying?" I tipped my wineglass over but ignored the deep red that spread across my napkin like a bloodstain and soaked my plate.

Karo looked up at me with surprise. "We saw soldiers trying to run over people with a truck. Chia said we had to film the scene and send it to the international media, like they'd give a damn. But he insisted it would shock the world."

"I don't understand." The drinks muddled my thoughts, and I struggled to process Karo's words. "Chia was the one filming? Why was it on your phone, then?"

"Mine had a better camera," he explained matter-of-factly. "Chia liked to borrow it to film."

I shook my head. "No."

"No what? It wasn't his first time doing that. All the photos he took when we went out were taken by my camera. You can't say you don't remember that."

I did. Of course I did. Right at that moment, several clips of Chia asking Karo to use his phone played before my eyes.

I stood from my chair and took a step backward. "You never told me that." I grew conscious of the tremble in my voice.

"You didn't know that? God himself couldn't stop your brother when he made up his mind about something."

I wanted to run away from the table, but my head swam, and the dizziness made me sit back down. I pressed my throbbing temples.

He bent forward. "Are you all right?"

I fidgeted, adjusted the strap of my dress. "Why didn't you tell me?"

"I didn't think I needed to. Don't say you assumed it was my idea all this time." His fingers gestured to his chest, his face a combination of surprise and defensiveness.

"You're the one who took Chia out that day. You knew how dangerous it was. You showed us some videos yourself!" Spittle foamed at the corner of my mouth, but I didn't wipe it away.

"Surely you knew I wouldn't film a thing like that on my own. It was a suicide mission. There were too many fucking soldiers around us. We were lucky we weren't shot on the spot!" I had never heard him swear like that.

My heartbeat wouldn't slow down. "You can't assume I know everything if you won't tell me. I am not a mind reader."

He drew his fingertip around the edge of his wine glass, which produced a faint squeal. His gaze was blank. "You keep pushing me to tell the truth to others, for everyone else to face these realities that hurt like hell. Look at yourself. If I tell you the truth, can you handle it?"

"Yes, I can." I crossed my arms.

"All right then . . . I spent a hundred days in a solitary cell. Nobody knew. My parents didn't know, didn't want to know. And telling them the truth about it now would only bring more pain." Karo spoke as if I weren't there.

He trailed off. "We had orders to shoot, but how could I . . . ?"

I squinted, trying to understand. "When you and Chia were arrested?"

There was a fierce glint in his eye. "No. I was released and conscripted shortly after. A fucker told on me. He said that instead of butchering the protestors, I'd let them run away. I was certain no one would notice. I was a good actor." His left cheek went up in a half smile, his raven hair covering his eyes.

Words evaporated from my mind like smoke. Under the pressure of this new truth, I silently lay down my invisible armor and weapons.

I paid the bill. He didn't argue. We walked toward the ferry terminal and sat on the green slats of the bench without speaking. I shivered mildly even though the night was warm.

I'd been wrong the whole time. It was Chia who had gotten Karo into trouble, not the other way around.

"Was that why you never contacted me all that time Chia was in prison?" I stammered.

"What did you think? What do you really think of me, Leila?" Karo faced me. He looked as though he'd aged a decade that night. "There's so much I've wanted to tell you . . ."

"Why didn't you?"

"The timing was never right. You were always angry, always under all sorts of pressure. I thought sharing my ordeal was either useless or would only increase your burdens." He turned and looked away. "I can't believe you didn't know your brother was the fearless idealist, not me."

I looked down in embarrassment. "It seems so obvious now that I hear the words, but things in my head . . . All this time it seemed that you had gotten him arrested, saved yourself, then abandoned me when I needed you most. Can you try and see things from my perspective? After he was killed, you reappeared and started acting like my savior. Even that made you look like you were ticking boxes to eliminate guilt." I shook my head, unable to continue speaking.

He held his face in his palms. "Two months after I was freed from prison, I saw that I couldn't resume my studies. I just couldn't keep up the charade. Of course, that meant I was conscripted and was assigned to the *yegan-e-vizhe*. Because I was big, they decided I should become one of the elite guards trained to crack down on protesters. But I wasn't capable of it. How could I be? I mean, how could anyone attack unarmed people?"

His voice grew hoarse as he summarized the tale of his torment in as few words as possible. Over his shoulder, a band of moonlight glistened on the water.

"I ended up being charged with disobeying orders and was put in solitary confinement. For a hundred days my only companion was a starving rat."

What did a hundred days in solitary confinement feel like? And that was on top of the three months that he'd spent in the custody of Intelligence for allowing his friend to film the state's murder scene. His parents knew nothing about Karo's time in prison, so the cover-up of our "marriage" didn't seem like such a big lie by comparison.

As the ferry swung toward the dock, the moonlight brought his profile into sharp relief. The scene kindled a nostalgic feeling in me and a deep kinship, as if I had known him for eternity.

The ferry arrived at the terminus at the foot of Bay Street. We walked out through the iron gates, hands clasped, leaning close to each other like never before.

The station walls zipped by quickly as the semi-empty subway train swept through dark tunnels. Karo placed his head on my shoulder, and as I laid mine on his, the plans I had eagerly conceived unraveled, the dream of a stalwart, independent Miss Free.

Once we got off at the train station, I said that I wanted to walk the rest of the way home. A part of me was still terrified of being alone in the dark, but Yonge Street was busy enough, safe enough to let me clear my head.

"See you at home," he said. "Call if you want me to pick you up." I embraced him, and he placed his lips on my neck, bare for once.

From an Iranian supermarket I bought an international calling card, entered the codes into my cell phone, and dialed Joanna's phone number. I needed to share the news, to tell her that Karo hadn't put Chia in danger or ignored me on purpose. That I'd been so stupid. So blind.

Her phone rang and rang, but she didn't pick up.

I dialed again, entering the code wrong a couple of times, then redialed and redialed. I was desperate to ask Joanna if it was okay to allow myself to love Karo fully, to allow all I had tamped down over the years to finally surface. An angry woman who wasn't Joanna finally answered, saying Joanna had moved and no one knew where. She then reminded me that it was early morning and hung up.

I didn't know what else to do. I needed to speak with someone immediately, so an email to Shiler wouldn't do. I had to speak what I'd learned aloud, talk it over with somebody so I could believe and digest it.

I called my parents. The last time I'd called Baba had picked up, but he immediately hung up when he heard my voice. This time Mama answered, telling me about the pomegranate trees in full bloom. Mama went on about herself and forgot to ask how I was getting by in this foreign land or if I'd gotten into a university yet. "How does Baba like being back home?"

"I don't think he will ever truly be joyful again. But he looks calm. The happiest I've seen him in years. He has friends here, childhood friends."

I asked where Joanna was. She said Baba believed she had left Mariwan to join Shiler. I held my phone to my chest. We said goodbye. I kept walking up Yonge Street in vain, looking for a familiar face in the crowd.

A young man embraced a girl in the alley by a nightclub and kissed her passionately. Her fingers raked his hair as she opened her mouth to his kiss. I hailed a cab.

CHAPTER THIRTY-NINE

KARO HAD CRAWLED under the blue coverlet on his mattress, his white undershirt tight across the muscles of his chest. When he saw me, he looked at my packed suitcases and directed his gaze back at the ceiling.

I stood by the bed. "Karo, you are a much better person than I am, than I can ever be. I was so absorbed by pain, I couldn't see anything or anyone else. I'm sorry."

He searched my eyes and opened his arms. I leaned in and stroked his chest.

I wanted to pounce on him open-mouthed, to take him for mine. The sudden yearning threatened to break open my skull.

"So you'll stay?"

I nodded.

His eyes brightened into a smile. "Will we get married for real?"

"One day," I said. "One day. I need some more time."

He got up in one fluid motion, a surfer standing on his board, and he sat by my side on the bed.

"I never wanted you to think that I expected you to fall in love with me because . . ." He shrugged. "In return for helping you. But I certainly hoped that you'd get to know me and like me as I am." Karo held my hand, gently squeezed it, and seemed to gain confidence and fluency in his speech. "Leila, I always liked you. You seemed uninterested."

"Are you crazy? Why didn't you ever say anything?"

"I loved my friendship with you and Chia so much that I was terrified of risking it by asking for more. When I was finally ready to ask you out, one tragedy followed another."

"And now your mother does not approve of me."

"Nor does yours of me. We can live somewhere else though. We don't have to live in this basement. I can look for work in Vancouver, St. John's, anywhere, as long as you . . ."

"As long as I . . . ?" I had an overwhelming desire to bite his biceps.

"Can you honestly and truly stop blaming me for Chia . . . ?" He caressed my hair. "I see it in your eyes every day. You must promise not to rub it in my face every time we have a disagreement."

"The truth is . . ." I swallowed. "I'm still grieving. But I realize that you aren't to blame." And his mother was a lonely woman, deceived and abandoned, who had never learned how to accept herself or other people.

His palm reached my cheek, and I moved it to my lips, planting a kiss on it. He untied my ribboned pigtail and tangled his fingers in my hair, caressing my scalp. Our foreheads touched, followed by our noses. "May I kiss you?"

"Wait, Karo. I want to be with you, I really do—but I also want a life for myself. This is my one chance to start over."

He waited, his lips still inches from mine.

"I've applied to a few universities, to film programs. I can't delay my education—I won't put my dreams on hold any longer."

"Of course. Of course." He cupped the back of my head and pulled it toward him, and I leaned in for a long kiss, tasting his lips between my teeth, their liveliness and sweetness. For once I didn't fight my powerful attraction to him, and I slid my hands under his shirt, over his hips. He moved his lips to my jawline, down to my clavicle.

"Slowly," I whispered. I wanted to savor it.

"Okay," he said, smiling into my eyes.

We kissed for a long time. A hand held my waist and the other my cheek and neck. I lightly stroked his arms and closed my eyes to focus on the taste of his lips, take in his woodsy, sultry scent, the sweet aroma of his aftershave. Opened my eyes to prove this was not yet another fantasy. Closed them again so his piercing eyes wouldn't distract me from his lips. Unlike the actors in films and the couples I'd seen on the streets, he kept his eyes open while kissing, as if he were afraid I'd disappear if he blinked. I felt the heat of his body, the warmth of his breath that kept getting shallower. This was it. The moment that we'd each thirsted for, unbeknown to the other. I broke off our kiss abruptly.

I got up, feeling dizzy and ecstatic. I was shedding skin, breaking open my cocoon.

I wriggled out of my dress. He took off his undershirt and unbuckled his belt. I sat at the edge of the bed in my underwear. After a momentary pause, Karo laid me back, crept on top of me. I was in life's twilight, in an in-between state where I yearned for Karo in a vacuum, with nothing and no one else around him.

His warm mouth traveled from my neck to my breasts and down to my belly button. His hands ran over my thighs and between my legs. He took off my bra and kissed underneath my left breast. A pleasurable shiver ran down my spine, and heat radiated from deep within me. He lifted the edge of my panties, and his tongue darted between my legs after he gently removed them.

"Is this good, darling?" he whispered ever so tenderly.

There on the bed, the rain thrumming outside, the full moon shining, he took me in until I was gripping his hair and biting my lip to muffle my cries. I twisted to reciprocate, tugging at his briefs, but he moved up to kiss my lips, held my shoulders, and stared into my eyes as he tried to find his way inside me. My body tensed up and tightened.

"I can stop whenever you want." He kissed my forehead and eyes, letting me feel his warm breath on my cheeks and neck, calming my nerves with his tender kisses until my body relaxed.

I reopened my eyes. He smiled at me, his eyes full of unprecedented care. My chest was filled with a very fine mist.

I felt him inside me and left teeth marks on his arm.

The tense moment of pain was eclipsed by the bottomless pleasure I felt—and not just from what Karo did to my body. Life was this: the fleeting moment of bliss between one agony and the next.

He pulled out in time and came into his undershirt. I looked at the blood droplet on the sheet, at what used to be a new bride's badge of honor. "That was another reason I was so afraid of touching you." He pointed.

"You didn't bleed, so I assume you weren't a virgin."

He smiled. "I was in a relationship for about a year before I met you."

"Another important thing I didn't know about you. Ever robbed a bank? Dumped a body?"

He rolled onto his back and held me against his chest. "No. Been waiting to do those fun things with you."

We lay like that, tangled in the sheets. His fingertips caressing my hair, my ear pressed against his thumping heart. "We're probably the only couple to wait this long to consummate their marriage," I said.

"Will you teach me to speak Kurdish? Our children should speak and write their mother tongue fluently," he said.

"Children?" I raised an eyebrow.

We laughed relaxed, gratified laughter in each other's arms.

I padded down the hallway, filled the bath with hot water, and lay down in it. When I closed my eyes, Chia nodded and smiled at me.

"Karo!"

"What, love?" He appeared at the door, his arm bearing the mark of my teeth.

I wasn't sure what I wanted to say. "I've just realized—after everything that's happened in my life, I can finally just be. I can end at 'I am.' Regardless of what the rest of the sentence is. Actually, my story can end right there."

He tilted his head, his brows drawn, his face a question mark. "Okay?"

"I mean, I don't have to think 'I am a Kurd' or 'I am Chia's sister,' right? I can just be. Only say 'I am.' Full stop. Do you know what I mean? Just be."

An eyebrow went up, and the frown was gone. "Okay," he agreed. "You are. I am. Full stop." He kneeled by the tub and puffed the suds away to sneak a peek. I laughed. We kissed. He held my wet hands, touching my forehead with his. Water and foam dripped down our tight grip.

I washed off and teetered out of the bathtub. Karo hovered in the doorway, watching. Soapy water dripping from my hair streamed over my collarbones, around the mole on my left breast, and down onto the tiled floor. He kissed my clavicle and licked away the beads of bathwater on my navel. I directed the hairdryer into his face.

I wiped the mist off the mirror. The girl glimmered at me from behind the bars my fingers had drawn. "You're free!" I whispered as I wiped the mirror. "And you are beautiful." She shone a face-wide smile on me.

In the bedroom, Karo's long limbs were stretched over the stained sheets, one arm dangling over the side of the bed.

I searched through my suitcase. Once the carefully folded shirts and pants were unpacked, I reached for the books at the bottom.

The folder. I held it to my chest. I was ready.

Life was a landfill. What made one humane was the ability to convert the waste into a valuable resource and to enjoy the occasional flowers that bloomed in the refuse. Or perhaps life was compost. Our experiences piled up, broke down into a rich soil, and in the heat of life, some seeds buried in the dark began to sprout.

Karo read Chia's slanted writing on it: "From Self-Reign to Self-Immolation: The Paradoxes in Kurdish Women's Lives."

"Will you help?"

He held me from behind, and his breath caressed the back of my neck. "Of course."

The future with all its blithe abundance belonged to us. The full moon of my childhood smiled.

EPILOGUE

ALAN'S SKINNY LIMBS were hidden under a sky-blue blanket, and three pillows were supporting his back and neck. Folded tissues, a bottle of Scotch, ice packs, and boxes of pills had each claimed a space on the rug his mother had woven for him decades ago. Munching on a vanilla cake, Hana was rocking in a faded wooden chair, the fat on her thighs drooping down from the sides of the seat. A rotten tangerine let off a fetid odor that no one seemed to notice.

Alan and Hana were watching a Kurdish satellite TV channel based in Sweden, which announced that even though the Islamic State no longer ruled over a specific area in Syria or Iraq, their sleeper cells continued to carry out random suicide attacks.

The sun was shining over the city of Halabja. Outside their window, some of the bright red flowers hanging from the glossy, oblong leaves of a twenty-foot tree were beginning their unhurried transformation into pomegranates. Their bungalow opened onto a park with a popular playground where children with disabilities could play on handicap accessible, colorful play equipment. The children who had been exposed to helium during the genocide were now parents of children with birth defects.

A framed picture of Chia's graduation hung on the wall across from the bed and the chair. A wreath was hanging from his neck. In a corner of the frame there was a small picture that showed him as a child holding hands with his young parents. But if one inspected the picture blurred by old dust, they would notice Chia's sneaky look toward the right corner of the photo. A little girl's green spotted skirt overlapped his pants, but her body had been crudely cut out with a pair of cheap scissors. In the photo, Alan's stare was blank, Hana's proud.

On the television, panelists in suits discussed the importance of ideological confrontations post-liberation. The screen was dominated by a video clip of the cities and villages turned into rubble, the destroyed ancient sites and artifacts, the half-burnt buildings, the walls perforated with innumerable bullet holes, a three-legged cat mewling through the dust and destruction.

"Nothing has changed." Hana sat back in her chair and rocked a few times. The hopeful faces of refugee kids, smiling shyly as they stared into the visitors' cameras, sharply contrasted with the footage of devastation shown only seconds ago. "We were killed a hundred years ago; we are killed now. Homes smashed down then and now. Pulverized heads then, pulverized homes now."

Alan wiped his sweat with a hand towel. His week-old stubble was fully white. "What are you talking about? The world itself depends on Kurds to defeat the Daesh murderers. My father and uncles predicted this day."

Hana scanned the room and groped for her glasses on the floor, but they were out of reach of her pudgy fingers. She grabbed the wooden handle of her cane. The wall behind her was stained by the old coal heater. With her full weight on the cane, she took a step forward before she bent to pick up the glasses. She winced and cursed in her attempt to straighten up again. "When is she going to be on? You said 5:30. It's 5:40. Maybe you have the wrong channel." She limped back to her chair, trailing cake crumbs behind her. Alan squinted at the TV in silence.

A group of young boys was getting ready to play football in the park, showing off new shoes and boasting about kicking butts while the coach urged them to warm up properly.

Hana ran a hand through her hair, a messy tapestry of gray, henna-orange, and black. She then reached for the remote on the corner of Alan's bed and flipped through more Kurdish channels broadcasting dance, music clips, and politics from Europe.

"So what inspired you to make this very powerful movie?" asked the bright-faced, bespectacled presenter. The camera then turned toward the smiling face of the guest on the program. Hana gaped, and her finger twitched against the button of the remote control. The channels began to automatically scan, losing the interview.

Alan and Hana looked at each other for a few seconds, the longest in years, searching for confirmation. Alan didn't notice Hana's trembling hands when he snatched the remote, pressed and repressed the buttons of a tool only half-responsive because of its dying batteries.

"This is it! This one," Hana called out when she saw the face of the interviewer for a brief moment. "Go back! Go back! Give it to me!"

"Be quiet for a second." Alan focused on the remote and found the program again. His face had grown craggy with age.

"*Warrior Butterflies* is the story of three Kurdish women, people like you and me; one is a school dropout, one's a university student, and one's a mother . . . but when a barbarous group attacks their hometowns in Rojava, despite the fact that the majority of the population flees the war zone, including these women's immediate families . . . they stay." The interviewer's glasses had slid to the tip of her nose, giving the impression that they might fall off any second. "With no military training. Knowing that if they are captured by the enemy, they will be raped and trafficked as sex slaves, these women join a merciless fight . . ."

"Let your guest talk, you stupid woman." Hana white-knuckled the arms of her chair, impatient for the camera to pan back to the show's guest.

Outside, the crescendo of cheers from the football players reached its peak as one team scored a goal. A bride and groom by the splendid fountain were posing for their photographer.

"So these three women . . . for political and personal reasons, these women who could not kill a mouse if it marched into their kitchen . . . they become fighters." The interviewer reached out with her hand as if to grab the right words. "Their purses and backpacks that used to carry books and makeup are now filled with grenades and bullets. This is a movie about war and demolition, corpses and illnesses, and yet . . ."

The camera showed a glimpse of the guest, looking down, blushing. She had bangs, and her ponytail was tied with a green spotted ribbon. A butterfly brooch was pinned to her lapel.

The interviewer scratched her cheek and moved forward on her chair, still hogging the camera. "When the war ends and they rescue the kidnapped Ezidi women, they establish Jinwar, this women-only village where they build their houses brick by brick, plant crops, learn medicinal uses of herbs, swim in open pools, cook together, and heal together. This is the most poetic movie I've ever seen. How can I describe it? It was dreamlike, it was beautiful, even sensual . . .

"The fighters, the songs they sing—one of them, the homemaker mother, is a closeted poet, eh?—and the friendships and competitions between these women who wouldn't have found common ground outside of a battlefield is inspiring. These characters—they have such distinct and charming personalities. I guess my question is, how did you manage to balance these contradictions?" Before the director could answer, she rambled on. "It's such a subtle production, so moving. It received the longest standing ovation at the Cannes Film Festival, and now it's been nominated for Best Director . . . tell us about it! Go ahead."

The entire screen filled with a close-up of a woman in her thirties, her dimples deep when she smiled, a glimmer in her eyes. "The film is based on the true adventures of my childhood friend Shiler. And in making this movie, I'm following my brother's path."

Hana and Alan clasped hands in pride and excitement, watching the close-up of their daughter, whom they hadn't seen in years. Ever since they'd read in Kurdish papers about her successful film, they had been monitoring the television schedule to catch an interview with her.

"Yes, Chia Saman. *Al Jazeera* named him one of the most influential persons of 2010."

"He still is influential, what he stands for. The authorities thought—or they hoped—that Chia's cause would die if they placed the noose . . ." Leila swallowed. "But in death, Chia and people like him are invincible. Assassinations don't help dictators because . . . because the pain that is aroused in the victims' society can become a strong source of artistic creation or activism, resistance in so many different shapes."

The TV presenter nodded. "And in this . . ."

"The effect is not always the same." This time Leila spoke over her. "It's not only our nishtman, our homeland, that is colonized. Our self-worth is hijacked too. Tyranny can stimulate unwitting self-sabotage. Pain needs to be managed—perhaps, in a sense, outsourced." Leila placed one hand over the other, a ring glinting on her left hand. "I'm indebted to my brother and others who taught us to rise above oppression and not be swallowed by it. I was about to . . . At one point I gave up, but I owed this to him, not only for his awareness and courage, but for his sincere and indiscriminate compassion."

"To my brother, who . . ." The interviewer shuffled a few pages on her lap as the camera zoomed out to capture them both in the frame. "Yes, the dedication is right here. 'To my brother, Chia Saman, whose love breathed purpose into my life long after his physical presence was removed.'"

Leila's face glimmered, and she placed her hand on top of her stomach. Her forest-green dress fit snugly across her abdomen.

"She's pregnant!" Hana cried.

"So the women of your film are heroines and fighters who are brave, and at the same time they have plenty of fears. Why is that? Why aren't they larger than life, so to speak?"

"It all paid off. All the sacrifices . . ." Alan whispered, his calloused hands gripping the blanket firmly.

"Because I'm weary of superhuman representations as much as victimized portrayals. I think we Kurds have a long history of being talked down to. And then came the Islamic State, causing a lot of harm but making the rest of the world reevaluate its attitude toward us, seeing us as its shields, if not outright saviors. We no longer feel so neglected. There is respect out there, admiration for the Kurds' fearlessness and their gender-egalitarian, environmental, democratic values. In the nineties, Western media portrayed us as victims. Gassed and displaced. And now we are presented as champions. From being labeled 'terrorists' for resisting the politics of annihilation, we are now the peacekeepers. I look forward to a time when we are not talked down to or talked up to. I want to be talked to. The world needs to accept us as people with strengths and weaknesses. For generations of Kurds, life has begun and ended in violence. I hope that time has passed."

Leila rested her hand on top of her stomach again, sanguine and self-assured.

In the park a high-pitched ululation announced the arrival of the wedding guests, who then played music and danced in a circle, waving colorful handkerchiefs.

"Ms. Saman. Tell us. How do you feel about being a Kurd? Are you proud?"

"Am I proud?" Leila squinted into the studio lights. Silence. She shook her head. "'Proud' is not the right word."

The interviewer straightened in her armchair and frowned.

"I'm not proud to be a woman either. Nor to be human. I didn't work hard to be any of those."

The presenter removed her eyeglasses and pursed her lips.

"But I am happy to be one. It was awfully tough, and it took a while, a long while, but I learned to appreciate being a human, a woman, and a Kurd."

A tear streaked down Alan's face. He didn't reach to dry it. Instead he composed his first email with the subject line "My daughter."

AUTHOR'S NOTE

THE UNITED NATIONS and several human rights organizations have reported* that, as an ethnic minority in Iran, Kurds are often the majority among political prisoners and suffer the most vicious torture. Kurdish regions have been intentionally kept underdeveloped, resulting in entrenched poverty and all the trauma and trouble that follow the plague of poverty. Kurdistan also has alarming rates of female suicide. All the mistreatments and attacks against the Kurds mentioned in this novel, whether through snippets of television and radio broadcasts or Baba's impassioned speeches and childhood flashbacks, are historically factual.

FARZAD KAMANGAR, THE person who inspired this novel, is my teacher. We never met and he never knew of me, but he shifted something fundamental within me.

He was an elementary school teacher in an impoverished village in Kurdistan when Iran imprisoned him, accusing him of belonging to a Kurdish opposition party and therefore being an "enemy of God." Since Iran's supreme leader is officially the "representative of God on earth," opposing the state is blasphemy, a crime punishable by death.

* "Special Rapporteur on the situation of human rights in the Islamic Republic of Iran," UN Office of the High Commissioner for Human Rights, March 5, 2018, https://www.ohchr.org/EN/HRBodies/HRC/RegularSessions/Session34/Documents/A_HRC_34_65_AUV.docx.

Despite vehemently denying the charges, Farzad never received a fair trial. Instead, what he received in abundance was brutal and sadistic torture at the hands of the state. He wrote:

> *I was beaten because I was a Kurd, because my cell phone had a Kurdish ringtone. They'd tie my hands to a chair and pressure various sensitive points of my body . . . they would remove my clothes with force and threaten to rape me with a baton or sticks . . . they would chain my feet and electrocute me.*

Amnesty International reported* that Farzad suffered from spasms in his arms and legs because of repeated beatings, flogging, and electrocution. The organization also quoted Farzad's lawyer Khalil Bahramian as saying that the trial where he was accused of "endangering national security" lasted no more than five minutes, with the judge issuing his sentence without any explanation and then promptly leaving the room. "I have seen absolutely zero evidence presented against Kamangar," Bahramian said. "In my forty years of legal profession, I have never witnessed such a prosecution."

In the meantime, I was in Toronto, contemplating my freedom and isolation in exile. I had achieved many of my goals—winning a scholarship from the University of Windsor to pursue my master's degree in creative writing, signing my first book deal, and applying for immigration as a skilled worker. It was sinking in, however, that although I was not censored in Canada, I wasn't being heard either. While appreciating my adopted home for all that it offered me, I was taken aback by just how discriminatory the job market and the publishing industry were. I had several part-time jobs and could barely afford a studio apartment or time to write. What was the point in storytelling anyway? Then I came across Farzad's letters, which he'd been writing from his cell in a nefarious prison and had been shared on social media. I read and reread them.

> *One [interrogator] hit me for my ethnicity, the second for my words, the third said I had endangered national security, the fourth hit me to see where in the world my screams would reach.*

* "One Year After Execution Kurdish Political Activists Still Persecuted," Amnesty International, https://www.amnestyusa.org/one-year-after-execution-kurdish-political-activists-still-persecuted/.

I fainted and later regained consciousness in my cell. I kicked and screamed in pain and told myself that they were the signs of life. All newborns squirmed and screamed.

Farzad then quoted the legendary poet Ahmad Shamlou: "A mountain begins with its first rocks and a human with the first pain."

Farzad was merely one of the countless thousands who have suffered excruciating torture at the hands of Iranian authorities. But he was one of the rare few who possessed the ability to safeguard his inner life: "I will eventually get out of here. 'The butterfly that flew away in the night told me my fortune.'" He turned his pain into poetry and relied on his imagination to survive in a place that tried to annihilate his hopes before destroying his body. In one of his letters Farzad wrote about almost choking on his own blood after a severe beating. Then he heard the faint music of a wedding happening nearby. If I were he, I'd think, *How are people celebrating while I'm being tortured? The very people I fought for?* But no, of course he didn't think like that. Instead, he relied on the music to leave his anguished body and imagine himself the groom, dancing with his bride, giving a toast in honor of all those who risked their lives for freedom and all the parents who were awaiting a reunion with their brave children, now kept behind bars.

That's who Farzad Kamangar was and that's how, on his own, and only with his words, he won millions of hearts and shook the foundations of a theocracy that fed—and feeds—on division, despair, and apathy. Farzad knew that every time people like him lost hope, submerged in self-pity, or were overcome by fear, the oppressors became a little stronger. Despite his obvious innocence—and perhaps because of his influence and resilience—on May 9, 2010, at the age of thirty-three, Farzad Kamangar was executed; alongside him Shirin AlamHoli, Farhad Vakili, Ali Eslami, and Mehdi Eslamian were hanged. Contrary to Iran's own law, his family was not informed.

"He had such a tender soul," Farzad's mother later said in an interview I came across online. "He loved his students to pieces. Spring was his favorite season. He was born in the spring." Tears stopped her from continuing. I realized he'd been killed during his favorite season.

I WAILED AND sobbed for hours upon hearing the news that Sunday morning, feeling thwarted and tormented, feeling guilty that political prisoners were killed and I could do nothing, feeling desperate that Kurdish women set their bodies on fire to end their torturous lives and I was helpless.

Farzad's murder by the state left me with many questions that whirled in my head. What are you and I to do when we can neither bear to face the atrocities, nor overlook them? If I recuperated the eagerness to push on and write about the Kurds, would it be read? I had noticed that, even in North America, certain lives were valued more than others. Whose stories are heard?

Whose lives are saved? Whose losses are mourned?

What if Farzad Kamangar was released from prison but drowned in a sea on his way to imagined safety, like Alan Kurdi?

What if he survived the ocean but was detained in an immigration center where he witnessed numerous refugees commit suicide, like Behrouz Boochani, author of *No Friend But the Mountains: Writing from Manus Prison*?

And yet, I had just learned from Farzad that giving up was the worst idea. I believe that when humanity grows truly sick of inequality, we will push toward forming a global community, above narrow identities, and build a fierce and intensifying coalition that values all lives indiscriminately. What can get us there?

Literature cultivates our senses by humanizing the unpeople—the "ungrievable lives" in Judith Butler's words—by encouraging us to recognize our (un)conscious human/less human binaries. Literature fuels us to bring awareness to and change our conditioning formed over thousands of years, according to which a person who looked different was equated with danger.

I saw that I was standing on the shoulders of giants, as the saying goes. When people like Kamangar fought tirelessly for justice even from inside the most wicked prisons and didn't lose hope, there was much I could do as a free woman, despite xenophobia. There was no time for disappointment or doubts, for fear or despair.

So I picked up my pen again and have never put it down since.

I started crafting a novel, the one you've just read, about siblings, and in honor of one of my friends (a Kurdish activist who risks her life in Iran to save lives) I named the sister, the protagonist, Leila. At the same time, I commenced my efforts to decrease suicide rates in the Kurdish region of Iran. I have written and spoken publicly about self-immolation—including at the United Nations, the video of which is posted on my website—and I work with a reliable team who educates suicide-prevention strategies in Iran, away from the eyes of a government that wants us dead and desperate.

THIS NOVEL WAS inspired by Farzad Kamangar's resilience, but claims no resemblance to his actual life or family history—it is entirely fictional. Fiction imitates life, but unlike life, it is required to have a reasonable sequence of cause and effect. Fiction is expected to be sensible and have a resolution.

For example, Farzad's body (like the bodies of many others who were executed) has not been returned for proper burial. His family visits a ceremonial grave when they miss him. They know it's empty. They also know any part of their region could be an unidentified graveyard.

So this book only touches the tip of the iceberg. And yet, perhaps it's no coincidence that the book is released on the tenth anniversary of his execution. Tyrants fall one after another. Farzad Kamangar and his likes transcend.

ACKNOWLEDGMENTS

IN THE DECADE it took for this book to come to fruition, the only thing that was more difficult for me than writing was not writing. I had a dozen reasons to give up and yet how could I? The story demanded to be written. The story was mightier than my doubts. I am grateful to my family and friends, professionals, and institutions who supported this undertaking.

Chris Kepner, my warrior agent, I am indebted to you for fighting for this book when I had little hope left in me, for supporting diversity with more than words.

Chelsea Cutchens, my wonderful editor at The Overlook Press, your superb editing skills and your dedication to this book enriched the manuscript and most importantly warmed my heart in ways I could not have predicted. I am indebted to all you have done to guide and support my writing. You are my book's godmother. Infinite thanks also to your entire team at ABRAMS.

Jennifer Lambert, my incredible editor at HarperCollins, thank you for having faith in me, for stirring the book with your skills and wisdom. I also extend my gratitude to publisher Iris Tupholme and to the HC team in Canada.

Ehsan Attar, my beloved, my reliable travel companion, I am truly grateful to you for sharing our life's journey with so many invisible characters, for believing in me when I struggled to believe in myself.

My amazing editors/friends Susan Walker, Dr. Jenny Ferguson, and Dr. Brandon Moors, thank you for going through earlier drafts of the novel. For friendship, sympathies, and sharp eyes, thanks to Gavin Wolch, Karen Heading, Rachael Rifkin, Neda, Dr. Philip Loosemore, Dr. Zeinab Mcheimech, and

Dr. Kamal Soleimani. My talented critique group, OC Fictionaires, it's been delightful to be a member of such a vibrant group of professionals.

I owe thanks to my mentor David Bezmozgis, PEN Canada, and the Humber School for Writers for the scholarship, to the Joy Kogawa Historic House and the George Brown College for the residencies, and to the Toronto and Ontario Arts Councils for the grants.

Ako and Azad, my brilliant brothers, I have loved you ever since I have known you. Together, you're my muse.

To my family and relatives whom I miss dearly in the cruelty of exile, your love has put borders and distance to shame. I cherish you with all my heart and I know that we will meet again one day. To my new family in Canada and the US, your love gave me back the home I thought I lost.